D.A. MASIERO

The Chains of Malice

Those Who Suffer: Book One

First published by D.A. Masiero 2026

First edition

ISBN (paperback): 979-8-9952231-2-2
ISBN (hardcover): 979-8-9952231-3-9

Cover art by Matt Hubel

This book was professionally typeset on Reedsy.
Find out more at reedsy.com

To Jon,
My friend, I wish I could have told you this story; it's a doozy. I suppose settling for the time we had together will have to be enough. Now, this duo is just a solo. See you on the other side.

1

Awake

June 1st, 2053

Fields of Bastion

If it weren't for its tendrils, Zora would have already sedated it and brought it back to Bastion. Blights like the one that lie before her are of high order. *Special.* Regal, even. In all her years of working in Errant Recovery, she's never seen a Class A escape.

Judging from the gratuitous wounds across its drearily grey mottled skin—and the nearly identical Class A less than fifty yards away, which lie with its head cleanly detached at the neck—the pestilence didn't let her go without a fight.

IT, Zora reminds herself. *Not her.*

Though morally—albeit only internally—she'd rejected the missive that Blights are no longer entitled to pronouns, she's historically signaled only perfunctory acceptance of this. True, they can no longer reproduce sexually, giving their "sex" little value, but they *were* a "she," or a "him," or a "they" at one time. Such dehumanizing rhetoric has already contributed to the Culling, she thinks, and to do so again is foolish.

This final thought she's only ever spoken aloud to herself in the mirror one night; shaking, as she imagined pleading her case to Director Joshi.

"What do you think it looks like, under all of that grime?" says a small, yet pleasantly indifferent voice beside her. It has been years since Zora aged out of her own immunity, but that isn't why she harbors disdain for the girl. Handpicked little orphans; trained, sheltered, and spoiled by the Directors. The same platitudes weren't afforded to Zora when she was but one of many such meat shields for humanity.

"I think it's irrelevant," Zora scoffs dismissively, though she appreciates what the Waif is really asking. *Do you think that* she *was pretty before she was taken?* "Just, stay close to me. It's still breathing."

The girl nods placatingly, apparently sensing Zora's misgivings, which she feels a little bad about.

A *little.*

Doctor Zora Manzurova and Waif Karima both kneel inside of the cramped hunting shed, sheltered in the bosom of Bastion's southernmost—and heartiest—forest. Before them is the—sleeping—body of the Blight they'd been called to capture, tucked into the corner of the shed. She can hear the stalking footsteps of their military escort in the grass around them. *Hopefully,* she thinks, *the sergeant won't ask me—*

"How long until transport?" a male voice asks from behind. The question is an accusation, if the brusqueness in his voice didn't give it away. She *has* been neglecting to actually stabilize her "patient," opting to spend the last ten minutes either forlornly staring at it or checking its vitals repeatedly.

Protocol is clear: Should an Errant escape from beyond the Pale Wall—the rampart between humanity and its greatest enemy—all necessary steps shall be taken to preserve its life and bring it to Bastion for study. *Study.* Zora has performed such "studies" firsthand. She isn't eager for new patients, though in the past, she has reluctantly complied.

But this is different. *She.* Zora cannot see her as anything but this. *A woman, like me.* The Blight's wounds ooze with viscous obsidian blood. *With purpose.* Her chest crackles, rising and falling, a stubborn metronome. *She's special.*

"I, uh…" She clears her throat. "I would like a second opinion. I need…our Pilot."

A moment after she finishes speaking, the group hears a distant *thump. Director Joshi must have been listening in.* Zora isn't surprised at this. She also isn't surprised when the sergeant exhales a peevish sigh and grumbles his way out from the doorway, resuming his watch.

What *is* unexpected is the elbow that nudges her side. The Waif flashes her a subtle—but clearly delineated—smile, and gives an equally subtle nod. *Of course she would know.* The Waif's apparent foreknowledge irks her some, but she's thankful for the reassurance that she's doing the right thing.

Zora cannot help but stand and make the two-step journey to the doorway to watch the Pilot's landing. She wonders how long it's been since he's used the cannon. Then she wonders if it's something a person could ever get used to; being reduced to a projectile. She faces Bastion, swallowing a mouthful of apprehension as the city's distant grey enormity makes Zora feel as if she's the size of a pinhead.

It's subtle, but she can hear his thrusters whine as he approaches, the crisp sound silencing the forest denizens. Almost too quickly to comprehend, he's just a moment from touchdown, still moving fast enough that Zora thinks he'll crack the earth below him. To her shock—and relief—the Pilot emits a tart column of heat from his palms, slowing him to a near stop, and he lands gently on his two feet.

A second wave of apprehension rolls over Zora as she watches him approach. Such little fanfare for easily the deadliest person in this city, and yet here he is, outfitted for war, strolling across the grass. She feels no logical fear toward him, but for Zora, this man is the same as a domesticated predator. Something preternatural. Some*thing* powerful.

"Sergeant," the Pilot drawls abruptly as he passes the man. If the sergeant is still peeved that Zora has called for the Pilot, he gives no indication in the affirmative. The men exchange polite, yet terse, nods of recognition. "Doctor," he continues as he reaches Zora. "It's been years. They been treating you well?"

It *has* been years. Roughly sixteen since the Calamity. Since they'd seen each other in reeking casualty tents, tight-lipped in the chow line, in the blood-soaked trenches. His question makes her regret her thoughts about him. *He's still human; must be.*

Her neck cranes back as she looks up at the Pilot, his above-average height compounded by the added stature of his armor. *Human.* As human as a person can be with irises so large that they nearly eclipse the whites of his eyes, and so obstinately red that they seem to glow, even in the hearty daylight they're bathed in.

Zora clears her throat. "Yes, Pilot Parker," she answers curtly. "You?"

He gives her a wry smile in return and shrugs his armored shoulders. The Pilot's eyes wander to the headless Blight's corpse, its black tendrils lying motionless across the grass like fallen vines. Soldiers have formed a cordon around the area, with two assigned to—reluctantly—keep a watch on the corpse, should it decide that being a corpse isn't ideal.

His attention passes to the girl, who's followed Zora to the door. "Waif Karima, keeping out of trouble?"

"We're not authorized to get into trouble, Pilot," the girl teases.

Parker hums lightly in amusement. "I see. In here, I assume?"

Zora speaks before Karima can answer. "Yes, Pilot." The Waif is here to be her shield, not to speak on her behalf. She won't allow these two—who see each other on the daily—to usurp her purpose here.

The Pilot seems unfazed by Zora's frustrations. "Karima, step out. Too little room for the three of us," he orders with a jerk of his head. The Waif complies, and the Pilot steps past Zora and into the shed. "Has she said anything?"

The use of a pronoun stutters Zora's words. "She, uh— *it* hasn't," she says as she follows him inside.

"I take it they weren't friends," he adds, motioning his head in the direction of the fallen Blight outside.

"That's part of why I wanted you to come out here." Parker sets his eyes on her, but doesn't offer any words, leaving Zora to elaborate. "It, um…fled, and fought, and then came here to die. I thought…" She hesitates, knowing that Director Joshi is (certainly) listening through his suit's microphone. "There must be a reason."

"Maybe she just wanted to be free," Parker says contemplatively. Before Zora can correct him again on his use of pronouns, he speaks loudly. "Doctor Manzurova, I am taking charge of this Errant." She knows this proclamation isn't for her. "How long does she have?"

A loaded question, and not one without a plethora of variables. Blights should—and often do—recover from wounds that would be fatal to their human hosts. *Especially* in the case of Class A's. But beyond the sickly borders of the Exclusion Zone, their strength wanes. All Blights are linked through a sort of telepathy that humanity hasn't deciphered, and without their "master's" direction—and *gifts*—their bodies simply shut down. Even if this Blight wasn't seriously injured, it'll waste away in hours, or days, at best.

"I have no earthly idea. The fact that it's alive at all is astounding.

If she died right now, I'd be less than surprised." *Shit*, she let that one slip. Internally she curses him for tainting her already wavering thoughts on the matter.

Parker drops to a knee, the parched floorboards squealing under the weight of his armor. He studies the Blight in silence for a full minute. Zora stays equally silent by his side. In this quiet, watching the Blight's labored sleep, Zora can't help but think how utterly human it looks. *She* looks.

That's partly because the Blight *is* human. Depending on who you ask, of course. There's no consensus among the philosophers or doctors; the former argues that without free will—a supposed staple of humanity—Blights cannot be considered human, whereas the latter believes that regardless of the DNA corruption, what began as a human—no matter how ill they've fallen—cannot be anything but.

"Wake her," the Pilot says suddenly. Doctor Manzurova's training kicks into action as she opens the leather medical bag on the floor beside her. *An epinephrine injection would be the fastest.* As she palms the injector, she thinks better of it. Zora digs through her bag, muttering to herself. *Eh, no need to antagonize its system any further. Methylphenidate has worked for me before, but it takes a while to kick in, and I don't know how soon he—*

Zora feels a heavy hand on her shoulder. "You could just tap her," he muses, his tone politely patronizing. Her rueful expression urges him to clarify. "I've got your back. Just can't touch her myself. And at this range—"

"I can't be infected, yeah, I know," she finishes smartly. Not only does the Blight's dominion over its victims fade beyond the zone, but its ability to infect new hosts does as well. *Not like that makes this easier.* Zora takes a half-step forward, swallowing hard. Like a viper, she reaches and taps the Blight's shoulder before quickly backpedaling. The Pilot stares incredulously at her, his eyes rolling. This frustrates her, as even in *this* pitiful state, the Blight could easily end Zora's life in the blink of an eye. Zora spies the Blight's tendrils, four in number, which lie languidly around it. Any hint of motion, and she swears she'll break for the door and leave the Pilot to deal with it.

A sheepish Zora steps forward again and taps. Nothing. "H—hey," she whispers as she taps the Blight further. "Hey, you." Not a hint of motion. Tap, tap, tap. Her touches become firmer, the Blight's clammy skin cold on her palm.

"Hello? Hey, you. Wake up." *Shove.* "Ma'am?"

Zora falls squarely on her backside as the Blight rouses with a jolt and a sharp teeth-filtered inhalation of air. It scrambles back into the corner, pressing its back against the boards. Parker hasn't so much as flinched. The Blight's glossy black eyes flit between the two guests, wearing an expression Zora is familiar with.

She's...confused. Like someone being lifted from a deep sleep or clinging to consciousness after a concussion. For a moment, she's not a Blight at all to Zora. Just a lost, disoriented woman. The Blight's mouth goes agape as it searches their faces for something, and at first Zora doesn't know what it is looking for. But, as the Blight's countenance melts into resigned despair, she knows what it wants.

To be told that this was all a dream, and that she's home safe, among friends.

The Blight's barely focused gaze settles on the Pilot. "Fr—free..." her lips tremble out. Zora covers a gasp with her hands. In the years since the Blight first ravaged the land, when one *does* speak, the vulgarities it spews are second in severity to the rancor that drips from its tone.

"Yes," Parker says softly in return. "You are free now."

The Blight swallows with relief, its eyes closing for just a moment.

It mumbles something, forming the word slowly, one syllable at a time, as if it's creating the word right then and there. "Jo—Joshi?"

"That's right, Director Chandrima Joshi sent us," Parker replies, but not without a dash of reticence. Zora thinks that perhaps it's an issue of secrecy, but is relieved when the Blight shakes its head in the negative, as if this wasn't what it was asking.

She's nude—and featureless from the neck down—save for a hearty brown jacket two sizes too big. Her hands pat it down with a drunkard's demeanor, and after apparently feeling what she's looking for, she pulls a modestly sized journal from it.

An effort begins, and as the Blight agitates, the Pilot extends his arm and firmly ushers Zora back a step. Distant, torment-laden nothings spring from its vocal cords; its tendrils rouse themselves, seemingly at odds with this development as they haphazardly—and feebly—lash out at the Blight's own arms as they carry the journal away from its body, urging the Pilot to accept it.

With somber reverence, he does, plucking the journal from its tight-fisted grasp. One of the Blight's arms drops, exhausted, but the other forms its fingers into a stern point, commanding the Pilot to obey. *"Joshi,"* it repeats, spoken like an order.

"I'll make sure she gets it," Parker says. The Blight shakes its head, and Zora's eyebrows arch in disbelief. Its hand is still outstretched. *She...wants to shake on it?*

"You shouldn't—" Zora begins and stops short as Parker's hand clasps with the Blight's. Something like a shockwave surges through it; its hand sizzles and smokes. Zora expects it to recoil, but instead, it locks eyes with Parker and moves its arm up and down, once. The two separate, and the Blight collapses back into the corner, drops its arm, and leaves its now scalded hand upturned on the floor beside it. Its eyes quiver as red irises bubble up from the blackness.

"She's still in there..." Zora says as she and him watch the Blight in stoic appreciation. "Isn't she?"

Parker nods and looses a shiver as steam wafts up from the collar of his armored suit. A tendril of his own—red as blood and eager—slithers up from his back and sets itself swaying above his shoulder. "Close your eyes," he says, and Zora knows he's not talking to her. Her lips quiver as the corners of the Blight's mouth upturn into a relieved smile, eyes closing.

His tendril burrows into the Blight's forehead and out of the other side whipcrack fast, poking through the wooden plank behind it. It retracts just as quickly, and Parker shivers a second time as it slides [SL1] into the back of his suit. The Blight shudders a death throe, then falls silent, motionless.

"Thank you," Zora blurts before she can stop herself. Can't have the Director think that she sympathizes with the Blights, especially because she does. But the Pilot did assume responsibility and could have as easily ordered her to stabilize the Blight for transport. *I've done nothing wrong.*

The shed rattles as the Pilot unceremoniously falls onto his armored ass; sunlight seeps through the weathered rafters, cutting rays of illuminated dust kicked up by his weight. Crossing his legs, his head cocks as he examines the journal. "Why don't you do it?" he asks, offering it to Zora. "It feels delicate."

"Shouldn't we wait until we get back to the city?" she counters.

Parker firmly shakes his head. "Director Joshi wants to see what it says. Now."

Though Zora—obviously—didn't hear it, she gathers that the Director is giving him orders in real time via his suit's speakers. The doctor accepts the journal warily and joins Parker in sitting cross-legged on the shed's floor. Unbeknownst to them, Waif Karima, ever the curious soul, has crept back into the doorway.

It's so brittle. Every sensation her hands are feeding her say that this object is one jolt away from disintegration; the leather cover is dry as a bone—cracks in the dried flesh spider to the edges; its spine is taut and stiff—she worries it'll rend the book in two if she opens it. But it's what the Director wants, and Zora won't be the one to disobey her.

The journal naturally opens in the center and a pressed flower falls into Zora's lap, having been concealed by the pages. "Oh…" she whispers, as if she'd dropped something insignificant. She sets the book down and examines the flower; it's sealed in plastic—sloppily, with irregular edges and angles—and nearly flat.

"*That,*" Parker says as he snatches the flower from her hands, so fast that she at first thinks that she's dropped it, "is probably something we shouldn't touch. Waif! Biohazard!"

Karima moves with a startle, bashing her shoulder into the door— that she's been half-concealing herself behind—and briskly takes the flower, and before Zora can turn her head to see, she's gone from them.

"Right," Zora concedes. She carefully flips the journal to its first page and begins to read. *Read.* As if there's any structure or organization to the blasted thing. Each page is as disjointed as the next, the words as nonsensical, as if a gaggle of people had written it all at once. She can't read all of them—the majority are written in languages foreign to her. Some words she recognizes: *shame, penance, repose, fury.* They're repeated at irregular intervals throughout the pages.

Some sheets pass by without words, only drawings. Drawings of— human—viscera, drawings of graves, and—sprawled across two pages at the very center of the journal—a drawing of a tree whose branches are heavy with osiers and budded flowers.

But farther past, the variety of words begins to decrease. The tone shifts, apparent in the depth of the letters and the pivoting of the ideas they're meant to evoke. Zora's stomach knots itself as she turns the pages, mirroring the apparent panic the author—or more accurately, *authors*—felt as it was written.

"Tell me what you've read," the Pilot whispers, his tone offering comfort as he leans over to her. The manic, individualized entries have ceased, and *one* ultimate theme has emerged. Not a theme, but a word. Zora feels that—even without knowledge of the foreign languages—she can read every word that is written. And it's the same one, again and again. It dominates the pages, its letters spilling over the edges as cramped hands fought for page space. She can feel the desperation, the pleading, pathetic supplication of what she is convinced is one hundred *million* souls all vying to be heard above the screaming hellscape they're trapped within.

They *beg* her to listen.

"I, uh…" Zora begins, squeezing the tears from her eyes. "I only speak Dutch and English, so I may be missing—"

Parker cuts in. "I know what it says. I want to know if *you* know what it says."

Zora exhales a quivering, barely audible breath. "Yes, I know what it says." Her hands disagree, flipping rapidly through the rest of the book to try and disprove what she already knows.

We're not ready. An innocuous word. *Not yet.* It isn't complex, nor sizable. *I don't want to die.* Not one that may have been yelled in jealous rage, or righteous wrath. *If I leave to the Americas, I can stay with my mother. We can...end it there.* No cruelty is assigned to this word, regardless of how it may change in shape and meaning through every language and dialect humanity has ever uttered. *No, nowhere is safe.* But to Zora…

…it is the most vulgar word she has ever read.

Zora feels the Pilot's heavy, armored arm across her shoulders. If nothing else, she doesn't have to live this wretched moment alone.

"What does it say?"

Her hands acquiesce. The book snaps shut with a thud. Holding it with what little strength she can rouse, she lowers it to the floor, her muscles giving up, leaving her posture to her skeleton. She takes a breath—her last, true breath before her world collapses around her—and prepares herself. It feels dirty even saying it aloud.

"...awake."

2

Caged Bird

August 27th, 2053
Wilted Rose Asylum for the Criminally Insane, North American
Union

Without a clock—or another device of similar purpose—Curiesay's circadian rhythm is all she has to tell the time with. The sun isn't up yet, but she feels as if it's closer to midnight than to dawn. Dry and itchy linen lies underneath her—she hasn't had one of her predictably sweaty night terrors. *Why am I awake?*

Thick-soled boots strike cheap linoleum flooring and send echoes down the hall, ending at her cell door. *That's why.* She's grown used to the rhythm of the guards' gait and can—usually—surmise who is on duty given that information. The sudden, and rushed, pace of these footsteps tell Curiesay that this guard isn't here for his rounds.

It's been awhile since she's been accosted. She had *thought* that the defensive injuries she'd inflicted across Orderly Peck's face—or the scream he let loose when she nearly cleaved his nose off with her incisors—would have dissuaded any potential attacks for years to come. The notion that Peck may be the one marching to her door now sends adrenaline pouring into her blood. *This time*, she thinks, *he isn't here to fuck.*

A tart *clang* strikes her ears as the sliding hatch slams open. "Aye, wake up, you have visitors," a fed-up voice demands.

"For one thing, I don't take visitors at butt-fuck-early-o'clock," Curiesay retorts sharply. "And second, anyone who knows I'm here is someone I don't want to see. Leave me alone."

"I *wasn't* asking," the voice strikes back, doubly impatient. Curiesay, who's covered up to her nose by her thin—piss-poor excuse for a—blanket, sets her gaze on the opening in the door. She's intending on indicating her obstinance with her eyes, but with the light from the other side shining through and blinding her, she's unsure if he's even watching. "I won't tell you again," he warns, and Curiesay can hear the familiar sound of epoxy-covered wood rubbing against metal as the guard unsheathes his club. "Get yourself up and—"

"She doesn't need to move a muscle, we're just here to talk," an offensively pleasant female voice chirps. Curiesay can hear the hubristic tone of absolute authority in her voice, and suddenly she thinks she'd be better off if it *were* Peck coming to have his revenge.

"Ma'am," the guard begins, his voice mollifying as it quivers. "Visitation doesn't take place within the cells. If you would simply return to the waiting area, I'll—"

"That won't be necessary. I'd like to see her accommodations," the voice interrupts, not missing a crumb of tact. Curiesay hears the guard start to protest when the voice speaks again. "Give me the key and go take a break. Put your feet up; call your significant other; pleasure yourself in the reeking bathroom stalls for all I care. Come back in thirty minutes."

Curiesay hears what she believes is the clinking of keys being passed over, followed by the receding footsteps of a man wearing thick-soled boots on linoleum floors. Unbelievably to her, she wishes he had stayed.

There's some whispering from beyond the door, and Curiesay realizes that the voice is not alone. "Hello, Curiesay," it says. "Or, good morning, rather. We'd like to come in and speak with you. As a show of goodwill, I've brought some *fresh* food, *not* from your cafeteria. Can we come in?"

Can you? Is that...rhetorical? Even so, to be given a choice as to whether her cell door opens is so utterly foreign that she doesn't respond for nearly ten seconds. "Uh, no," Curiesay musters, shaking off the surprise. "No, you can't come in, but feel free to *fuck. Off.*" Oftentimes, Curiesay's recalcitrance sets itself at odds with her survival instincts, and this is no exception. A yapping little dog versus whoever has the authority to admonish the guards like that.

"Oh dear, I've already messed this up. I'm afraid that we *must* speak with you." A face interrupts the light shining through the port in the door, though Curiesay cannot make out any features. "We're coming in now." A short pause. "Lights."

Before she can protest further, Curiesay's pupils burn and she snaps her eyes shut; her guests have turned on her cell's glaring white lights. She hears the insertion of the key followed by the clang of the bolt. A moment later, she watches as the door swings open.

The first one in is—she assumes—the source of the voice. Though, she'll admit, she wasn't expecting the person it came from. A corpulent, compact, and offensively inoffensive woman whose crow's feet seem surgically implanted on the flanks of her eyes. Curiesay figures she's some kind of doctor—by the lab coat she's wearing—and wonders if her primary psychiatrist has finally given up and sold her off to some research facility. The woman's smile, which also seems to be a consequence of elective cosmetic surgery, curls with bother as she examines Curiesay's cell.

Following her is a man who sets Curiesay more on edge than before, if solely for the fact that he *is* a man. *Tall, check; square-headed, check; stupid, check.* He more than fits the bill for the types of people they hire to patrol the halls and keep Curiesay—and the rest of the patients (though they don't call them that anymore)—in check. A pang of remorse strikes her as she locks eyes with him. Across his eye sockets, from temple to temple, and touching his nose is a scar as thick as her pinky finger. One eye shimmers emerald green below his brow, while the other is a wind-swept baby blue. He has heterochro*hwhatever the fuck it's called.*

He nudges the female guest, who clears her throat. "Yes, well, uh, it's nice to finally meet you. Not that we've formally met yet. As, well, I *can* only see your eyes. But you can see me, so t-take a good look." In contrast to the unbothered temerity her voice carried when she was speaking to the guard, the woman's speech is reduced to a wavering, choppy mess. "Not in a weird way. *Not* that I would care. It's just, um…"

"I understand that this may be uncomfortable for you," the man butts in, and Curiesay sets her critical eyes on him. The depth of his voice *should* give her pause, but he speaks with sincerity. "But we aren't leaving until we speak with you. If there's anything we can do to make you more comfortable—"

"I sleep in the nude," Curiesay barks out, her body still covered by the blanket.

The woman's face seems to try to eat itself in mortification. "Oh dear," she wails. "I'm so sorry. I should have asked before I barged in here. I just got so excited about the prospect of—"

A hand covers her mouth as her male counterpart comes from behind, puts his other arm around her waist, and drags her still-rambling body from the room. The heels of her shoes squeak across the floor, leaving black marks in their wake. "Please, be quick," he says.

Curiesay's eyes don't stray from the doorway as she slowly uncovers herself. She pulls on her top and bottoms, flipping the waistband of the latter over itself—she's not allowed to have strings, and the bottoms are quite baggy—then rouses her locs and ties them back with a piece of fabric she's torn away from her bedspread. Sitting cross-legged on her bed, she sighs. "*All right*, come on."

Her guests reenter, and the woman takes a neutral stance across from her. The man removes his backpack and drags Curiesay's small nightstand—the only piece of furniture in this room besides her bed—between them. Containers of food—eggs, meats, muffins, griddle cakes, and diced potatoes—are unloaded onto the table, seemingly only enough for one, which gives Curiesay pause. It wouldn't be the first time that—

"These aren't drugged, if you're wondering," the woman says, apparently homing in on Curiesay's hesitance. "Not that you believe me. Parker?"

Her words are taken as a command as the man—apparently named Parker—moves to pluck a sausage from one of the containers. "No, not him," Curiesay demands. She figures if one of them can shrug off sedatives—or something more diabolical—it's the big guy. Curiesay points at the woman. "*You.*"

"Of course," she responds and grabs a plastic fork—*Smart to bring plastic instead of metal*, Curiesay thinks—before sampling a bite from each container. She talks while she chews, covering her mouth with her free hand. "You know, I'm not really supposed to eat carbs like this. I've been trying to cut them out on account of my weight. My ex-husband always said I was fat. I mean, *I* didn't think I was fat. Not that there's anything wrong with being fat, or overweight rather. He said it would kill me someday, that my *big fat heart* would give out. Well, joke's on him, because he's dead." Curiesay furrows her brow in response to this. "Oh, no, I didn't, uh… It's not funny that he's dead. And I didn't kill him, if that's what you're wondering. He was hit by a bus." *She definitely pushed him.*

"Satisfied?" Parker asks abruptly, interrupting his cohort's rambling non-confession. Curiesay responds by pulling the nightstand close to the bed. *Eh, what does it matter? If they wanted to drug me, there's easier ways.* With this, Curiesay starts in on her food.

"Fresh" is the *last* word Curiesay would use to describe the food she's served at the institution. She's been assigned to custodial duties every other day, and while cleaning the kitchens—which is too strong a word for what they are—she's well aware that there aren't any actual appliances save for rows of thirty or so microwaves. Their food is always cold in the middle and scalding on the outside.

If her memory serves her, this meal isn't *that* spectacular. But all things considered, it's the best food she's eaten in a very long time. With reckless abandon, she shovels the eggs into her mouth, chewing little as she swallows them down. She spends a little more time masticating the sausages—only enough so that she doesn't choke—before moving on to the griddle cakes. She rolls one up like a newspaper and eats it like a banana, pouring a small container of syrup into the middle.

Watching Curiesay feast, the woman gives an amused hum. "You remind me so mu—" This sentiment is cutoff as Parker nudges her *hard* in the ribs. Curiesay takes note but doesn't offer any acknowledgement. "Ahem, right. My name is Chandrima Joshi, and this is Adam Parker. We come from the city of Bastion, a city in the country formally known as Belarus. Perhaps you've heard of it?"

Curiesay waves her fork around, unimpressed. "Mankind's last hope, something or other."

"*Something or other* indeed. Let's cut to the chase, shall we?" The unbothered and airy tone in her voice sharpens so quickly that

Curiesay nearly chokes as she eats. "I am here to offer you a job. You meet the requirements for our Pilot program, of which Parker is our only current member. The specifics are classified, unless you accept. If you do, I will sponsor your immediate and permanent removal from this facility"—at this, Curiesay finally meets eyes with Chandrima—"and you will be remanded into my custody. But I must warn you; once you have been indoctrinated, there is no leaving the program. You will remain to exercise humanity's collective will until our victory or your death, whichever comes first."

Curiesay begins to ask what will happen if she insists on leaving the program, but given the firm—yet eerily pleasant—tone of Chandrima's voice, she's already certain of the answer. "What if I refuse?" she asks.

"Then nothing will change," Chandrima says. "We will leave here and never return, and you can spend your years rotting away in this decrepit asylum, sleeping on dirty linens and dining on the kind of food I wouldn't serve to a stray dog." She takes offense to this, though she isn't sure why. There's a haughty undertone in Chandrima's voice that Curiesay cannot shake.

Chandrima waits patiently for Curiesay's response as she tracks down the dregs of her breakfast in the corners of her mouth. She snaps her fingers at Parker, who rolls his eyes in response. He hands her a water bottle and she drinks it heartily, imploding the bottle with negative pressure. The air conditioning in Curiesay's wing kicks on, rumbling through the vents. It squeaks and coughs and pumps musty-smelling air into the room. Curiesay rubs her eyes; it always makes them water.

"Lady, whoever you're looking for, it isn't me." Curiesay's tone bites. "I don't give a shit about your program, humanity's will, or whatever else you're blabbering about. I want you to *leave*."

If Chandrima is fazed by—or even listening to—Curiesay's words, she doesn't show it. "I can see it in your eyes; I made the right choice to come and speak with you. The flame you coddle deep within you needs a purpose. Without a purpose, it will consume you or simply die out. Trapped in such a place, with nothing but your thoughts and solace, you're bound to immolate. But I can *give* you a purpose. Or, more accurately, guide you toward one." Chandrima's voice brims with conviction, and although Curiesay has no interest in her words, she cannot help but appreciate her sincerity.

Chandrima steps closer to a still-seated Curiesay, who watches her carefully. "It would be the greatest disappointment for me to leave you here to rot. I know what you've done, and I don't think it justifies a lifelong sentence. You're not insane; you're wounded. If you come with me, I can help you."

You don't know me. Again, Curiesay's stubbornness poisons her words. "I belong here, *bitch*, and if you don't leave in the next ten seconds, I'll prove it to you." This threat is followed by the terribly non-threatening process of Curiesay turning her back to Chandrima while her legs are still crossed, scooting on her butt in a circle.

Parker huffs and begins to speak when Chandrima makes a slicing motion with her hand. Her smile, which has hardly wavered since she entered, redoubles. "You have quite the appetite, don't you? I've been told you have a proclivity toward sweets. How does unlimited *chocolate* sound to you?" It's been *years* since Curiesay has had chocolate, and the last time she did—when the inmates were given a packet of hot cocoa mix on Christmas Day—Curiesay's tongue told her that chocolate wasn't the main ingredient. "Or how about hot water? A hot shower in your own private bathroom. There's a movie theater, an arcade, a spa. So many possibilities, my mind is racing! What would you *do* with all that freedom?"

Freedom. Curiesay thinks that she and Chandrima have different understandings of what that word means. It isn't freedom if it depends on your employment. It isn't freedom if the alternative is a living hell. *But*, she thinks, *I do have a choice.* Curiesay's rarely given a choice beyond wiping her ass with her left hand or her right. She has a feeling this choice may kill her—that choosing to go with them would be the *wrong* choice. *Even if it kills me, that's what I want, isn't it? And if I can get some perks out of it in the meantime, what's the bother?*

Curiesay collapses unceremoniously on her side and turns over to face Chandrima. She isn't proud of how pathetic she sounds, but she can't bring any of her bravado to the surface. "Can I have a nightlight?" she whispers.

3

Bastion

August 28th, 2053

Bastion, Second Floor

"Oh?" Elva comments as she steps into the kitchen. "I thought you'd be sleeping in."

Her brother has long held the habit of oversleeping, a proclivity that even three separate alarm clocks can't break. And on a day like this, when he doesn't have to rise to meet the school bus schedule, he's apt to care even less—she's surprised to see him sitting at the table. Elva lightly brushes his shoulder by way of greeting as she makes her way to the pantry.

Sitting with all the posture of melted ice cream, her brother neglects to lift his eyes from the table. "Couldn't sleep," Arthur says weakly, as if inebriated. Before him is a bowl of what *was* hard cereal that has since devolved into a mushy sugar soup. He lifts a spoonful and turns it over, letting it plop back into the bowl. "I've…been having that dream. Almost every night."

Elva does her best to keep her tone neutral. "Oh? Was it the tree again?" Mother always told her not to pry; *acknowledging a wound will only make it hurt more.*

He's already hurting, she used to reply, and would again, were her mother around to hear it. She prepares herself a small breakfast in the kitchen nook: plain yogurt, cinnamon granola, and a splash of raisins.

"No, it was the city," he responds. Elva shudders for an instant but doesn't look at him. "I don't remember much of it, even after having the same dream so many times. I'm in the street covered in blood and crying. I feel..." Arthur shakes his head, questioning his own recollection, "...thirsty? Then the sun rises, and I wake up." His voice is near a whisper now, forcing Elva to prepare her breakfast more quietly so she can still hear him. The spoon clinks as he drops it into the bowl, watching as it's swallowed up whole by the cereal mush. "But it was different this time," he adds.

"Oh?" Elva quietly brings her own bowl and sits across from Arthur, but she doesn't lend him her gaze.

"Yeah. You were there, and Mom too."

"I see. Was there anything else that was different?"

He doesn't answer for a long while. Elva is counting the beats of her heart as it pounds in her ears. *You'll only make it worse.* When she can no longer stand pretending that everything is all right, she meets Arthur's crestfallen gaze.

"She looked scared. Scared of *me*," Arthur says, followed by a singular, muffled sob.

Elva stands and moves behind him with a quickness, draping her arms over him and putting her head on his shoulder. "It's just a dream, okay? It's going to be all right," she says encouragingly, though she can't help but hear her own defeated tone. "It's a long walk. Why don't you go wash your face and I'll lay your clothes out—"

"Elva, just stop. I'm not a kid anymore," Arthur insists as he shrugs her off and stands. "You don't need to coddle me," he continues, storming to his room and into the bathroom in the back. Elva takes a few deep breaths, steadying her quickened heart, then follows him.

She leans against the doorframe behind him. The sink runs, though Arthur doesn't make use of the water. It pours out and circles the drain as he watches with a stillness so complete that he seems content to stand here until the supply dries up.

His eyes rise to the mirror, watching Elva's reflection. "I'm sorry, I know you're just trying to help," he says, sorrow tugging at his vocal cords. "It just felt so real. I'm having a hard time grounding myself."

"It's all right, I—"

"It's *not* all right," he cuts in. "Why do you always say that when I snap at you? I shouldn't talk to you like that. I just—"

Elva reaches out and touches Arthur's shoulder with the same care she'd handle fine china with. "What I'm saying is that I understand. Dreams can feel very real, but they're just dreams. If mine were real, I'd be dead a thousand times over! Falling and drowning and being eaten by zombies, being eaten by *coyotes*…" She continues this morbid list for a few moments with light-hearted spirit as Arthur watches blankly.

"Can I ask you something?" he asks suddenly.

"Of course. Anything."

Arthur motions for Elva to come to his side, and they stare at the mirror together. A mop of jet-black hair sits messily atop Arthur's head—a strand or two sometimes strays into his vision, which always draws an annoyed huff, so he elects to keep it short. His eyes, emerald green and serious, sit inside deep sockets, his thick brows an awning that shadows them. A handsome boy—as his sister would say—whose face is hardening in late-stage puberty, his facial muscles cutting attractive lines along his jaw. His skin is the complexion of a bleached olive as faint earth tones color him. At a glance, most would pin his heritage somewhere in the Mediterranean.

And for his sister, they'd guess that her ancestors were about one thousand miles north of Arthur's. The most color her skin sports comes in the form of the freckles that appear irregularly across her body. Brilliant orange hair drapes over her shoulders—Arthur has expressed both envy and awe at his sister's hair—and gives her eyebrows a fiery look. Beneath them are cold grey eyes which seem to suck all the life and color from her face. Though she is certainly narrower than Arthur, whose shoulders have nearly finished broadening, she's a bit taller. At twenty-two years of age—and six years his senior—she figures he'll catch up soon.

The stark contrast in their appearances hasn't gone unnoticed by Arthur. "We look nothing alike," he says breathily, as if he's realizing it all over again. "Why?"

And all over again, Elva sighs as she attempts to reassure him. "We've talked about this. Mom was a busy woman and never had the chance to settle down, and we ended up with different fathers. So, we look a little different!"

"Is that the truth?" he asks, turning to face her.

Arthur, you already know the answer. "Yes, I would never lie to you." *So, please, just drop this.*

His lips purse as he gives a skeptical, downturned series of nods. "Okay then. I, uh…" He squeezes his eyes tight and clears his throat before looking at his sister. "I'm sorry about all that."

"Don't be! It's all good, little bro," she quips with a hard pat on his shoulder. Arthur grimaces—he doesn't like being called *little*.

Elva finishes her breakfast while Arthur gets dressed, then the latter waits while Elva does the same. The two meet at their apartment door a short while later. "Aren't you forgetting something?" Elva asks, holding a glass of water and a pill bottle.

Arthur groans. "Oh come on, you know—"

"Yes, I *do* know. *You're* the one whose headaches are getting worse, along with your nightmares." She also knows that these pills will do nothing to help that. It's always worse this time of year. "So do what the doctor told you do and take these *consistently*."

Arthur accepts the bottle reluctantly and swallows two pills from it, downing the water afterward. "Happy?" he asks.

"Yup!" Elva chirps as she flings the door open.

The pair exit their apartment and shuffle onto the sidewalk. Between Bastion's climate control being on the fritz and the geo-engineers' design of having the interior weather correlate with the seasons, it's quite cold on the street. Luckily for Bastion's residents, there's little wind inside of the dome.

Both siblings are dressed warmly as they make their way to the elevator banks, ride one to the First Floor, and head to the pedestrian traffic exit. It's past rush hour, so the crowd is thin. They make it outside of Bastion's walls in minutes. South of Bastion is her sister city, Respite, the only other human settlement for thousands of miles. Elva and Arthur walk on the sidewalk alongside the main road connecting the two cities, though their destination is much nearer than Respite is.

"You've been wanting to see her more often," Elva says innocently.

"It's her birthday," Arthur responds.

"Yeah, but still. We went last week, and the week before too. Something on your mind?"

* * *

Yes. There is *much* on Arthur's mind.

Foremost is the inescapable feeling of guilt that pervades every moment of his life. Sometimes it's small, sometimes it's large, sometimes it is all. But it's always there. For whatever reason, he can't remember what he feels guilty about. It's something…distant.

Like his dreams. Real, but only when he closes his eyes.

This same guilt is only worsened when he's beyond Bastion's walls. The moment he steps outside, it's as if the world pours it into him, making his flesh squeal with strain. It wasn't as bad when he was younger. He's always had a penchant for nature and wildlife. Hours upon days upon weeks he'd spent in the southern forest, forcing his sister and mother to stay with him as he reveled in his human heritage. After his mother died, the intrinsic guilt he felt boiled to the surface, *especially* when he would enjoy himself outdoors. Elva took notice—she figured it was just how Arthur was grieving—but doesn't know the truth. That ever since that day, the gentle touch that nature obliged him made him feel vile and unworthy. He hasn't been to the forest since.

It passes on their left, and Arthur can hear the beautiful nothings of life filtering through the foliage. He longs to be among them, and his heart aches as punishment. *You deserve* nothing, *you wretched thing.* If his mother were still around, he thinks she would agree.

* * *

After a long while, Arthur answers. "I let her down somehow. I guess visiting her makes me feel like I'll find the answer if I just listen hard enough. But whenever I'm there, I just feel...empty."

The two turn right onto a trampled footpath into a short-shorn meadow. "You didn't let her down."

"You were intentional. I was a mistake."

"You were *unexpected*, not unwanted," is the best Elva can do.

"I guess," he responds.

A tree rises to meet them on a small climb in the landscape. Its leaves have just begun to turn, the first of many lifeforms to respond to the coming autumn's touch. Just below, recessed into the ground, is a rose marble plaque.

Amiree Emerson, 2003-2031, Beloved Scholar, Friend, and Mother

"Look! Chandrima must have visited recently," Elva remarks. Leaning against the trunk of the tree is a bouquet of flowers. The pair stop when they reach the plaque. Elva crouches to wipe away a trio of leaves that have fallen on it. She runs her fingers across its surface, feeling the gentle slope of the engraving and the grit of the marble that has just begun to deteriorate from the occasional rainstorm.

Elva stands and looks at Arthur, whose eyes are misty as he stares at the plaque. "You all right?" she asks.

Arthur shrugs. "I guess I just feel like I'm the reason she did it, you know? Like she couldn't live with me any longer."

She turns and grips him hard by his shoulders. "Don't you ever say that. What she did, she did for herself. It was selfish and cruel. It wasn't your fault."

Another shrug from Arthur loosens her grip. Before she can follow up, there's a sound from the canopy of the tree. "Shh…" Arthur whispers, his attention fully migrated upward.

Elva complies. She knows what's coming. She's seen it hundreds of times, but it's no less exciting. Arthur croaks and caws, his voice deep but forgiving. He sticks one arm straight out to his side as a raven descends from the canopy and lands on his wrist. It cocks its head with clockwork motion, examining the topography of his face. His calls continue, gently now, beckoning the bird closer. Making its way up his arm, it finally arrives on his shoulder. Arthur curls his arm and places his fingers under its chin, stroking its hackles. Elva cannot help but smile—*Enjoy it, dear brother.*

"Hey there, friend," Arthur says as the raven trills. Then Arthur stops moving, as does his guest. Dead still. A gust of wind rolls across the meadow, and Elva's skin tightens—it's ice cold. Suddenly the raven hops and takes flight, heading northeast.

"Arthur, what just happened?" Elva asks as she moves close to him.

He shakes his head, puzzled. "I think I've met that one before," he says with a gulp. "Let's, uh, head back. Maybe you can still make it to class on time."

The pair turn back, heading down the path. "Worried about my attendance, huh? Most of my classes are elective at this point, and I'm way ahead. *You're* the one who is falling behind," Elva responds with a smirk.

"It's boring. They're not teaching me anything I don't already know. Even the advanced classes are putting me to sleep," Arthur grumbles. He has a habit of overscoring during placement testing and then dragging his feet with his classwork. The only reason why the administration hasn't dropped him as a student is due in no small part to Elva's steadfast advocation and some favors called in from their aunt.

"You still have to attend. We're lucky enough to still live in Bastion," Elva reminds him. No residents of Bastion are there on accident. Amiree was allowed to have her family stay with her while she tended to her research duties. Without her as their sponsor, it is—again—only by the grace of their good aunt that they still have residency. A teenager and a college student don't provide anything useful for Bastion. "The least you can do is get your diploma."

"Paper and bureaucracy; it's meaningless," Arthur huffs. "I've already outgrown my studies."

She pauses for a beat, then responds with acute sarcasm. "Quite the rebel, aren't you? So, once you've 'broken free of these chains,' what will you do?"

Arthur rolls his eyes, still looking forward as they turn onto the main road toward Bastion. "Don't know, never thought about it."

Elva gives a sly smile. "Oh, you haven't? So, you're not hoping, let's say, that you can be a Pilot?" Arthur doesn't respond. "You know,

Pilots have to fight. You've said it yourself that you've no stomach for violence."

He shakes his head. "But that's all I'm good for."

"Don't say that! You're good at plenty of things." Arthur looks at her, goading her into backing up her claim. Her eyes dart back and forth as she thinks. "Nature! I mean, like animals and stuff. You could become a veterinarian, or a botanist. Then you could spend all day outside."

Arthur looks back down the road as Bastion's figure begins to rise far above them. "I…don't think that would be a good idea."

Elva stutter-steps as Arthur stops in his tracks. He turns, facing west, and Elva moves closer to try and mirror his sightline. There's nothing, save for the rolling fields and clear sky. For a minute, at least. A low percussion strikes her ears and slowly builds until she spots a helicopter approaching Bastion from the southwest. It passes in front of them, its flight path mirroring the road below. The two stare at it for a few moments in silence.

Twenty minutes later, the two disembark the elevator onto the Second Floor and make their way home. As they approach their apartment, they see several black-suited men and women crowded around their door while one knocks. Arthur steps defensively in front of Elva, who whispers something into his ear, causing his body to immediately relax.

"Can I help you?" she asks, stepping up to the men.

The man who had been knocking faces them and bows slightly at the waist. "I apologize if we've startled you. Director Joshi asked us to escort you two to the Third Floor. The others will pack your belongings while you're away."

"What?" Elva asks breathlessly, head shaking. "Why?"

The man cocks his head. "She hasn't told you? You're both moving to the Third Floor."

* * *

Curiesay wonders if the figures that stroll upon the road below have any idea how close they were to being vomited on. *"I need fresh air"* may not have been the best thing to say, as the crew had slid the door open, allowing Curiesay's eyes unfettered access to the ground below.

The irony of her apparent fear of heights isn't wasted on her. During her years at the Wilted Rose Asylum for the Criminally Insane, she'd made a habit of bird watching while spending time in the recreation yard. She'd even taken one as a pet, for a time. She envied their flighty souls, their freedoms, their feathers of tan and white-gold and black. She wondered what it would be like to soar high above it all, untouchable by all those beneath you. Imagining herself as one of them, she'd close her eyes and dream of flying up over the fences topped with prickly barbed wire and off to somewhere more appropriate.

Now, she's glad she was born with arms instead of wings. *I wouldn't make a very brave bird,* she thinks.

A little over twenty-four hours ago, Curiesay had agreed to Chandrima Joshi's terms—the latter's insane smile led Curiesay to immediately regret her decision. Since that time, everything's been a blur for Curiesay. She'd checked out of Wilted Rose—using a piece of paper from Chandrima that made the secretary sweat as she read it—and followed Parker and Chandrima out the front doors. The whole thing seemed surreal, like a dream, until Curiesay spied Peck watching her from behind the glass in the lobby. *Better luck next time, asshole,* she'd thought as she flipped him off.

Several flights and thousands of miles later, the three of them had boarded a helicopter out of—the country formally known as—Poland for the last leg of their trip. Curiesay had been (mostly) fine up until this point. But as they approached Bastion, her stomach began a somersault routine.

The city is enormous, if such a word is even encompassing enough. Its exterior is rather uninspired—it's simply a dome. A large, grey, oppressive dome, whose footprint makes the trees around it look like toothpicks that someone has staked all around it. To Curiesay, it almost looks like a *ball* that has been dropped from a great height and plunged its lower half into the earth. As they approach, her nerves tell her that they're about to strike the façade of the city. "Hey, fucker! You're about to smash right into it!" she implores.

Chandrima and Parker—who are sitting across from and facing her—share amused glances, but don't comment. Curiesay perceives this as a smug kind of insult that she'll file away in her *reasons why I hate these people* folder.

"Don't worry about it; a lotta people freak out on approach," the pilot comments over the intercom. It is another forty-five seconds until the helicopter reaches the very peak of Bastion. Curiesay realizes that the city is simply so *large* that even from a few miles off—when it is already swallowing most of your vision—it seems like you're right on top of it.

Curiesay squeezes her eyes shut as the helicopter descends into Bastion through an opening at the very top. The sound of the rotors changes in pitch as they pass the threshold. A few moments later, her stomach jumps as they touch down gently on the hangar deck.

She nearly stumbles out of the aircraft, fighting the urge to press her lips to the concrete floor. Chandrima and Parker disembark, and the latter retrieves and hands Curiesay her singular duffel bag of belongings from underneath her seat. Curiesay snatches it from his hands, but if it bothers him, he doesn't show it. Her eyes wander to the handgun he has holstered on his side. She's seen that he carries himself stoically, and wonders if he's just come along for the trip as Chandrima's bodyguard.

Curiesay follows Chandrima and Parker across the hangar deck. She cannot keep her eyes from drinking in this new space. The hangar is massive; several static aircraft are being accosted by maintenance personnel, running in rows of ten as far as her eyes can see. Several sets of eyes watch dubiously as the trio pass by, with some fingers pointed and whispers exchanged.

The pace is quick as the three enter a small elevator and ride it down. Another first for Curiesay; her beleaguered stomach performs lazy acrobatics. They exit into a long hallway and pass through a security checkpoint, then enter what Chandrima says is the *Third Floor*.

"So what am I doing here again?" Curiesay asks as she struggles to keep pace—she won't stop turning her body every which way as she desperately tries to orient herself. It's no use—this place is too large, too new, and her current situation doesn't allow meaningful connections to be made inside of her brain.

"Hmm?" Chandrima hums. For the duration of the trip to Bastion, Curiesay had been expecting her new *boss—Fuck, I hate that word—*to explain…anything really. Why she's been chosen, what she'll be doing, will she be paid. Chandrima hasn't offered more than a perfunctory smile in Curiesay's direction. "Oh, yes. It'll be easier to explain once you're suited up and—"

Curiesay's patience has shriveled up. "You haven't tried to *explain* anything since I agreed to this." She's aware that Parker is walking beside her and prepares to bite his head off if he offers anything more than quiet breathing.

The hallway they walk in is wide, lined with doors on both sides. On their right is a woman who beckons for Curiesay's bag. "I'll put that in your room for you," she says.

"But I—" Curiesay begins.

"It's fine, you won't need it today. It'll be locked up safe in *your* room," Chandrima implores. Curiesay's white-knuckled grip on her bag is a struggle to relax, but with some effort, she does so and passes it off to the woman. Everything she owns—which is almost nothing—is inside of that bag. The woman gives a confident nod and steps inside the room.

"Quickly now," Chandrima says, beckoning Curiesay along down the hall.

The lack of answers and the loss of her bag have pushed Curiesay's nerves to their breaking point. She's afraid, she's confused, and she's *very* angry. "Lady, you need to tell me what the fuck I'm doing here. I've waited long enough."

Silence from Parker. His lack of concern or acknowledgement of Curiesay's words frustrates her more than if he had spoken. The same goes for Chandrima. Perhaps she isn't being loud enough.

Chandrima doesn't miss a step, walking briskly into an open area at the end of the hall and taking a right. Vaulted ceilings and columns comprise the architecture of this space, though Curiesay can also see other hallways in the distance. "I already told you, just have some patience—"

Patience? "Patience?!" Curiesay echoes aloud. *This* does arrest Chandrima and Parker's motion as they stop and face Curiesay. "I've been goddamn patient since I agreed to this!" She steps closer to Chandrima, their noses nearly touching. "I won't move another inch until you tell me what the fuck is going on!"

The reverberation of her voice drops off quickly as it races down the hallways. Doors in the hallway nearest to them swing open and dozens of people poke their curious heads out, drawn by the tirade. Chandrima's smile softens from performative into genuine goodwill. "You're right, I've been rude," she says as she takes a half-step back and turns toward Parker. "Go ahead and get yourself ready. We'll be there in just a bit." A grumble is muffled by his closed mouth, but he simply nods and continues in the direction they were headed in. Strangely, Curiesay feels *less* safe as he departs. "Let's talk in my office."

4

Pilots

irector Chandrima Joshi's—Curiesay read the plaque above her door as she walked in—office is as scatterbrained as she imagines the owner's mind is. A quaint desk sits on one side, with a laptop computer covered by papers, flanked by mountains of folders. The rest of her office is more of the same: stacks of boxes teeter haphazardly against cabinets; loose papers nearly eclipse the carpeting; file folders sit open on the cushions of the couch that is against the wall.

Chandrima takes a heavy seat in her chair, and it lends a creak in response. "Please, just sit anywhere," she says.

There's nowhere to sit, you messy bitch. Curiesay swallows these words before they can escape her mouth as she spots a chair with a plate and a cup of moldy coffee on the seat. She debates kicking it over and leaving the mess for someone else to clean up—which is what she desperately wants to do—but bites this back as well. *Just take it easy; you got your way, after all.*

She clears the seat *properly* and drags it in front of Chandrima's desk before plopping down in it, letting her legs splay open, arms crossed. It would please her to know just how defiant she appears in Chandrima's eyes.

"Wow," Chandrima says in an awe-filled whisper. Curiesay scrunches her face and gives an unimpressed shrug. "I'm sorry. This is, uh, just as sudden for you as it is for me. I've a lot on my mind; these last few weeks have been a whirlwind. Thank you for coming, truly."

The sincerity of her tone softens Curiesay's guard a bit. *She sounds tired.* "Yeah, well, as long as you hold up your end of the bargain. Speaking of which…" She feels her own voice shrinking as she fights through the embarrassment. "How soon until I get some chocolate?"

"Of course!" Chandrima exclaims. She uncovers a grey box on her desk and presses a button on it. "Kitchen, chocolate for one, thanks!" Chandrima meets Curiesay's skeptical gaze. "They'll be by shortly."

Curiesay does her best to ignore the anticipation of her sweet treat. "So, go ahead. Explain."

Chandrima's smile fades as she sighs. Curiesay mentally recoils— this is the first time she's seen her placid expression change to what she perceives as grief. "Sixteen years ago, just five months after the Calamity, the Blight retreated into the Exclusion Zone. Contrary to what you may have been taught in school, we have no earthly idea why."

Curiesay's *schooling* consisted mostly of untrained orderlies poorly reading pre-built digital presentations for a class of poorly motivated—and drugged—patients. Most of what she knows is what she read herself from secondhand materials. "They said it was the bombs."

"That was the easiest explanation. Morale was low and we needed a win." Chandrima shrugs as she says this, as if the choice were obvious. "But, as most people have pieced together, if the bombs were so effective, why didn't we just turn the Exclusion Zone to glass?" This time, it's Curiesay's turn to shrug. "We didn't know if it would kill it entirely. It's a disease, like nothing we've ever seen. We don't even have a traditional classification for it. It's not a virus, bacteria, fungus, or even a prion. So instead, we built the Pale Wall and Bastion and have spent the years since trying to find a way to combat and eliminate it. Which brings us to *you.*"

A barging knock at the door startles Curiesay into silence. "Come in!" Chandrima says.

Lanky and pale-faced, the man opens the door and places a silver tray atop Chandrima's desk—she shoves a stack of folders onto the floor to make room. "Your chocolate, as requested," he says sharply.

"Oh, it's not for me, Frederic. You should know better." Chandrima gestures at Curiesay. "This is our newest Pilot, Curiesay. She has quite the affinity for sweets."

Something like nostalgia washes his expression as he faces Curiesay—she can feel his curious eyes all over her. "You are... Curiesay?" he says quietly.

"No shit, that's what she just said," Curiesay spits back. She doesn't like being gawked at.

Instead of his expression fouling at her snarky retort, Frederic's face lights up. "Of course you are!" he proclaims before bowing aggressively at the waist. His accent is crisp and from *somewhere in France or something.* "I am the Pilots' head chef, and it is an honor to meet you, ma'am. Please, if there's anything you'd like prepared for dinner tonight, I'd be thrilled to know."

The prospect of food—and meeting the provider of such—forces Curiesay to reconsider her tone. "Do you have any raviolis? Like, the ones from the can? Those are my favorite."

Curiesay has shot his proverbial dog. The light fades from his eyes as he stands, his gaze cast downward on her. "Ma'am, I will *die* before I ever feed you such filth. I will make a meal so exquisite that you will curse the day you ever ate *raviolis from a can!*" His final words are mocking, but less of Curiesay and more of the concept of such a meal.

I hope his food is as flamboyant as his passion. "Well then, Mr. Frederic, I look forward to eating your food." This seems to please him, as he grins widely, bows to both women, and excuses himself from the room. "He's pretty excited huh?" Curiesay takes a handful of dark chocolate squares and stuffs them into her mouth. She wishes she had the self-control to allow them to melt on her tongue, but she quickly chews them into a chocolate blob.

Chandrima has been fidgeting with a pen on her desk as they talk, and Curiesay finally takes notice; she's missing her ring finger on her left hand. Well, it isn't *missing,* but it *is* made of metal. The gentle whirring of the mechanics within when Chandrima uses it are well beyond Curiesay's hearing. She also takes note of Chandrima's eyes—brown, with irises closer in color to yellow than to black. She wears glasses so thick that Curiesay is floored that they stay on the bridge of her nose without succumbing to gravity.

Chandrima nods. "Yes, he is. We *all* are. Curiesay, we need you."

Though she's skeptical, the notion that she is significant to the world in any manner pleases her. "To do what exactly?" She chews loudly, mouth open, lips smacking. "I'm not a soldier or a scientist. Surely there's someone more qualified." *Try not to talk yourself out of a job, dipshit.*

"On the contrary, there's no one more qualified than *you*. Your purpose here is to pilot an Arbiter, an armor system that is designed to mimic the speed, strength, and robustness of the Blights. Think of it as a genetic lottery. Your DNA is a suitable match for the suit, and as such—"

Curiesay swallows hard, interjecting. "My DNA? Aren't they made of metal?"

Chandrima slows the pace of her words, speaking deliberately. "On the outside, yes. The innermost layer is made of lab-grown flesh, which—"

Another interruption. "But you just said they're made to mimic Blights, right? So—"

Chandrima interrupts back. "It's not going to make you sick, if that's what you're worried about. And it's not *Blight* flesh. It's lab grown. Sterile. Safe."

This mollifies Curiesay. A bit. "Sterile. Safe," Curiesay repeats. "You better hope it is, or you'll be the first one on my list when I get infected." Chandrima nods, acknowledging the threat. Curiesay feels she's—*maybe*—being too harsh. After all, she received chocolate, which in her book makes Chandrima an ally. Though the thought of considering her as such concerns Curiesay greatly. "So, I wear this suit, you point out the Blights who are giving you trouble, and I, what? Shoot them in the head or something?"

Chandrima giggles at this prospect as if it's obviously ludicrous. "We haven't found firearms to be particularly effective against the Blight's regenerative abilities, especially concerning the Class A Blights you're meant to combat. Hand-to-hand confrontation, coupled with extreme violence and overwhelming force, is the only way to put them down for good."

The idea of fighting *up close and personal* with diseased and contagious Blights doesn't excite Curiesay, but she bites her tongue. *I'll have to see what these suits can do.* "All right, let's say that I believe you. When do I get this *suit*?"

"Today! I'm actually expecting—"

Chandrima's words fall short as the door to her office swings open, hard. "Time's up," Parker rumbles. "I'm fed up with waiting."

"You didn't knock," Chandrima says firmly.

"*You*," Parker says, pointing at Curiesay. "Get down to the Dock and get suited up. Now."

What composure Curiesay had been building up shatters completely at this show of hostility. She stands and steps up to him, only to realize that he's *wearing* the armor she's supposed to receive. It bolsters his already imposing stature, and although she's quaking on the inside, she doesn't let it seep into her words. "Hey, motherfucker, we were in the middle of something here! Don't order me around, I'm not the one, you understand?!"

Curiesay recoils a bit as Parker bends forward at the waist, his face close to hers. "That's the spirit, see you soon." With this, he exits the office. A woman in a lab coat peers inside from just beyond the door.

"Well, I suppose he's right," Chandrima says as she stands and stretches, suppressing a yawn. "Go ahead and follow Doctor Neer to the Dock. She'll show you what to do."

This change in pace puts Curiesay on edge. Suddenly, she's *very* hesitant to do anything they ask her to. "Wh—what happens now?" she begs as Chandrima ushers her out of the office.

"Trial by combat, of course!"

* * *

Bastion, Third Floor, Dwellings Wing

"You really have no clue why we're here?" Arthur asks skeptically as he and Elva—along with their escorts—bustle down the wide hallways of the Third Floor. Dozens of doors line both sides of the hall, and on one side, a horde of eyes peer at them as they walk by. Arthur recognizes their uniforms—*Waifs*. Little girls immune to the Blight. A few wave their little hands and snicker as he walks by, and he realizes that they're only watching *him. Can they see me?*

Elva sighs, having repeated herself more than once. "I promise I have no idea." This surprises Arthur—she usually knows everything. They have just been shown their rooms; a pair of them, side by side, in the same hall they're walking down. "But I can't imagine why she would move us both up here."

Yes, you can, he thinks. There's only one possible explanation, and Arthur isn't sure how he feels about it yet. Elva's reticence is so heavy that he can feel it in the air, so he makes a point not to mention his thoughts. "Kinda weird that we have adjoining rooms."

"Is it?" she responds innocently. He knows she's more excited about it than she lets on. "I mean, you still have your own space."

"Yeah, with a door on the inside that leads to *your* room."

"I told you that you can leave it locked, if you want," she says. Arthur had considered this before flipping the deadbolt open.

Their escort stops in front of a black door that nearly blends into the dark grey concrete wall it's set in. "We're here. Please, step inside. You're expected." He opens the door, and the siblings sheepishly oblige.

Inside, the din of conversation overwhelms their ears. It's as loud as a convention center, but more cramped. Hundreds of people fill the space. From left to right is a half-oval glass wall that overlooks a demolished city, a half-circle desk with a row of computer workstations behind it, and a vaulted viewing gallery that ascends upward for a dozen rows.

The people, mostly wearing white lab coats, talk amongst themselves, pointing at the hanging screens above them or studying each other's notepads. An electric mood colors their auras—*Something big must be happening*, Arthur thinks.

"Hello there!" a familiar, cheery voice calls out. They two look toward the front and spot Chandrima, also clad in a white coat, and make their way to her. "I'm so happy to see you two!" she exclaims as she tries to hug both of them. Elva takes a polite step back, pulling out of her reach, but Arthur falls into her arms. He knows that Elva's feelings toward her have soured over the years, but his haven't.

"What are we doing here, Chandrima?" Elva asks flatly. Arthur doesn't like that she doesn't call her "aunt"—even though, by blood, she's not—but doesn't comment on it.

Chandrima separates from Arthur. "Yes, well, there's been some questions raised about your continued residency in Bastion without a sponsor, and I'm quite at the limit of my power. So, I put in the paperwork…" Arthur braces himself for what comes next. "And Arthur here is going to be our third Pilot!"

Elva pushes Arthur back and steps between them. "Like hell he is. He's sixteen and doesn't need to drop out of school to be one of your puppets." Her curt speech and mannerisms begin to draw attention as the conversations begin to still.

"I've already spoken with his teachers, and he is well ahead of his peers in terms of ability. Based on his previous test scores, they've agreed to grant him his diploma. So, if that's what you're worried about, it's already taken care of." *This isn't good.* Chandrima's placating tone is paper-thin in its sincerity—his sister isn't going to like that.

"Oh, don't act like it would stop you either way," Elva spits back. "You don't care about anything that isn't useful to you." She pauses for a moment, seemingly putting something together in her head. "Did you…keep us here, keep *him* here, just so that he could Pilot for you one day?"

Chandrima shakes her head dismissively, but Arthur has the impression that it's *exactly* as Elva has said. "I kept you here because your mother was a dear friend, and her children should enjoy the fruits of her labor. Which is why, in addition to Arthur being a Pilot, *you* will be his Steward!"

"I refuse," Elva says brusquely. "And so does Arthur." It's nearly dead quiet in the room as everyone watches the two women. "Let's go," she says, nudging Arthur as she turns on her heel and heads for the door.

"Will I be able to help?" Arthur asks quietly. Elva's shoes squeak as she halts mid-stride. "I mean, if I became a Pilot, could I help people?"

Chandrima nods. "Yes, Pilots—"

"Have one purpose, and that's to kill!" Elva roars back as she steps to Arthur's side, a sharp finger pointed at Chandrima. "Is that what you want? To make your nephew a killer?"

"I want him to help us save humanity. There are precious few people who qualify for the program, so we need everyone we can find." Despite Elva's insolence, and the concerned stares of Chandrima's subordinates, the latter still wears her signature smile and speaks calmly.

"He's not doing it, end of story. Arthur, let's—"

"Why don't we let Arthur decide? It's a volunteer outfit, after all," Chandrima says.

"Arthur…" Elva says sternly as she leans toward his ear.

"Please don't," he responds. *Please don't take it away from me.* Elva hesitates, then steps back.

Arthur takes a few deep breaths—the room is silent otherwise. "If…it will help fix things, then yes, I will do it. I will be a Pilot." A smattering of applause breaks out, hesitant in its percussion. "It's going to be okay," he whispers as he turns to his sister. "I have to do this." *You, more than anyone, should know that.*

"Fine," Elva resigns. She looks at Chandrima, her cold grey eyes narrowed. "I'll be his Steward. *Someone* in this family ought to protect him, don't you think?" she spits contemptuously.

"Of course, I wouldn't have it any other way," Chandrima responds. The door on the opposite side bursts open as a lab coat-clad girl bustles through it, clutching an electronic tablet in her hand. "Director, she's ready!" she calls out. She makes her way to one of the workstations directly behind the half-circle desks. Beside her sits a woman, clad in the same attire, who's wearing a headset with an eyepiece. A glance and a smirk is all she affords to her compatriot before she turns her attention back to her monitor.

Chandrima claps her hands together. "All right, people, showtime!" Any lingering conversations are shunted as the attendees scramble to their desks in the viewing gallery, with a few braver ones flanking the edges of the viewing glass. "Arthur, come along," Chandrima says as she beckons Arthur to the glass, pointing. "Watch down there, she's about to come out."

"Who is?" he asks.

"Our newest Pilot, Curiesay." She turns her head and flashes a smile so wide that her crow's feet turn into crow's hooves. "You're going to learn what being a Pilot is all about."

5

Epiphany

August 28th, 2053
Bastion, Third Floor, Dock Wing

If the personnel have any qualms about seeing Curiesay naked, they don't show it. She'd stripped, as requested, and stood in front of them, shielding herself from their eyes. To their credit, they've been very reassuring. "This is all above board, believe me," one of the women had said as she folded Curiesay's patient clothing—an unflattering and unremarkable orange top and bottom—and uncapped a tube of *something*.

Unsurprisingly, their gentle encouragement and neutral words have done little to dispel Curiesay's fears. She protests, half-assedly, as the woman and another red-jumpsuit-wearing woman squeeze the tube into their hands and apply it to Curiesay's body from toes to neck.

She's a lean woman, not so tall, with skin a shade darker than nutmeg. Her locs have remained untouched throughout this ordeal, though they are frizzy and disarrayed, as they always are. Hair products were hard to come by in Wilted Rose, so whatever oil she happened to procure—often illegitimately—is what she used. High cheekbones flank her sharp face, and two hazel eyes stare widened at the scene that is unfolding.

This shit is slimy. Another thing to add to Curiesay's list of *things that I fucking hate.* Whatever that stuff is, she hopes it's the last time she sees it. Once she's thoroughly covered, they bring a one-piece garment for her to wear. They tell her it's called an "Interface Suit." It's tight, and she realizes what the gel must be for as they wrangle it onto her with help from her slick skin. She feels no less naked wearing it and isn't keen on the idea of leaving the locker room they're in like this. Notably, she feels terribly cold, as if the heat from her very core is being drawn up through her skin and wicked away.

She's asked *What is going on?* no less than four times and is met with vague answers like *Annata will explain* and *We're running behind.* Both of which do nothing to inform her. Though she feels like little more than an object to these people. She follows the two out of the far door of the locker room, entering a long bay with low ceilings. "Hey, can y'all just relax for a second? What is going on? What am I about to do?"

To her surprise, there are twenty people waiting on either side of the hall she is ushered down, the majority of which are women. All are clad in various colors of scrubs: blue, red, and black chief among them. Every set of eyes is on her, save one. A singular girl wears a white coat and is standing in the center of the hallway, holding a tablet in her left hand and tapping her toe impatiently.

"Pilot, there is no time for idle talk. You are about to be fitted with your Arbiter, please follow me," the girl says in a self-important tone, standing a full head shorter than any of her coworkers. *What is this kid, ten years old?* Curiesay is concerned that the person in charge is a child but senses that she doesn't have much of a choice. She follows the girl down the hall, the spectators following along the walls single file, eyeing the would-be Pilot with fantastical curiosity.

The hallway opens up on the right side, revealing ten identical workstations with red toolboxes and computer monitors atop rolling carts around them. In the center is a circular recession on the floor and a bright LED light overhead. Behind each workstation is what looks to be a mannequin, and every one of them is without dress except for the second workstation, and on the wall over top is a digital sign reading *CURIESAY*. The mannequin is clad with a suit of armor.

She thinks it looks akin to a medieval knight's armor, albeit much slimmer. Its surface is glossy black, polished beyond reflection. The upper body is hearty, starting with a broad chest plate that narrows and wraps around the neck. Its midsection is more modestly armored, keeping the waist slight. Like her Interface Suit, the armor spans from toes to neck. Strangely, she thinks, it doesn't seem to have a helmet.

Without looking up from her tablet, the girl points at the circle in front of Curiesay's suit. "This one, Pilot. Go ahead and stand in the middle." A moment later she finally looks up to find Curiesay glaring at her. The girl rolls her eyes. "Please."

Curiesay reluctantly complies and steps onto the circular plate. The moment she does, a group of five workers in red scrubs hurriedly move to the suit of armor behind her and unmount the pieces, one at a time, from their mannequin display. Her eyes dart to and fro, realizing that this suit is certainly meant for her, as if the name placard didn't give it away.

"I'll give you the basic rundown as they install your suit, so listen carefully," the girl begins. The technicians move between the mannequin and Curiesay, installing the pieces as she waits nervously, surrounded by gawking eyes. *They don't see me as a person; I'm just a tool.*

The girl taps away on her tablet. "The suit is called an Arbiter. Underlayers of cloned muscle amplify your physical force..." Curiesay struggles to listen as her attention is on the technicians that scurry around her. First, they bring the boots, and she instinctively lifts her feet so they can slide them on, up to her knees. *Already I've fallen in line.*

"...provides moderate impact resistance, and an integrated cooling system helps to regulate..." Next comes the thigh plating, two halves of a single piece. The technicians clamp them together with her thigh in between and bolt them to one another. Curiesay's attention is torn between the strangers assembling her casket around her and the child who's doing her best to educate her.

"...thrusters on the feet, hands, legs, and back allows for three-dimensional movement, and excess biomass allows for ejection of projectiles and formation of solid beams of projected..." Only half-listening, Curiesay does her best to accommodate the technicians as they bring forward the torso section of her armor. Maybe if she's helpful enough, someone will come and save her. If only they knew how agreeable she could be, they wouldn't make her do...whatever she's about to do.

"...located on your back, in line with your spine, to allow smooth transitions of your tendrils from the underlayer to the surface of your suit. They are controlled by your will, like your limbs, and can..." The technicians fit her abdominal and chest plating together and move to fetch her gauntlets.

It makes her cringe, but Curiesay learned long ago how to appease people. Not long after she'd arrived at Wilted Rose Asylum for the Criminally Insane, she realized it was in her best interest to come off as meek and non-threatening as possible. But every time she had to flutter her eyes to get what she wanted, she felt like gagging. How humiliating, she thought, to sell her dignity in exchange for common courtesies. In this strange city, however, in this room, in this suit, surrounded by people who she feels do not care for her beyond their feelings for a common hand tool, she knows that there is no one to leverage.

"...monitoring your performance from my workstation and providing real-time feedback. Any questions?" the girl finishes, taking a gasping breath after her long speech. The technicians slide Curiesay's gauntlets over her hands and up to her bicep plating.

Of course I have questions! What happens now? Is this safe? Shouldn't I have a class or something? Curiesay's mind races with questions, but she knows they're irrelevant. She feels that regardless of her protests, what happens next is out of her control. It's as she figured—*different dictator, same servitude.*

Curiesay manages to ask the only question that doesn't provide her with a useful answer. "Who are you?"

The girl looks up from her tablet and smiles as if pleasantly surprised. "My name is Annata, and I am your Steward. We've waited a long time for you, Pilot." Curiesay's brow furrows with confusion, as the answer has only provided her with more questions. The technicians finish installing Curiesay's gauntlets and step back, admiring their handiwork.

"So, how does it feel?" Annata asks. Curiesay bites her tongue, her mind having neglected the possibility of being asked anything by these people.

She shifts her feet from side to side as the metal plates clunkily contact each other. "Uh, it...feels a bit loose. I don't think the pieces are connected." In fact, she *knows* they aren't connected to each other. They are simply bolted to one another with her body in between.

Her Steward smacks her own forehead with her palm. "Oh, right! Sorry, one moment." She taps on her tablet and Curiesay feels a burning sensation over her entire body for a split second. Each joint of the suit snaps together and her posture tightens. She can no longer feel the suit on her skin. The cold feeling is replaced by the feeling of being…*embraced?* For a few moments, the staff watch Curiesay in awe, like they're seeing a fawn walk on its own for the first time.

Curiesay shrugs once, twice, rolling her shoulders like a boxer stepping into the ring. She rocks her head and taps the floor with her toes. The echoes of the metal to concrete contact reverberate down the corridor. Her hands are next—she flexes them, squeezing hard, and she has the feeling that she could draw water from a stone if she so chose to. She taps her palms with her fingertips from thumb to pinky and back again and is pleased to find that a delicate touch is still within reason.

The butterflies in her stomach have met their fate. Curiesay paces in a circle, carelessly shaking her arms. Logically, she's still in the dark. But this suit, this *blessing* and the feeling it provides, tells her more about her role than any words can. She wonders if the people fawning over her with captivated eyes have any idea how dangerous she is now. Curiesay bounces up and down, hardly making a noise as she contacts the floor. *Light as a feather.*

She recalls Chandrima's words to her a short time earlier: "On the contrary, there's no one more qualified than you." *She had that much right.* Her casket turns out to be the embrace of God. Though she is no longer Christian, she had, as a child, once wondered what it might feel like to be Raptured, to be lifted from her earthly form and brought high. She no longer wonders.

At last, she holds her gauntleted hand in front of her, turning it over from palm to back, her eyes sparkling with awe. On her tongue, the sensation of a taste arcs across and disappears into the ether. *Tastes like…peppermint?*

Annata interrupts her Pilot's train of thought. "You're all set! We'll have to forgo a detailed calibration as we are very behind, but I will be watching and making adjustments as you fight."

Curiesay snaps her head to the side to meet her eyes. "Fight? Who…

" She trails off with an acknowledging grumble. *Who else?* Annata grins deviously, sensing Curiesay's understanding. She motions for Curiesay to follow her, and the Pilot obliges.

The crowd of staff whisper amongst themselves as they follow loosely behind the Pilot and her Steward, making their way down a hallway opposite the Arbiter's assembly area. Unbeknownst to them, and jarringly surprising to Curiesay, she can hear even their most carefully whispered words.

She has no further questions for this girl. Being directly responsible for giving Curiesay this armor, this *gift*, Curiesay feels gratitude. As this feeling fades, she mentally dismisses her. *I've no use for you any longer.* The pair reach a door large enough for a truck to pass through. Annata taps on her tablet, and the door hisses open.

The dark hallway is filled with light from the Arena and Curiesay shields her eyes with her arm. An instant later, she no longer feels the need to do so, as her eyes have adjusted, her pupils rapidly constricting. *That...was fast.*

This new space is enormous—a sprawling city lies before Curiesay. The door opens to a road, with rows of small structures on either side, and farther down, the city opens up with ten-story and higher buildings. It looks abandoned or even created solely for aesthetics. Burned-out cars litter the streets, glass lies in roughly rectangular patterns on the sidewalk in front of stores, personal effects lie scattered.

Curiesay steps in—without instruction—and hears the door begin to close behind her. This seemingly sticks a needle in her inflated ego as she whips around to face Annata. "Wait, what now?" She curses herself for not asking more questions, for being so lost amongst her own bravado. Logic sets in and reminds her that she is alone and ill-informed. *Perhaps I wrote her off too soon.*

"Now you fight! I'm rooting for you. I'll be in your ear and on your shoulder the whole time," Annata says, the split door between them closing vertically. "And one last thing: don't hold back!"

The door clangs shut, leaving Curiesay standing alone on the pavement.

She stares at the door for a moment, then turns on her heels and looks at the city. Craning her neck back, she spies the light fixtures that line the ceiling, hundreds of meters above, which provide enough light to the space that it is as bright as daytime. Walking down the road, heading nowhere in particular, she feels as if it's the right direction to go. Eyeing the windows of buildings, bus benches, orange construction cones, the handful of intact automobiles, she searches for life, hoping to see anyone but who she is expecting.

* * *

"There she is!" Chandrima shouts as Curiesay enters the Arena. Several large TVs hang from the ceiling in the booth which show Curiesay from different angles as she walks. The rapacious staff have quieted, taking their seats and watching the screens intently. Arthur is pressed up against the booth's forward-facing window, opting to see the action with his own eyes.

Elva is beside him, holding his hand. Arthur's eyes scan the city and focus on Curiesay. His neck hair stands on end as he grimaces, pressing his fingers into his temples. Elva sees this and gives a solemn nod.

The woman who sits beside Annata speaks, but not to the room. "Pilot, she's on her way to you, from the east, one hundred and sixty-seven meters until visual."

Not a person in the room moves or speaks, save for Chandrima, who rushes to the window as Curiesay turns her head to look. Chandrima waves obnoxiously with both arms, pressing her face against the window and grinning from ear to ear.

***

Blank white walls surround the city, save for the one sporting the Observation Booth's window. It's a few meters above street level, bulging into the Arena in a half-oval shape. Curiesay looks and sees a frenzied Chandrima flailing her arms at her. *What a weirdo.* She returns a curt nod.

A minute later, Curiesay reaches a four-way intersection; off to her left is another road, leading directly below the Observation Booth, so she turns right, and hears a voice.

"About time."

He's distant, one hundred meters or so. Curiesay isn't surprised at who she sees. Parker waits for her like a statue in the street—he's clad in armor like hers, his own titanium vanity. As she examines him, she ponders. *His stubble, it's dark.* She can nearly see the individual follicles of his beard. *But he's so far? Isn't he?*

Parker smirks. "Are you ready?"

She's been in fights before. A thieving block mate who plundered her spare hairbrushes, an *over-eager* orderly who caught her working alone on the night shift, a social services worker who denied advocating for her release because she was "an ungrateful bitch." In none of those cases did she consider herself a winner. Until now, that is. This moment. The righteous bravado she had been swimming in a short while ago wells up again, her ego becoming so full she feels that it may prevent her from moving through doorways. She rocks her head from side to side, bounces her shoulders, and locks her eyes on Parker.

"I'm ready," she growls.

6

I'm (Not) Alone in the Dark

August 28th, 2053
Bastion, Third Floor, Arena

She is *not* ready.

A blur of motion is all Curiesay can comprehend before Parker's punch connects with her midsection. It feels like she's been hit by a truck and is sent tumbling backward across the pavement. Her armor lessens the blow, barely; she suspects a cracked rib.

"Get up!" a voice in her suit yells. She's barely to her feet when Parker follows up with a kick that sends her liver into shock. His speed is unreal to her—his attacks kick up the stagnant dust on the street. Curiesay is again sent to the ground as she tumbles backward. This time, she doesn't wonder about her ribs; every inhalation sends waves of pain through her torso.

"Quit daydreaming and move!" the voice yells again—she recognizes it as Annata's. *You're not helping.* She feels that her entire abdomen will fall to pieces if she stands. A thousand errant signals per second torture her nervous system, emanating from her liver.

She turns her head upward as footsteps approach and she is violently yanked to her feet by Parker's grip on her chest plate.

"What are you doing?" Parker scoffs. "Do you even care if you die?" Face to face with him, Curiesay can see what she is up against. His irises shine a piercing crimson-red against the bloodshot whites of his eyes, a black pupil swimming in the center. Every vein on his face is visible and raised, the beats of his heart detectable as they pulse.

He looks upon her with repulsion, seemingly disgusted to be sharing the same air. To Curiesay, he looks like the kind of exaggerated caricature someone would commission to portray their political opponent as a demon.

"You broke my fuckin' ribs, asshole," she growls through pained breaths. Her last surviving shred of bravado spits a mouthful of blood onto his suit. He doesn't seem to care. She can feel heat emanating from his armor, as if he's a roiling furnace.

"You're not going to kill me, so just fuck off already," she gasps out, barely able to string words together as her abdomen spasms. She doesn't believe them as they leave her mouth.

He eyes her for a moment more, then speaks. "Jordan, do me a favor. Tell the runt to get her Pilot in order. She has sixty seconds."

He abruptly releases his grip on her armor, turns, and walks away. The pain from standing unaided drops Curiesay to her knees. *What the fuck is happening?*

Annata again speaks to Curiesay, the speakers just below her armor's collar crackling to life. "Okay, Pilot, don't worry. We'll get you back on your feet."

Curiesay snaps back. "I don't think so, kid. I can't even stand. I need a hospital." *I sound like a whiny bitch.*

"You're *wearing* the best hospital money can buy. Your suit can heal you, you just have to concentrate. The fractures aren't complex, so it shouldn't take long. I should warn you though: it will burn," Annata says, speaking matter-of-factly and seemingly unaware that Curiesay is fighting for her life.

Curiesay suspends her disbelief for a moment. "Uh…okay? So, like, how? Concentrate on what, not having broken ribs?"

Annata parrots like she's reciting a passage from a textbook. "These functions are autonomic and somatic, like breathing. Your body will do it on its own, but you can consciously control it as well. Just like you can take a deep breath and hold it, command your cells to repair your broken ribs."

"What the fuck does that mean? How am I supposed to—"

"Just humor me! Close your eyes!" her Steward yells. Curiesay pants for a few moments, stubbornly refusing. *What have you got to lose? Let her help you.* She grudgingly concedes, closing her eyes and listening intently.

Low and deliberate, Annata takes on an earthly tone, the voice of a soul shaman in a time where humanity revered them. "You know how to do this. You have always known how to do this. Every cell is yours. They exist solely to do your bidding. Command them. Your injuries do not serve your needs, and thus must be rectified."

The feeling of connection to her primal self Curiesay had felt when she donned her Arbiter, she again is at the precipice of an epiphany. *They all live to serve me.* It makes sense. Not logically, but spiritually. She has no need to understand how, as it already is and always has been. She knows it as surely as she knows her own name, as surely as she knows that she exists.

What begins as warmth in her abdomen rises to seething temperatures as cells flood to her broken ribs. White-hot tendrils of agony emanate from her wounds and seem to stretch to every corner of her corporeal being. The heat tugs at Curiesay's conscience, screaming *Go no further, we cannot bear this.* A crescendo of agony chokes incomprehensible vulgarities from her mouth, her breath steaming as if the words themselves are inflammatory.

After ten seconds, the pain subsides and Curiesay takes a deep and pain-free breath. She can see the waves of heat subtly rolling off her armor, but she doesn't feel warm at all.

"Hey! That was pretty fast, good work," Annata says proudly.

No time for niceties. "Repeat everything you tried to tell me in the Dock. I wasn't listening. Quickly." Curiesay finally reassesses her surroundings; she is on the street, buildings reaching up on either side of her, a window full of curious spectators and a very violent man standing just ten meters from her, watching. As Curiesay struggles to her feet, she flips him off. *How you like that, fucko?*

Curiesay hears Annata take a deep breath. "Okay, suit, cloned muscle, jump high, run fast, hit hard." *I've seen that much.* "Circles on hands, feet, back, legs, port excess heat, make you go fast. You can throw bits of biomass like little grenades, or concentrate them on your palms and basically, like, shoot like this laser thing." *Excuse me?* "And then there's your tendrils… They're like snakes. You can wield four of them, two on either side of your spine. Think of them like arms, if you like…say instead of arms you had, like, snakes where your arms go. Except they're not where your arms go; they come from your back. Have you seen *Spider-Man 2*? It's this old movie that—"

"Okay, enough with the fuckin' snakes or whatever. How do I beat this guy?" Curiesay interjects, her eyes locked to Parker. He hasn't moved a muscle, and she's a bit irritated that he can probably hear both her and her Steward talking from that distance.

"Your genome analytics indicate that you possess superior speed when compared to him. He is quite a bit stronger however, so I recommend keeping your distance. Strike, reposition, strike, evade. But Curiesay, Parker is a veteran Pilot. Whatever you do, do not underestimate him, do you understand?" Annata says, and Curiesay gives a determined nod.

"One final thing: you said before that he wasn't going to kill you." Curiesay's ears perk up, her internal clock telling her that she only has a few precious moments left before her sixty seconds of respite are up. "You were wrong. He *is* trying to kill you."

With only a moment or two to spare, Curiesay asks one final question before Parker resumes his attack. "Why?"

Seconds tick by.

"Doctor's orders, Pilot."

Curiesay identifies the blur of motion as Parker charges forward. She pushes off with all her might, propelling herself out of the way of his elbow strike. Leaving the ground in a diagonal trajectory, her apex is three meters high, and she lands with a shuffle of her feet.

"Whoa," she says aloud, appreciating her deftness. Parker launches himself forward again, feigning a right hook as he shifts his weight, the momentum traveling through his hips and down to his leg as he whips it forward, aimed at Curiesay's recently healed ribcage.

In a flash, Curiesay bends backward, splays her legs, and drops to the ground like a limbo competitor. She sees his heel rapidly approaching as he follows up on his missed kick with a stomp. Curling her legs up to her chest, Curiesay transfers her weight onto her upper back, braces on the ground, and pushes off, somersaulting backward and out of the way, but not before delivering her own heel strike to Parker's chin.

She lands silently a few meters back and flashes a shit-eating grin as she sees blood trailing down from Parker's split lip. *Oh, so sorry, did I do that?*

Parker stares her down—steam crawls up from his wound as the gash closes itself. She knows that she'd healed her own body a short time ago, but seeing the freakish speed at which his wounds knit themselves up, she can't help but feel a pang of horror. *What the hell are these suits made of?*

Her eyes take notice of Parker's arm as he raises it, palm up, and just above it hovers an orb the size of a marble. *What is that?*

Parker thoughtlessly tosses the orb toward her, and when it lands between them on the ground, it erupts with shocking force and smoke. Curiesay's teeth rattle, but before she can fully process what has happened, Parker cuts through the smoke in an instant and delivers an uppercut that sends her tumbling through the wall of a half-demolished building behind her.

Curiesay scrambles to her shaky feet, diaphragm spasming. No quarter is given when Parker pursues her and follows up with a palm strike squarely to her chin. Bone concedes to force as her jaw splits down the middle—white-hot pain travels from the wound and drills into her temples.

For a solemn moment, Parker stands before her. Her awestruck eyes widen—behind him are what seem to be four red snakes, peeking around his torso, swaying lazily. Curiesay eyes them, the momentary fascination providing a distraction from the pain.

It is short lived for poor damned Curiesay. Parker digs in and launches a hailstorm of attacks. His fists shatter bones and crush soft tissues while his tendrils strike at the lightly armored joints and cleave skin apart. Annata rails into Curiesay's microphone, begging her to "Move, fight, do something!"

But she does not.

In mere moments, Curiesay's body is in tatters. Parker's right hand shoots forward and clamps onto her throat. She can feel her feet leave the ground as he holds her aloft.

Though she's squeezed her eyes shut, she can feel his critical gaze on her skin. "Are you finished so soon?" *Please, don't hurt me anymore.* "Why did you bother coming here if you were just going to quit?" *I had nowhere else to go.* "Is this your heart?" *It's all I have.*

Then, a familiar voice. "Parker…" *Chandrima, thank God, maybe she will—* "…I didn't tell you to stop," Chandrima says flatly through Parker's speakers. *You wanted this?* "Adam! Continue!" *You brought me here to die?*

As Curiesay waits for the inevitable, she can feel quaking from the hand that chokes her. "I can't see you, Curiesay," he whispers. To her, it sounds like an apology. "I can't see you at all."

Parker releases his grip, and she crashes to the ground in a heap. Her eyes open and she watches her assailant shiver as he retreats, his tendrils slithering into his back.

* * *

"Parker, I didn't tell you to stop," Chandrima says. A few murmurs roll across the crowd. Elva snaps her head toward Chandrima and glares. *Arthur thinks so highly of you, and this is what you show him? I was right about you. You're as bad as mom was.* "Adam! Continue!" she follows up.

Annata is staring at her monitor as her fingers dance across her keyboard. Her opposing Steward, watching forlornly with crossed arms, declines to speak.

The tension evaporates from the room as its occupants relax their taut spines—Parker has dropped his prey and is heading to the Dock. With the chance of a televised execution averted, low whispers break out as they discuss the scene.

"I'm done," Parker says, transmitting to only Chandrima's headset. "Come clean up your mess."

The Director falls into her chair with a grumble. "Parker, you jerk. I told you not to hold back."

* * *

Curiesay lies on a bed of rubble, eyes upturned and unfocused on the ceiling of the Arena far above. The single-story building she's in has crumbled further from her tussle with Parker. Naught but dust, debris, and blood exists here.

Taking stock of her injuries, she'd panic if she had the strength. The task of breathing feels monumental—her right lung, full of blood, is useless, leaving the left panting and working double. Broken, jagged ribs tear her lungs with each breath.

Her left hand feels far away. If she were aware, she'd realize her shoulder is dislocated, leaving her left arm lower than normal. She *is* aware that her right forearm is broken because it's folded over itself, her right hand resting on her bicep. Luckily, she thinks, she can feel nothing below her waist.

Her normally symmetrical face has suffered a series of defining gashes. Bone beneath shines white as the blood runs from her wounds. A broken and offset jaw doesn't help matters, and she tries in vain to squeeze her muscles just enough to keep the two halves from scraping each other as she breathes.

Curiesay cries in short, pain-filled coughing fits. Little red rivers of blood and tears cut through the grime on her face, carving out paths of clean skin on their way to the ground. *Is this how I die?*

Primal instincts analyze her agony and provide her with a grim conclusion—*This is the end.* Her groans drift uselessly through the ruined building she's entombed in, dying out before reaching sympathetic ears. *Is anyone there? Is someone coming to help me? Why don't they want me? Why don't they want me around? Doesn't anyone want me?*

Of all her deathly dreams and ill-fated attempts on her own life, she never expected *this* to be her end. She yearns for her little white room. For abusive staff. For disgusting cuisine. For safety. Her first real decision in years—the one that brought her to Bastion—was a mistake, and she curses her foolishness. As her vision fades to black, she drifts into the ether, down into the dark, into the abyss, and thinks back to when she had first experienced staring death in the face.

* * *

"Curiesay! Move your ass!" a woman shouted from the window of her idling sun-weathered sedan. The July sun glared down upon that Texas town. Little Curiesay stumbled out the screen door, right down the steps, and flat onto the concrete path.

Oh no. She'd torn her white stockings and scraped her knee. The blood quickly wound a path through the fabric down to her ankle. With more deftness than led to her fall, she leapt up, patted away the concrete dust which powdered her black dress, and booked it to the sedan.

Her butt narrowly contacted the seat when the car lurched forward, and her door was slammed shut from the force. She was eight. Much of her short life was spent with this foster family.

The Calamity was six years past, and the world still reeled from the devastation. Economies shuttered, workforces stretched thin, and orphans abounded. Mankind abandoned most of Asia, Europe, and Africa, leaving the Americas and Australia as the last habitable continents. A flood of foundlings inundated the Americas, and any open door who would take one got one. Any *good faith* vetting went out the window.

Her parents were dead, or abandoned her, or were missing. She never knew either way, as she was told to stop asking. *You got a new family now, who gives a shit where you think you came from?*

"They all waitin' for us at the church and you're out here fuckin' around," the woman began, driving erratically. Curiesay fought against the turns as she struggled to fasten her seat belt. The woman had been in several accidents, three with Curiesay in the car, and the headaches she suffered after the one last winter had just began to subside recently.

"And we're late cause you wanted to bring your fuckin' bag," the woman scolded, swatting behind her with a wide, angry palm. Luckily for Curiesay, the blow glanced off her calf, her dark skin barely reddening in response.

Too focused on covering her damaged stocking, Curiesay didn't react fast enough to stop the woman from wrenching her backpack away. "I'm keeping this. You don't get to do whatever you want; not on my time, not in my house," the woman spat as she sped through the streets. Curiesay braced the best she could around the curves.

The sedan screeched to a half, sitting cockeyed on the street before the church steps. "You better keep your bitch mouth shut and not whine a single peep, or you'll be the next one whose ass is in a casket," the woman snarled, her rank breath combined with the summer heat—the car's A/C was on the list of things to be fixed, right behind the cracked windshield and the brakes—curling the hairs in Curiesay's nose. It smelled of alcohol, as it often did, and she could hear the clanking of empty bottles from the front seat. *That explains the driving.*

A kind gentleman in a grey suit opened Curiesay's door and helped her onto the sidewalk. Curiesay eyed her backpack in the front seat as they ascended the steps. *My teddy is in there.* Her uncle had gifted her a small stuffed bear, with eyes of black plastic and a felt-like exterior. She carried it when she was feeling lonely.

The church was hot and stuffy, just like her bedroom. Pews upon pews were brimmed full of those who'd come to pay their respects. Though she thought of him as a god among men, Curiesay couldn't believe how many people her uncle knew.

Curiesay and the woman made their way up the rightmost aisle, moving to the front pew and shuffling in. Her "brothers" were there, the biological kin her foster family provided her, and after lifting their legs to let the woman take her place beside her husband, who sat in the middle, they did not give Curiesay the same courtesy.

"'Bout time, you always slow as hell," the oldest boy snickered as Curiesay sheepishly tried to move past him, nearly tripping over his purposefully flailing legs.

"Watch your step, dummy," the second one said as he waited for Curiesay to pass and then stuck his legs in between hers and kicked hard, throwing her to the floor, her fall partially broken by her foster mother's shins.

She felt weightless as the woman yanked her by the back of her dress and tossed her onto the open spot next to her. "Sit. Down," she growled through gritted teeth, the pastor only a few steps away, having begun his walk up to the podium to speak. Young Curiesay sat in silence as he spoke, his words giving life and color to the cold grey that had become her uncle's life.

* * *

In the Observation Booth, half of the spectators have already left. Chandrima and Annata, equally melancholy, sit haphazardly in their chairs, like bags of liquid people. Arthur and Elva are still up against the window, watching intently for movement from Curiesay.

On Annata's screen—which displays the status of her Pilot and Arbiter—the rolling barrage of vital signs take an unexpected turn.

"Um…Director?" Annata says warily, sitting up with the assistance of her hands on the arm rests. "Can you come look at this?" Chandrima perks up a bit, seeing the same numbers crawling across the screen in front of her, but opts to move to Annata's side.

As Chandrima comes around behind her, Annata's display begins to throw red rectangular flashing warnings, indicating alarming vital signs. "Her body temperature…is skyrocketing!" Chandrima says with a squeak. The ears of the spectators—who are making small talk by the door as they filter out—flutter, and they hurriedly take their seats.

"Cerebral cell activity is stable, blood oxygen within limits, internal temperature forty-five point two degrees Celsius and rising," Annata says calmly, shifting excitedly in her chair.

Chandrima keys the microphone on the headset she wears. "EMS, call off your team. Do *not* enter the Arena."

* * *

Surely, Curiesay had always thought, Uncle Thomas must be from a different family.

In terms of his capacity for kindness, he may as well have been a different species than her foster mother. She could hardly recall a memory of him where he wasn't smiling. As far back as she could remember, Thomas had always brought her candy in secret during family gatherings.

From beyond the wench's eye, they'd snack and talk for hours. Thomas always had stories to tell: his glory days as a young lieutenant stationed in the French Foreign Legion; competing on a local wrestling team; business trips where he met beautiful women only to spend scant days with them, their memories tugging at his heart as he grew old as a bachelor. Curiesay had made a mental note that when she grew up, she would be sure to appreciate a kind man, should one cross her path. He was the only person she knew that treated her as a person and not as a child or a burden.

The summer prior, he had confronted her foster mother, frenzied on liquid courage during a cookout, and publicly scolded her for her treatment of young Curiesay. As a result, he was estranged from the family for months. Curiesay called him in secret one night and begged him to apologize so she could see him again.

With repugnance, he conceded, telling his sister-in-law pretty lies about herself to soothe her ego, and he was allowed to visit once again.

The first time he attended a family function afterward, Curiesay pulled him aside. "I don't need you to protect me. I just want to spend time with you." He nodded solemnly, lamenting with great sorrow that things couldn't be different.

The father wasn't often around, working long hours, so Curiesay was left to be tended to by a woman with a sour soul, and her treatment only became more brutal as she grew older. She couldn't imagine why—she wasn't a terrible kid.

She did her chores and kept her room clean and excelled in school. Still, the mother was ruthless. She wasn't allowed to have friends over, nor visit their homes. Most times when the family would go out together, she would be left behind at home.

She grew to prefer that, as it was less hassle overall. Plus, she'd call her uncle and pester him to come and visit in secret. He'd park on the road behind their house and Curiesay would hop the fence so the front neighbors couldn't report on her clandestine meetings. Thomas would fatten her up at the pizza parlor and fill her pockets with candy before returning her home.

Hershey's Kisses were her favorite, mostly for the fun of unwrapping the foil they came in. Thomas would take the wrappings and add them to an ever-growing ball. Whenever one reached softball status, he would chuckle, toss it into his glove compartment, and start another one. In such a life of strife, Curiesay took comfort in treats, and Thomas was more than happy to oblige.

But happiness wasn't in the cards for young Curiesay.

Spring brought with it an unexpected guest—kidney cancer. After fainting at a barbeque, Thomas stayed at the hospital for nearly a week. At his insistence, Curiesay's foster mother allowed her to visit. While the mother went to the cafeteria to indulge in bland, heartless food, Curiesay begged Thomas to tell her everything.

His kidneys were beyond saving, and the cancer had also staked claim in his liver and the lower lobe of his left lung. He confessed that his doctor had given him six months to live, twelve if he was lucky, and less than that if he opted for the aggressive treatment plan which was one of his two options.

In a moment of weakness, he asked Curiesay what she thought he should do, and she gave him the same answer that his eyes gave her at every goodbye—*Don't give up.* She didn't know if that was the right answer, but it's what he'd taught her. It was the only answer she knew to give.

He told his doctor to give him the drugs, insisting that he would go out fighting if that were to be his destiny.

A short eleven weeks later, his family rushed to the hospital to witness his dying breath. The chemo had boxed his already distressed liver, and no transplant committee would pin a healthy liver on a would-be corpse. Her foster father insisted that Curiesay be brought along, commenting that she "was the only person he asked me about."

Thomas' room was filled from wall to wall with people, and Curiesay could only catch glimpses of him through their legs. She heard some whispering as the adults looked around, then down, and made way for her, ushering her to the front. She felt ashamed, but sometimes she'd wished they hadn't.

Curiesay learned that day that even the brightest twinkle in a person's eyes could vanish in a puff of rancid smoke.

There was hardly anything left of the man who she clung to so dearly. The cancer and chemo had stripped the cherry from his cheeks, the fullness from his lips, and the hair from his head.

She thought that he looked awfully hungry.

Through desperate gasps behind his oxygen mask, he whispered. "Curiesay. Come," he managed with a lazy flick of his wrist, urging her forward.

In her shaking hands she gripped a toy tightly. "Hi…Uncle Thomas. I brought you my Gumby… I thought…you might be bored here so I wanted you to have something to play with," Curiesay squeaked. Unable to manage the words themselves, Thomas outstretched a trembling hand, took the toy, and gave a nod in thanks.

With much concern from those closest to him, Thomas sat up. Shushes and hushes and gentle hands urged him to stay laying down, but he protested. "What's…a bit…of pain…at this point?" Eventually the hands turned to helping him, the group spreading like the sea in front of Moses as Thomas swung his legs around and faced Curiesay.

He removed his oxygen mask, letting it drop around his neck, and took forceful breaths with great effort, his lungs clamoring for the pure oxygen they had been receiving. He denied them, locking eyes with Curiesay. Then she saw it—the flame. It was still there, but it was faint. With furrowed brows and furious hazel-brown eyes, he told Curiesay what she told him just eleven short weeks prior: *Don't give up.*

He motioned to the men nearest to him, then to Curiesay, and they picked her up by her arms, bringing her close to Thomas as he put his hand on her shoulder and took a deep, raspy breath. Of this memory is Curiesay most fond.

"I'm…proud…of…you…"

* * *

The group by the door have now all crowded around Annata's

workstation—unnecessarily, as the readouts are available on the big screens—as Curiesay's vital signs bounce back and her readouts all begin the same flashing routine as the others.

"That's extraordinary; her energy output is ten thousand watts and climbing!" Annata exclaims to a flood of gasps from the crowd.

"She's getting up!" Arthur shouts, still glued to the window. The spectators take their eyes from Annata's display and scramble back to see the overhanging televisions that are broadcasting live from the Arena.

Curiesay hobbles onto the street, facing down the road at Parker's back. Her wracked body pours steam from every wound and orifice. Her Arbiter's cooling fins, mounted between the gaps in her armor plating, glow red as they struggle to keep up with her demands. Joints pop, bones crackle, cuts sizzle as she commands her cells to obey, pushing them to the brink. She raises her jaw back to its rightful place with her hand and it pops into place.

His eyes crawling over her, Arthur stares, entranced. "She's... beautiful," he whispers.

* * *

As the pastor gave his closing remarks, he invited the immediate family to kneel at the casket, its dark red exterior and gold handles commanding its presence at the front of the congregation. Curiesay moved to follow and was pushed back down by her foster mother, a stern look thrown her way.

They never loved him like I did. Her "brothers" seemed to enjoy her exclusion a bit too much, as they glanced back with rueful smiles. *They didn't know him like I did!* As they knelt, Curiesay sprang up and rushed to the casket, squeezing her way in between her foster family. The observing congregation shifted uncomfortably in their seats at this break in decorum.

A moment later, Curiesay was thrown backward, tumbling down the stairs that led to the pews.

* * *

The trepidation they feel is so thick it's tangible, like breathing in clouds of vapor. Their pupils constrict; their skin crawls; their instincts scream. But they are frozen in place.

Only Chandrima and Annata are actively working, the air heavy on their shoulders. "Director, sync rate is nearly seventy-five percent. She's about to Cross," Annata says with a tremble in her voice, though on her face is a satisfied smile.

"Hey, Parker… Turn around," Jordan says shakily into her mic as she mirrors Curiesay's display onto her workstation. Two warnings flash continuously.

TEMP HI

1ST CROSSING

In the Arena, Parker stumbles.

His legs feel heavy, the hair on his neck standing on end. The trepidation experienced in the Booth is nothing compared to the crushing weight of rage given form that tugs on his every cell.

With a relieved sigh, he turns on his heel, facing down the road toward Curiesay. "Finally."

Curiesay's body radiates intense heat, the waves lapping at the light around her. The heat, combined with the steam pouring from every seam of her suit, sends arcs of heat lightning crackling across the air surrounding her.

I can't hold it. Something wicked grows within her. *I don't want this.* Her irises boil to red, her brow furrows, and she bears down until her teeth splinter and crack.

* * *

The pastor rushed to Curiesay's side and helped her to her feet. "My child, are you all right?"

Curiesay looked up the steps as the woman came barreling down at her. "You disobedient brat!" The pastor's assistants held the unruly woman back, the rest of the foster family frozen in wide-eyed shock.

Without a word, Curiesay surged forward, seeking to bypass the scuffle altogether and get to Thomas' casket, but the pastor held her back as the woman continued her tirade. *I can't hold it.*

"I should've never agreed to this! You're just as naïve as he was!" the babbling woman declared as she swatted at Curiesay.

Curiesay stood her ground, eyes moist. "I just want to tell him that I love him."

"Child, I don't think that's such a good idea right now, let's get you sat back down," the pastor insisted. Curiesay didn't budge. This was too much for her young mind to process.

The congregation, her uncle's friends, gawked at her—*What must they think of me?* As her eyes darted between the wench and Thomas' casket, she could feel something vile rising from inside of her.

Her pupils constricted, hyper fixated on the large metal cross hanging from the pastor's neck, its bottom pointed to allow him to insert it into the holder by his bedside.

That...looks sharp. On the precipice of complete ego death, Curiesay's hearing betrayed her to a ringing tone, her eyes neglected the true colors of the world, her mind neglected its trained niceties.

Her face contorted, she took a deep breath, and...

* * *

She can hear air rushing past her ears as she plummets toward the blood ocean below. She passes through the surface, the red abyss welcoming her without contest. The speed of her descent does not slow. A singular light is suspended far above, and to her it is the only light and will be the last light she will see as it diminishes. It's so warm down here, she thinks.

So dark.

And so, she sinks. No endeavor is launched to resist her descent. No hope for absolution, or forgiveness, or mercy. The urge to breathe becomes too great to ignore, and she gasps for nothing but blood as it races into her lungs. She welcomes it, as soon the last sparks of life within her mind will be stifled and there will be no more pain.

She closes her eyes, being consumed by somber silence as the light is not more than a distant memory. It's slipping. My mind, she thinks, it's fading. Taking one last look at infinity, her eyes open, and she can see Thomas' face, his eyes furious with defiance, looking down toward her.

"W—wait..." The blood muffles her words. Her legs, weighty with deprivation, kick. "Wait!" Arms of pins and needles reach out and swing down, reach and out swing down. "I don't want to go!" She commands her apathetic body to fight, to swim, to climb, but it is much too late, and she is much too far.

Inundated by the dark.

She sets herself in a fury, kicking and grabbing and gasping in futility for the air she so desperately needs. She knows that her last moments, so precious a set of them, are now destined to be gorged with rage. It is futile, it is pointless, and it hurts. Yet, she persists, determined to enact a furor so tremendous that, even at this depth, a singular bubble shall rise to the surface to mark her passing. As her last moments draw to a close, she musters her strength, kicks a final time, and reaches up with all her might. A hand plunges into the deep, gripping her wrist and dragging her upward with terrible force.

She surfaces, gasping as the blood runs from her eyes. It holds her above the blood, its grip crushing Curiesay's bones, and upon her savior's face

revealed, she draws a deep breath, and...
...she screams.

7

Good L_ck, Yo_'re F_cked

August 28th, 2053
Bastion, Third Floor, Arena

Curiesay howls into the air, loosing a dirge of pent-up energy. The shockwave races across the ground with a crack, buffeting Parker's eardrums. Curiesay arrives an instant later, her fist drawn back as she strikes him squarely in the chest. Her momentum is imparted into him, sending him tumbling end over end down the ruined road and impacting a wrecked car.

His Steward yells through his suit's speakers, "She's right on top of you!"

Parker is well aware.

He is half-stuck in the crushed body of the car when Curiesay comes skidding to a halt in front of him, her own tendrils having burst from her back, four in total, arched over her shoulders. He sees the glint of the same orb he had tossed at Curiesay a short time ago—she holds one in each hand, and at the tip of each tendril. Curiesay begins a flurry of throws, six limbs all working in series, and Parker disappears in an ever-growing cloud of smoke as the explosions rattle

75

the windows of the not-so-distant Observation Booth.

I can't see him! With a mass of dark smoke concealing Parker, Curiesay is essentially throwing these orbs into the ether. Suddenly, she can feel her eyeballs burn white hot, and through the smoke she can see an orange outline, roughly Parker-shaped. With great vitriol she draws her right arm back, gripping one of the explosives tight as it materializes through her palm, and throws with all her might.

Slashing through the smoke, the projectile parts it, a straight path being revealed to Parker. The orb detonates on his chest, and he is propelled backward through the air. *Direct hit!* As he tumbles, his hands and feet emit a dull blue glow. His thrusters stop his roll, and he lands thirty meters back. He is given no respite as Curiesay pursues him with the deftness of a young falcon chasing its prey through the foliage.

She hardly touches the ground as she uses her own thrusters to maintain her forward momentum, keeping her opponent on the back foot. *Strike.* Using her tendrils to slap aside his blocking arm, Curiesay delivers a straight kick to his shoulder.

Reposition. Barreling through the ruined cityscape, Curiesay pushes off a bus bench, tearing it from its moorings in the process, and crosses in front of Parker, his eyes struggling to keep her squarely in his sights.

Strike. Just as he locks his eyes to her again, she spins in the air, striking him across the chin with the back of her closed fist.

Evade. As he attempts to retaliate by commanding two of his tendrils forward like whips, Curiesay uses her tendrils like a monkey swinging from a tree, wrapping one around a light pole and quickly redirecting herself.

Rapidly approaching a fork at the end of the road, the two crash through the wall of the two-story building at the end, the windows bursting out with flashes of light and concussion as they clash throughout. Like many of the buildings in the Arena, this one is on its last legs—so to speak—and in a moment of clarity, Parker targets the support columns as Curiesay pursues him, crashing through them like a bull. The upper floor collapses atop her as Parker bursts through the far wall onto the next street over and out of danger.

Or so he thought. Curiesay comes charging through the falling rubble, drop-kicking Parker with all her remaining momentum and sending him sliding backward on his feet in a daze. A moment passes and Parker clears his head, his arms up in a defensive boxer's stance as he awaits the next attack. But there is none.

Slow idiot fuck. Intrinsically, Curiesay knows how to use her thrusters to great effect. She bides her time as she dances around him, in no hurry to land another attack. *I wish I had more time with my playthings.* Internally, she brims with vengeful joy as she watches Parker desperately trying to keep track of her. But everywhere he looks, she's already gone. For all he knows, she isn't even in the same dimension as he is.

Like a buzzing gnat that cannot be seen for more than an instant, Curiesay enjoys the anonymity. *Can't hit what you can't see.* Her enhanced hearing can pick up his conversation as he speaks to his Steward.

"Jordan, where is she?" Parker asks into his microphone.

A beat passes as the hair on his neck stands, telling him the same thing as his Steward. "Behind you!"

Parker turns as Curiesay charges feet-first into him, the titanium plates on his chest cracking as she sends him sailing down the road. She tumbles for a moment and springs to her feet as she skids across the ground. Wrapping all four of her tendrils around her right arm, she summons another orb in her palm, this one the size of a baseball, winds up like a pitcher from the stretch, and throws with all her might.

"Bye, dipshit!" she roars.

The projectile rockets down the street at a blistering velocity. Curiesay stands with one foot forward, having finished her throw and awaiting the *kaboom*, when her pupils rapidly constrict, tracking a new target. It is the sphere, returning to her *much* faster than she had thrown it. With scant moments to spare, Curiesay swings her left arm, palm out, across the front of her body, slapping the sphere an instant before it impacts her, deflecting it behind her. It impacts the far wall with an unfortunately wasted explosion.

The shockwave races across the ground and passes by Curiesay as she turns to face Parker. With every ounce of spite she can manage, she smiles snidely. *Tch, well good for you, asshole.*

Parker had willed his tendrils to wrap around themselves, forming into a club, and batted the sphere back toward Curiesay. A half-smile flashes across his face as he rocks his head from side to side, feeling the satisfying *crack* sound as the air bubbles between his vertebrae find their way free. The two Pilots settle into defiant stances, facing each other down the long stretch. They catch their breath, their eyes furious, irises crimson-red. Their bodies and Arbiters work in unison to power their actions—they radiate the heat waste into the air, their auras weighing heavy on the eyes of their spectators.

* * *

Stewards know well enough that when their Pilots are in the zone, they shouldn't interrupt them. Any words of advice would come too little, too late at the pace they fight at. Annata and Jordan monitor their respective Pilot's vitals, making small adjustments to their suits as they take mechanical damage from the clashes, but otherwise sit in silence, as do the crowd of spectators.

Chandrima has moved from behind the desk and is standing near

Arthur by the window. Elva is close by, not nearly as enraptured as Arthur is by the violence. She spends more of her time watching him and his expressions than the fight taking place beyond the thick glass.

Chandrima sports a deviously satisfied grin as the action unfolds in front of her, standing in stoic silence as her eyes struggle to keep up.

* * *

The Pilots charge forward, meeting with exchanged blows. *She's fast; wait for her to make a mistake.* Curiesay is far more agile than her larger Pilot counterpart, seemingly dancing across the ground and air as she dives, swings, and leaps, using her thrusters to amplify her force, like a mechanically augmented Olympic gymnast.

Despite her superior speed, now that Parker has settled into the battle rhythm, she is unable to inflict any significant damage. *Sloppy; I saw that.* Her moves are highly telegraphed, allowing Parker a moment to dodge, block, deflect, and in the case of the snap kick Curiesay launches, a hard parry!

Parker catches the inside of her thigh with his arm, opening her torso to attack, and strikes hard at her chest plate with a closed fist. The lighter Curiesay is thrown back, tumbling for a moment before springing to her feet. In both hands and at the tips of all four tendrils, Parker wields a total of six marble-sized explosives, and in unison throws them forward. Not one misses Curiesay as she's enveloped in a cloud of fire and smoke, and Parker gives no quarter as he charges through to follow up.

She's gone. Coming out of the other side of the cloud, Parker swats at nothing. *I can still see you.* His peripherals track her movements— Parker looks straight ahead, an impatient scowl on his face. *Foolish, trying the same trick twice.* The silvered lamppost to his rear right, the pavement on the left, leaping over his head, off that car. He cannot see the "gnat," but he can guess where it'll be next.

Her diversions become predictable as Parker stands immobile, waiting for the perfect moment to—

There! Parker swings a straight arm out to his side, catching the incoming Curiesay at throat level, her momentum carrying her past Parker as she skips across the ground. She crashes into a building at the end of the road. Parker turns to face her, willing his arms forward as his tendrils wrap around them, down to his palms.

Curiesay drags herself from the rubble, her face contorted with vengeful rage when her jaw drops. Parker's hands crackle with barely contained energy as he wills all his excess heat and biomass forward into his palms, igniting it in a flash and sending a white-hot beam forward from his fingertips, leaving red molten pavement below as it races toward Curiesay.

In stubborn defiance, she throws her four tendrils in front, bracing herself for the attack. They're all burned away in a terrific flash of fire and smoke as the explosion consumes her, sending a plume of roiling smoke mushrooming into the open air above.

Parker falls to his knees, barely able to hold himself up with his hands. He leans forward, sucking air hard into his lungs. *That was too much.* He feels as if he has sprinted for an hour straight as his cells clamor for oxygen and glucose. *She's done. She must be.* He is (fairly) certain she will survive, though he may have put her in the hospital for a few weeks. *She fought well, I'm sure she'll—*

* * *

In the blink of his eyes, Parker is no longer in the Arena, nor in Bastion, nor on any earthly plain known to man. Infinite darkness surrounds him in all directions, save for the circular ray of light that illuminates him and the area immediately around him, like the star of some clandestine one-man show.

She couldn't have.

She wouldn't have.

He's wrong.

Looking wildly in all directions, he tries to track her down. She must be here. *Like a waking dream, visions unfold before him. Fading in from the infinitude of nothingness he exists in, these memories are not his own. He can feel her presence—out of reach, out of sight, out of time.*

A figure casts a long shadow down upon him as the door behind it closes, the light that filters through being choked out as it shuts. She's closing in.

The bird's crooked wing sits in a clumsy bandage before an unyielding heel crashes down upon its skull. You don't have to show me.

The wet sits atop her forehead, awaiting its companion which leads to pain and rebirth, the smooth mouthpiece itching the back of her mouth, and she convulses. She's here.

"Can you see me now?" Curiesay asks with shame-filled eyes.

* * *

"Curiesay, that's enough!" Chandrima roars into her microphone, but it's no use. Curiesay has charged through the smoke and resumed her attack, redoubling her furious efforts as her rear thrusters scream with overstress, punishing Parker through the cityscape. The spectators can see little as they zip to and fro, crashing through rubble and leaving only blood and refuse behind.

Elva and Chandrima see the incoming threat and scramble backward. The booth overflows with sound and devastation as Parker crashes through the window, smashes through the semi-circle desk, and comes to rest in a divot in the concrete floor.

Chandrima looks back at Parker, his eyes fluttering open as he tries, and fails, to stand. Curiesay leaps into the booth through the hole she created. She looks unnatural, feral, the whites of her eyes bloodshot and her irises screaming crimson.

"Make it stop!" she cries as she grips her head, the titanium armor on her Arbiter glowing red-hot as its cooling systems fail. Like a rabid animal lashing out, Curiesay puts her arms forward and bears down. Chandrima can see the arcing light between her fingers and knows that this is the end. What's coming will surely leave everyone in this room no more than ashes.

Chandrima braces herself as the room floods with light. To her horror, she sees Arthur dash in front of Parker. "Arthur, don't!" Chandrima cries out before it all goes dark.

* * *

The injured have all been removed from the Observation Booth when Chandrima finally leaves the scene. She has some mild burns on her forearms, a gash on her cheek, and her hands ache, but she is mostly unscathed. What concerns her the most is the headache—and the seeming gaps in her memory—but she won't allow herself to take a spot in the MRI machine until the rest of the injured are attended to.

One hundred and seven personnel are injured: triage estimates twenty-nine head injuries; eleven broken bones (between six victims); a yet uncounted number of burns; every person has, at the least, minor hearing damage. Remarkably, there were no deaths. Both Pilots clung to life, and with the added weight of their Arbiters it took specialized hydraulic gurneys to move them to the Medical Wing. Chandrima refused treatment on the scene, insisting that her staff be treated before she was. She limps down the hall, declining help from anyone who offers.

She enters her office and plops into her chair, putting her hands over her face, smearing blood from her cheek onto her palms. Her respite is cut short by a knock at her door.

This gives the injured Director a painful jolt. "Come in!" she shouts with some effort. The door swings open, revealing the exasperated grin of a tall, tan-skinned woman. She's dressed casually, if that can be said for the designer button-up tucked into her high-waisted denim jeans, topped off with a diamond necklace that rests between her breasts.

"Zochitl! Oh, thank God," Chandrima says with a sigh.

"Expecting someone else?" Zochitl says as she enters, closing the door behind her.

Chandrima allows herself to relax, melting further into her office chair. Her lab coat is stained with blood and the fringes of it are burned. "Prefect Typher was here earlier, I was worried they'd already voted me out," she says with a defeated chuckle.

"For? You were acting within your power. They'd be fools to terminate you over this," Zochitl responds as she strolls to the Director's desk. In Bastion, power is shared between three branches of government: science, headed by Director Chandrima Joshi; civil, headed by Prefect Typher; military, headed by Garrison Commander Cutter. It takes a two-thirds majority to replace one of the leaders, and since Chandrima can't vote on herself, the World Congress also has a say.

"That hardly matters. I'm sure the Congress will want some sort of punishment. They're always swinging their you-know-whats around," Chandrima responds, closing her eyes for a moment.

"Well, as the Assistant Director, Typher and Cutter have already asked me to conduct a formal investigation," Zochitl responds, giving Chandrima another jolt as she nearly falls out of her chair. Zochitl gives her a reassuring hand gesture, pressing her hands down, suggesting that Chandrima crush her anxieties. "Relax, there's nothing to it. I won't throw you under the bus, not that there's any wrongdoing to be found. I'm to return west by the end of the week to present my finding to Congress."

Chandrima runs her hands down her face, stretching her skin as they reach her chin. "I did the right thing, didn't I?"

"I suppose. She Crossed, did she not?"

"She did. She was…magnificent."

"Shame I missed it. Fuel shortages are such a nuisance. I had to fight tooth and nail to get another flight."

"Be glad you weren't here, or else I'd have another injured person that I'm responsible for."

"Director, stop. This is the job, you know this." Chandrima doesn't respond to this, her gaze drooping down to her desk. "So, what happened?"

"What do you mean?"

"Well, I've already started my interviews. Been talking to some of the staff who are still conscious," Zochitl begins. Chandrima's eyes remain lazy, but inside of her leather flats, she curls her toes as Zochitl speaks. "It seems no one actually saw what happened before the explosion. What's even *stranger* is when I tried to view the video, there's nothing after Curiesay tossed him through the window. The file is missing. Nothing from their Arbiters' onboard cameras either."

Chandrima sits up suddenly, as if a previously drank shot of espresso has made its way into her grey matter. "You know how it goes with Crossings. Electro-magnetic interference and what not. Curiesay's Arbiter suffered a catastrophic failure before she got the blast off, so I'm sure that didn't help matters," she says with her usual cheery tone.

"That would distort the video, not erase it."

"You'll have to talk to tech support about that."

"Also strange for her Arbiter to just fail. I've never seen one fail like that during testing."

"Well, Curiesay produced quite a bit more energy than I anticipated. It's possible—"

"They're tested to two-hundred percent capacity, so it wasn't that. And what about the staff? How is it possible that, in a room with over one hundred people, nobody saw anything?"

"I mean, the concussion from the energy expulsion alone—"

"I obviously only spoke to the ones who *don't* have head injuries, and they don't remember anything after the window breaking."

"They're in shock! It was a near-death experience and—"

"Shock doesn't erase memories." To this, Chandrima does not respond. She finally turns her eyes upward, meeting the gaze of Zochitl as she leans over her desk. "They may ask these same questions, just so you know. For your sake, have some better answers by the end of the week," Zochitl follows up. Chandrima takes a breath of relief with the rapid-fire questioning over. They lock eyes, with Zochitl staring emotionlessly at the seated Chandrima.

* * *

Chandrima can feel footsteps in the sands of her mind. All her life she has been alone within her skull, and now, a stranger is present. They move like peripheral smoke—gone the moment she turns her head.

Never has she felt such intrusion, immodesty so visceral, it's as if she's being held down and violated as the pages of her mind are rifled through. How impossibly obscene, a place where none but her ego should stroll, invaded by this...ghost. This erasure of solitude jars her, the epiphany working its fingers into the cracks that have begun to form in her soul. No, she thinks, not fingers, but—

* * *

85

"Hey, take it easy," Zochitl says as Chandrima snaps back into reality. She had nearly fallen out of her chair, and Zochitl struggles to pull her back upright. As quickly as the intrusion had come, it dissipates.

"What, ah… What happened?" Chandrima asks with a wince. A wave of nausea rolls over her and she dry-heaves. Zochitl brings her a trashcan. With some effort, Chandrima manages to calm her spasming abdominal muscles. She fights to recall the trauma of her immediate past, but it is rapidly fading into the ether of her mind.

"What *happened,* is that you need to get seen by a doctor. Your pupils are mismatched, you're nauseous, and you just fainted. You have a blast-induced concussion," Zochitl says as she takes a step back, allowing Chandrima a moment to sit with the trashcan on her lap as she tries to get her rapid breathing under control.

"I'll…get seen…once the last person has been treated. Not a moment…sooner," Chandrima responds stubbornly, tossing the vomit-less trashcan to the floor. *It's gone.* Whatever it was, the only thing that remains of it is Chandrima's notion that *something* happened. She can feel her beleaguered brain fighting for coherence.

Zochitl sighs, placing her hands on her hips. "Whatever you say, Director Joshi. I'll leave you to it then." She makes her way to the door, looking back before she walks out. "I'm telling the attending doctor to personally check on you in one hour," she says with a flash of her pearly white teeth. Chandrima nods in agreement, managing a weak smile in return as the door closes.

Chandrima's head pounds, and she struggles to keep her eyes focused, but she has work to do. She listens for Zochitl's receding footsteps to cease, and once she is sure she has gone, Chandrima sits up in her chair and taps her keyboard, bringing her computer to life.

She does feel a modicum of guilt for lying to her subordinate, and realizes that concealing evidence, especially now that she's being formally investigated, won't go over well if it's found out. However, she knows better than Zochitl, Typher, Cutter, and Congress. What did, or didn't, happen in the Observation Booth is frankly none of their business. Using her cell phone to move the existing video files to her personal desktop took her only a few moments in the hectic aftermath of the explosion, and her staff know well enough when something isn't to be spoken of. Still, it *is* a lot of mouths to silence.

Chandrima's fingers move sluggishly as she struggles to remember her password, but she eventually gets herself logged into her desktop. A second set of credentials is required to access her hidden files, and she obliges after a few moments of contemplation.

She had copied the video files from the cameras in the Observation Booth, cut the interesting parts, and reuploaded the edited files into the shared drive. It was sloppy, but Chandrima didn't have much time, or processing power, to think of a better solution.

She opens the file, and the screen loads up an image of the Observation Booth. The camera is mounted inside the observation window, with the camera pointing back toward the viewing gallery, and the semi-circular desk is up front. It is empty, as the recording started a few minutes before anyone entered the room. She scrolls forward. People rapidly appear and move around the room, then Arthur and Elva enter as well. She continues to scroll, observing the reactions of the people in the room to the fight that was taking place. The tape gets staticky for a few moments. Then it clears up, and the video resumes.

She pauses and moves forward frame by frame. Parker's limp body entering the frame, crashing into the desk, onlookers staring at Curiesay, Curiesay's suit glowing red-hot, her arms pointing forward—

"There!" Chandrima says to herself and quickly covers her mouth, looking at the door. At the very bottom of the frame, Arthur and Elva stand. She zooms in on them and advances the frames again. Elva leans toward Arthur's ear, and a frame later, he is between Parker and Curiesay, his arms braced in an "X" in front of him. A frame later, the screen goes blank. She scratches her chin, then returns her gaze to Elva. She rewinds.

She zooms in farther on Elva. Chandrima leans forward, her face only a few centimeters from the screen. Frame by frame. She can see her lips move. Rewind. Frame by frame. She mimics the motions of Elva's lips. Again and again Elva whispers into Arthur's ear. Chandrima tries different words to see which one fits as she whispers to herself. "Black, bank, bleed, bonk, blank, block…" Her eyes widen, and she sits back in her chair.

"Block," she concludes. For a moment, she exists in silence, her weary brain attempting to make sense of what her eyes are seeing, but she comes up short. With a gasp she sits up and leans forward over her keyboard. *Where the hell are they? You old fool!* How could she have missed them? She had personally witnessed every single person leave the Observation Room. Her fingers dance quickly over her keyboard as she logs into the shared drive, pulling up the camera feed from the hallway just outside of the Observation Room.

Rapidly scrolling, she spots the moment when the door is flung open by the force of the explosion, black smoke pouring into the hallway. She sees Arthur and Elva as they come through the smoke, moving quickly down the hallway, somehow avoiding the first responders who had passed by them a moment earlier. Elva walks with a limp, ushering her brother forward. Chandrima pauses the tape and rewinds it to a point where they are both clearly in the frame.

"Oh my god," she whispers as she presses play. While Elva wore tattered clothes with trails of blood running down her from multiple cuts, Arthur was completely nude, leaving steaming footprints behind on the concrete floor.

8

Waifs and their Flocks

Early Morning, August 30th, 2053
Exclusion Zone

The girl is *trying* to nonchalantly peer through the telescoping device as the corporal jots down positional coordinates of their quarry in their notebook. Behind the two prone spotters is the third member of their trio, an officer. The captain is vigorously, but quietly, stirring what is to be their dinner. She had opted to remove her camouflage blouse and has her undershirt tucked neatly into her trousers—she firmly believes in maintaining a professional military appearance even while in the field—as she prepares their meal. Her standard-issue sidearm is locked securely in its holster on her leg.

The girl gives an obnoxiously exasperated sigh as the corporal nudges her away from their sighting device, denying her curious eyes their prize. "If she's not moving then why can't I look!" she whines.

The man doesn't flinch. "Because as soon as you *do* look, she's going to move, and I don't want to lose her again."

"She's asleep," the girl responds in sing-song. They're lying on a dust-gray concrete floor, the remnants of a carpet providing disjointed patches of cushion. A second room is connected by an *unplanned* hole in the wall, allowing the trio to utilize both rooms to their fullest.

Twenty stories up, they are in one of the taller buildings in this dreary city. The moon is waning, its crescent reflecting a meager amount of light down to the terra, and the once illustrious Lake Narach Hotel stands like a soulless monolith, its vine and moss-ridden exterior exclaiming to the world: *Look. Where man once was, nature has reclaimed.*

Structurally, the building is sound—as much as the captain can tell—and serves its purpose as a high vantage point. Additionally, any threats would have to climb many flights of boobytrapped stairs—the hotel was plentiful with furniture whose legs were easily removed and whittled into foot-seeking spikes by busy hands—and with a total of two-hundred and thirty-two rooms, the Blights would be hard pressed to locate them.

Frustrated by the lack of response, the girl stands and walks away in a huff. "You should tell him that I get to have a turn," she says as she lightly stomps her boots on her way over to the captain, who shoots her a sympathetic, but firm, glance. A downward glance, as the girl barely comes up to the captain's chest.

"He's right. Surely you don't want to carry your gear every which way as we try to track her down again. We only just got back to this side of the city," the captain replies gently, lifting the ladle from the pot she was stirring and pouring its contents into a steel canteen cup, one of three. She then plops a spoon into it and passes it to the girl, who accepts it with a sour look.

"Thank you, Jess— I mean, *Captain Pullhum,*" the girl responds.

"You're welcome, *Waif Karima,*" Pullhum says, causing Karima's cheeks to run cherry-red.

* * *

For whatever reason, when the Blight's war sixteen years prior was in full swing, humanity noticed that of all the refugees they accepted, an overwhelming majority, were girls under the age of twelve. Most confessed that they were front and center during the outbreaks, but had been passed over by the infection, resigned to watch their families and friends have their wills ripped from them.

It didn't matter much why, but for the first time, mankind had *some* kind of weapon against their enemy. The girls were dubbed "Waifs" because they were often frail and malnourished by the time they were recovered by friendly forces. In short order, the girls were conscripted and attached to combat units, using their immunity, and the Blight's aversion to them, to provide much needed protection to the soldiers.

Years later, all the prior Waifs have "aged out" of their usefulness. Bastion now accepts volunteers, often canvassing the plethora of refugee camps and orphanages around the world for little girls who would accept the call to protect their fellow humans. Many of them jump at the opportunity, and Karima is as eager as any.

* * *

Karima stares at the steaming cup pensively, the smell of salted ham and beef broth tickling her nostrils, then walks over to her corporal. He's still lying prone, his right eye shielded by the rubber eye cup of the device, and the girl not-so-politely taps his ribs with the toe of her boot. "Here," she says as she places the cup on the floor next to him.

He doesn't budge. "I'll eat it in a minute."

"You'll eat it now," she says flatly, kneeling. She raises a spoonful of the soup from the canteen cup and positions it close to the prone man's lips. He turns his head slightly and glances at her, furrowing his brow with a *stop being an ass* look on his face and returns his gaze to the device.

Unfazed, the girl taps the side of his cheek gently with the spoon. "Do you want me to make airplane noises?" she whispers, and behind her a mist of soup spouts from the captain's mouth, her shrinking stomach being denied its first spoonful by a spasming diaphragm as Pullhum desperately struggles to contain herself.

Without a word, the corporal opens his mouth, and the girl feeds him a spoonful, then two, then a third as he keeps his focus squarely on his target who is, as the girl had said, sleeping in a mess of mismatched linens in the aisle of a corner store three blocks away. In her eagerness, the girl narrowly misses the corporal's mouth on a fourth scoop, spilling the spoonful onto his sleeves.

"Oh for fu—" he starts loudly, shaking his forearm vigorously to keep the hot broth from scalding him. He takes a deep breath. "Okay, fine. I know what you're doing. If she moves at all, say something," he says as he pushes himself up from his prone position, his abdomen aching from the hard floor beneath. The girl quickly drops to her chest and scoots into position behind the optics as the corporal grabs his canteen cup and walks to where the captain is sitting: a makeshift dining area with a few sofas and two coffee tables pressed together. Atop them is a dim lantern, their only source of light save for the waning moon.

"You sure that's a good idea, Corporal Clark?" Pullhum remarks as Clark takes a seat across from the one she's sitting in.

He nods in the affirmative as he swallows down another spoonful. "Yes, ma'am. She knows how to operate it. She's been trained after all, probably better than I have," he responds with a scoff.

* * *

Of course I was, Karima muses to herself. Assistant Director Zochitl Bottazzi insists that all Waifs receive adequate training on the gear their team uses. *If you're going to be out there, you may as well make yourself useful,* she had said. Karima didn't care one way or the other, but it does give her an excuse to watch her friend.

She does think of her as a friend, in the deepest sense of the word. The connection she feels is genuine, like a sibling she always had but never knew until she saw her. They haven't met, not in the common usage of the word. But on the contrary, they had met dozens of times in the girl's dreams.

At first, she thought them to be simple night terrors—she's used to those. Days passed in the Exclusion Zone, and as more of her nights became filled with flashes of red light and pain and sorrow, she realized that she wasn't dreaming. She was seeing something, *someone.* It was the same girl every time; around her age, maybe eight or nine years, with ratty, stained clothes that would be at home in a refugee camp and silky black hair. As with most dreams, there wasn't much to recall. The nose hair-curling smell of body odor and cigarettes, the streams of red light through the windows, the needles.

She hadn't been able to make much sense of it at first, but as she grew accustomed to the sensations that poured into her psyche, she felt as if they weren't her own night terrors, but someone else's. As disjointed as most dreams are, these felt real. Logical. She began to recognize a pattern, the same few moments played on repeat. And every time it was the same girl.

She certainly looks like her, Karima thinks as she eyes the woman sleeping in the rotten linens. *Or a grown-up version of her.* A bolt of regret strikes her when she realizes that the woman is dreaming alone this time. In every instance of their shared dreams, a flood of loneliness threatened to drown Karima's heart. She feels the sudden urge to leap up, barrel down the flights of boobytrapped stairwells, and run the three blocks over to the woman to tell her, *You're not alone, I'm here.*

When the woman hunted, she was a blur of claws and tenacity, leaving the cries of her prey echoing through the city. Their death knells alone were enough to jolt the nerves of any other would-be prey. Even other Blights flee from her. But at rest, she looks like a person Karima could have met at any of the homeless shelters or joint living spaces in her home country. Someone that needs help, needs to be seen.

Through the lenses of the long-range scope, she feels that she is helping her, in a sense. She doesn't know what Bastion's plan for her is, but she knows they don't often stake out specific Blights. Especially not ones that look so human. She knows what the other adults think of Director Joshi, but Karima can't relate; Chandrima is ruthless, sure, but primarily in her righteousness. If this Blight can be saved, it'll be Chandrima who makes it happen.

As she watches the woman's chest rise and fall, Karima gives a sorry sigh. After all her whining, *now* she wishes that Clark would take his post so Karima can rush to sleep and be with her friend. *Silence.* A neuron sparks, calling her attention elsewhere. *What is different?* Her comrades who had been, up until just now, talking lowly amongst themselves, are quiet. The talk has ceased, and Karima becomes aware of the silence. It's the kind that's found between the fumbling of a teacup and its inevitable shattering upon the tiled kitchen floor, and she knows before she turns around that they are not alone.

* * *

The room they are in is trashed: the paint has begun to peel from the walls; the cheap carpet is torn and stained with ancient blood; the furniture is broken and disheveled. The first day that they arrived, Clark toured the adjacent rooms and scrounged together the handful of intact furniture pieces they are enjoying. The two soldiers practically sink into the soft cushions of the sofas.

"How's it taste?" Pullhum asks her corporal. She already knows the answer, but she enjoys making him uncomfortable. Fraternization is frowned upon—to put it lightly—but if it wasn't, she can think of less attractive men to be stuck in the field with. She is a few years his senior, but already his face has settled into the grizzled look of man nearly twice his age, with a five o-clock shadow showing up unwelcomed by noon every day.

Clark gives a coy grin. "Well, if the taste doesn't kill me, the diarrhea will. You think they'll send Ursula back with some better food?" he responds as he places his empty canteen cup on the table, tinted red by the lantern's glow. Regardless of how he feels about the quality of the food, he must eat.

"This *is* the better food. Not much you can do about preserved cans of ham," she quips as she puts her hands behind her head and stretches until her feet kick like a small dog.

"Haven't been sleeping much, have you?" Clark asks, watching her intently. Pullhum shakes her head. Clark nods, glancing across the room and out the window, the distant stars providing a sobering atmosphere. "Me neither. Karima says she sees a girl too." Pullhum's eyes widen as he says this. "It *has* to be her."

"You can't be sure of that. All..." She hesitates a moment with a grimace as she presses her fingers into her eyes. "All I see is horror."

"Same. But that's not what Karima sees. She thinks she wants to be seen," Clark insists.

"That's unprecedented," she begins before she tempers her surprise. "If it's true that is. We'll mention it in the next outgoing report."

Clark nods in the affirmative. The two soldiers exist in silence for a moment. A gentle breeze from the adjacent room—whose window is shattered—rolls into and across the room. They close their eyes, stealing a few moments of microsleep for their fatigued brains.

"I'm gonna get her dinner since she gave you hers. Take a few hours and try to get some sleep, then come relieve me," she says, standing. Clark puts both hands over his face and rubs it slowly as the captain moves back to the kitchenette where the cooking pot is suspended over a stainless-steel propane heater.

Pullhum ladles a hearty scoop, scraping the bottom to ensure that her Waif gets at least a few pieces of ham. As she drops a spoon into the cup and is about to take it to Karima, who is nearest to the window on her right, she hears the creak of an opening door.

That's odd, she thinks. The figure that has walked in did so casually, as if this is a room it has rented. She glances down at its feet and can see tar-thick black blood leaking from its soles. It wears tattered blue jeans, fibers thick with grime, and a t-shirt for a band she cannot identify in its dirtied state. It turns its head toward the captain, who is still holding the canteen cup in one hand, and looks her up and down with lazy jet-black eyes. In its hand it holds a dimly shining flashlight that it points to the floor.

It has been such a long time since she has seen one in person. Pullhum had been a Waif herself during the Calamity. She had seen the stolen and twisted bodies face to face, using her presence as a shield for her comrades. Back then, she felt little fear of monsters like the one that stands before her. Once she aged out, she enlisted in the Bastion Home Guard, and learned how to kill, rather than how to protect.

But she knows she's no longer safe. She knows that this thing sees her as prey as much as any other human. This time, she feels the hunger they emanate, and knows it means for her to be its victim. *So this is how they felt.*

She hopes that Clark is paying attention. Even if she could draw her pistol before the Blight closes the two meters that separate them, the gunshot would surely draw more to their location, and they would be done for. Their rifles have silencers, but are leaning against the wall near their dining area. With no right choice to make, for the moment they are—human and Blight alike—calculating their best course of action. Even more odd than its sudden appearance is its hesitation. *What could it possibly be thinking about?*

Suddenly, Karima dashes across the room, drawing the Blight's attention as she puts herself between the captain and her foe. The disheveled being grunts under its breath, then moves forward.

* * *

I hope this isn't a mistake. She figures the captain hasn't drawn her weapon because she doesn't want to draw any attention to them. Clark should have seen her move and is hopefully readying the rifle. That is, if he hasn't fallen asleep already.

Her training takes over before she can react on her own. *Separate. Distract. Admonish.*

The Blight takes a step, and Karima calls out, voice quivering, "Shame!" The Blight's feet stutter, then step, leaving black footprints on the floor behind it, its feet still seeping. "Shame!" she repeats, a sureness settling in her tone. The Blight stumbles, catching itself against the short counter just a foot away from her. Karima can feel the captain gently pulling back on her shoulder, but instead, Karima pushes forward out of her grasp.

"You're pathetic. Hideous. Unclean." Karima has lowered her voice a bit, painfully aware that she may draw more attention if she yells. As she speaks, the Blight repeatedly tries to move past her and—she imagines—toward her friends. She refuses to allow it, placing herself directly in its path each time. It has been refusing to look at her, its mannerisms akin to those of an abused dog seeking to avoid its scornful master and go about its business.

"Look at me," Karima demands. The Blight shields its eyes with its arm, reaching out with the other one to try and navigate its way to the soldiers. Karima puts her arm out and pushes back on the Blight, her inferior height landing her outstretched hand on the creature's abdomen. *He's so cold.*

"Please, look at me," she repeats in a gentle tone as her foe shakes its head. Karima pushes it, lightly, but the gesture is enough for the Blight to backpedal. She pursues it, reaching her outstretched arm up and pulling the Blight's arm out of the way of its face. Its eyes dart back and forth between Karima and over her shoulder. Karima snaps her fingers crisply in the Blight's face with her other hand.

Its eyes, watering, struggle to lock with hers as she speaks. "How dare you. How dare you bust in here and try to harm us. Shameful. You hear me? You should be *ashamed.*" She's speaking as if she is a scolding mother, giving her disobedient child an earful after returning home many hours after dark. She is on the precipice of a flinch, anticipating a gunshot that has yet to come. *What the hell are they doing?* On the word "ashamed," the Blight gives a sharp exhale through its teeth.

Clark bolts past Karima and an instant later her face is sprayed with what feels like tree sap. It gets into her eyes, and she pulls her shirt to her face to wipe it clean. Not only are her eyes sprayed, but so is the rest of her, a mist of black blood tainting her clothes. Karima clears her eyes enough to see Clark—his face is covered by a towel tied behind his head, eyes shielded by his standard-issue goggles. He wields a table leg as a club, with which he had bashed the Blight's head in. *No wonder he took so long.*

* * *

"I'm okay," Karima assures Pullhum as she rushes to her side. Clark had noticed the commotion and went to intervene when Pullhum ordered him to protect himself and strike the Blight in the head with a series of hand signals. She had her rifle shouldered as she took aim at the Blight from behind Karima—if the Blight had made a move she would have fired—but had chosen to take a quieter approach. Both soldiers abandon their weapons and try to approach Karima, like parents seeking to comfort a child with a scraped knee.

Karima backpedals, shaking her head. "Nope. Gloves and goggles. Corporal Clark should watch the door." The soldiers freeze in their tracks. *Damn, she's sharp*, Pullhum thinks as she rushes to her backpack, retrieves her protective gear, and dons it. Karima moves into the adjoining room which they had mostly been using as a refuse dump—a good place for her tainted clothes.

Pullhum follows behind her, nearly rolling her ankle on the mounds of rubble as they make their way to the washroom. "He should have been more careful. You're covered," Pullhum says frustratedly as she kneels to help Karima undress. Karima waves her off as she puts her hands over her head and begins to remove her shirt. Pullhum watches and waits, her heavy breaths fogging her goggles.

"You can't expect him to know which way blood will splatter. You both did good, I'm fine. But I only have my pajamas left," Karima says as she removes her trousers. *Leave it to a Waif to comfort her flock.* The top and bottom are both camouflaged but are much smaller than the ones Pullhum and other adults wear.

"Lift your feet," Pullhum says as she slides a piece of plastic between Karima's discarded clothes and the soles of her feet. Pullhum pulls a pouch of wet wipes from her pocket. Unlike the ones the trio had been using for their "baths," these are much thicker, and their smell will make you lightheaded if you inhale too closely. In near total silence, with only the moonlight and Pullhum's flashlight—which she's holding in her mouth—illuminating Karima, she wipes her clean.

Once she is done, Pullhum brings Karima her pajamas—with freshly changed gloves—and carefully bags up her soiled clothes as she slips them on. "Oh! Don't throw it away," Karima says as Pullhum ties the plastic bag tight. "My patch is in there." She dresses quickly, feeling a bit embarrassed to be out of uniform.

Pullhum nods. "Gotcha. We'll go through it tomorrow and dig it out." Karima flashes a smile and slips her feet into the slippers Pullhum had brought. The two ladies leave the room and return to their living area.

Clark had just finished giving the stairwell a once over—no others seem to have followed their unwelcome guest. He had torn up the hallway carpet and laid it overtop of where the Blight's blood had pooled on the floor and dragged the body into the hallway. Using a pillow to further muffle the sound, he put two silenced rifle rounds into its head for good measure. He slips into the closet, using the door as a privacy barrier, and changes into a fresh pair of camouflage utilities.

"You did good, Waif. Textbook, I'd say," Clark says as he walks to Karima. Captain Pullhum takes a seat on the couch for a breather.

Karima rolls her eyes as she retrieves her own wet wipes from her pack which sits nearby on the floor. "Oh, we're not done yet, Corporal. Come here," she demands as she pulls a wipe from the pack. Clark grunts but complies, moving to Karima and dropping to his knees so his head is at her level. With the nonchalance of a veteran barber, Karima manipulates his head, eyeing it up and down until she finds a mistake.

"Don't. Move," she whispers as she carefully takes the wipe, putting a corner of it to his upper cheek, just below where his goggles cover, and dabs a speck of obsidian-colored blood from it. Without another word, she motions for him to spin around as she checks his hair thoroughly, the corporal shuffling in a circle on his knees.

After checking his neck, Karima gives an affirmative nod. "All done! You…" she says with a half-joking scolding tone, holding the wipe with the speck of blood on it up to him, "… should be more careful."

The captain giggles, having watched this process unfold from the couch, her rifle across her lap. "She's right, you know. Can't afford to lose Karima's favorite corporal." Karima shoots her an embarrassed glare, her cheeks cherry-red. She had confided in her captain that she had developed a crush on him—as children sometimes do—and she feels her secret is on the edge of being revealed.

A scratch at the door interrupts their momentary peace, with the captain springing to her feet and pointing her rifle toward the door as Clark stands aside of it, sidearm drawn. A second scratch, then a tap. Standing out of the captain's line of fire, Clark flings the door open with a swift motion, and a Siberian husky comes scampering in, heading straight for Karima.

"Ursula!" she exclaims as she throws her arms open, embracing the husky as it crashes into her, its tongue checking to see if Karima's face still tastes the same. It does. The two soldiers sigh with relief as Clark closes the door. After a few moments of hectic reunion, Pullhum clicks her tongue and Ursula breaks off, neglecting Karima and heading to the captain, taking a well-behaved seat as she reaches her.

Pullhum takes a knee. The dog wears a secure-fitting harness with several zippered pouches. She quickly empties them: five cans of potted meat; two bags of rice; two canisters of propane; a folder with documents enclosed. She gives Ursula a pat on her back and rubs her head. Ursula's water bowl is brought and filled, and their courier gulps it down with great vigor.

Grabbing the folder, the captain stands. "I need to decode this and write my report. I'd like to get her moving by tomorrow night," Pullhum says, rubbing her tired eyes. Regulations state that teams must decode communications immediately upon receipt.

Karima makes her way to the window, their telescope sitting unattended on its tripod. "Corporal Clark, I'm wide awake. Can I watch for a while?" she asks, fluttering her eyes in a manner that she'd learned usually got her what she wanted.

Clark gives a sly smirk. "Sure. Let us know if she wakes," he says as he makes his way into the dining area, grabs his rifle, and heads to the side of the room where their sleeping mats are. Taking a hard-earned rest, the corporal eases himself onto the mat, laying his rifle beside him on the floor.

The captain retrieves her writing gear from her own pack, sits on the sofa next to the exhausted Ursula, who has passed out on the opposite cushion, and puts her feet up. She has a *lot* to tell Bastion.

Karima sights in and sees her friend right where she left her. She sighs, settling into a comfortable prone position. Then the tears start.

The night has taken its toll on her young heart. She'd never seen someone die before, never seen a head caved in with a cudgel right in front of her. Never had to use her training to protect her friends.

As the adrenaline wears off, she sobs quietly, her tears dripping into the eyepiece. Unbeknownst to Karima, both Clark and Pullhum can hear her, and decide that it would be too embarrassing for her if they acknowledge her cries.

9

Little White Lies

August 30th, 2053
Bastion, Third Floor, Dwellings Wing

Arthur wakes with a shout, his t-shirt soaked with sweat, an Arthur-shaped wet spot revealed as he sits up. He looks around for a moment—this room is foreign to him. *How did I get here?* Swinging his legs off the side of the bed, he stands uneasily. *I feel so heavy.* His new room is moderately sized, with a dresser and accompanying vanity next to the door to the living area and a small nightstand near his bed. There are no windows, so he moves to the door and slides it open, letting the light from the living area strike him.

"Hey," he says as he steps out.

Elva sits up from the couch where she had been laying, throwing off her blanket. She moves to him, stepping around the three-sided sectional. "Hey! Good morning. You hungry?" she says cheerfully. He looks at Elva for a moment, then spies the rest of the room.

"Where are we?" he asks. His voice is low, his speech mildly slurred like someone recovering from a night of drinking.

"It's your new apartment. Remember? Chandrima moved us up here."

"Did she? When did… What…" Arthur subtly shakes his head, digging. "When was this?"

"Yesterday," she responds quickly.

"Was it? I don't… I feel like it's been a long time…since I fell asleep." *What day is it?*

"Yeah, well, moving is a lot of work. I was pretty tired too."

"Are you sure… That doesn't sound right." *Is she lying to me?*

"It's been a hectic couple of days!" Elva says loudly, tapping Arthur reassuringly on his shoulder. "We watched the demonstration, came back, and spent yesterday getting settled in."

"Did we? The demonstration, what…happened?" He shakes his head again. *It's slipping, I'm losing it.* "That girl…was fighting that Pilot. And they… She…" Arthur drifts off, squeezing his eyes tight as he freezes in place.

* * *

Please, just forget it. Arthur stands motionless, Elva's eyes locked onto his face. This goes on for a few moments before he opens his eyes, his expression pleasantly surprised.

"Hey, when did you get here?"

Thank God. Elva freezes for a beat, then smiles. "I stayed overnight. It's a bit embarrassing, but I'm not used to sleeping in a room alone."

He looks her over, noticing the faint shadow of a bruise on her cheek, a broken and bruised pinky fingernail on her left hand, and a few scabbed-over scratches on her face. "What happened to you?" he asks sternly.

"Just forget about it," she responds with the same tone.

Arthur's expression blanks and he rubs his eyes. "I'm hungry. How, uh…how do we get food here?"

"There's a cafeteria, but I already had some food sent here. It's in the kitchen, let's go sit down," she says as she walks to the breakfast nook, her groggy brother following just behind her.

Their new apartments are a bit smaller than their old one on the Second Floor, but they're aesthetically pleasing. The front door opens into the living room, with the kitchen off to the left (a two-burner stove, microwave, and dishwasher), a full-size bathroom at the back of the living area, and two rooms on the right (a bedroom and a study). On the left side of the living area is a door that leads to Elva's apartment.

"I didn't know what you'd be in the mood for, so I got a lot," Elva says as Arthur sits on one of the stools and leans onto the counter. She grabs two large bags of to-go containers and sets them in front of him. He tears the bags open and, without giving much thought about what's in them, begins to eat ravenously—with his hands until Elva passes him some silverware—and in a few short minutes, Arthur eats nine and a half containers of food. Seven turkey sausage links, an entire container of perfectly fluffy scrambled eggs, four pancakes, three bowls of oatmeal (with brown sugar), six pieces of toast, three muffins, and a cup of yogurt.

He finishes eating, his breathing heavy as his airway finally receives priority over his food, and Elva dutifully clears the empty containers from in front of him, sliding them off the counter and into the trash can. *That should do it for a few hours at least.*

Color rushes to Arthur's cheeks as he puts his arms above his head and stretches. "I'm thirsty," he says as he finishes, moving to stand up from his stool.

Elva motions for him to stay and passes him one of two plastic gallons of water on the counter. "Here, drink." In less than five minutes, he's finished it, and she passes him the second. He polishes it off in the same amount of time.

"So, you ready?" she asks as he rubs his stomach.

"Ready for what?"

"Chandri—*Director Joshi* wants to show us around. Since we'll be working here and all," Elva says, and Arthur quickly sits up straight.

"That's right! We're… I'm gonna be a Pilot. That's…" he begins as he locks eyes with her. "That's a good thing, right?"

No. It's going to ruin everything. "Yes, Arthur. It's a good thing, I'm proud of you. Now go get ready," she says.

A short while later, the two meet in the hallway. They begin their walk down the wide hallway, with doors appearing on either side in pairs. The last two doors have placards on them that read *Adam Parker* and *Jordan Graft*.

The central area of the Third Floor is wide and circular, with a handful of benches and lounge areas scattered around between several thick support columns. The ceiling here is much higher than it is in the corridors, and above, the lights, though shining brightly, are barely visible. Elva and Arthur approach one of the benches and sit, waiting for some time, and chat about their new accommodations.

The pair hear the faint sound of footsteps clacking on the concrete floor as Chandrima approaches. She's wearing her usual white lab coat, and her hair is put up in a long ponytail. Elva notes that she looks particularly worse for wear: she has a butterfly bandage on her left cheek; her hands are bruised on their tops; her gait is minutely unsteady.

Now that Elva is grown, she looks at Chandrima with far less reverence than she did as a child. Her mother, Amiree, and Chandrima were inseparable when she was still alive. Chandrima would often come to dinner at night and work with Amiree on the Third Floor during the day, even spending most holidays with them.

After Amiree died, Elva saw less and less of her "aunt" and holds some contempt for her in that regard. Elva had kept herself strong for Arthur's sake, but spent countless nights mourning into her pillow, wondering why her mother's closest friend had abandoned them. Although she is thankful that Chandrima had advocated on their behalf to allow them to stay in Bastion, she felt as if it were only to Chandrima's benefit, and now that she has recruited Arthur as a Pilot, her suspicions feel vindicated.

"Good morning, my dears! Are you ready for your tour?" she chirps. The two siblings nod and stand.

Chandrima gives them a glance up and down. "You both look well!" she quips. Arthur catches sight of her injuries, and he casts his gaze to his sister, who gives him a subtle shake of her head. "Shall we?" Chandrima follows up, waving the two along as they begin their tour.

* * *

The Third Floor is circular, but not symmetrical, with nearly two-thirds of it being taken up by the Arena. The Dock Wing runs alongside its inner wall and provides the only access point. In this hallway is the Dock itself, the Arena and Observation Booth, the classrooms, the Briefing Room, and the Command Center.

Chandrima's office is in the Medical Wing, down at the very end. This hallway is considerably more furnished than the nearly barren Dock Wing, with several framed pictures—including a young Chandrima and Amiree standing in a half-finished Third Floor with workers in the foreground passing wiring along the drop ceiling—on the walls, a few intentionally overgrown ferns and a handful of waist-high coffee tables. The Infirmary is here, staffed with doctors from every specialty, ten operating theaters, and fifty-two patient rooms. A few more doors exist, but they are not labeled and require a fingerprint on their nearby scanner to enter.

The Medical Wing's traffic is rivaled only by the adjacent Recreation Wing. Nearly one thousand staffers cycle through the Third Floor each day. The laboratories run non-stop, and they are afforded ample time for rest, relaxation, and most importantly, good food. Although the cinema is quite popular (able to accommodate seventy people at a time), and the recreation room is wall to wall with all manner of games (from the very first handheld to advanced virtual-reality booths), the real star is the cafeteria.

Serving four meals a day—and quick/easy food in the interim—the kitchen and cafeteria serve nearly one hundred thousand meals a month. When the funding for the Third Floor was divvied up during its first year in operation, Chandrima and Amiree were adamant that the kitchen receive no less than ten percent of the budget for the cooks' salaries *alone*. They knew what would be asked of these people, and along with happy workers being productive workers, satisfied employees don't steal classified data—most of the time.

The Dwellings Wing houses the Pilots and Stewards, as well as the Waifs on the opposite side of the hall. Being the top floor in a dome, the Third Floor has limited space, and as such, all the rest of the staff live on the Second Floor, sans the Director and Assistant Director, who enjoy the convenience of having their rooms adjacent to their offices. This wing also houses a spacious gymnasium, with enough equipment to film several unique Hollywood training montages, an Olympic-sized swimming pool, and a fully staffed massage parlor.

Finally, the Administration Wing. Largely serving as overflow office space and storage, the residents of this wing change often. The only permanent installation is the office of the Assistant Director at the very end of the hallway.

* * *

"Any questions?" Chandrima asks as the trio return to the rotunda from which the wings branch off. They had been walking at a brisk pace as Chandrima talked at lightning speed. Elva and Arthur look at each other, then back at Chandrima. "Many, I assume?" she continues. The siblings nod. "Don't worry, my dears. There's a lot to take in, but you live here now! You'll have plenty of time to familiarize yourselves. For now, the important bits are the Classroom and the Dock. You'll see the rest of it eventually," she says, and the siblings nod again.

The three exist in an awkward silence for a moment, shifting uncomfortably on their feet. "Well, uh, okay," Chandrima says, clearing her throat. "It'll be a few days until our other Pilots are back on their feet, and we won't be fitting your Arbiter until then, Arthur. So you two have the run of the mill! The rest of your belongings should be up here by the end of the day, so keep an eye out. If you need me, you know where to find me," she finishes as she gives a wave and walks off toward the Medical Wing, leaving the siblings standing alone.

"So, you wanna go check out the Rec Wing?" Elva asks as she pats Arthur on the back. He turns and nods, and the two cross the rotunda and enter the Recreation Wing. The first door in the hallway is a double door and has a plaque above it:

KITCHEN

Elva feels excited on Arthur's behalf; he'd always had a voracious appetite, and having a personal chef is a gift to him that she cannot overlook.

"Let's go meet the chef! Chandrima said he's really talented, world renowned even," Elva says, ushering Arthur toward the door.

"Well, we can't just barge in there. I'm sure he's busy," Arthur protests as he leans back against his eager sister. *You deserve this, dear brother.*

"They're here to cook for *you*, Arthur. I'm sure he wants to meet

109

you too. Besides, I wanna see what the kitchen looks like."

Arthur grumbles and reluctantly pushes open the double doors.

Inside, the space is massive. Along one wall are stoves, hot-top grills, and oil baths. Along the other are several large ovens recessed into the walls and two large refrigerators at the end. In the center is a working area, with pans and utensils hanging from above. The row of workstations extends down in both directions, and are currently staffed by tens of cooks, as are the hot-tops and the stoves. They move frantically, with expletives being shouted across the room at each other as they hurriedly make breakfast for the Third Floor staff.

"See, they're busy, let's go," Arthur says as he begins to back out of the doors. Elva sees a tall man with an apron, wearing a tall white hat. She points at him, grabbing Arthur's sleeve and pulling him back inside. *Stubborn, stubborn boy.*

"That must be him! Frederic, hello!" Elva yells as she drags Arthur across the kitchen, drawing the eyes of the frantic staff.

Frederic smiles widely. "Ah! You must be the new Pilot and his Steward. Chandrima told me about you two—you are siblings, yes?" he asks, ushering them to a less crowded part of the kitchen. The cooks and wait staff carefully move around them since they're blocking one of the walkways.

"We sure are! I'm Elva. Arthur here is my little brother, *and* the soon-to-be third Pilot," Elva says as she puts her hand out. Frederic takes it and kisses it, causing Elva to blush. Frederic looks at Arthur, who is standing uncomfortably.

"Monsieur, Mademoiselle, it is a pleasure to meet you both. Tell me, Pilot, what is your favorite food?" Frederic asks, leaning his long torso over Arthur.

Arthur hesitates. "Uh, I guess pasta mostly. And bread."

Frederic raises an eyebrow. "Ah, I've forgotten, you two have only ever lived on the Second Floor?" The pair nod.

Frederic stands up tall and puffs his chest out. "Well, in *my* kitchen, we serve our Pilots and Stewards only the best. We are staffed at all hours, ready to prepare anything you desire. As well, we import specialty items at our Pilots' request." He is speaking ecstatically, grinning from ear to ear. He looks a bit disheveled—he has been here for five hours already this morning—and the bags under his eyes threaten to close them against their will.

"I apologize, I am a bit excited. Just a few days ago, Curiesay arrived, but she's been in intensive care since then, as has Parker. But now with a conscious Pilot, my purpose here is renewed!" he says, throwing his hands up.

Arthur laughs. "Well, I'll do my best to keep you busy."

Elva puts her hands on his shoulders. *That wasn't painful now, was it?* "Let's let him get back to work, Arthur." They exchange smiles and wave goodbye to Frederic as they make their way out of the kitchen.

The rest of their morning is spent touring the Recreation Wing: they spent some time in the lounge in the big leather massage chairs; watched half a vintage movie in the theatre; visited the arcade. Laughing to themselves, they leave the arcade, heading to the cafeteria.

Arthur had grown colder and more unsure of himself as he had gotten older, and Elva worried about his happiness. After their mother died, he took a turn for the worse, and things that once interested him became irrelevant in his eyes. As a boy, he would clamor to leave Bastion and spend time in nature. He envied Elva's skill as an artist and would watch her for hours as she would sketch the landscape or the occasional passing rabbit.

In recent years, she found it hard to coax him to leave his room at all, and she mourned the erasure of sense of wonder from his soul. Elva's heart warms—*Arthur is laughing.* She so seldom sees joy on his face these days. *Maybe this will all be okay.*

It's lunchtime in Bastion, and the siblings enter the cafeteria. Complementing the kitchen's large footprint is a doubly large dining area. Standard picnic tables, with seats attached, run ten rows deep, stretching nearly wall to wall. On the far right are a handful of tables against the wall, and on the left is the long serving line, cut up into three sections for the meal of the day, halal/kosher meals, and vegetarian at the end.

As much as the architects of Bastion tried to create a noise-dissipating space (insulating the walls with open-celled foam, like that of a recording booth, and painting the walls with microporous paint), the cafeteria is consistently one of the loudest places on the Third Floor.

Personnel occupy the seats by the hundreds: doctors in their crisp lab coats; mechanics with grease handprints on their coveralls; technicians wearing color-coded jumpsuits. They intermingle, talking and laughing amongst themselves as they dine. It doesn't go unnoticed by Arthur that two-thirds of the people here are women. As Arthur and Elva look for a place to sit, they see a hand waving near the back. It's young Annata, sitting next to her fellow Steward, Jordan. The siblings make their way to them.

"It's Elva, right? And Arthur?" Annata says, setting her fork down for a moment. In front of both her and Jordan are metal trays with the day's lunchtime meal: meatloaf with tomato sauce, along with a variety of sides from potato salad to boiled eggs.

Elva cocks her head. "Yes, that's us. You…" she starts, pointing to Annata first, then to Jordan, "…were both in the Booth that day. So you must be their Stewards, right?" she asks, receiving impressed nods from the seated pair.

"That's us! Why don't you take a seat?" Annata follows up with a sweeping hand gesture.

The siblings oblige. "You know who we are?" Elva asks as Arthur sits quietly, putting his hands between his knees.

"Well yeah! The Director told us all about you. You're gonna be the new Steward, and Arthur the new Pilot. You'll be spending a lot of time with me and Jordan as we show you the ropes," Annata says with a smile.

Elva nods in understanding, then glances at the serving line. "So, do we just walk up there? And get in line?"

"No. Well, yes. Kinda. Us Stewards can request custom meals like the Pilots, but we usually just have what they make for the rest of the staff," Jordan says, then looks at Arthur. "And you, Pilot. If you try to eat what they've prepared for everyone else, you'll give ol' Frederic a heart attack," she continues. She casts her gaze across the cafeteria to see Frederic rapidly approaching their table with a notepad in his hand.

Jordan leans forward and half-whispers, "And he often takes the Pilots' orders personally."

Frederic swiftly arrives, face flushed. "Monsieur, what would you like me to prepare for you today?" He looms over the table, his notepad raised in front of him.

Arthur hesitates for a beat. "I don't see why I'm the only one who gets *special* food. It...doesn't feel right."

Frederic goes to speak, but is cut off by Jordan. "If it makes you feel any better, Frederic would be more upset if you *didn't* request custom meals, isn't that right?"

"Surely. Pilot, my sole purpose is to keep Bastion's Pilots well fed and satiated. Please, allow me to do my job," Frederic says firmly.

Arthur nods in reluctant agreement and thinks for a moment. He winces, eyes twitching. "Okay, uh...halibut? And three steaks, rare. Mashed potatoes, some steamed vegetables, fried okra, and a slice of carrot cake." Frederic writes furiously, his pen strokes becoming ever more exaggerated as the order increases in size. Elva watches

Arthur carefully, giving a somber smile.

Frederic bows as he steps back from the table. "Excellent! I'm pleased it's more than simply 'pasta and bread.' I will have it to you shortly." As quickly as Frederic had arrived, he retreats to the kitchen.

"Well, I'm gonna grab a tray for myself," Elva says. She heads to the far end of the cafeteria and gets in line. Arthur watches her, lips pursed.

"It's fine, Arthur, really," Annata says as she observes his guilt. She waves her hands to draw his attention. Both her and Jordan extend their hands to Arthur, and they exchange shakes.

He eyes the two Stewards: Jordan has a long, slender frame, with fair skin (lacking in Vitamin D, a consequence of too much time on the Third Floor) and shoulder-length brown hair. Annata is her junior, with legs not long enough to touch the floor while sitting at the table. She's a dark-skinned girl, her hair braided and tied back with an elastic band, and has soft, pre-pubescent facial features, which contrast against two sharp brown eyes, seemingly belonging to a soul much older than she currently possesses. Jordan's tongue drips with Southern charm, though her vernacular is (usually) proper, while Annata's high-pitched voice contradicts her seasoned vocabulary.

They converse while Elva waits in line, eating in between sentences.

"Stewards…I keep hearing that word," Arthur says.

"While you Pilots are out fighting and saving the world, we Stewards monitor your vital signs, suit diagnostics, and provide you with current tactical information. We can make adjustments to your suit on the fly, even if you are unconscious. We also keep you focused, making sure you don't lose your bearings in tough situations," Annata answers quickly.

"So, you're basically, like, guardian angels?"

"Oh, you flatter me," Annata says with faux modesty and a dismissive wave. "Yes, that's exactly what we are."

"Pretty cool to have your sister Stewarding for you," Jordan adds.

Arthur shrugs his shoulders. "I guess."

"You guess? It's awesome! She'll have a front row seat to…" Annata trails off.

Arthur nods solemnly. "Yeah. She will."

"Y'all will be all right. Stewards gotta get used to the bad stuff," Jordan says, her tone unbothered and light.

Arthur shrugs again. "I suppose she will have to."

"You are being so dramatic! We're gonna have *three* Pilots now! You'll be unstoppable together," Annata exclaims triumphantly.

Jordan sees Elva, tray in hand, only moments away from getting back to their table. "Don't worry about Elva when you're fighting, Arthur. Do what you must to survive. It don't matter how it looks to us," Jordan says as she locks eyes with him. He nods, and Elva returns to the seat next to him. Her tray has a slice of meatloaf with mashed potatoes and a cup of soda.

"This smells so good!" Elva says with a smile as she takes a bite.

Annata puts her arms above her head, stretching with a half-yawn. "Yeah, it's pretty awesome."

A waiting cart rolls up to their table. The waiter quickly unloads Arthur's substantial meal and gives a half-bow before returning to the kitchen before Arthur can thank him. Without thought or hesitation, Arthur starts in on his meal, tearing through the steaks in a few minutes and inhaling the halibut immediately after. He devours the sides and cake shortly after. After just two minutes, his plates are all clean. Annata and Jordan share impressed nods.

"And you ain't even Piloted yet. Reckon you'll be plenty hungry after your fitting," Jordan quips.

Arthur casts his eyes to her. "What do you mean? Does Piloting make you hungry?"

Annata interrupts Jordan as the latter goes to answer. "Though most of the biomass consumed *does* come from your Arbiter, you still burn a lot of calories when you're wearing it, even at rest."

"How come? I mean, why is it so taxing? When you say biomass…do you mean, like, flesh? I thought they were made of metal," he asks, eyelids fluttering.

"Well, you'll hear all this in class, but the suits are synthetic muscular systems…" Jordan begins, her drawl permeating through her textbook answer, "…and the armor plating is attached to the outside. You and your Arbiter will depend on each other and share resources, including oxygen and nutrients. So, when you're using it, it's normal to feel…" Jordan trails off as she sees that Arthur's eyes have closed completely, his arms falling to his sides.

Elva's cheeks run red. "He's, uh, been really tired, since—"

Jordan interjects. "It *was* a big meal, ain't no wonder he's out cold." Elva matches her gaze, taking a moment to process. Annata casts her eyes off to the side, suggesting that her ears will follow.

"Yeah, yeah, he does tend to get pretty tired after he eats," Elva starts as she begins to stack Arthur's empty plates and tray together with hers.

Jordan waves her off. "Why don't y'all just head back to your rooms? I'll bus your trays."

Elva nods and nudges Arthur awake. "Hey, let's head back." She lends him an arm, helping him stand from his chair. He doesn't speak, but does give a half-wave to the two Stewards as he turns, his eyes hardly open.

Elva doesn't turn back, guiding Arthur to the far door. The eyes of the patrons—who sport bruises, cuts, and bandages—follow him as he shuffles along. The corners of their mouths betray the upturn of nearly concealed smiles. Once the siblings have left, they turn their attention back to their meals.

* * *

"So, how is he?" Annata asks as the pair bring the trays to the drop off.

"Doctors say he'll be awake soon, hopin' he'll be fully healed in a few days. Raw biomass infusions, oxygen exchangers, the works," Jordan responds. The two Stewards exit the cafeteria, heading toward the rotunda. "And Curiesay?"

Annata is taking twice as many steps as Jordan, as her short legs struggle to keep pace with her taller counterpart. "Same. Worse, actually."

"That ain't a surprise."

"It was to me."

"You didn't do anything wrong," Jordan implores. The Stewards walk in silence for a moment, their tailored white coats almost skimming the floor as they cross the rotunda and turn toward the Medical Wing.

"I didn't expect it to be that bad," Annata says finally.

"Nobody ever does."

"Are they gonna make them do the same thing to Arthur?"

"I doubt it. Word is the Commander ain't *thrilled* about how it went down, neither is the Congress. Reckon they'll try a different approach with him." The two finally arrive at a door labeled *ICU* and enter.

Annata cocks an eyebrow. "There's a different approach?" she asks as the two stop at the first door in the hallway.

"Not that I know of," Jordan says as she enters. Annata sighs, then enters the next room down.

Jordan stutter-steps for a moment as she spots Chandrima, who is speaking quietly to the attending doctor. "Director! I didn't expect to see you here."

"I'm here to check on him. I'm not *that* heartless," Chandrima replies with a smile.

"Coulda fooled me," Jordan blurts out, quickly covering her mouth. Chandrima waves the doctor off, and he briskly leaves the room, closing the door behind him.

"I'm sorry, Director, that was inappropriate," Jordan trembles out.

Chandrima gives a firm nod. "But not uncalled for. You're concerned for your Pilot, which is part of your job. So just forget about it," she says flatly.

Jordan steps up to the bed—it's gotten no easier for her to see him. Parker is wrapped nearly from head to toe in bandages, and what little skin is visible is discolored. Tubes run into his arms and hands, and an oxygen mask is secured to his mouth.

"He's going to be all right. I've seen him in worse shape," Chandrima says, then turns to leave the room.

Jordan whips around. "Was this really the only way, Director?"

Chandrima speaks without looking back. "I don't know," she responds as she exits.

The Steward pulls a chair to the bed and pulls her knees to her chest. Her tears bridge the gap and drop onto her coat as she watches him sleep. It is silent in the room, save the metronome beeps from Parker's heart monitor. Its steadiness keeps her grounded.

Without provocation, his eyes slowly open, focusing themselves on Jordan's gaze. "Hey," he mouths breathlessly through his clear mask.

Jordan puts her hands over the rail, clasping his hand. "Hey," she says with glistening eyes.

10

Strange Places

August 31st, 2053
Bastion, Third Floor, Medical Wing

A cart rolling. A steady beeping. People talking as they walk, passing by, conversations fading.

Curiesay's eyes flutter open. The thin, itchy sheets she lies in remind her of the asylum, and for a moment, she forgets where she is. She feels a slight uncomfortable feeling in her elbows and examines them to find an IV in each arm—she winces. *Ugh, needles.* Beside her bed is a monitor which displays readings she's not familiar with.

Patting herself down, she's relieved to find all her parts intact, albeit quite sore. She scans the room: door, sink, trashcan, cart, door, chair, man.

Man.

Rapid blinks assure her that her eyes are functioning properly. The man is Parker, slumped over in the chair, seemingly in good health. Curiesay stares at him for a long while, satisfied with lying in this bed for now. The last time she saw him, they were trying to kill each other, an endeavor that *he* incited.

"Good morning, sunshine," he says dryly as he opens his eyes. He's dressed for comfort, wearing dark blue sweats and a beanie on his head, pulled down to his ears. Like the first time she saw him, and unlike the last, his eyes are neutral, his one blue and one green iris peeking out from under heavy eyelids, a scar across his temples and nose.

"Yeah? Is that all you have to say?" she snaps back.

He puts his hands up in surrender. "Curiesay, please." Her upper lip trembles but eventually relaxes. She sighs, rubbing the back of her neck. Parker sits up in his chair. "How do you feel?"

"I have all my parts, no thanks to you." She cannot hold her tongue. Parker stares blankly, then stands and makes a move toward the door when Curiesay grabs his sleeve.

"Wait!" she yelps, and Parker turns to face her. She tries her best to quash the desperation in her voice. "I mean…tell me what happened." Their eyes lock. *Don't leave me here alone.* When they'd fought, she felt every ounce of his strength. It scared her then, but now, she wants someone strong around, if only so that she can feel safe.

Parker sits back down, elbows on his knees. "I'll do my best to fill you in. You've been here for three days. The doctors are sure that you will fully recover. Doctor Joshi stops by quite often, as does Annata."

"I assume you didn't actually want me dead, given that I'm in a hospital."

"I didn't, and I don't."

"Sure have a funny way of showing it."

"It wasn't my decision. I didn't want it to go down like that."

"Bullshit. You seemed to be enjoying yourself as you beat the fuck out of me."

"I… You're right. I let myself get carried away."

"Yeah, no shit." With this, the room falls silent. Curiesay turns her head away in disgust. Her monitors beep diligently. Footsteps approach and pass in the hallway. Fans gently whir, feeding the room's air vent.

Parker lowers his voice, his tone restrained. "Do you remember what you saw?" Curiesay crosses her arms. "It's important that we talk about it, you know. It…isn't pretty."

He is the *last* person she wants to talk to. Well, other than that crazy bitch who dragged her here. Although she feels surprisingly *whole,* she still has some aches, especially her head, which currently feels like she has a boiled cabbage for a brain. He had nearly killed her, and *now* he wants to talk about—

"How do you know I saw something?" she asks, slowly turning her head to him. She studies his face for a moment—his eyes are soft, mourning.

"Because it happened to me too. Once," he responds.

Curiesay appreciates this candid expression internally. The wound is still fresh, but she *does* so desperately need to make sense of it. "I don't…remember a whole lot." She speaks slowly, uncovering the words in her mind. "My uncle was there… I mean, my memories of him. I remember his funeral. I remember the exact moment I saw his face before they took him away from me. I was so…angry. And then suddenly, I was…somewhere else? I don't know, it was…different."

Parker leans forward, his voice low and soft, hardly broaching a whisper. "What did you see?"

Curiesay shakes her head, delving deep and thinking hard. "Blood. Like I'd never seen. So much, and I just…fell into it. Was that…my… blood? It felt familiar. I was pulled down and I…could feel it filling up my lungs and weighing me down, and I sank for so long. I felt so wrong…out of place…out of time. I…resigned myself for a while and just waited to die. I felt…despicable, vile, alone…but…I didn't *want* to die. So I swam and swam, and I knew I'd never make it to the surface…but…" Curiesay takes rapid breaths as the emotions flood out of her mouth.

"I didn't want to die!" she yells, voice cracking. Parker doesn't flinch, watching intently. She shakes her head, lip twitching. "And then something just clicked, and…I wasn't alone anymore," she finishes, her voice now reduced to a whisper.

Parker moves closer and puts his hand out to her in a gesture of comfort, but she waves him off. "You'll learn more about it later, but we call that a Pilot's *Crossing*. It's required to use your Arbiter to its full potential."

Curiesay scrunches her nose, exchanging her melancholy recollection for aggression. "Oh, is that so? I can only Pilot that fuckin' thing if you beat me half to death?"

"It's a bit more complicated than that but—" Parker begins, but is cut off by an increasingly loud Curiesay.

Her heart monitor beeps at an accelerated rate as she sits up and rails against him. "Well, I wouldn't know since your boss kept me in the dark! You really had to do all that?! Is that why she didn't fill me in on the details? Since she knew if she did, I'd tell her to fuck off, right?" she finishes, taking a few deep breaths as she glares at Parker. She's still quite weak, struggling to stay upright.

Parker contemplates for a moment, sitting unflinchingly beside her bed. She's used to her temper scaring people away, but he's unfazed.

"I don't know if it was necessary, but it worked. You piloted your Arbiter, and pretty damn well I'd say," he affirms with a nod. Curiesay notes this, sensing that he's pandering to her ego.

Which works.

"Thanks," she says grudgingly. "Speaking of… Are you okay?"

"Never been better," he responds patronizingly.

"Oh…well good. I thought… I mean I *do* remember that part. You know, when I tried to kill you," she says frankly, searching his face for a reaction.

"Ah, you need some practice, 'cause I'm not dead."

"Clearly."

Parker smirks. "I don't expect an apology, but—"

"Why would *I* apologize?" Curiesay interrupts, but Parker continues without missing a beat.

"I forgive you." Curiesay stares at him in stunned silence, her heart monitor winding down from her earlier tirade. She thinks back to her Crossing. To their meeting in the *other*. *What did he see?*

"What was that?" she asks with a swallow, her lips pensively searching for the words. "Right before I lost control... I was somewhere else. You were there. You saw me. You saw...things about me."

Parker speaks flatly. "That is called your Dominium Animae. It's where your soul resides. It's well-guarded, but the veil thins once a Pilot has Crossed."

Curiesay has never bought into any spiritual bullshit. God died for her long ago, and she thinks nothing of herself more than blood and bone. But he *was* there. Somehow, in her most sacred place, he walked. It's both unbelievable and undeniable to her.

"Why were you there?" she asks accusingly.

Parker shrugs. "You tell me. You're the one who brought me there." Her cheeks flush red in embarrassment; he'd *seen* her. He'd seen— "I won't ever talk about what you showed me. I promise," he follows up.

Curiesay stiffens her lips. "Damn right you won't," she snarls, but still, Parker remains unfazed.

"I'm sorry. Maybe this wasn't the only way. Chandrima... Doctor Joshi cares more about results than she does about people, even me. I mean, hell, you almost *killed* me." Curiesay relaxes her expression, feeling a pang of remorse. "But in the end, the result was acceptable. We both survived and you completed your First Crossing with your

Arbiter. From now on it will be considerably easier to Pilot it."

Curiesay pauses for a long while after Parker finishes. *First? He can't have said that by mistake.* "And if I refuse? I mean…if I won't get in the suit again, what happens then?" she asks dispiritedly. With how things have gone thus far, she already knows the answer to that question.

"You will be considered a threat to the secrecy and integrity of the program; Director Chandrima Joshi will have you imprisoned or killed," he responds without hesitation.

Curiesay nods with an abdicating grin. *Looks like I'm stuck here.* "So, what do I do now?"

"*You* just focus on resting and healing. They should let you out by tomorrow, and in a few days, you'll be ready to begin formal training. You know, what we should have done in the first place," he responds. She allows herself to fall back onto the bed. *Kiss-ass.*

For a few moments she stares blankly at him. "You know… I still haven't forgiven you. I think as an apology you should go get me some food," she says coyly. Parker stares, stone-faced. "Please…" She crosses her arms and looks away, bested.

"Frederic has been waiting for you to wake up. I'll let him know you have." Parker leaves the room, and the moment the door closes behind him, Curiesay kicks her feet childishly under the white blanket. *I'm so fucking hungry.*

* * *

"Come in," Chandrima says, answering the knock at the door to her office. Parker enters and collapses onto the sofa up against the wall opposing her desk, knocking loose papers and books onto the floor. He squishes his face with his hands, covering his eyes.

Chandrima's eyes are glued to her computer monitor. "Good to see you, Parker. You look well." He doesn't respond. Running errands for her as soon as he's back on his feet has put a sour taste in his mouth. "So how is she?"

"Well, she's pissed. But coping. I think. Hard to tell, she's kinda erratic," he responds wearily. He's too prideful to show his exhaustion in front of Curiesay, but on this sofa, with cushions that feel like clouds, his mind yawns.

"I see. Does she remember anything?" Chandrima asks as she dutifully types away.

"Yes, quite a lot actually." He pauses for a long while, contemplating. Finally, he uncovers his face and adjusts his position on the sofa, turning his head to face Chandrima. "She recalls her Dominium. Memories. The blood, and the fall. And then…" His tone is grave. Hesitant. As if he's sharing a private matter, one told in confidence, with an outsider. Someone who could *never* understand. "*It* was there." A long exhale marks the end of his thought. Chandrima has not looked up from her computer, typing away cheerfully, her mechanical finger providing a different tone than its flesh counterparts when it strikes keys.

Parker swings his tired legs around, puts his feet on the floor, and sits up. "There's something else. In the Arena, right before she…lost it…I *saw* her." Chandrima's fingers hesitate for an instant. Parker doesn't know if she's taking notes, working on another matter, or even listening at all. She should know that it's ingrained in him to replace exhaustion with anger, and she just gave him a reason to do so.

"You know, if you're gonna have me running around doing *your* bitch work, the least you can do is look at me when I'm talking," he spits. If she was going to respond in the half-beat that Parker waited before he shot to his feet and marched to her desk, he'll never know. His Southern accent leaks out as his voice fills the room. "I ain't your servant boy! You wanna tell me what your plan was?"

Chandrima looks at him, her fingers hovering above her keyboard. "I don't appreciate your tone. Change. It," she responds with the same cheerful smile on her face as is commonplace.

Parker's fists press into the top of her desk. "Tough. Shit." Chandrima locks eyes with him. Her smile fades. Parker mentally recoils—*I must have struck a nerve.*

"I didn't have one. I expected my *veteran* Pilot to be able to handle a novice," she says vindictively. Parker crosses his arms. "She Crossed, as I intended, and her capabilities were only *slightly* beyond my calculations. You know how perilous Crossings can be, so if you felt unprepared, that's on you." Her tone is flat, like an educator scolding her thousandth student.

Parker rolls his eyes as he musters up a retort. "You were supposed to shut it down if she lost control. I wouldn't have overextended if I knew—"

"I tried, but her Arbiter wouldn't accept the command. Too much interference. And your inadequacies are not my responsibility. If you were *so* worried that she'd kill you, why didn't you do anything about it?" The moment the words leave her mouth, the mood in the room shifts. She leans back as Parker absorbs her words.

"You wanted me to Cross? Again? That...*that* was your plan?" He shakes his head with indignance. Chandrima opens her mouth, but no words come out, offering only a subdued shrug of her shoulders. Parker looses a hearty sigh. "So, what now? Any more candidates in mind?"

The Director's face droops with this change in direction. "Yes, but unfortunately I am not on good terms with Congress, so I haven't received the go ahead to make contact."

Parker's anger fades. "How bad is it?"

"I'm being formally investigated in relation to the accident. Zochitl should be reaching out to you for your statement."

"What should I tell her?"

"Tell her the truth."

"You *need* to stay in charge. Especially after what I found."

"I know."

"You don't sound very worried."

"I am," she says flatly.

Parker gives a compassionate half-grin. He lowers his voice, speaking just above a whisper. "What did Nerezza say? About the Blight with the journal?"

"She's just as puzzled as I am," Chandrima responds just as quietly. "Our estimates aligned, putting her age at roughly twenty-five years. That means that Waifs *aren't* immune, but are avoided for some other reason. Why it chose her specifically to infect, and why she was able to exercise that level of free will, we still don't know."

He somberly nods, rubbing his eyes with his hands. "So what does this mean for us?"

Chandrima flashes a devious grin. "Congress has rescinded my authorization to recruit more candidates from the general population. They didn't say anything about Blights."

"You can't be serious?" Parker asks incredulously.

"She had tendrils, did she not? If we could cure one, then—"

"You *are* serious," he interrupts as she talks over him.

"—I see no reason why they couldn't Pilot. I already have one in mind. Thanks to Karima."

A jolt of nerves shivers through him at the mention of Karima. Living and working so close to the girls has left a soft spot in his heart, and he hasn't slept much in the weeks since the Director had sent Karima into the Exclusion Zone. "I'm still sour that you sent her at all."

"It's her job. We're not a daycare. And who better to send? She'll be fine," Chandrima responds dismissively. Parker's tight glare gives her pause as she reconsiders. "She *is* fine. Just heard from them. I've reassigned them from canvassing to tracking down the Blight they've spotted. Similar age to the one you found, similar…*disposition.* There isn't another Blight within twelve square kilometers. Apparently, she's not very friendly toward her kind."

The revelation softens Parker's expression into eager curiousness. "She kills other Blights?"

"They haven't witnessed it personally, but they've heard clashing and seen her return to her hobble covered in black blood. She's also been communicating. With Karima primarily. Bringing her into her Dominium." Parker's face flushes red. "She's okay, I just told you that. Karima seems to think that she's lonely, and besides being a bit unsettled by the experience, she's coping with it well. In fact, she says that she doesn't mind it."

"That Blight knows she's being watched. And if she knows, then *it* knows. You should pull them out."

"If she wanted them dead, they'd have ended up like the Blights she harasses. Karima is quite fond of her, so I doubt she'd come back even if I ordered it," Chandrima responds matter-of-factly. *Reckless.* The Blight communicates with its thrall telepathically, using magnetic waves to carry information. If one Blight knows something, they *all* know. Though Parker wonders if that applies to rogue Blights like the one he killed or the one Karima is stalking.

He shakes his head with disgust, taking a drawn-out breath through his nose. He knows it's folly to argue with the Director, especially when she's made up her mind. "So, how do you plan to cure her? Or even get her back here to begin with?"

Chandrima coyly shrugs her shoulders, giving Parker a wide-eyed half-smile. "I'll figure it out. *You* just worry about getting Curiesay and young Arthur up to speed."

Another jolt of nerves perks his weary brain up as he hears his name. He'd known that Chandrima had been planning to recruit him, but he hadn't formally met Arthur yet. For some reason, the mention sends the rusty wheels of his mind turning.

"What, uh… Tell me again what happened in the booth. You said… that her Arbiter failed?" Bruised and staggered, his brain struggles to make the connections he is so desperate for. He closes his eyes, recollecting the moment Curiesay stood before him, then the blinding light.

"Yes. Given the amount of damage it sustained, I'm not too surprised," she responds. Parker's ears tense as he senses her carefully measured tone. *One of your suits malfunctioned, yet you don't seem all that bothered. Before the light… What happened before the light?*

"Is that what happened? I thought…the *kid*… Eh, I don't know. It's all fuzzy to me."

"You sustained injuries to your head at the end, it's a miracle you can even remember your own name," Chandrima chirps with a smile. Parker nods skeptically. He knows that if she's lying to him, it's in his best interest not to challenge her. As well, all this excitement is eating through his precious mental focus—he is beginning to disassociate.

Chandrima notices his eyelids flutter and honeys her words. "Thanks for helping me out today, truly. Go get some rest." She flashes a smile that Parker perceives as genuine—a rare sight.

"Say no more," he says as he makes for the door. *Get the fuck out before she thinks of something else for you to do.*

* * *

Room, food, sleep. Room, food, sleep. The exhausted Pilot repeats this mantra as he walks down the Medical Wing hallway to the rotunda, turning down toward the Dwellings Wing. He sticks close to the wall,

129

and as he enters the hallway, he nearly runs into another person.

You gotta be kidding me. It's Arthur, the soon-to-be third Pilot and Director Joshi's nephew. Just behind him, standing a hand's width taller than him, is his sister, Elva. *They're gonna want to talk to me.*

He is right.

"Oh, hey! You're Parker, right? You got back on your feet *fast!*" Elva beams as she steps up and shakes his hand. He manages a sincere smile even if he's mentally shrieking at this further delay.

"That's me, and thanks. Modern medicine and all. You're the Director's niece and nephew, Elva and Arthur?" he responds, and Elva nods earnestly. Arthur stares at him, his gaze shy. Parker recognizes Arthur's uneasiness and addresses it. "We'll be seeing a lot of each other, so it's good that we've met. You been settling in all right?"

Arthur perks up, maintaining eye contact as he speaks. "I guess. It's kinda overwhelming, but I'll get used to it eventually," he responds.

Parker's eyelids flutter again, and he gulps down a breath. Elva grabs Arthur's arm. "It was nice to meet you, we'll let you get going," she says quickly as she ushers Arthur into the rotunda, their course heading toward the Rec Wing. Parker turns and glances back at them, the shadow of a memory crossing his grey matter as he looks at the back of Arthur's head. *I need to lie down.*

Luckily, his room is nearest to the rotunda, and in half a minute he is opening his door. His eyes glaze over the figure on his sectional as he enters, more concerned with maintaining an upright posture and closing the door. It isn't until he turns back around that his mind makes an effort to identify them.

Please, have mercy. "Jordan, hey," he says with an overacted sigh. His Steward, easily able to access his room from their adjoining door—which he never locks—is lying on his couch and watching the wall-mounted television.

"You ain't seem too excited to see me, Pilot," she says with a sly grin.

"I was worried about you. Been waiting all day. Don't you ever check your phone?"

I don't even know where I've left it. "Apparently not," he says as he crosses the room. Jordan watches her Pilot longingly as he steps into the kitchen, fills a glass of water, and downs it. He does this a second, then a third time, breathing heavily as he tosses the glass haphazardly into the sink.

Jordan stands and moves to the breakfast nook opposite the sink, leaning against it. "You know, I don't feel like getting another Pilot if you die," she says sarcastically.

Parker is firmly gripping the edge of the kitchen counter as he reluctantly makes eye contact with her. "Thinking of replacing me already? I've only been out for a few days." He tries to come across with the same level of sarcasm, but it falls flat. More of a resignation than anything else.

"Yeah, a few days in the ICU."

"It was necessary."

"You sound like her."

"The results *more* than make up for it."

Jordan furrows her brow at his seeming lack of self-awareness. "Now you *really* sound like her. I don't see how you ain't the least bit upset."

Parker grumbles. He has already made amends with Chandrima, and now he is tasked with calming his Steward. "I am, but I knew the risks back when I first became a Pilot. And after *my* Crossing, I should have expected this. I'm almost back to one hundred percent, and in a few days, Curiesay will be too." He pushes himself away from the counter and heads to the couch, collapsing with one leg hanging off the side.

To his chagrin, Jordan follows and sits next to him. "She's strong."

"Yes, she is."

"I think she's dangerous too."

"I certainly hope so. For my sake."

"Just keep yourself safe, please."

"No promises, I don't like to lie."

Jordan forces a weak smile, then sheepishly says her next words. "She's pretty."

Oh my God. Parker gives her a sour look. "I'm nearly twice her age."

She waves her hands dismissively. "I'm just saying! I happened to notice."

"I wouldn't worry about it."

She scoots closer, tapping his head with her pointer finger. "I worry about *you*." Parker obliges and lifts his head as she slips under it. He turns onto his side, head on her lap. The weight of his eyelids doubles as he gets comfortable, the heat radiating from her lap calming his shot nerves.

"I'm fine, can't you tell?" he asks as he curls up, using his Steward as a pillow, and begins fading out of consciousness. He reaches around her side and grips her thigh like a pillow, curling farther up onto her.

"You're paler than a bedsheet right now. Surprised you made it through the day like this," she teases, stroking his head. "I will say, you're never this lovey. I changed my mind—get your ass kicked more often."

"Now *that's* a promise I can keep," he responds with a yawn as the day's errands finally catch up with him, his mind drifting to sleep. Jordan remains for about an hour, lightly petting his head, until she (carefully) substitutes her lap with a pillow and slips into her own room.

A few hours later, a knock. He shoots up in a panic as he moves to the door, his mind vaguely aware that he's forgotten something important.

"Assistant Director, hi," he says as he swings the door open, taken aback. A tall, tan-skinned woman stands opposite him, her lab coat hanging just a hair above the floor below, a red knapsack over her shoulder.

"Don't look so happy to see me! I'm here to deliver your infusion since you declined to attend your appointment. And please, after working hours just call me Zochi," she says with a purr, inviting herself in. Parker clumsily steps aside, the sudden waking and prior exhaustion combining forces to keep him off balance. Zochitl grabs the coat rack near the door and drags it into the living room.

Unshouldering her bag, she unzips it and pulls out an IV bag, tubing, and a catheter, all sterilely packaged. She motions for the Pilot to sit, and Parker can do little else but comply like a lost sheep.

"Sorry to make you come down here yourself. I've, uh, been pretty out of it today," he says apologetically as he watches her prepare to run the line into his arm, pulling out a disposable alcohol pad and some tape.

"It's fine, really. You're barely out of the ICU and already Chandrima has you running errands. It's understandable that you're a bit tired," she says as she expertly inserts the catheter into his right arm, securing it with medical tape.

She connects the bag and hangs it from the coat rack. "All right! Get comfortable—it takes about forty-five minutes."

Parker rearranges the cushions on the couch, making a comfortable spot to lie. "Ugh, I'm glad this is my last bag."

"Oh really? Why's that?" she asks as she takes a seat across from him.

"Even with the sterilization cycles…it gives me nightmares," he says, putting his hands over his face. *So much for a good night's sleep.*

"I see. Well, occasional psychological discomfort is a reported side effect of—" Zochitl begins before stopping short. "I'm sorry, I know it's uncomfortable. But like you said, it's the last one."

His upper lip twitches. "Yeah, until the next time Chandrima sends me to get pummeled." He knows he shouldn't complain, especially to his *other* boss, but this sudden waking has made him cranky.

"I wanted to ask you about that actually. How are you alive?" she asks bluntly. Parker's breathing pauses for a moment. "You may know I'm conducting a formal investigation, and you are my last interviewee."

He removes his hands from his face and turns his head to her. "No idea. I don't remember anything after I hit the glass. I hit my head pretty hard, and it was lights out. Woke up two days later in the ICU." He hates its necessity, but if he has learned anything from Chandrima, it is how to lie. Discussing his doubts with Zochitl seems unnecessary, especially considering that Director Joshi's job is at stake.

"Ah, I see. Well, if you do happen to remember anything, you know where to find me," Zochitl says as she stands and gives a slight wave. "Oh, I almost forgot! Prefect Typher has requested your presence tomorrow at eleven at the Spire. You are a key witness, after all." *Is she being vindictive?*

"I'd honestly rather spend another week in the ICU," he responds, taking the pillow from behind his head and placing it over his face. This new development has pushed his exhaustion to a new level, and he wishes to be buried under a mountain of linens and sleep for ten days.

Zochitl doesn't comment on his childish actions. "Get some rest, Pilot. See you around." She exits and closes the door behind her. Parker lies there in silence, fading into a sleep drenched in nightmares and terror.

11

Congress

September 2nd, 2053
France

The conversations within the café reverberate gently off its vaulted windows as the midmorning light casts diagonal shadows across the floor. An unspoken agreement to keep the sounds of the daily bustle at a low level exists here; cargo haulers, soldiers from overseas, and researchers seldom catch a break from their demanding schedules, and a place of quiet respite is a rare delight in this busy port city.

At the rearmost section, an odd pair of patrons share a booth. Both are females of significant stature, though lean of build. Verlean is a dark-skinned woman, with powerful legs concealed by a flowing white and pink sundress, her forearms highly tuned and taut. Her braided hair sports a variety of colorful beads, tied back with a purple ribbon. She has modest facial features, a defined yet feminine jaw, and piercing brown eyes which seem to take on a personality of their own with their criticality.

Opposite her is Sadie, who is a bit shorter, but still well above average. She's a weight class below her counterpart, with far more of her skeleton making her corners and crevices sharp. Her skin is a shade darker than pastel white, with shoulder-length blonde hair and cloying baby-blue eyes that mesmerize those who are unlucky enough to get lost in them. A yellow spring dress, held up by her upper arms, exposes her collar bone. She stares at her compatriot with an obnoxiously impatient look, as if waiting for a comment they're both expecting.

Verlean looks disgusted as she examines her own attire. "It's a lot…*brighter* than I thought it would be."

Sadie giggles. "Oh, Verlean, I'm glad you like it. I think you look beautiful! It really contrasts the whole 'I'll tear your head off' vibe you have."

Verlean exhales forcefully. "Keep it up and I'll show you first-hand, brat."

Their waiter approaches the table. He first asks if they speak French, to which the two women respond in the affirmative, and they converse as such. Much to the Frenchman's displeasure, this establishment, like many others in Europe, has become increasingly Americanized, and their order reflects this. That's what happens when three continents lose ninety percent of their population.

Sadie speaks over Verlean as she rattles off the order. "She'll have six eggs, sunny-side up, half a sliced and toasted baguette, three fruit crepes, three stacks of pancakes, and a coffee. And I'll have…" she rocks her head back and forth, a scornful grin forming on her face, "…uh, I guess just the veggie omelet, with egg whites, and a coffee."

The waiter reads their order back to them. "That's a lot of food, are you sure—"

Verlean cuts in. "I'd appreciate it if you didn't comment on my figure. You may go." The man gives a disapproving grunt and leaves without a word, Verlean's sharp eyes following him as he enters the kitchen.

"Geez, Verlean, could you at least *try* not to draw any more attention," Sadie says in English, exasperated.

"These fucking maggots don't deserve an ounce of kindness." She turns her eyes to Sadie. "Don't ever order for me again," she continues with a snarl.

Sadie responds with a smile. "I've been around you long enough to know what you like. You miss me when I'm gone, don't deny it," she chirps, bouncing in her seat. Verlean gives a sour expression. "You see, this is why you need me around. Our natural arrogance aside, can't you tone it down at all in public? You stand out enough as it is."

Verlean's eye twitches as her nostrils flare and she gives a long exhale through her nose. "Ugh, I know, you're right. How do you do it? Bastion is so tightly packed—don't they get on your nerves?" The coffee arrives, and the two remain silent until the waiter departs. Verlean takes her mug. Dash, dash, dash of sugar.

"They're not so bad! Sure, they're vermin, but they're the best humanity has to offer. I actually..." Sadie closes her eyes for a moment, "...enjoy my time there. And besides, as a child I was always interested in science. Our current *situation* aside, I am living my childhood dream." Verlean nods, though with a half-disgusted look on her face. Her eyes widen a bit as she locks onto a spot just above Sadie's left eyebrow—a quarter-sized section of skin has rapidly turned a light brown shade.

"You've, uh, got a little somethin'..." Verlean trails off as she points to her own forehead, indicating the spot to Sadie. Sadie's cheeks flush as she pulls out a miniature mirror from her purse. She examines the spot, using her free hand to shield her eyes from any other patrons that may be watching. Verlean scans the café as Sadie's irises glow faintly red. The brown patch of skin quickly reverts to a shade matching the rest of her face.

The café's hanging bell rings as three more patrons enter. Soldiers, dressed in their camouflage uniforms, take their seats a few booths away from the two women. Verlean eyes them discreetly for a moment.

As Sadie puts her mirror away, Verlean clears her throat. "So, what came of it?"

Although they are companions, Sadie is reluctant to share all that she knows. Her soft heart has become far too invested in her work, even if she owes Verlean this favor. That is, the favor of feeding her information on Bastion's doings. "They've recruited another Pilot. Zone security is increased, and they're mustering a ten percent increase in overall manpower at the Wall," Sadie says carefully, with an embarrassed quality to her hesitance. Nothing of their Waif and the team in the Exclusion Zone. Nothing of the revelations Chandrima had shared with her about the errant Blight that Parker had found. Nothing of Curiesay's outburst and the miracle that came with it. *I'll tell her...eventually.*

"How did she make it that far? Samael is slacking," Sadie continues.

Verlean nods. "These things happen, I suppose. No word on what his punishment will be." Both women shudder. "In any case, my instructions are clear. Maintain your cover."

Cover. She'd never intended to be a spy, but a favor should be repaid. Though, Sadie had never expected this. "Understood. My clearance level is adequate."

"And Doctor Joshi?"

"Sharp as ever, but that matters not. I'm doing well, working as her direct subordinate."

Verlean grimaces. "Subordinate? Quite humble of you to reduce yourself to such a word. Do you kiss her feet as well?"

A muscle in Sadie's jaw feathers for a moment before she tamps down her aggression. "You know me—I have no problem being dominated," she responds with a wink. Verlean's dark cheeks lighten as they flush, poorly concealing an entertained smirk.

Two waiters arrive carrying large trays of food. They unload them, leaving no table left to be seen. They wait for a thank you that they never receive before leaving. The two women eat quickly and savagely, with Sadie finishing her small meal in a scant few moments. Within minutes, the plates of food disappear into their stomachs.

Sadie stifles a burp and giggles, annoying Verlean. "You know, I've been meaning to ask, have you lost weight?" Verlean asks, her eyes crawling over Sadie's figure.

"Uh, well, the thing is…" Sadie's eyes drop to the table. "I have been able to avoid detection thus far, but they're adding scales to the checkpoints."

Verlean cocks her head. "*Really*? She's as sharp as I remember."

"Quite. As a result, I've had to…slim down. Shrunk a bit. But I'm confident they won't detect me," Sadie says, managing a weak smile.

"Let's hope so. I must say, I'm surprised…" Verlean starts, leaning over the table with a wicked grin. "I never thought you could *be* so weak."

"Ah, Verlean! You are always a riot! If we weren't out in public, I'd rip your fucking throat right out of. Your. Pretty. Neck," Sadie responds with an equally insane grin, pointing at Verlean's neck as she annunciates.

Verlean scoffs, then leans back. "Fair enough. I do commend you though—keeping myself at even *this* size is…unpleasant." Sadie accepts the compliment, sporting a satisfied grin. Verlean rolls her eyes. "Anything else?"

Sadie clears her throat, fidgeting in her seat. "The Pilots."

"What about them?"

"Well, there's that white guy, Parker."

Verlean's left eye twitches as she grits her teeth. "Don't remind me."

Sadie looks down at the table, drawing imaginary figures with her pointer finger. "And a new girl. She's…formidable."

Verlean's eyes widen and she cocks her head to the side. "Quite an endorsement."

"She's at least as strong as Parker, maybe even more so. Here. Take these." Sadie reaches into her purse and retrieves a small plastic case and a photograph. She hands the case to Verlean, who examines it. "Some footage, all I could manage."

"Footage? I don't give a shit how she fights. Pilots are inconsequential," Verlean snaps scornfully.

Sadie stumbles over her words as she avoids eye contact. "Verlean, she…well…it's *her*," she manages as she slides a photo of Curiesay across the table. Verlean's eyes widen; the veins in her neck and face inflate themselves; her mouth forms into a tooth-shattering scowl. She closes her eyes, calming herself, and sighs loudly while placing the plastic case into her purse.

"Of course," Verlean says, exhaling a lung's worth of air.

"You know, it's a miracle that any of us exist with *that* kind of a reaction," Sadie remarks.

Verlean shakes her head with disapproval. "Well, yes, they're disgusting, vile little creatures." A beat passes as her face relaxes, eyes softening. "She has his eyes."

A nostalgic smile creeps across Sadie's face. "Yes. She does."

"How long have you known?"

"For a while. But I wasn't sure if she would agree to it. I didn't…" Sadie's voice soften, "… want to cause you any distress if it ended up not happening."

Verlean studies her critically, then gives a slow, acknowledging nod.

Business in the café carries on as usual, the morning crowd giving way to afternoon travelers. A sizable cargo ship must have made a port call, as dozens of sailors, with grizzled complexions and oil-stained clothes, enter the café, talking loudly and disturbing the quiet contract that they are unaware of. The two women watch them with disdain, as if the sailors are here without their blessing.

"I should get going," Sadie says as she grabs a paper bill from her purse, lays it on the table, then scoots out of the booth. "I have to brief them before the interrogation begins."

Verlean reaches out quickly and grabs her arm. "Be careful. Please."

Sadie flashes a grin and blushes. "Always am."

* * *

Bastion, Second Floor, Government Sector

Chandrima waits patiently in the hallway outside of the meeting room, just next door to the Prefect's office. It's in the government sector of the Second Floor, at the top floor of the tallest building there—the Spire. She doesn't often get vertigo, but she is undeniably afraid of heights, and she can feel the building swaying ever so slightly under her feet, even though the building contacts the bottom of the Third Floor at its peak. That fear, in addition to her apprehension about the imminent meeting, makes her queasy.

Pacing nervously in front of the door, she counts her steps. A handful of curious eyes study her as residents of this floor go about their daily business. The hallway smells of carpet and fresh paper copies, with the faint aroma of coffee wafting over from the break room.

Contrary to her public perception—that she has so carefully crafted—Doctor Chandrima Joshi is a neurotic, anti-social, and uncertain person. As far back as she can remember, she's been an insomniac, her racing mind making use of every moment the days have to offer. Hours of second guessing, impossible scenarios, and past embarrassments keep her up until her brain shuts down against its will, savoring a scant few hours of rest.

Peers have remarked that she is aging gracefully, and at the age of fifty-two, they are right. But they are unaware that her morning routine involves a plethora of "beauty" products, with some intending to turn back the time on her skin while the others seek to cover up the years entirely. The stress of her station only makes matters worse. Her brown skin has begun to spot, and the crow's feet that flank her eyes only grow by the day.

She does hold a sense of pride in her ability to put on a show. Long ago she realized that her neuroses were here to stay, so she worked to hide rather than cure them. Behind her back she had been called "ruthless" or "cruel," but *at least they don't call me "weak."*

Wearing a freshly bleached and pressed lab coat, along with some modest gold jewelry and leather flats, she feels she looks as good as is possible for her. She goes over the potential line of questioning again and again, positing her answers in the exponentially increasing scenarios. She realizes it's futility—no amount of preparation could account for every situation. If there is one thing that she takes solace in, it is her massive intellect, which will help her bully her way through this.

She hopes.

The door opens suddenly, startling her and interrupting her stride. "Director Joshi, we are ready for you," Prefect Typher says as he gestures for her to enter. He's a stout man, a hand taller than Chandrima. He wears a professional-looking grey suit, his salt and pepper hair slicked back and his face cleanly shaven. Chandrima gives him a courteous nod and walks through the doorway.

The room is small and dark, with a chair near the front, facing ten or so chairs on the opposite side. Behind them are a dozen rectangular screens positioned long ways on the floor, so that they tower above the other occupants of the room. Parker is in attendance, sitting in one of the chairs, as is another man.

A tall man, with dark skin and a grizzled complexion, wearing his military dress uniform, olive-green, with several rows of bright ribbons adorning his breast, and a pair of quadruple stars pinned to his collar. He doesn't regard Chandrima as she enters.

Typher directs Chandrima to the chair on the left side of the room, facing the other chairs and screens, and takes a seat opposite her. She sits, crossing one leg over the other, intending to show her relaxed state. In truth, she feels like she may vomit.

The lights in the room mainly shine upon Chandrima's assigned chair and remind her of so many stereotypical interrogation scenes in action movies, with her detractors shrouded in darkness across from her.

A moment after Typher sits, the screens behind them flicker to life, and upon each one are several lines of text: country; position; name; local time. Each screen represents a different country, with their leaders or representatives transmitting their voices through the screen's internal speakers. There is no video, which Chandrima feels is a psychological tactic to make it difficult to defend herself against a faceless critic. Representatives from Cairo, Sydney, Tokyo, Washington, D.C., Quebec, and Brasília are all in attendance.

"Ladies and gentlemen, thank you for taking the time out of your day to be here. We will be discussing the recent demonstration of our Pilots in Bastion, as well as the outcome and consequences," Prefect Typher says flatly. Chandrima has known Alexi Typher for many years and is quite fond of him.

He'd fallen into the job by the simple misfortune of having *built* Bastion—and the Pale Wall which encircles the Exclusion Zone—and when the world's government needed a third head for the city, they could think of no one better. Apparently they didn't think all that hard, as Alexi is an architect, not a politician. Though, Chandrima has been continually surprised by his innate political wherewithal. She doesn't know if she feels more or less at ease with him leading this inquisition.

"Director Joshi, please explain to us what happened, in your own words," Typher says. Chandrima can hardly see him with the lights shining at her, and does her best to keep her eyes on Parker's silhouette. Though he is here to essentially testify against her, his presence is calming.

Chandrima takes a deep breath through her nose. "Our newest Pilot, Curiesay Richardson, successfully synced with her Arbiter and Crossed. In the ensuing confrontation, both her and Pilot Adam Parker were seriously injured. I've been told that they will both fully recover. As well, their Arbiters were severely damaged, but were able to be salvaged."

A small white light on one of the tall black screens turns on. "Ensuing confrontation? You make it sound as if it wasn't at your direction," says the representative from Washington.

"It certainly *was* planned, at least up until the end," Chandrima responds.

"Do your plans often result in the near death of your *entire* cadre of Pilots, as well as your staff?" he retorts. Chandrima struggles to keep her temper down—it is frustrating enough answering to a bunch of pencil pushers, let alone ones whose faces she cannot visualize herself spitting onto.

"No, not at all. This was simply an unfortunate mishap," Chandrima says coyly. If she can't let her temper flare, she can certainly be a smart ass.

The man's voice scoffs loudly through the speakers. "That's one way to put it," he responds.

Before he can speak again, another screen's light turns on. "How much does each suit cost, Director?" asks the representative from Cairo.

Chandrima's eye twitches a bit. *You already know the answer.* "Approximately one point three billion credits." With the dire state of the world economy, she may as well have denied food to the thousands that money could have fed with her own bare hands.

"And *two* were damaged. Quite brazen of you to gamble that kind of money, no?" the voice responds.

"Everything in life is a gamble, and…" *In Bastion, I'm the house, and the house always wins.* "…I felt confident that it was the right decision to make," she finishes.

The light on Tokyo's screen comes to life. "I see that the required repairs to the Third Floor exceeds ten million credits. My people largely live in squalor as you siphon our resources for your Pilot Regiment. Do you feel no remorse at all?" a female voice says.

The room falls silent for a moment when Typher speaks, still facing Chandrima. "If we expect the Director to operate under the assumption that she is not allowed to spend the money that you have allocated to us, I fear that our efficiency here would be greatly impeded." Chandrima's relief is tempered with frustration. If he shows that he is not impartial toward her, he'll surely be replaced.

The light on Washington's screen comes to life again. "I doubt her efficiency could be any lower, Prefect, as after nearly fifteen years you have a grand total of *two* Pilots. Maybe in another hundred you'll have enough to make a difference." Chandrima can see Parker quietly shifting in his chair and prays that he will keep quiet.

She sits forward and tries to keep her tone neutral even if her words are not. "Sir, we are doing our best, and we have come a long way. The newest iteration of our Arbiter allows us to more easily find suitable Pilots. A third is already attending classes. We're working miracles here, so I feel a bit of thanks is warranted." A pause follows her statement, clearly intended to make Chandrima sit with her words. Although she is quite socially inept, unable to make head or tails of casual conversations, she has a razor-sharp tongue that is difficult to control when the pressure is on.

Brasília's representative is the next to speak. "How many Pilots do you need to penetrate the Exclusion Zone?" she asks.

Chandrima ponders for a moment, knowing that she doesn't have a good answer. "If you're asking how many we need to effectively combat the Blight's armies, I am sad to say that we are nowhere near that number. However, with even two fully qualified Pilots, we will be able to launch *productive* missions into the Exclusion Zone."

Brasília's representative speaks again. "And what do you hope to accomplish? Do you have any immediate plans?"

The military man interjects, his voice commanding, yet tactful. "I'm afraid we cannot discuss those types of details in this setting. That information is highly classified, for appropriate reasons." A long silence follows, with a sense of unease being shared between all the occupants of the room.

Without speaking, all those in attendance know the real reason why it won't be discussed here. In the years since the Blight appeared, a group had begun to worship the pestilence. What Chandrima calls a "cult" is the largest religion in the world, and it isn't exactly a secret that many of the representatives in attendance rely on the congregation's support to stay in power. Although it isn't said explicitly, the distrust between Bastion and the rest of the world is well known.

Finally, Tokyo's light flicks on and a woman speaks. "Prefect, nearly one quarter of the global GDP is being funneled into Bastion, with almost half of that being consumed by the Third Floor. I'd like to know what Bastion's conventional armed forces could do with that kind of money." Chandrima curses silently to herself; *All you people care about is money.*

Typher looks at the military officer. "Garrison Commander Cutter?"

"It would certainly be appreciated, especially to fund the *Goliath* project. But the promise of the Pilots cannot be denied. I've personally witnessed Parker in combat, both *before* and after he was a Pilot, and the difference is clear. I'd wager that he alone is as effective as an entire regiment of my soldiers," the Commander affirms loudly.

Tokyo speaks again. "Were you not the one only a few months ago voting against an increase in budget for the Pilot Regiment and requesting it be directed toward the Bastion Home Guard? What changed?"

The Commander speaks his next words in a mournful manner, as if reading an obituary. "Our enemy is no longer at rest."

A thick air settles upon the occupants of the room, and unbeknownst to them, the representatives in their home countries can feel the same. Not one person shuffles, exhales too loudly, or thinks too selfishly. For a few moments, they are all in agreement.

Commander Cutter clears his throat, snapping the trances of those in attendance. "The new Pilot's Crossing isn't a surprise to me, as we had an arguably *worse* outcome after Parker's First Crossing. The fact that no one died this time shows that despite her, what I consider to be, *reckless* methods, Director Joshi is trying to improve from a safety standpoint."

A short silence falls over the room as Chandrima feels a stake driven into her heart upon mention of Parker's Crossing. She silently curses the lights which are blinding her from being able to see him.

Next to speak is the representative from Quebec. "Commander, you work side by side with Director Joshi in the defense of Bastion and, as such, the defense of humanity as a whole, do you not?"

"Yes, that is accurate," he responds flatly.

"You have personally seen her Pilots in action, correct?"

"Yes."

"Given that, how confident do you feel depending on Director Joshi, and her Pilots, to assist you in the defense of humanity?"

Cutter doesn't hesitate in his response. "Supremely confident." Another long silence falls over the room as Chandrima wonders what kind of leverage the Commander seeks to gain over her. They have butted heads for years over the budget, and she always thought he would throw her under a bus should one happen to pass by.

The screen transmitting for Sydney speaks. "I want to hear from your veteran Pilot," the male voice says in an upbeat manner.

Parker shifts uncomfortably in his seat. "Yes, sir." Their exchange proceeds rapidly, with questions and answers being traded in quick succession.

"How are you feeling? I understand that you were gravely injured."

"I am nearly fully healed."

"What do you think of your new comrade?"

"She's capable."

"Is she stable?"

"Are any of us?"

The male voice chuckles. "Fair enough. How do you feel about Director Joshi risking your life?"

"It was necessary."

"Do you think she would do so again?"

"Should it be required, yes."

"And you trust her judgment?"

"Yes."

"You bet your life on it?"

Parker responds emphatically. "Yes."

"Ah, good to hear. As always, I appreciate your candor and

conciseness, Pilot. Well, I think that's all we needed to hear. The Prefect, the Commander, and her Pilot all agree that she was well within her rights to do as she has done. Assistant Director Bottazzi has also submitted her recommendation, in which she is adamant that no consequences are necessary. I see no reason to spend all day debating this. Bastion is manning the fort, and we should do our best to support them. I hereby motion to disband these proceedings. All in favor?"

A moment of silence passes, and one by one, the representatives' screens flash the word *aye*, signaling their approval. Chandrima feels a sense of relief flooding her body, only to be dragged back to reality a moment later.

The representative speaks again, his tone far more malicious than before. "You have escaped punishment, Director Chandrima Joshi, but make no mistake—you are not God. It is by the good graces of your peers that you continue to serve, but the Congress is less forgiving. Is that understood?"

"Yes, I understand," Chandrima replies, chin high, stomach turning. A moment later, the names on the screens fade to black, and Typher stands. Moving to the door, he flips the light switches, turning the lights facing Chandrima off and turning on the overhead lights.

"Well, Rima, it seems all's well that ends horribly," Typher says with a chuckle as he steps toward Chandrima, who is still seated. The Commander stands and briskly heads for the door.

"Commander!" Chandrima calls out when he reaches the door.

Cutter turns slightly toward her before he exits. "Don't thank me," he says gruffly. Chandrima eyes the doorway for a few moments, then turns to look at Typher and Parker, the latter of which has stood up and is moving to her.

"I've never seen someone who hates a person so much speak so highly of them, Rima," Typher remarks.

"Yeah, well, he was just being honest. I think," she responds with a sigh. Typher extends his hand to help her stand, but she waves him off. "I think I'll just sit here for a minute and collect my thoughts." Typher nods and exits the room. A moment passes as Parker and Chandrima are left alone. Apparently, he can see the beads of sweat forming on her forehead—he pulls out a plastic bag from his pocket and hands it to her, closes the door.

Chandrima empties the contents of her stomach, which consists of a granola bar and a cup of coffee, into the bag. Parker puts his back against the now closed door, ensuring nobody can enter as he watches his boss gag and spit. Parker is the only person living who truly knows the depths of her anxiety—this show of weakness isn't anything new to him.

"You really can't control your tongue, can you?" Parker remarks.

Chandrima waves her hand dismissively. "Those assholes need to mind their own business and focus on getting us more money. They're not the ones within a stone's throw of our greatest enemy." She spits into the bag and leans back in her chair. Then she turns her head to him and continues, her eyes soft. "He shouldn't have brought up your Crossing. It was uncalled for."

Parker shakes his head with a smile. "Doesn't bother me anymore." *Liar.* He motions for her to hand him the bag, which she does with some reluctance. He carefully ties a knot into it and helps Chandrima to her feet. They exit together and he tosses the vomit bag into a trash can as they pass a stranger's office on their way out of the building.

* * *

In the late afternoon, Curiesay was discharged from the ICU with explicit instructions—*Do not exert yourself.* She feels the words were wasted on her as she hardly has the energy to make the long walk back to her room. *Her* room, which she hasn't had the pleasure of seeing yet.

Some welcome party, she muses to herself as she walks. The spaces she traverses seem much smaller than she had remembered on the way in, as if the massive concrete walls seek to close in upon her. She wonders if her perception is the result of the cocktail of medications she has received—she's a bit of an expert on the misuse of pharmaceuticals.

The medical staff gave her a set of white sweats to wear, and as she approaches the door with her name over it, she digs in the pockets for the key they'd also given her. She holds it in front of her face, studying it with reverence. *This is my key. To my room.* In foster care, all that she "owned" was borrowed, and she was gifted less than nothing at Wilted Rose.

It's so pretty. How strange, she thinks, to feel so attached to something so inconsequential. She puts her ear to the door and inserts the key, listening to the lock's gentle clunks. Opening the door, she hesitates at the threshold, casting her gaze down both ends of the corridor. No one is there to admonish her; no one is there to ask her where she's supposed to be. She wonders if the feeling of *being wrong simply by existing* will ever go away.

The door is locked with haste after she closes it behind her.

It's not large, but it is quite cozy. *Fuckin' sure better than a cell,* she thinks as she stalks her apartment with curious eyes. *Big television, couch, oh, a little kitchen. And a fridge? There's already food in here. What the hell is "kefir"? Ah, next. Bathroom... Oh.* She isn't used to seeing toilets filled with water—the doctors at the asylum deemed it *too dangerous* for "unstable" patients. Curiesay had thought that if she were to kill herself, it wouldn't be by drowning, and she sure wouldn't do it in *shitty toilet water.*

She steps back into the living area and spies the two rooms on the side with sliding doors. *I get two rooms?* One has a bare wooden desk, an empty bookshelf, and an office chair. The other is her bedroom.

A king-sized bed takes up nearly a third of the space and is accompanied by a matching set of nightstands, two dressers, and a full-size vanity mirror. The dresser in front of the bed has a ratty green duffel bag atop it. Curiesay inhales sharply when she sees it.

She hasn't had time to think about anything since she'd gotten to Bastion. All she knows is that her bag—in which is everything that she owns—has been out of her sight. Frantically she searches through the pockets and finds her mark—a cardstock envelope à la cheap amusement park photo booths.

Its brown construction has darkened over the years from constant handling, its edges frayed and held together by tape. As if disarming a bomb, she opens and squeezes it, bowing the edges inward as she reaches in and pulls out three strips of photographs.

The summer before he died, Thomas had taken her to the state fair. Even now, as she recollects, she can remember the smell of hot funnel cakes, of dirt and dust, of livestock and their shit. He spoiled her that day, letting her have the run of the park, moving from ride to ride, from booth to booth, from sweets to snow cones to carnival games, giant houses full of mirrors, and she even got to pet a goat! Somewhere in the chaos, her and Thomas had slipped into one of the photo booths.

Curiesay lays the three photo strips down gently onto the dresser, caressing them softly. Thomas had taken her to a face painting booth, and she'd *insisted* that he get his painted as well. With Curiesay's face sporting a bird's yellow beak and feathers, and Thomas' a zebra, they laughed and smiled their way through the photos, and in each one she sees a little girl who was as happy as she'd ever been.

Her lips tremble as her eyes moisten, and she thinks that even though her life back then had been hell, she would certainly relive it just to spend more days with him. In the end, all that remains of him for her are these aged strips of photos. She nods to herself—*I know you'd be proud of me.*

A knock at her door startles her. She instinctively puts the photos away and returns the envelope to her bag. *You're not a prisoner anymore,* she reminds herself. She smirks—she doesn't entirely believe that.

Curiesay walks coolly to the door, moving slowly as she opens it. "Who are you?" she says stiffly to her visitor.

Arthur stammers a bit as he responds, "Uh, hi. I-I'm Arthur."

Curiesay shakes her head dismissively. "Okay, and?"

"And... Sorry, I'm supposed to be the third Pilot. I had heard that you got released from the ICU and I wanted to introduce myself."

Curiesay eyes him down—he's just a bit shorter than her, his posture reserved and timid. "How old are you?" she asks accusingly.

"I'm sixteen."

Curiesay laughs aloud. "Damn, Chandrima is recruiting kids now?"

Arthur responds innocently. "I guess? She just moved me up here from the Second Floor last week and told me I was selected to be a Pilot. But since you and that other Pilot were hurt, I haven't really been doing much."

Curiesay tilts her head. "Second Floor? You lived there?"

"Well, yeah. Most people in Bastion live there, except for the soldiers. They mostly live on the First." A silence falls over the two as they stand on opposite sides of the threshold to Curiesay's room. As much as she wants to know more about Bastion, her patience for socialization is wearing thin, and she's becoming increasingly frustrated with this intrusion into the first moments of solitude she's had since arriving in this city.

Suddenly, her eyes grow wide. Neurons flicker and spark between each other as she studies his face, a face that... *I've seen before?* That can't be it. She's only met Chandrima, Parker, and her Steward. She would have remembered meeting another Pilot. *So who is—*

The memory flashes across her mind and is gone in an instant. But she *knows*; this boy stopped her from killing Parker. She is certain of it. The same boy she is staring at had stood between herself and Parker that day with gritted teeth and fire in his eyes.

The notion of demanding an explanation evaporates as quickly as it had formed. A lightning bolt of trepidation arcs across her chest, and from a place beyond her sight, an innate—but unknown—presence urges her not to ask. She has been unwittingly staring at Arthur in silence for nearly a full minute, a consequence of her narcotic-influenced mind.

Arthur shuffles his feet. "Are…you okay?" It is a valid question. The only sleep she's had since she arrived was courtesy of being beaten half to death. Her thick hair is frizzy and unkempt, eyes bagged, face thin.

This question snaps Curiesay from her trance. "Yeah! I mean, yes, I'm fine. Why don't you come in?" She steps back and motions for Arthur to enter. In a leap of faith, she plans to sacrifice a few moments of solace to learn more about this stranger. Not only is he supposed to be a fellow Pilot, but he is also a resident of Bastion, and yet, there is something even greater about him which she *needs* to know but dares not ask directly.

Arthur obliges and enters, with Curiesay closing the door behind him. His eyes scan the barely lived in room. "Just getting settled in, huh? Me too. Well, me and my sister." He walks into the living area, asking with his eyes, *May I sit here?* Curiesay nods and takes a seat across from him.

"Your sister? Both of you live up here?"

"Yes, but only recently. Aunt Rima said she is gonna be my Steward. She's in classes right now."

Curiesay leans forward and exclaims, "*Aunt?!*"

Arthur puts his hands up defensively. "I mean, not by blood! She was best friends with my mother, so we spent a lot of time together." *Good, this is good.* She has no interest in sharing anything about herself, and Arthur seems to be the perfect person to get some information from. Feeling some resentment about Chandrima's apparent ability to decide her fate, she hopes that maybe she can gain leverage over her through her *nephew*.

But somewhere deep inside, she feels guilty. She does not sense a modicum of ill will from Arthur. Her instincts, trained for years under the thumb of the oppressive institution staff, scream at her to take everything she can from this stranger. A gentler part of herself, the part she knows speaks on behalf of Thomas, urges her to exercise kindness.

Curiesay resigns her line of self-serving questioning for something more genuine. "So, what do you think so far? I mean, I haven't gotten to see much of this place other than the Arena and the hospital. Is it nice?"

Arthur's eyes light up. "Yes! Way nicer than where I used to live. There's a lot to do, and the food is amazing." Before Curiesay can respond, Arthur continues. "Are you feeling better? I saw you get hurt pretty bad."

Curiesay can't help but jump at the opportunity. "Saw? Saw me when?" She takes a cue from Chandrima and feigns a smile. Though when Curiesay does it, using all the muscles in her face, she looks insane.

"Uh... I was there. Aunt Rima brought us up to watch the demonstration."

Ahah! It was you! But how? She cannot help herself, and guilt aside, she decides to press the question. "My memory is still a bit fuzzy. What happened?" Curiesay's heart is in her throat as she asks, the trepidation again pleading with her to drop this. Her ears ring.

Arthur shakes his head slightly. "Well, you…you had…" He trails off as he shakes his head again, pressing his fingers into his temples. Curiesay watches him carefully, neither speaking nor moving.

After a few moments he drops his hands to his sides. "So, what do you think? The rooms are nice, huh?"

What just happened? She can't put her finger on it, but she feels as if she has dodged a bullet. Before she can respond, there's a knock at the door. *What now?* In a huff, she quickly moves to the door and flings it open, startling the woman on the other side.

"Arthur!" the woman says as she sees him on the couch. She quickly switches her tone, speaking more nonchalantly, a shadow of panic behind her eyes. "I was wondering where you'd run off to. I just got out of class."

Curiesay senses that this woman isn't comfortable with Arthur being there. "We were just having a little chat; he wanted to introduce himself."

"I see! Well, I'm glad to hear you're acquainted. I'm his sister, Elva." She peeks farther into the room and extends her hand to Curiesay, who declines to shake it. "Arthur! I wanna tell you about my class, why don't we head home?" Elva says as she motions for Arthur to come with her.

He nods and stands when Curiesay butts in, a hint of challenge in her voice. "We were kinda in the middle of something."

Arthur watches as the two women lock eyes, his face tight with a visible awkwardness.

Elva steps closer to Curiesay, less than an arm's length away. Curiesay doesn't budge, steeling her gaze. "Arthur, come with me," Elva says flatly. Arthur's face blanks as he walks to the door. He brushes past Curiesay without a word and stands next to Elva.

Curiesay's brow furrows. "Well, Arthur, it was nice to meet you. And you too, I guess, *Elva*." Elva nods in agreement, but Arthur does not speak. Elva puts her hand on his back and guides him to his room, following him inside. Curiesay peeks her head into the hallway, watches them enter, and slams her own door in anger.

12

Pilot Regiment

September 4th, 2053

Bastion, Third Floor, Dock Wing, Classrooms

"Four days?! I almost killed him. How the hell did he recover in *four* days when it took *me* seven?!" Curiesay rages.

She's seated in the front row in the classroom, half-standing at her desk. Annata is on her left, watching her crazed Pilot with wide eyes. To Curiesay's right is Arthur and Elva, and behind them sits Parker and Jordan, seated at the rearmost of the three rows.

Atop each desk is a pen and notebook, save for Curiesay's and Parker's. The latter has his feet on his desk, arms crossed. Annata has two in front of her—Curiesay declined her offer to borrow one with a huff.

Front and center to the Pilots is Chandrima, wearing her usual lab coat and standing at a wooden podium, a large screen behind her. The screen has an image titled *Casualties*, with a long list of specific injuries the Pilots incurred during their fight.

Chandrima rotates her hips cheerily as she sees the livid Curiesay's reddening face. "My dear, if you would allow me to continue, I am getting to that." Curiesay looks around, now fully aware that the rest of the room is gawking at her. She relents and falls back into her chair. Annata attempts to console her with a pat on her shoulder and is repaid with a death stare. The young Steward hardly shies as she turns her attention back to Chandrima.

"As I was saying, both Pilots sustained major injuries, with Curiesay's being more dire," Chandrima continues as the notebook-equipped attendees take notes while Curiesay glowers and Parker simply listens. "In fact, Curiesay's most serious injuries were a result of her own actions." The Director clicks the remote in her hand, changing the image on the screen. Curiesay's discolored skin: arms; legs; back. Cropped for modesty.

"Our readouts indicated that Curiesay's external body temperature reached one hundred and three degrees Celsius. The damage to her skin and suit was severe." Chandrima clicks the remote. "However, Curiesay's *internal* body temperature was nearly ninety-seven degrees Celsius." Elva gasps, while Parker simply shakes his head. Curiesay nods, looking confused. Annata quickly scribbles on a piece of paper and passes it to Curiesay.

Her handwriting reads: *97 c is 206 f.* Curiesay gives her Steward a shocked glare, then looks back at Chandrima. "Your blood boils at one hundred degrees Celsius, my dear. Get *that* hot, and no hospital in the world can save you."

"Wait... You're telling me that my temperature was two-hundred and six degrees *Fahrenheit*?" Curiesay begins in a near shout. "I had a fever of a hundred and four as a kid and thought I wasn't gonna make it till morning." She has the exposing feeling that everyone in this room knows more than she does concerning just about everything.

"But you are not a kid anymore, Curiesay. You are a Pilot. Handpicked for your resilience... And your suit does a lot of the heavy lifting in the survival department, but we'll get to that," Chandrima responds with a smile. *Click.* "Let's break down the bout itself." The screen displays two images, filmed by mounted and free-floating cameras in the Arena. On one side, Curiesay stands in the Arena, her body like a furnace, boiling the moisture from her skin. On the other side, a list of her vitals from that moment. Curiesay shoots bolt upright, intensely curious. She curtly taps the desk to her left, and Annata discreetly passes her a notebook and pen.

"Curiesay's initial injuries were severe, but not unmanageable, and she healed remarkably fast. With no prior training, I attribute this to Annata's concise instructions to her Pilot, which she executed expertly," Chandrima proclaims, a woeful smattering of applause being heard from the class. Curiesay stares daggers at her Steward through the corner of her eye, and Annata shuffles uncomfortably in her seat.

"Curiesay! This is *not* a competition," Chandrima barks. "Your Steward is your lifeline and is dedicated to caring for her Pilot. Show her the appropriate respect." Curiesay's cheeks rapidly flush as she melts into her chair. Chandrima is cheery to a fault. Being chastised by her makes Curiesay feel impossibly tiny, and she debates pulling her sweater over her head to hide her embarrassment. *Click.*

Seemingly unbothered by her Pilot shrinking to the size of a pinhead, Chandrima continues. "We were able to capture this image *during* her Crossing, and I must say, it is *spectacular.*" The image shows Curiesay the moment she Crossed, her tendrils extending from her back, the shockwave forming a circle a short distance from her, eager to resume its march.

Curiesay perks up, her eyes studying the image carefully. *It was spectacular.* Although much of it is still blurry to her, she can recall this moment down to its tiniest detail: the air thick with the smell of ozone; the heat wicking itself from her skin. The liberation. The pain.

It had been the most harrowing moment of her life. She cannot recall a greater upheaval, a greater endeavor. Her soul had turned itself inside out and set itself aflame. But for all the grotesqueries she'd experienced in that moment, in that bloodied corner of her soul, she'd never felt as complete as she had when she Crossed.

Chandrima interrupts her recollection. "I feel like I may cry! I should get this framed," she says with a snorty laugh. She lifts the remote to move on to the next image.

"Wait!" Curiesay blurts out, drawing eyes to her.

"You have another question?"

"Obviously! What do you mean when you say 'Crossing'? And…" She trails off, trying to think of a way to make her question sound less insane. "Why did I explode?"

Chandrima flashes a grin that Curiesay perceives as genuine, because instead of it being cheery, it looks deranged, like an inebriated sports fan seeing an opposing player get seriously injured. "Well, dear Curiesay, to use your Arbiter to its full potential, you must *Cross*. Crossing is a heightened emotional state which drives your body to action. Your Arbiter recognizes your body as an extension of itself, and the potential energies sometimes overflow and burst from within. Essentially, it is a manifestation of your emotional state, and if your emotions are particularly…*unruly,* the effect is amplified."

Curiesay nods. "So that won't happen every time?"

"Not if you can keep your temper in check," Chandrima responds. *We'll see about that.*

Click. The screen changes again. The freeze-frame shows Curiesay's tendrils, their ends formed into curved scoops, in various stages of slinging the small round projectiles at Parker, who is enveloped in smoke.

Chandrima studies the image for a moment, tapping her chin.

"Curiesay, of this I must say I am impressed. Without any training, you not only managed to produce these Gripes, but used them quite effectively." Curiesay nods proudly, looking around with a smirk. A moment later, she clears her throat and awkwardly raises her hand. *What the fuck is she talking about?*

Chandrima detects her subtle confusion. "'Gripes' is their designated name. They're made of solid biomass, ignited and conflagrated in an instant. Effectively, grenades."

Arthur's hand shoots up. "How could Parker have stopped them?"

"Good question. The quantity and velocity were certainly—" she begins before Parker interjects.

"I was caught off guard. Once the first one went off, I lost my bearings and couldn't re-establish a guard."

"And your infrared?" Chandrima asks.

Parker shakes his head, arms crossed. "The heat obscured my sight. I could see her outline, but only intermittently. Had no idea where I was." Arthur and Elva write furiously as they listen.

"Infrared..." Curiesay begins, her mind digging deep to recall some weathered VHS tape she had watched a dozen times in the institution's recreation room. "Like the *Predator*? I remember that... I could see him when this happened. He was red, or orange. But my Arbiter doesn't have a helmet, or goggles, so how could I see him?" Curiesay's pen is in hand, awaiting Chandrima's response.

Chandrima's eyes drift to Parker's for a moment, the two sharing a sly grin. "Arbiters can alter your biology. If the necessary ingredients exist in your Arbiter's biomass, and it is physically possible, your Arbiter will make it a reality." *That's so fucking cool.* She wonders if she could make herself a pair of wings. This job is quickly becoming *much* more interesting to Curiesay. *Click.*

The Director resumes the review, moving through the slides recapping the battle. Questions are asked, at first primarily by Arthur, but as time goes on, Curiesay gains more interest, her notepad rapidly filling with writing.

They approach the moment Curiesay lost herself. The moment that, in her own recollection, she had brought Parker into her Dominium and showed him her most sorrowful moments, then tried to end his life. Parker has swung his legs off his desk, with all eyes on Chandrima and all butts on their respective seat edges. *Click*. The last still image is replaced by a blank slide, with the words *Any Questions?* written in bold letters. A collective sigh is heard amongst the group.

"Wait, isn't there more?" asks Arthur, rising from his chair. Elva puts her hand on his shoulder, suggesting him to sit. Curiesay narrows her eyes as she watches. *It doesn't seem like he remembers.*

"No, there is not. Nothing after the previous slide is any different than what we have discussed. We are only here to discuss highlights and how we can improve as Pilots and Stewards." Chandrima looks at the eyes of each of her students, urging questions.

Curiesay speaks up. "So...can you explain how I survived?"

"Once a Pilot has Crossed, they are able to heal faster than a normal person. While not wearing their Arbiter, the effect is diminished but still accelerated," Chandrima begins. *It...changed me?* "The Third Floor also employs only the best and brightest doctors, whose sole purpose is to keep our Pilots alive. Artificial biomass grafts, intravenous feeding, oxygen exchangers, and groundbreaking pharmaceuticals allow our staff to treat virtually any injury a Pilot may sustain."

Curiesay follows up as soon as Chandrima finishes speaking. "And how did I get my injuries? You said I did it to myself, right?" Curiesay feels a pang of embarrassment every time she asks a question, thinking she is showcasing her ignorance, but she is determined not to be left in the dark. *This is my life now, and I'll be damned if I lose again.*

Chandrima cocks her head. "Arbiters allow Pilots to push their bodies *beyond* their natural limits. You burn calories at an accelerated rate, and a consequence of that is excess heat production. Arbiters are designed to withstand that kind of stress, but Pilots, especially a novice, are not. The heat can cause internal burns, and the strain on your muscular-skeletal system can result in fractures and connective tissue damage. Although your Arbiter will sacrifice its own biomass to heal you, eventually its reserves will be depleted, and you will be wearing, essentially, a *very* expensive coffin." Curiesay listens intently, trying to tune out the rapid scribbling sounds from Arthur and Elva's desks. "Arbiters only have so much biomass to work with. The more you demand, the sooner it will run out. You demanded too much, too fast, and your body paid the price."

"So, I pushed my suit beyond its limits, while Parker didn't. That's why he recovered so much faster?"

"More or less."

"Because I'm inexperienced?"

"Partly. It is expected that a Pilot's First Crossing will be…*dramatic*," Chandrima says, rocking her head from side to side. *First? Parker said the same thing.* "I wouldn't worry too much about it. Win or lose, you were spectacular." Curiesay manages a weak smile, feeling pandered to, but accepts the compliment.

"Any other questions?" Chandrima asks. Her students look around at each other, then back at Chandrima. The Director gives a nod. She motions to Zochitl, who up until now has been sitting off to the side and observing. The tall woman stands, herself dressed in a lab coat, with flashy gold earrings and her black hair tied up neatly atop her head in a bun.

The class eyes her as she steps up to the podium. "I am Assistant Director Zochitl Bottazzi. Since we are soon to have three Pilots, I wanted to formally introduce myself," Zochitl says with a cool wave, to which only Arthur reciprocates. Curiesay grumbles—*nobody is keeping score of your courtesies.*

"I am second in command of the Pilot Regiment, of which you are part. As such, my authority is surpassed *only* by Director Joshi. This is not my only duty on the Third Floor, but I am here to take some of the pressure off her." Unlike Chandrima, she gives off an air of *genuine* delight, as if there isn't a thing in this world that could rock her spirits. "And with that, Pilot teams, you are released to leisure hours until zero six-hundred tomorrow morning." She gives a slight nod as both her and Chandrima exit the room. After they are gone, the remaining occupants talk amongst themselves while gathering their belongings.

"Did you take lots of notes, Annata?" Jordan teases.

"Didn't need to, my Pilot is *naturally* talented, like me!" Annata responds with the same competitive energy. Jordan scoffs and begins to respond, but is cut off by Parker.

"Stop. We are a team, *not* rivals," he says, looking at Curiesay directly.

"Lucky for you," Annata says, sticking her tongue out.

"Annata, please. I got more fucked up than he did, *and* I did it to myself," Curiesay sulks, looking down at her desk.

Parker puts a hand on her shoulder as he steps up to her. "You did well," he says candidly.

Curiesay flashes a brief smile, then gently removes his hand. "Enough with the sappy shit, you big douchebag. I was only being nice. Next time, I'll be the one visiting *you* in the ICU."

The Pilots and Stewards exit the classroom and head to the cafeteria, finding a large table near the back to sit at. The three Stewards grab trays and enter the serving line while the Pilots give their orders to the waiter. The Pilots make small talk until the Stewards return; their trays have lamb chops, string beans, and scalloped potatoes on them, as well as their drinks.

"Why don't you guys order food like we do? You're allowed to, right?" Arthur asks, the Stewards taking seats across from them.

"I can't speak for them, but *I* don't because I ain't special. I've got a job to do like everyone else. Besides, the regular food is good too," Jordan responds as she starts in on her meal.

"If you're allowed, then you should do it. Apparently, they think you *are* special," Curiesay says unapologetically.

"It's just a personal choice. If Annata or Elva wanted to order, I wouldn't think any differently of them," Jordan responds with a full mouth.

"Personally, I don't want to wait for my food. I'll be almost done by the time your fancy Pilot food is even rolling out of the kitchen," Annata says between bites.

Curiesay nods as the Pilots watch their Stewards eat. Her eyes wander the cafeteria. A bloodshot eye. A bruised arm. A leg in a cast. Sprinkled throughout, dozens of staff sport a variety of injuries. Curiesay doesn't ask, but she's sure that it's her fault. She wonders how much worse it would have been if Arthur hadn't stopped her. *They must hate me.*

"So, have you two met yet?" Parker asks as he turns to Curiesay, who's sitting between Arthur and him.

The words reset her brain, giving her a moment of pause. "Ye— yeah, yesterday. Uh, he came by to welcome me to the Third Floor," Curiesay begins, turning her attention to Arthur. "So, you said you're supposed to be the other Pilot?"

"Yeah, that's what they've told me. What made you want to be a Pilot?" Arthur asks.

Curiesay snorts. "It was either that or rot away at a mental institution." The table goes silent for a few moments. *Too candid.*

"We told her that she could have all the pancakes she wanted, and she agreed right away," Parker comments with a laugh, breaking the tension.

"Yeah, that part is pretty cool. Whooping your ass was a nice bonus though," she responds. Jordan glares at her from across the table. Curiesay pauses for a moment before furrowing her brow.

"But! It all turned out okay. We're both alive and healthy," Parker says quickly, causing Jordan to relax her stare ever so slightly.

"You're awfully defensive over him, aren't you?" Curiesay accuses with a playful grin. Jordan's face flushes red in an instant. *Oh?*

"We can track your injuries in real time with the Arbiter's monitoring software. Every broken bone. Every ruptured blood vessel or organ. Brain injuries. It's upsetting to watch, if we're being honest. Stewards are supposed to care for their Pilots, so we take it personally when you get hurt," Annata interjects, drawing the gawking eyes off her fellow Steward. *Running interference, are we?*

"You knew what was going to happen to me, didn't you? You didn't seem too concerned when I was being forced into my armor," Curiesay says.

"I'm just doing my job, Pilot. There's a lot more where that came from," Annata responds matter-of-factly. Curiesay eyes her for a moment, again noticing that unlike everyone else at the table, Annata is barely an adolescent. A few tables over from them is a group of young girls, Annata's age or younger, who are eating while swinging their short legs under the table.

Curiesay opens her mouth to speak, curious about the presence of children on the Third Floor, when a waiter rolls up with a serving cart. Plates bustle as he carefully unloads the Pilots' substantial orders, the Stewards moving their own trays closer to make more room. The man gives a courteous bow as he takes his leave. The three Pilots begin to eat ravenously, the Stewards stifling their laughter at their Pilots' appetite.

"You guys are three peas in a pod," Annata remarks with a grin, and Elva and Jordan giggle. Curiesay can't help but notice that even though Parker has more food than herself, Arthur has nearly twice as much. *Where does he put it all?* In just a few minutes, the Pilots are finished, catching their breath as they lean back in their chairs. In her digestive stupor, Curiesay is done asking questions, and is eager to return home and sleep this meal off.

Parker pats his stomach, then turns his head to Arthur. "Make sure you get some rest. Tomorrow is your big day," Parker says as he stands, carefully stacking his plates. The others follow suit, bringing their trays to the drop-off near the door and heading to their rooms.

* * *

Just after midnight, September 4th, 2053
Exclusion Zone

She knew they were here for her the moment they set foot in *her* city. It was comforting to know that she hadn't been forgotten about. That the Blight hadn't been forgotten. There were people, somewhere, that still railed against it. Against *her*. The scant moments of acquiescence that she shared with the child filled her with hope, but she never let it grow large enough to make a difference.

She is too far gone. It had told her so. The Willow would never allow her to leave, not with her life. It is too deep, too vital. All that remains of her is the same putrid memories it keeps repeating in her dreams. But with this girl, she doesn't feel so alone.

And so, with less hesitance than she has felt in years, the woman nestles herself deep in the dirty linens. She closes her eyes and drifts into that eternally sorrowful place.

* * *

"Hello," she whispers.

Karima steps through the shroud of dust, taking a seat next to her on a floor-bound mattress. The room is hardly tangible. As if she could fall through at any moment.

"Hi," Karima responds quietly. In this place, the woman is just a girl—her frail, childlike body is much smaller than Karima's. "You...you can talk." The girl nods somberly, staring blankly at the unpowered television on the floor. Karima scoots closer to her on the soiled mattress, careful not to startle her away. "How long have you been here? I mean, the city, not this place."

"I do not know," the girl responds. "A very, very long time." The girl turns her head, her brown eyes set inside of bruised sockets. "What do you want from me?"

Karima hesitates. She hadn't expected this when she lay down to sleep. Normally, the place they meet is far more unstable, with only whispers of nonsense permeating the din of howling wind and the sounds of liquids running. Now, it's as if she is truly here with her, in this place. Though, she isn't sure how long it will last.

"I want to be your friend," Karima says finally. "I don't know what the others want with you. We were sent to—"

In a flash, the girl covers Karima's mouth with gentle swiftness. "Don't," she pleads. "They'll hear you."

Karima nods in agreement, and the girl removes her hand. "What's your name?"

"My...name? I don't... Nobody has... I don't remember," she squeaks out. "Do you think...I still have one? What if it's gone?" The girl's lips quiver as she takes clipped, shallow breaths. "What if they took it?! Oh God, my name. I don't have a name!"

Taking a leap of faith, Karima puts her hands on the girl's shoulders.

The girl recoils, as if her hands burn, but doesn't shake them free. "You have a name. Everyone has a name," Karima insists.

The girl nods reluctantly. "What's yours?"

"I'm Karima."

"Kah-ree-mah. Karima. That's a nice name. I wish I had a nice name," the girl says, crestfallen. She turns her head away, facing outward on the trodden mattress.

Karima scoots closer still, gently putting an arm around the girl's waist as their hips meet. "I'll help you find it. I promise. And if we can't find it, I'll help you pick a new one!"

"You'd...do that? For me?" the girl asks hesitantly. "You know it's dangerous here. Why help me at all?"

Karima takes the girl's hand, placing it softly on her knee. "Because I know what it's like to be alone.

13

A Natural

September 4th, 2053
Bastion, Third Floor, Dock Wing

"Arthur, are you ready?" Chandrima asks. They're in the Dock, standing just in front of the Arbiters' armor stands. Arthur nervously rocks on his feet, his skintight Interface suit making him feel immodest. He knows that this is what he wanted, to be a Pilot. Any excitement he feels is tempered with apprehension. *Don't hurt anyone.*

In front of him sits a suit of armor, black, with his name on a placard above it. The two armor stations to his right are empty, as are the seven stations to his left.

His eyes crawl over his armor, from the gauntleted hands and forearms to the thick chest plating, the more thinly armored abdomen and the generic legs. He cocks his head, moving closer, peeking around the backside. Four ports exist alongside the spine, a handful more spread along the legs and back for his thrusters.

Taking a step back, he nods his head uneasily. "I guess so."

Elva is off to his side, wearing a new white lab coat, her orange hair set loose down her back. As Arthur steps into the assembly circle on the floor, the technicians who have been patiently waiting—wearing red scrubs and with tools in hand—spring into action. Chandrima is showing Elva, who is using her issued tablet, how to navigate the Steward's software program.

Arthur lifts his feet, and they slip his boots on. The lower leg plating is clamped together and bolted. Then the upper leg, groin, chest, and arms. His gauntlets are the last thing to be installed. After a few minutes, Arthur stands motionless in his black Arbiter which covers his body nearly up to his chin.

Chandrima smiles ear to ear as she speaks. "Arthur, you look magnificent! What do you think of the black? Would you like a different color?" Arthur shakes his head. *This smell... Who is this?* He moves around, his armor plating contacting itself and clunking.

Chandrima doesn't wait for an answer. "In the assembly screen, click here to open the activation menu, then click confirm," she directs. Elva complies, her fingers dancing across the tablet, and a moment later, a clicking sound is heard followed by a light hiss. Arthur's armor snaps together at the joints, and he springs upright.

* * *

He is not alone in his armor. Of that he is certain. A presence nips at the edges of his thoughts.

You're too kind! Ah, this embrace. It is invigorating. So warm. What's that taste, candy? What? Why would you say that? I haven't done anything wrong. Where are you going? Hello?

* * *

He grimaces and looks at Chandrima, who returns a concerned stare.

"Arthur, is everything okay?"

No. "Yeah, I think so. I just… I felt strange for a moment. I don't know, I think I'm still half-asleep," he says with a nervous laugh.

Chandrima walks up to him. With his armor supplementing his height, he is a bit taller than her. "Don't worry, we'll wake you up! Parker and Curiesay are already inside. Let's head to the Arena and see what you can do!" she exclaims, motioning for Arthur to follow. They cross the hallway and enter an adjacent passage, the one Curiesay used to enter the Arena on her first day.

After a short walk, they arrive at the large metal door. Chandrima presses a button on her tablet and the door creaks open. The pair step through and begin to walk down the rubble-littered street when a voice calls out to them.

"Aren't you forgetting something?" Zochitl yells as she enters through the same door. In her hand she carries a thick tube, grey in color, with a steel fitting on the end.

"Oh dear! Yes, of course," Chandrima says as she begins to turn back.

Zochitl waves her off. "I'll get him sorted, Director. You can go on ahead." Zochitl steps closer to Arthur, who is notably shorter than she is.

Chandrima nods and walks down the street toward the center of the Arena. "Don't keep him too long. See you soon, Arthur."

Arthur watches her as she goes, suddenly feeling very alone. "What is that for?" he asks Zochitl.

Zochitl suppresses a rueful giggle. "You know, her classes *do* lack some of the important stuff. Your Arbiter begins consuming biomass the moment you activate it. Though it's cumbersome, while you're in here, this feeding tube will keep your Arbiter at one hundred percent capacity," she says, then twirls her finger. "Turn around."

Arthur does so, and the Assistant Director drops to her knees, careful not to kneel on anything sharp. Near his tailbone is a port that is different from the rest: the feeding tube's home. Zochitl inserts it and gives it a turn, a satisfying *click* following shortly after.

Zochitl stands, dusting her knees off as Arthur turns to face her. "There are feeding apparatuses spread among the city, so just get yourself plugged into whichever is most convenient. If you need to remove it for some more *dramatic* training, be sure to hook it back up when you're done," she says breezily, her infectious smile putting Arthur at ease. For a moment.

* * *

It isn't as she expects as she closes the door behind her. She is not a mover, but a guest. It's timeless here. Stable. She finds herself, this time, in the light. Beyond her is darkness—the silhouettes of the doors make their edges known.

He is watching.

"Who are you?" a male voice booms out from the abyss that surrounds her. Frantically she spins, searching for the source. This isn't possible—How can he see me?

"I won't tell if you won't," he says. Seeking to conceal, she concedes. She opens the door she came through, moves past the threshold and—

* * *

"Are you okay?" Arthur asks as he moves to Zochitl's side. She has fallen onto her backside, and as she shakes away the confusion, she presses her knees together, attempting to keep herself modest since her skirt has hiked up.

She makes eye contact with Arthur, the shocked expression she wears instantly evaporating and being replaced with a blushing smile.

"Yes! I'm fine, just got a bit lightheaded. Shouldn't have skipped breakfast," she insists with a chuckle as Arthur helps her up. She gives a thankful nod and turns, walking back into the doorway from which she entered. As she leaves and the door closes behind her, Arthur winces, pressing his fingers into his temples.

"Arthur, get moving," Elva says into her microphone, feeding into her Pilot's speakers. Without a word, he turns and heads down the street, dragging his twenty-meter-long feeding tube with him. The scars from his fellow Pilots' battle are still fresh. The ruined city doesn't look much different from before—it is now just slightly more ruined. He thinks it curious how much like a real city the Arena looks. He had seen war movies growing up where factions would construct mock neighborhoods and cities for their soldiers to train in, *but this is something more.*

The architecture here is strikingly similar to that of the Second Floor where he grew up. The storefronts seem unique, with novel names, their wares spilling onto the sidewalk. Sedans, minivans, short-bed trucks, scooters. Most of the vehicles here are burned or otherwise damaged, but a handful seem to be intact enough to be brought back to life with some elbow grease. Arthur inhales through his nose. *Blood and terror.*

"Hey! Over here!" Parker yells, waving. Curiesay and himself are standing at a four-way intersection, wearing their Arbiters; they seem to be fully repaired, or brand new. Curiesay's is completely black while Parker's is navy-blue. Arthur approaches them, noticing that Chandrima is standing between the two, shrouded by their stature.

"Are you sure you want to be in here while we're Piloting?" Parker asks.

Chandrima throws her hands up, responding ecstatically, "Of course! Look at you three! Indominable! Between the three of you, I'm standing in the safest place in the world." The Pilots collectively blush.

Chandrima steps off onto the sidewalk. In addition to her normal attire, she wears a pair of safety glasses and a white helmet.

Parker directs Arthur to a fire hydrant-sized bright orange apparatus poking out from the sidewalk. Tubes leading to Curiesay and Parker's Arbiters are already plugged into it, and Arthur, after a moment of examining the connectors, hooks his up as well and returns to the center of the intersection.

"Okay, Arthur, tell me, what do you remember from the crash course I gave you this morning?" Chandrima asks.

Arthur's eyes twitch. "Extension of yourself, it has its own biomass, can...*make* extra limbs, or tendrils rather. Thrusters on the feet, hands, back, and legs. I'm sure there was more."

Curiesay nods sarcastically. "Well, he knows more than *I* did my first time."

"And still, you performed exquisitely!" Chandrima responds loudly. Curiesay rolls her eyes. "There's a *lot* more, Arthur, but those are the core concepts. Let's run some simple drills to get you moving." The other Pilots back away, standing opposite each other in the four-way intersection, with Arthur in the middle.

"Now, opposed to Curiesay's first time, I'm not planning on you Crossing today. You should be able to use a portion of your Arbiter's power, if we're lucky, up to fifty percent," she says as she reaches into her lab coat's pocket and retrieves a remote with a plethora of buttons.

"Crossing? Don't I have to? To use the suit?" Arthur says as he hears the whir of a mechanical target popping up in the distance, atop a four-story building.

"Don't worry about that for now, let's get started. I want you to knock that target down, without moving from this spot," Chandrima says. Arthur turns to face the target, nearly a block away. It's a red bullseye, mounted on a metal frame with a small motor underneath.

"Okay, how do I do that?"

"That is up to you, my dear."

"I don't know… Those little balls? What did you call them? Gripes? Is that what I use?"

"Yes, that is what you will use. To form them you will want to—" Chandrima says as Arthur lifts his right arm in front of him, palm up. A moment later, a sphere the size of a marble materializes, drawn up from liquid flowing on his palm, floating just above his skin. It's black and smooth all around.

A fleeting thought rockets across his mind, a glimpse into the fog of his past. He's seen these things before, long before he'd come to Bastion. He chases it, but as quickly as the thought comes, it disappears into the ether, and he forgets ever thinking of it.

"Oh my, that…was fast," Chandrima says, shaking her head. Parker's blank expression dissipates as he looks worriedly at Chandrima, then back at Arthur.

"This is it, right?" Arthur asks. His eyes crawl over it, neurons firing en masse. As much as he tries, he can no longer recall where he's seen this before. He can see the shock rolling over his aunt's face. He wishes she was excited instead.

Chandrima clears her throat, forcing a smile. "Yes…it is. So, now knock the target down."

A wicked gust of air hits Chandrima and sends her stumbling backward, knocking her helmet off. Curiesay and Parker rock back on their heels, the combined mass of their bodies and Arbiters just enough to keep their feet on the ground. Arthur had swung his arm forward, launching the sphere at incredible velocity and striking the target. A small explosion tears the apparatus from the rooftop and sends it crashing to the ground in a heap.

Arthur rushes frantically to Chandrima as she stumbles. "I'm sorry,

Aunt Rima! I didn't mean to throw it that hard. Are you okay?"

She's patting her rear end, having backed into the side of the building on the sidewalk, the grey dust leaving a mark on her lab coat. "Arthur, that was magnificent! You're a natural! I should have had my helmet strapped." She bends and retrieves her helmet, dons and straps it tightly, then confirms with a tug. "But from now on, just *knock* the target down, don't blow it up." Arthur's face runs red. Curiesay gives a short laugh and glances over at Parker, who is clearly not amused. He's narrowed his eyes, watching Arthur carefully.

Arthur nods apologetically. "Okay, sorry."

Chandrima clicks her remote a few times and more targets pop up on rooftops around them. One at a time, Arthur forms a sphere in his hand and knocks them down. He throws gently now, with the subtle pings of metal echoing through the city streets. *Click, ping. Click, ping. Click, ping.* Chandrima pauses as she clicks, letting Arthur identify and strike each target before she raises the next one.

"Now, I don't expect you to be able to do this, but just humor me," Chandrima says after some time has passed. *Click, click, click, click.* Four targets rise atop various buildings, at different heights and directions. Parker and Curiesay do a slow spin, identifying the targets' positions. "I want you to knock all the targets down at the same time."

"Okay, how do I do that?" Arthur asks.

Chandrima gives a coy smile and shrugs. "That's up to you." Arthur nods cautiously and stands motionless, eyes closed.

Putting his fingers to his temples, Curiesay can feel the hairs on her neck flutter for a split second. Steam begins to pour from Arthur's back through the four ports running alongside his spine. Slowly, his tendrils emerge, forming themselves at the base and extending until they're three meters long. They dance carelessly behind him, side to side, up and down.

Chandrima's eyes grow wide as Parker snaps his head toward her. "Rima! I think we should call it a day," he says firmly.

The Director waves her hand dismissively, never letting her eyes wander from Arthur. "No! It's fine, let's see what he can do." A beat passes and Arthur whips each tendril in a different direction, with four metallic pings being heard at the same time as the targets fall.

"Director, what just happened?! Arthur's sync rate is at one hundred percent!" Jordan yells, speaking into Chandrima's earpiece. She brings her own tablet up, her fingers dancing across the screen as she accesses Arthur's vitals, and her screen shows the same reading. Arthur's ears twitch as he faces her, his tendrils having returned to their lazy dance.

The box on Chandrima's tablet shows his sync rate glitch for a moment, showing a *null* reading, before recalibrating. "Oh, wait. No, it's at eighty-six, shit, no it's eighty…eighty-two…one…" Jordan is transmitting with an open microphone, correcting herself as the number stabilizes at eighty point zero. "Sorry, ma'am, must be a software glitch. But still, how is he at eighty percent? Did he Cross?"

Chandrima doesn't respond. Arthur smiles gently at Chandrima, his irises glowing bright red. Calm. Collected. No fury bursting forth nor vendetta against another. The veins on his neck and face are slightly raised, glowing the same color as his irises, but he seems to be more relaxed than she has ever seen him. Parker's disdain has grown as he scowls at Arthur, and Curiesay takes notice.

"Arthur…that was incredible!" Chandrima exclaims as she throws her arms over Arthur's armor-plated shoulders. She inhales through her teeth as the heat rolling off his Arbiter lightly scalds her forearms.

Motioning toward one of his tendrils, Arthur wills it forward and lays it on her outstretched hands. She examines it, grabbing it like a butcher would a sausage and turning it from side to side. Her eyes sparkle with awe; liquid flesh held together by their Pilot's will, the tendrils are never static, constantly varying in shape and size, like earthworms inching across the pavement. They're partially translucent and red, with the occasional glowing vein being visible from inside.

"Arthur…this is magnificent. You're going to be a great Pilot," Chandrima says, choking the words out as she fights back tears. *Say that you're proud of me. Please.*

Arthur smiles weakly, again putting his fingers to his temple. "Could we be done for today? I've got a bit of a headache."

Parker steps up, putting a firm hand on Arthur's shoulder. "Yeah, that's a good idea. Let's head back to the Dock." Chandrima looks at him and nods. Taking it upon herself, Curiesay goes to the apparatus feeding their Arbiters and disconnects their tubes. The three Pilots and Chandrima begin to walk, heading down the main street that leads to the Dock. Behind them, the feeding tubes drag, still attached to their lower backs. Parker walks just behind the group, his eyes locked on Arthur.

* * *

A short while later, after being freed from his Arbiter and having changed into his plain white sweats, Arthur, alongside Elva, walked back to their rooms. In the time they'd been living on the Third Floor, they'd become less concerned with memorizing their surroundings and more interested in the quality of their environment.

Each hallway has a handful of high tables and sofas where people sit and chat or work on their laptops. The Dock hallway, at least the side opposite the Dock itself, seems to always have children—little girls—milling around the doors or the couches.

They are professionally clad, with tailored uniforms: jet-black long coats down to their ankles (with bright red buttons running down left of center); crimson-red berets; shiny little shoes. On their right shoulders are embroidered patches—a shield with a bleeding heart pierced by a nail. Elva had noticed that they took a particular interest in Arthur whenever he passed by, exchanging excessively bubbly waves with him.

Today is different. As Arthur and Elva pass, the girls all scramble into their respective rooms. They stack their heads over one another as they peek into the hallway, smiling deviously as he walks by. Arthur gives a courteous wave, and their little hands return it in kind. Elva notices this but doesn't comment.

As is usual, when they arrive at Arthur's door, they both enter, as Elva spends most of her time in his room. Inside, there are boxes spread out in the apartment. Although the movers had their belongings delivered within the first few days, Arthur hasn't gotten around to fully settling in.

"Since we got off early, why don't we get some of this put away?" Elva asks as she drags a box to the couch. Arthur declines to respond, moving to the couch and falling onto it face-down, his legs hanging off. "Or you just relax, and I'll work on it."

Arthur's words are muffled as he talks into the couch cushion. "Oo oon't ave to do tat."

"I'm still your big sister, and that's what big sisters do," she responds. Arthur lay motionless, with Elva watching him longingly. "Are you hungry?" A moment passes without a response from Arthur before he raises his head. He pushes himself up and sits, looking at his sister for a moment, then away, letting his gaze drop to the floor.

"Elva… Why…" he begins, his tone reserved. "I mean, when Curiesay used *her* Arbiter, it seemed like it took a lot to push her there. It's like she went crazy. And I…did it on my first try."

Elva playfully pats his shoulder, speaking with a smile. "You're just talented is all." *Leave this alone.*

Arthur shakes his head. "That can't be why. It's something else, I know it is."

His sister looses a pandering scoff. "And what might that be? You think you're sick or something?"

"No! I mean, I don't think so at least. And then there's... When she was fighting Parker, I could swear I had seen her before."

"But you hadn't, you'd literally never met her."

"That's what I'm saying, it's like—"

"I think you're looking too far into this." *Arthur, please.*

"I'm not! The dreams have been getting worse too. I've hardly been—"

"You're somewhere new! You're still getting used to it. It'll take some time."

"And my head has been killing me, every day."

"Have you been taking your medicine?" To this, Arthur doesn't respond, his eyes forlornly staring at the carpet beneath Elva's feet. "I'll be right back," she says as she rushes to her room from their adjoining internal door. A few moments later she returns, a thick book in hand.

"I found this book about déjà vu the other day." She sits next to Arthur and flips to her bookmark where she has highlighted some sentences. "'Some individuals are more prone to déjà vu than others... ' blah blah, oh! 'It has been observed that these people will often recognize people they have never met.'" She turns the pages until she reaches another bookmark and continues reading. "'Patients who routinely report instances of déjà vu *also* commonly report migraines to their physicians.'" She snaps the book closed as she finishes. "You see! That's all it is, Arthur. You just have a lot of déjà vu. You're normal. You're just a normal, talented young man. You should be excited about your success!" she exclaims elatedly.

Arthur turns to look at her and smiles genuinely, but after a moment, it fades. Elva can feel her neck hairs flutter. "You know, I can tell when you're lying to me," he begins, his voice low. "You're awfully insistent about this. Why?" Elva gulps, taken aback by this sudden change. She tries to look away, but she cannot. *Arthur, don't.* Her lips quiver but she struggles to speak, and for her, time stands still. The air becomes thick, like breathing through a straw. As Arthur glares at her, she can see his irises changing—

"Go to bed," she says flatly. After a moment, he stands. Without saying a word, he walks to his bedroom and closes the door behind him.

* * *

Chandrima is sitting in her office when she hears a heavy knock at the door. She sighs loudly. "Parker, please."

Parker lets himself in. "How the hell can he Pilot without Crossing?"

"I don't know, just talented I guess," Chandrima responds with a chuckle. Parker glares at her from the other side of her desk. "Okay. Truthfully, I don't know. It may be that he's already Crossed before on his own, but he's lived in Bastion his whole life, so I think someone would have noticed that. I think the most likely answer is that the Mark VI has lowered the threshold to such a degree that it is possible to use its full potential without Crossing."

Parker nods skeptically. "Or his DNA is so similar that the suit thinks it's a part of him. Which means that—"

Chandrima cuts him off. "That is an extremely serious accusation to make. You know the consequences."

"I don't see any other explanation."

"I just gave you one. The Mark VI is revolutionary, and Arthur is gifted. Anything beyond that is just reckless speculation," Chandrima responds firmly.

"You're one to talk about *reckless*. I hope you know what you're doing, Director," Parker responds as he leaves her office in a huff. Chandrima sits there in silence for a few moments before sitting up in her chair and tapping on her keyboard.

She logs into the program that manages camera footage. Reviewing the videos of Arthur from within the Arena, she has her tablet next to her that shows the record of his vitals, including his sync rate. It is as she had seen—it rose to one hundred percent before resetting itself and dropping to eighty.

It is strange, truthfully, but a software error *is* the most likely culprit. She opens a blank document and begins to type out a request to the I.T. department to review this record. Midway through, she stops. She returns to the cameras, rewinding the footage to when Arthur had entered the Arena.

Playing the footage back, Arthur's sync rate hovers around fifty percent, as expected. However, it does fluctuate by several points, with the number sometimes nulling out before resetting. *It's definitely a sensor malfunction.* She purses her lips; she'll have to rewrite the report for the technicians to look at his suit. She allows the video to continue to when Zochitl arrives. Arthur turns back to face the Assistant Director. At that same moment, the vitals playback begins to fluctuate wildly, with Arthur's EEG reports giving impossible readings, his sync rate reading one hundred percent or higher.

Chandrima pauses the video and locks her door before returning to her desk. She presses play, and Zochitl falls onto her backside. Arthur's vitals return to their normal readings, which are still inconsistent. He helps her to her feet and as she turns to leave, Chandrima sees Arthur put his fingers to his temples. *His headaches?* Checking his vitals again, they are not fluctuating like they had been but are firmly locked at a one hundred percent sync rate, his heart rate broaching two hundreds beats per minute.

She closes the video file and moves the file containing Arthur's vitals to her personal computer, erasing it from the mainframe. Tap, tap, taps her chin. Next, she opens the video file showing the view from inside the Arena Booth. Elva and Jordan are sitting next to each other, with Jordan showing her how to use her workstation. Annata is just off to their side, fully concerned with her own work.

Zochitl enters the frame a minute or so after she leaves Arthur's side. Chandrima plays the video, and Zochitl walks up to the Arena Booth window, looking outward. She stands motionless. Unbothered. Doesn't so much as rock on her feet for the entire duration of the training session.

At the same moment, Chandrima gets a notification on her computer. Another IP address, accessing the same file as she is. She has memorized every IP address that is authorized on the Third Floor, and *this* isn't one of them. After a few seconds, the IP disconnects. Chandrima opens another program and checks the *recently accessed* drop-down for authorized logins, but that IP she had seen isn't there, and the last login was *Joshi, Chandrima, DIR.*

Who is that? From memory, Chandrima quickly jots down the IP address on a notepad, folds it up, and places it in her glasses case. She opens the text document she had been working on, staring at it for a few moments.

Closing it, she drops the file in the trash. *It's not the software.* Her hands are clammy as she rubs her face, smooshing her features around and pressing her palms into her eyes. *It's not his Arbiter either.* She sits in solemn silence for a long while, having no one that she trusts enough to share what she knows. *It's Arthur.*

14

Arbiters

September 5th, 2053
Bastion, Third Floor, Dock Wing

Elva has been taking classes on Stewardship for more than a week, being the only Steward who is there to learn. Jordan and Annata attend, but the former simply listens, occasionally checking her phone, and the latter takes *some* notes but seems to be familiar with her duties.

Chandrima and Zochitl split the classes, alternating their instruction. Elva has noticed that Chandrima's style of teaching is more whimsical than Zochitl's, getting sidetracked easily. During Zochitl's classes, Elva would often ask for clarification of something that Director Joshi had said, and Zochitl would do so with an eyeroll and annoyance in her voice.

It is quite an affirming change for Elva. She had always been at the top of her class in school, taking college-level classes when she was eleven years old. Operating at a level above her peers, she had a sense of separation from those around her. Solemn superiority. Now, among those of a similar intellect, she doesn't feel so isolated.

Years of tending to her fragile brother have left little time for her to do much of anything else. Though she curses the predicament Chandrima has forced her into, having *anyone* else keeping Arthur busy is a welcome relief.

Briskly walking down the Dock hallway, she exchanges polite waves with the Waifs who are waiting for their own classes to begin. Tiny. Professional. Eerily upbeat. Assistant Director Bottazzi had told her that Waif classes run year-round. She envies their uniforms, their purpose. A job strictly for orphans, she sometimes (morbidly) wishes she had lost *both* of her parents and been given a great purpose as a Waif.

"Elva! Good morning," Annata chirps as Elva opens the door to the Observation Booth. Yesterday, Jordan had fulfilled the duties as Arthur's Steward, but today Elva would be allowed to Steward for her younger brother.

Outside of combat, it's a low-effort job. Arbiters are made to self-regulate, with their internal "computer" being entirely mechanical. A built-in thermostat to regulate temperatures to an ideal range. A neural link to control thrusters, communications, and most other functions. Fluid reservoirs within the Arbiter's biomass that feed liquid through its Pilot's skin. At rest, they are simple machines.

During high-effort activities, however, Arbiters are dangerous to their users. They are designed to operate at a higher temperature than their Pilot and could cook them alive should the cooling systems fail. Damaged or malfunctioning thruster ports could experience an "unplanned disassembly," sending shrapnel flying.

Asking a Pilot to adjust their fighting style to compensate for failing Arbiter systems *while* they are in combat places too much load on them. Stewards are meant to advise, make system adjustments, and keep their Pilots focused. After all: every Pilot needs a wingman.

"Hey, I'm not late, am I?" Elva asks. She knows she is early, but both

Annata and Jordan are already behind their respective workstations, dutifully plugging away on their keyboards. As usual, they are wearing their lab coats.

"Nope, we're early. Just running some system checks," Jordan responds without looking up from her screen. Elva sits at the workstation beside Jordan, who is in the middle. She opens the Steward's software and accesses Arthur's Arbiter while it sits on the Dock.

Jordan leans over to the junior Steward. "Mirror my screen to yours, I'll show you what I do before Parker suits up. It ain't required, but I like to be thorough." Elva nods and does so, watching Jordan's display from her own workstation, showing Parker's suit status.

A visual representation of his Arbiter is in the center, showing the individual parts and their status; green is functional, orange is damaged, red is inoperative, and grey is nonresponsive. On the right side are his vitals, with five available to view at one time. On the left are system advisements. There is only one present: *Pilot Not Detected*.

"So first I activate the internal claxon to warn the technicians in the Dock," Jordan begins. Annata isn't speaking, but is doing the same on her workstation to Curiesay's suit. The technicians on the Dock quickly step back from the area surrounding the docked Arbiters as they sound a harsh alarm. A moment later, Elva does the same on her own display, sounding her Arbiter's alarm.

"Then I override the thermostat to test the auxiliary cooling fins. Do *not* operate them for more than fifteen seconds at a time," Jordan continues. The Arbiters begin to heat up, dull red heat showing from in between the titanium plates. As the Arbiters exceed their normal operating limits, a handful of the armor plates extend from the suit, mostly on the back, allowing the cooling fins underneath to breathe. The technicians activate the cooling fans on the Dock as the ambient temperature begins to rise precipitously.

"The thrusters can cool the suits off pretty quick, so I test those next. Don't activate more than one at a time, and use the slider here"—she hovers her mouse over the slider on her screen—"to adjust the thrust to below ten percent. More than that and your Arbiter is bound to turn into a 'piss missile.'" Annata giggles at Jordan's Southern drawl and terminology. The Arbiters shake on their armor stands as the thrusters alternate, using the excess heat to produce thrust, rapidly cooling the suits.

"Then I just use the self-diagnostic tool to run the sensors through their paces. They're redundant, so if you have two showing the same reading, you'll know something is up. And that's it," Jordan says, tapping on the *self-diag* button on her screen and leaning back in her chair, stretching and being taken by a suddenly insistent yawn. Elva enjoys her presence. She had spent her childhood caring for a younger brother, and Jordan seems a perfect fit for an older sibling.

Elva sits back in her chair as well. Jordan again checks her phone, playing a golf minigame that uses irregularly shaped fruits instead of golf balls, while Annata is expertly switching between multiple views of her Pilot's Arbiter, checking and rechecking the sensor readings, biomass level, thruster settings. Elva eyes her for a moment, again noting that she is about the same age as the senior Waifs she had seen in the hallway.

Elva rolls her chair over to Annata's desk. "So, what made you want to be a Steward?"

Annata smirks, using her desk as leverage to rotate her chair toward Elva since her legs aren't long enough to reach the floor. "This seemed more fun. The classes got boring fast, and I didn't like hanging around those meathead soldiers during our field training. I *borrowed* a Steward's handbook from Jordan, made some suggestions concerning improvements to the Arbiter's systems, and submitted them to Director Joshi," she says, spinning herself around in her chair.

I bet she didn't take kindly to that.

"How'd you know so much about Arbiters? Not exactly common knowledge."

"It is for Waifs. They've been on this kick for a few years for us to assist Pilots directly in the field, so I've seen a lot of footage. The systems don't seem *too* complicated. Basic physics. Using the bioproduct of energy transformation to power the suits is ingenious," Annata continues with a shrug. Elva thinks it's quite a contrast between this girl's stature and high-pitched voice and her understanding of the suits. "I redesigned the thrusters on some craft paper and sent my blueprints about adding eject-able armor plating. Of course, Director Joshi was a bit...*perturbed*. Probably because she hadn't thought of it herself. Obviously..." Annata mock fans herself with her hand as if she were royalty, "...they implemented my suggestions. They'd be foolish not to. Then she offered me a job as a Steward, and I started training alongside Jordan."

"Don't get her going, Elva, unless you want to hear about how *great* she is for the rest of the day," Jordan says sarcastically.

Annata slaps her desk. "You're just mad that—" She's interrupted as the Observation Booth's door opens and the Assistant Director steps through. The Stewards quickly turn their attention to their workstations. Although Zochitl seems perpetually unbothered, she also brings an air of disdain for nonsense.

"Good morning, Stewards. It is good to hear that you have so much energy," Zochitl says as she moves to the semi-circle desk at the front of the room, just behind the large window. "I hope you're ready for your first day, Steward Emerson."

* * *

"How does it feel, Arthur?" Elva asks as she watches him enter the

190

Arena via the perimeter cameras.

"Fine, I guess. I mean, I don't really *feel* it, I just know it's there," he responds. His fellow Pilots are already in the Arena as he enters. He has a bad habit of sleeping in, and this morning is no exception. Parker sees him enter and waves him over to where he and Curiesay are.

"I mean, that's good, right? If you can't feel it that means you're synced adequately," Elva says as she glances up at her screen. On her desk, next to the display, is an open book. On the top of the page, it reads *Steward's Handbook, Chapter 3.*

"You've been reading, more than me at least," Arthur says.

"Sure have! And I know that *eighty percent* means you are properly synced, and look at that—you're at eighty percent right now," she says, her voice upbeat.

Arthur nods. "Oh, okay. That's…good." He reaches his peers as they stand in the street, their feeding tubes leading from their lower back running along the ground and into the orange apparatus nearby. Both have crimson-red irises, which contrast greatly against the whites of their eyes. Arthur quickly plugs his own tube into the apparatus and feels a cool sensation flooding his suit.

* * *

Curiesay has four tendrils out, forming at the holes parallel to her spine. At rest, when not given a command, the tendrils dance around behind their Pilot, swaying languidly. Three of Curiesay's tendrils are doing this, drifting with no direction in mind.

Curiesay holds one of her tendrils in front of her, examining it. Her breathing is steady, and her eyes watch the tendril carefully. It moves like a worm in zero gravity. Listless. A bead of sweat rolls down her cheek.

191

Parker stands in front of Curiesay, observing her tendril. "So, this will be a bit more difficult than last time, Curiesay. Seeing as I'm not trying to kill you."

Curiesay scoffs. "Why would that matter?"

"Your Arbiter's cells are programmed to fill in gaps of knowledge for their Pilot, but when you're relaxed, it takes a backseat. You need to be able to Pilot it *before* you're put in a mortally dangerous situation," Parker says. She nods reluctantly, not enjoying the idea of her Arbiter *thinking* for her, if that is even possible for a suit of flesh. "It works the same as any other aspect of your Arbiter. You must *will* your needs into existence. Tell yourself that you need a shield."

Curiesay's eyes narrow. Like a length of pizza dough being rolled out, one of her tendrils flattens itself until it's roughly one meter in diameter, but paper-thin. Its volume hasn't changed, only its shape. From Parker's perspective, it looks like a worm has emerged from Curiesay's back and is holding a large red trash can lid in front of her.

The tendril is so thin that light can penetrate through, and Curiesay can see Parker beyond it, as well as the veins spidering this way and that throughout.

"Right now, it's much too thin to be of any use. Any sizable impact will punch right through it. Try a bit smaller, but thicker," Parker says. Curiesay nods as the now circular tendril shrinks in diameter. Once it's about half of its original size, Parker puts his hand up. "Now *this* should protect you more effectively."

"But it's too small. I can't protect much with this," Curiesay responds.

"Trying to shield your entire body isn't efficient. Protect what is being threatened." Curiesay furrows her brow, and Parker senses that she doesn't get it. "If you need all four of your tendrils to block an attack, it's probably an attack worth dodging," Parker says, alluding to her defiance in blocking his attack during their fight, an attack that turned her tendrils into dust.

She senses this stab at her stubbornness. "Fine, whatever."

Parker thoughtlessly rocks his head from side to side. "Now, I want you to make a Gripe."

Yesterday, Arthur had—to the surprise of Parker and Chandrima—produced a Gripe with ease. With him watching, she's determined not to fail, though she doesn't know *why* she cares. She puts a hand out, palm up, as if she's presenting an award. From the gaps in her gauntlet's plating, she can see the black liquid seeping out. It rises in globules like a lava lamp, each one adding to the mass of the Gripe that is forming above her palm, suspended by nothing.

"Easy now," Parker says as the Gripe exceeds the size of a marble. "You've seen how dangerous these are. The one you threw at me was the size of a baseball and…" He points to the distant wall where she'd deflected it during their fight. The latticework is exposed, the plating on the wall having been annihilated in the blast. The adjacent plating is knurled inward and scorched black. "You can see how powerful it was. Any bigger than that, you risk blowing yourself up too. Plus, they use a lot of biomass; not the best option for longevity."

I'll have to keep that in mind. Without direction, Curiesay *thinks* about reabsorbing the Gripe into her suit, and it does, falling into her palm and receding into her gauntlet. It's hardly noticeable, but she can feel her suit "filling out" ever so slightly as the biomass redistributes itself.

Curiesay turns her attention to Arthur. Since her realization that Arthur had somehow stopped her from killing Parker, she's grown increasingly curious about his abilities, and after Parker's frustration at his aptitude yesterday, her curiosity has increased. "All right, your turn."

Parker nods carefully in agreement. "Yeah, kid, show us what you can do." Arthur steps forward and trades spots with Curiesay. He closes his eyes, and when he opens them, his irises glow bright red, floating in the whites of his eyes. Slowly, his tendrils make their way out of his back, forming themselves from the root up. Bit by bit, his Arbiter reroutes biomass down to his spine, building the tendrils out of its own flesh.

Parker's eye twitches a bit, then he smiles at Arthur. "You're taking to this pretty well, kid. How do you feel?"

"Fine, I guess," Arthur responds as he wills his tendrils from the left to right.

"I meant mentally," Parker follows up. Curiesay listens carefully, trying to keep a neutral expression on her face.

Arthur turns his head to Parker. "Um, fine?"

"You're not angry?"

"Why would I be?"

Parker's words stumble out. "W-well sometimes when… Piloting can make… Never mind." Curiesay's ears perk up at his hesitance. *Piloting can what? Make you go insane and try to blow people up?* "Let's see if you've been studying. How many tendrils do you have?"

"Four in total, two on the left and two on the right."

"How much do they cost?"

"Each tendril consumes three percent of my Arbiter's biomass."

"And how do they work? In your own words."

Arthur contemplates for a moment. "They have a set mass and can be formed into shapes. They can extend, becoming thinner, and retract, becoming thicker."

"Geez, kid, you memorize the entire manual already?" Parker says with a chuckle.

"I'm just getting up to speed, there's so much to learn," Arthur says, rubbing his neck.

Parker narrows his eyes as he watches Arthur. "Why don't you and Curiesay run the agility course?" He points down the street.

Red paint marks their route, painted on cars, lampposts, windows, balconies, benches. There are also red hoops along the course; some are ground level, others are atop the buildings or strung up between them. Pilots need to jump, swing, dive, and use their thrusters to move quickly through the course. The two Pilots walk to the red line painted on the ground in the middle of the nearest intersection.

"Okay, that's the starting line! The course is self-explanatory; just follow the red markers, and you'll end up back here again," Parker says from behind them. He keys his microphone and speaks again. "Elva, Annata, eject their feeding tubes." A beat passes, and Curiesay and Arthur's feeding tubes disconnect with a hiss, falling to the ground.

"Are you ready, Arthur?" Curiesay says as her thrusters spool up, emitting waves of heat and a quiet whining noise. She's determined to leave him in the dust. Arthur nods as his thrusters do the same. They crouch down, ready to explode forward.

"Begin!" Parker yells, and the two Pilots move forward in a flash.

* * *

Elva watches Arthur's progress as he keeps pace with Curiesay. The two Pilots jump, dive, leap, and sprint their way through the streets, using their thrusters for boosts in speed and their tendrils for quick changes in direction.

"Arthur…" Elva whispers into her microphone as Arthur begins to overtake Curiesay. "Slow down a bit." Unbeknownst to Elva, Zochitl's ears flutter for an instant as she says this. A moment later, Arthur begins to lag behind the deft Curiesay, who is moving nearly as furiously as when she fought Parker. On Annata's screen, Curiesay's temperature is at its upper limits, her biomass being consumed at a decently quick pace.

Annata looks over at Elva. "Looks like he needs a bit more practice, huh?" she says with a satisfied smile. Elva does her best to feign a frustrated expression, rolling her eyes. On Elva's screen, Arthur's heart rate is barely north of one-hundred and twelve beats per minute. Parker is not participating, so Jordan hasn't much to do. On her screen, she's brought up the vitals for Arthur and Curiesay, pinning their windows side by side.

Curiesay's heart rate, temperature, respiratory rate, and cortisol levels are all significantly higher than Arthur's. It isn't close. Jordan eyes the numbers, switching from one to the other. A glance. First to Elva, who stares forlornly at her display, then at Annata, who is making tens of small adjustments every minute.

Elva can sense eyes on her and turns her head, making eye contact with Jordan. As Annata types away and Zochitl stares out the window, Jordan winks before turning away.

* * *

Later, the Pilots are wrapping up their drills. Parker stands in the middle of the street and haphazardly tosses Gripes at the targets that Jordan is commanding to rise. He has his eyes closed, only listening to the distant and nearly imperceptible sounds of the target carriages as they push their proverbial boulders up their respective hills.

His Arbiter-enhanced senses are sharp, able to triangulate the positions of each target based on their sound waves' reflection off the surrounding buildings. Each Gripe lands not more than a few centimeters from the bullseye. *Ping. Ping. Ping.* Dutifully throwing, seemingly without much effort. Opening his eyes and turning toward Curiesay and Arthur, he tosses three at once, with each one heading in a slightly different direction, striking three targets.

Curiesay scoffs. "Pfft. Showoff." Truthfully, she's thoroughly impressed, but she won't admit that to him.

Parker shrugs as he walks over to his junior Pilots. "I've had a lot of practice." He stands in front of the two and puts a hand on each of their shoulders. "You know, you two are shaping up pretty quick," he says, a genuine smile following. Arthur returns one of his own, his eyes sparkling with affirmation, while Curiesay gives him a skeptical look.

"Before you know it, I'll be able to kick *both* your asses at once," she retorts, glancing at Arthur.

"You have *two* asses?" Arthur asks Parker in an unbelievable tone. Curiesay snaps her head toward him in frustration.

This elates a snorting chuckle from Parker, who covers his mouth for a moment as Curiesay stares daggers at Arthur. "That's the first time I've heard you say something unserious, Arthur," Parker remarks, and Arthur gives a satisfied grin.

"Jordan, send us some water, por favor," Parker says with an unfaithful accent as he steps past his juniors and onto the sidewalk. He puts his back against the concrete wall of the building and slides down. His armor scrapes, grating Curiesay's ears. Arthur and Curiesay follow suit, kicking rubble out of the way to make room for their armored *singular* asses.

"What are we doing?" Arthur asks.

"Taking a break," Parker says, resting his head against the wall behind him, eyes closed.

Curiesay playfully nudges Parker's shoulder. "It's cause you're old, isn't it?"

"Yup."

"How old are you?" Arthur asks innocently.

"I'm thirty-two," Parker says with a hefty sigh.

"Wow, you *are* old," Curiesay responds, giggling spitefully.

"Wait...so you...were my age when the Blight attacked?" Arthur asks. Both Curiesay and Arthur scoot closer to their larger and older counterpart.

"Yup." A silence falls over the three after he answers, the two junior Pilots staring at Parker as he *tries* to rest. A distant humming quickly builds until it's right on top of them. A flying rectangle zips past and drops three steel water bottles onto the pavement.

"What was that?" Curiesay asks, having narrowly missed the courier. She jolts a bit as Parker's tendrils crawl out from behind him, slithering onto the street. One. Two. And three. They return in short order, bottles in tow, and he passes one to his comrades, and one to himself.

His tendrils retract into his back, and he sips his bottle. "Go ahead. Ask."

"Did you fight?" Arthur asks flatly. Curiesay withdraws a bit, opening her own bottle and taking a swig.

"We all fought. Thirteen and up...for the males at least," Parker says.

"And the females?" Curiesay asks. Parker gives another heavy sigh, not answering as Curiesay stares at him.

"*I* was ten at the time, but I met girls as young as five or six," Jordan butts in, transmitting over all three Pilots' speakers.

Curiesay scrambles to her feet, facing the Observation Booth several blocks away. "What?! You were ten?!" she yells, seemingly preferring *not* to use her suit's communications.

"You were a Waif, weren't you?" Arthur asks aloud and receives a half-hearted nod in confirmation from Parker.

"There's not much work for little girls with post-traumatic stress disorder, so after the Blight retreated, I stayed with Chandrima and Amiree until Bastion was complete. A lot of us did, actually," Jordan continues.

Curiesay shakes her head, thinking back to the plethora of women she's seen milling about the Third Floor. "That's why there's so many women here."

"There ain't nearly as many of us around as there were. Most have moved on, or..." Jordan trails off. Her non-answer is enough for Parker to rile himself from his spot, rising to his feet before his comrades ask any more questions.

"I think that's enough for today. Let's get something to eat," he says, offering a helping hand to the two still-seated Pilots. They accept and he hauls them up with a grunt.

"Don't hurt your back, you old fuck," Curiesay says with snark as she nudges Parker. The three walk down the street, jeering each other playfully, heading to the Dock.

*　*　*

"Good afternoon, girls," Zochitl says loudly as she enters the classroom.

The twenty girls who had been, up until they heard the door open, engaging in childlike nonsense with their adjacent desk-mates, shoot straight up in their chairs. "Good afternoon, Assistant Director Bottazzi!" they respond in unison.

Zochitl cracks a smile as she strolls to the front of the room, the girls quickly and quietly putting their desks in order. She sets her bag down, unsnaps the clasps, and peeks obnoxiously over her shoulder.

The girls recognize this cue and fidget in their seats. "Hmm, I don't know," Zochitl purrs. "If you can't sit still now, I don't think giving you confectionary will help matters."

Shrill protests break out for an instant before the class leader slams her palm on her desk. The class jolts and falls silent. Zochitl turns to face them, her hands hidden behind her back.

"Ah, a girl after my own heart. You seem to have found your calling, Kashina." Zochitl urges the girl forward with an upward motion of her chin. With all the composure of a studious military scholar, Kashina stands and walks to the front. "Class leader, pass these out," Zochitl whispers as she takes the tray of neatly stacked brownies from behind her back, a pile of napkins on top.

"Yes, Assistant Director," Kashina responds with a nod. Taking the tray, she paces the aisles, laying down the napkins atop the desks and passing one square of baked goods to each girl.

"Karima is doing well," Zochitl announces, leaning against the desk at the front, ankles crossed. The girls watch her intently, waiting to indulge in their treats until every girl has one. "As always, I cannot say anything more about what she's doing or where she is. But she is safe. I thought you would like to know."

They do want to know. *Everything.* Karima is the first Waif in years to be sent into the Exclusion Zone. Of course, they aren't *supposed* to know that, but training these girls in what eclipses the skills learned at a military academy does grant them the ability to stick their little noses where they don't belong. They've gleaned enough from whispers and gossip to know that their former class leader is doing the job they've all volunteered for—and they are jealous.

Kashina sets the second to last brownie on the final girl's desk and makes her way back to her own. She stumbles, tripping over her own feet. The Waif and the glass container crash to the floor, the latter shattering and spreading across the room like a bucket of water on a frozen lake.

A silence so thick that it is all but palpable falls over the room as Kashina springs to her feet. She freezes, head downturned, embarrassment flooding her. Zochitl watches for several moments as every girl is stoic and unmoving in their seats.

"Why have none of you tended to your class leader's wound?" she asks finally, noting the blood dripping from the girl's shoe. An instant later, as nineteen girls make to stand from their desks, Zochitl speaks again: "Stop. I will do it."

She retrieves the aid kit from the wall near the door and places it on Kashina's desk. "Sit," Zochitl says, and Kashina silently complies. Zochitl opens the bottom of the Waif's long coat. A shard of the thick glass had gone straight through both her coat and the pants underneath. The cut isn't too deep, but it's enough to cause a bit of bleeding. "What's wrong?" Zochitl asks as the Waif bites down on a sniffle.

"I'm sorry," she despondently responds.

"You didn't answer my question." She tears, widening the hole in the Waif's pants so that she can tend her wound.

Kashina bites her tongue as the antiseptic burns. "I broke your dish."

Zochitl moves with grace and impartiality, paying no heed to what pain she may be causing the girl. "It's not about the dish. It's because you feel stupid." She takes an adhesive cloth bandage from the kit, dabbing the backside with a pinch of antibacterial gel. "Do you think that you're stupid?"

Kashina shakes her head meekly, her eyes downturned.

"I didn't hear you," Zochitl says, laying the bandage in her palm, adhesive side up. "Do you think you're stupid?"

"No, ma'am," Kashina whispers. She inhales sharply through her teeth as Zochitl applies the bandage, pressing down with a less-than-kind amount of force. "No, I don't think I'm stupid."

Zochitl looks at her until Kashina finally raises her eyes to meet her gaze. "I can buy another dish. Be sure to get new pants and coat."

She packs up the aid kit and returns it to its place on the wall. Turning to face the class, she can see the girls teeming with nervous energy, waiting for the silence to break so they can raid the broom closet and clean the glass from the floor. Kashina sits silently, her eyes wet with tears.

Zochitl hums a thought to herself; a single brownie sits glass-covered on the floor. Kashina's brownie.

Her diet has undoubtedly taken a toll on her temperament. A constant hunger gnaws at her, turning her stomach into itself. She had allowed herself to eat all the batter the night prior, allowing herself to clean the spatula as a compromise. And on the way to the Third Floor this morning, she'd huddled over the container in the ladies' room, mouth watering. But she did not make them for herself. Not all of them, at least.

She'd set aside a single brownie—it is atop her desk. She can feel it calling to her, begging to be consumed. She glares at Kashina, cursing both herself and the girl for what comes next.

"Ah, it's a good thing I have one left over," Zochitl says coyly. She retrieves the brownie square on her desk and brings it to Kashina. Her lips part with rising protest when Zochitl puts a stern finger up to silence her. "No buts," she says as she lays the brownie on the desk. "You will sit here and enjoy it with the rest of the class. That's an order, class leader." Zochitl flashes her teeth as she smiles down at Kashina, who blushes in response.

As the girls dig in, Zochitl pulls the retractable projector screen down and puts on an instructional video: celestial navigation and terrain traversal. They've seen it before, but it'll give them something to watch for the time being. She gets the broom and dustpan, quietly cleaning the glass from beneath their desks, her mouth watering as the scent of chocolate tickles her nose. Hungry, grumpy, and cleaning up after someone else. She smiles to herself—there's no place else she'd rather be.

* * *

Early Morning, September 5th, 2053

Exclusion Zone

"I feel kinda silly for asking, but what are you?" Karima asks.

The girl thoughtlessly rolls the ball toward her, leaving an undusted trail on the phantom floor in its wake. "What am I?"

Karima gives her head a spiteful tap and pushes the ball away. "Sorry. Like, where are you from? What, uh, ethnicity?"

The ball contacts her ankle before rolling up the inside of her leg. "Oh. I... It's been so long, but I think I'm from China. So, I guess I'm Chinese? Is... Does it still exist?" She again rolls the ball back toward Karima. The two are sitting across from one another, legs splayed out, and feet together.

"Well, the land is still there, but..." Karima responds hesitantly, "...most of Asia was wiped out. And Europe. And Northern Africa." She winces as she runs down the list. It's hard for her to imagine that four billion people lost their lives in a matter of months, or that four billion people could even fit on this planet. "But some have returned from overseas. Not many, 'cause, you know."

The girl's shoulders droop in shame. "Because of Master. Because of me—"

"No!" Karima interrupts desperately, startling the girl. "Not because of you. Never because of you."

The girl pushes the ball back with hardly enough energy to reach Karima, face blank. "Why do you want to know where I'm from anyway?"

Karima takes the ball in her hand, holding it above her shoulder before tossing it back. "I said I was going to help you find a name. Needed to know which baby books to get."

* * *

"She spends a lot of time sleeping lately," Clark says, watching Pullhum as she lays prone in front of the spotting scope. "I guess the good news is, she isn't roaming around as much." Pullhum doesn't respond. "They've calmed down a bit. My dreams, I mean. I think that spending time with Karima keeps her relaxed. Or, as relaxed as a Blight can be."

Again, the captain doesn't respond. Clark nods, taking this cue to stand from the recliner near the window and do his rounds. He slings his rifle over his body and unlocks the main door: hallways, clear; adjacent rooms, locked. Returning to their abode, he checks on Karima. *Like a log.* She's curled up tight, the cover of her sleeping bag barely covering her forehead. He envies her adolescent ability to rest so deeply.

"All clear," he says to the captain. She raises her hand and gives a thumbs-up. "I've been thinking—"

"Just spit it out already, Corporal," Pullhum says curtly. Her sleep debt has drained her reserve of niceties.

"What's the endgame, ma'am? Even if they found a way to cure her, they'd still have to get hold of her long enough to administer it. Parker is strong, sure, but I don't think he'd stand a chance."

"The Director has instructed us to report her doings and capabilities back to Bastion," she says flatly. "Anything beyond that is above my pay grade." A familiar silence falls over the two soldiers as the waxing moon peeks from behind the clouds, draping pale light atop the city. "You're worried about Karima."

"Aren't you?" Clark asks and receives no response. "I know. She's trained. It's her job. But you've seen what she can do. The thought of her spending so much time in her head just…it… I'd rather it be me."

Pullhum chuckles under her breath. "If she wanted to talk to you, you'd know it. You could always go down there and ask her to come back with us." Clark gives grunts in response. "Karima says that she's lonely. And it makes *her* happy. Maybe she can break through to her. I mean…" Pullhum takes her eye from the spotting scope and turns on her side to face Clark. "It's a miracle. That she's still in there. Well, maybe 'miracle' isn't the best word, but still—Karima is keeping her tethered. And with all the Blight has taken from humanity, if we can save even *one* of our own, I'd call that a win." She rolls back to her stomach and sights in again. "In fact, I'd *die* for that kind of win."

Clark smiles, sits on the recliner, and leans toward the captain, giving her a firm pat on the shoulder. "Let's hope it doesn't come to that, ma'am."

15

Scowls

October 3rd, 2053

Bastion, Third Floor, Recreation Wing

It's been four weeks since Curiesay had fully recovered and began her training, and she's finally settled into a routine. Every morning, before their classes, she is to report to the gymnasium in the Recreation Wing. She hasn't protested (much) about the daily exercise. Having dedicated tools for fitness invigorates her. The institution did not allow exercise equipment, so when she was restless, she took to running laps around the rec yard and clumsily performing her own brand of calisthenics.

This, however, did not provide her with the level of fitness that Parker demanded of her. Six kilometers on the treadmill, alternating muscle groups for weightlifting, deep stretching afterward. Every day. She kept her cussing as sharp as she could, intending to portray annoyance rather than desperation. In reality, her faith in herself to complete the workouts dwindled as the soreness in her muscles compounded.

Though, there is *one* thing to look forward to.

"About time," Parker barks as she enters. "Don't think you can skip out on your run, Pilot."

It takes every ounce of her composure not to stare slack-jawed at the man. She hates him for it, and herself for ogling. But she can't deny that she is reluctantly enjoying some eye candy. The only men she'd been around when she came of age were criminally insane inmates or the sturdy orderlies meant to keep them in check. She's never been around men in a casual sense before, and it's overwhelming.

Parker and Arthur have apparently already finished their run, standing just off to the side of the treadmills and stretching their calves. Their t-shirts are soaked through and sticking to their muscled chests. Although Parker's body is wider, taller, and more appealing, Curiesay can't deny that Arthur's body is just as incredible. She can see the striations of their shoulders pressing against the damp fabric, the beats of their hearts through their skin.

"You act like you've never seen men before," Parker remarks. He nudges Arthur, who meets Curiesay's blushing gaze and quickly averts his own, albeit with a grin.

"Still not used to seeing two sweaty dipshits every morning," she spits, walking to the last of the three treadmills and refusing to look at them again. "Though I don't think I could *ever* get used to it."

Her comrades step away, heading to the weight room section, down a flight of two stairs. "Believe me, I'm just as shocked when I see you," Parker responds. *Asshole.*

Curiesay drops her duffel to the side of her treadmill and begrudgingly sets the program for six kilometers, at a brisk five minute per kilometer pace. Two days prior, Parker had scolded her for shorting herself by a kilometer and had upped her speed as a punishment. Her vulgar tirade didn't land, and he'd responded that he'd only raise the speed further if she kept it up. *Fuckin' meathead fuck,* she'd thought to herself.

The belt picks up speed as she settles into a rhythm. She has always enjoyed running, but at her own pace. She supposes she'll be all the better for it, though she curses her expected submission to her senior Pilot. It *is* refreshing to receive a punishment which betters her overall, rather than a week in the padded room—which she's spent her fair share of time in—or a fat dose of sedative like she'd received at Wilted Rose.

She had purposefully showed up late today for one reason: to observe Parker and Arthur. The way Parker runs his programs requires the three Pilots to constantly switch out exercises, running a three-man circuit through the gym. Until today, she hadn't had a spare moment to watch. And she is *most* interested in Arthur.

She figures Parker knows. Not why she was late, that is, but rather that Arthur is *different*. She doesn't know that much about weightlifting, but Parker does. And he has yet to remark on Arthur's performance, other than the occasional "attaboy."

He is much too strong for his size. Although Arthur lifts less than Parker does, she suspects it's only for show. She can see the fakeness of his effort. The quivering before "failure" is a poor ruse. Overacted facial expressions.

As she runs, her comrades perform chest exercises. Parker goes first, and Curiesay hopes that he doesn't look over as she nearly drools over him. Or is it that she is drooling because this pace is hardly sustainable for her? She doesn't know. Seeing his gritted teeth and determined eyes as he presses more than twice his weight from his chest rouses something inside of her that she didn't know was there. On another note, she begins to wonder how she survived her fight against him at all, even *with* her Arbiter. Seeing his strength now has her fully convinced that he could put her through a wall if he so chose to, and ashamedly, she doesn't swat away the mental image.

The two have been doing sets of increasing weight and decreasing repetitions. Presently, Parker has increased the weight to his limit, hardly managing three reps before slamming the bar back onto the rack. Heaving, Parker rolls off the bench and drops down to do push-ups, with Arthur moving from the chest fly bench. *You're forgetting something, Arthur.* Whenever they switch exercises, each Pilot adjusts the weight to their own abilities. Except this time. In his haste, Arthur lays on the bench and lifts the bar from the rack, going through into his set. Lifting the weight that his substantially larger comrade was struggling against.

To Curiesay, the image would be comically obtuse if it weren't so shocking. Her mind can't comprehend that someone of his size could lift that weight even once, yet he is progressing through his reps without so much as a pause. Parker barely managed three reps, yet Arthur has passed ten and shows no signs of slowing. How his arms don't snap in two from the weight, she cannot imagine. She stops her treadmill so she can give her full attention. *What is he?*

* * *

"Arthur, did you just..." Parker trails off into a whisper, watching as Arthur sits up on the bench. He searches Parker's face for an inkling of the issue, then looks back at the bar. He meets his gaze again, his eyes trembling.

Parker puts his hands on his knees, feigning a need for deep breaths as he leans close to Arthur. "You need to be more careful." He turns his head, facing the camera on the far wall and pantomimes cutting his throat.

* * *

"Hey! I know you haven't finished already," Parker hollers over his

209

shoulder.

Shit. Seems like he knows. "I know you're too butt-ugly to be yelling like that," Curiesay responds, presenting a vulgar gesture as she hits the *go* button on her treadmill. *And Chandrima definitely knows, since she knows everything.* She picks up speed, the short pause giving her heart just enough cue to slow down before her body demands that it beat faster.

But *what* do they know? How did he stop her that day? How is he so strong? How can he Pilot without Crossing? She feels grossly underinformed. Parker, Chandrima, and surely his dear sister knows. *Why am I being kept in the dark?*

She feels a moment of frustration before it quickly fades. She had seen the fear in Arthur's eyes when Parker called him out. They're not keeping it from her out of spite; they're protecting him. *But why?*

Her memory of the event is still hazy, but she'd recalled it further in her dreams, her neurons striving to fill the gaps. Arthur had leapt between herself and Parker, bracing his arms in front of him, eyes alight with crimson fire. Like hers and Parker's are when they Pilot their Arbiters. But there's something different in his, something deeper. He had not been in his Arbiter. Hell, he wasn't even a Pilot yet. He'd drawn strength from somewhere Curiesay could not see.

Chandrima had said their suits were *designed to mimic the speed, strength, and robustness of the Blights.* Curiesay had thought, worriedly, that the cloned flesh was Blight in origin. But Chandrima *knows* something about Arthur, and she can't imagine that he's a Blight. He's something greater. Something older. *He must be.* Whatever the Arbiters are made from, she's convinced that it's related to what Arthur is. That must be why he can Pilot so effortlessly.

A word crosses her mind for an instant, disappearing into the ether before she can grab hold of it. *S...something. It starts with an S.* Is it some folklore term? She can't recall, but the circumstances have set her neurons firing. For the rest of her run, she tries every "S" word she can remember, mumbling them quietly to herself through her breaths.

She doesn't recognize it when she says it. "Scowl," she whispers. Over the sound of her breaths, her pounding feet on the treadmill, and Parker's masculine grunts of exertion, she knows he heard her. The moment the word leaves her lips, Arthur snaps his head to lock eyes with her. For an infinitesimal moment, before his eyelids wiped it away, she swears his eyes were burning a deep, crimson-red.

* * *

For the second day in a row, Curiesay shows up later than usual at the gymnasium. "Cancelled," Curiesay mutters to herself, staring at the paper sign on the door. "He could have fuckin' texted me before I—" Pulling her phone from her pocket, she realizes that Parker *did* text her. *Take the day off. See you around.* She's not owned a phone before and is struggling to adjust the volume or vibration of notifications. This isn't the first time she's missed a message.

She grunts, staring at the door for several moments, dressed in her sweats. *I could always workout alone.* She nearly slaps herself at the suggestion. Stepping back, she turns and lazily walks back toward her room.

Her *freedom* doesn't invigorate her as much as she'd hoped. Sure, she has some obligations to tend to on the Third Floor, but she has just as much free time and isn't sure what to do with it. This wrench in her daily regimen unsettles her.

Curiesay supposes she will get used to it. It is all a bit surreal. Sometimes, when she wakes, she panics at the sight of a ceiling that isn't the one from her cell. Hallways that she hardly recognizes. People talking *with* her, instead of *at* her. Weeks of catharsis have left her brain on autopilot, and now that she has nothing to do for the rest of the day, she feels a tide of uncertainty washing over her soul.

She takes the long walk back to her room, passing several Waifs, clad in their formals, heading to class as they exit the Dwellings Wing. "Good morning, Pilot!" they call out one after another. With all the politeness she can muster, she waves to each one, becoming increasingly frustrated at the never-ending columns of them.

Finally, she's in her room. *What now?* In short order, her eyes answer the question for her. She'd asked Chandrima to get her a laptop, and one has arrived, sitting on her breakfast nook. She grimaces at the idea of someone coming into her room uninvited, but she supposes she can be angry about it another time.

The "computer lab" at the institution consisted of relics of technology and terribly slow internet, but she does know how to use one. Of course, she hadn't told the Director why she wanted one. Other than choking out her own boredom, she intends to do some reading.

Setting it on the table in between her sectional, she gets to work. *Internet browser...here?* She deduces the correct symbol and clicks, opening a new tab.

Since she'd identified it, she has rolled the word around in her head. *Scowl.* She knows that as a noun, it means a foul-tempered expression. But she had heard it used as a *proper* noun before, and in the same vein as other mythical creatures. She'd heard of Bigfoot, the Loch Ness monster, wendigos, the plethora of Greek mythological creatures, et cetera. There was a book containing detailed histories of the origins and lore of such creatures and she had read it religiously—it was one of the many she'd hidden below the floor tiles while she was interred.

Strangely, she had thought, Scowls were not featured in that book. Unlike the whimsical and visceral tales that people would share about their favorite monsters, when they spoke of Scowls, their imaginations were hushed. It always sounded to her like they were recounting historical events. Never once did someone question the legitimacy of their claims as they often did with other creatures of whose existences were far more dubious. But although she'd heard them spoken of before, there isn't a single fact about them that she can recall, except that they *look* human, and that people trembled when recanting tales of them.

Unfortunately, as a noun, her search yields her no useful results. Screenplays, articles about lawsuits, a few dictionary entries. Strangely, *nothing* regarding their folklore. She hadn't imagined it; she knows she's heard the word used in that context. She scrolls and scrolls, page after page, the results becoming more muddied. *Nothing useful.*

"The 'Disciples of Willow,'" she says to herself, this particular link catching her eye. She recognizes the name of the organization. "Fuckin' weirdos," she had affectionately called them. Their core belief is that the Blight is a blessing, and not a disease. One of her orderlies was thoroughly obsessed with their congregation. Even showed up blindfolded once a month to observe some religious holiday they'd established. She did enjoy watching the buffoon stumble around all day, even if his devotions made her sick with disdain. She's not sure why it appeared in the search results.

She clicks the link. The webpage loads in a flash, with brooding symbols running along the edges of the page. In the background of the video and text window is an effigy of a large tree, its branches reaching off screen as it looms.

Curiesay glosses over the text but can find no mention of Scowls. The video window shows the "Allsister," their equivalent of the Pope. She is clad in obsidian robes, her face painted white like a porcelain doll with dark black lines running from her eyes to her collarbone. A crimson cloth is wrapped around her head, covering her eyes, and she stands before the congregation on a massive stage. Curiesay presses play.

"And what did we do? We strove to cast aside our godhood!" the woman calls out scornfully, her lips dripping thick with contempt. "Arrogant man! We denied our calling! We denied to Meld!"

"Meld!" the congregation called out, their voices joined in unholy unison.

"We denied our ascension! We denied submission!" The Allsister paces, viewing her audience with obstructed eyes. "And what was our price?! My brothers and sisters: hell on earth. Famine, plagues, squalor. Your pathetic lives, all, are our *just* punishment for such impertinence! How will you make amends?!"

"Submit!" the incensed audience cries out, their voices breaking.

"Prostrate before the Allmother!"

"Dissolve!"

"Join with the Willow!"

"Meld!"

A curt slicing motion of the Allsister's hand silences the audience. Curiesay's speakers don't register a single sound while Allsister paces, regarding the congregation with disdain.

"None of you are innocent of our collective sin," the Allsister growls. "We all bear responsibility for the Culling." Another long pause, the audience lowering their heads, bowing in shame. "Yes, you *should* be ashamed. For what did we do when our Mother sent us her angels? We struck them down! So fearful of our ascension were we that we denied breath to those already blessed by the Willow! For millennia did they deign to share our repulsive condition. We cast aside the Scowls"—Curiesay's ears perk up—"because we feared what we did not understand. And so, the Willow lashed out. Her war was one of abject sorrow, for we—"

The screen goes blank. "What the fuck?" She taps the screen with her hand. After a few moments, it turns back on. The webpage is closed. Curiesay opens the browser and searches again. She finds the link, but when she clicks it, a red screen with text appears.

Association with the Disciples of Willow, or worship thereof, is outlawed in the city of Bastion.

Goddamnit. Just when she was beginning to get some answers, they're ripped away from her. She wonders if this is Chandrima's doing and curses herself for being unaware that this laptop, and the internet, is likely monitored.

A knock at her door. Curiesay slams the laptop shut and stuffs it between her couch cushions. She debates answering it and wonders if she'll receive some sort of punishment. If they think that one of their Pilots is aligning themselves with a group that *supports* the Blight…

"Hey there!" Annata calls out as Curiesay opens the door. *Oh good, it's just her.*

Initially, the idea of having a Steward made Curiesay feel infantilized. *I'm an adult, I don't need my hand held.* Though she does sometimes wish someone *would* hold her hand, even against her will. The more time she spent Piloting, the more accustomed she became to hearing Annata's voice chirp over her suit's speakers.

"Biomass reserves at eighty-eight percent," she said after Curiesay had finished the agility course and was moving to plug herself back in.

"I can adjust your underfoot thrusters, put some more pep in your step." After Curiesay's second run when she stumbled, failing to clear an overturned trash bin.

Truthfully, she is most perturbed by the fact that she is paired with a child. If she's supposed to be some great warrior, why not give her an adult as a Steward? With her nerves still high, she focuses her frustrations on her partner.

"What do you want?" Curiesay says disdainfully.

Her Steward is wearing a white and black onesie with panda bears on it, her hair in locs and set back with a plain white headband. She looks up at Curiesay, her Pilot being quite a bit taller. If Annata is offended, she doesn't lend a reaction. "I have something I want to show you," she bubbles. "It's in my room. To which you have a door to *inside* of your room. I have to say, it breaks my heart that you never bother to open it."

Curiesay is stung by her admission. Up until now, she had only spoken with Annata during training or their meals. She wishes to be perceived as someone who doesn't need anyone. After all, she'd made it this far alone. She hadn't bothered to reach out to the girl who is supposed to help keep her alive.

The Pilot rolls her eyes and steps aside. Annata hurries in and to the right, entering the adjoining door to her room. "Promise I won't keep you against your will," she quips with a smile. Curiesay's eye twitches as she reluctantly steps inside.

Her room is nearly identical to Curiesay's, at least in layout. It is significantly more furnished, however. A hodge podge of bookshelves crowd every wall. Some jut into walkways, with longer titles sticking out even farther. Dozens of books lay haphazardly on every piece of furniture, except for two spots that look to have been recently cleaned on the couch.

Several picture frames of various sizes hang on her walls: a blueprint of what looks like an Arbiter, but far bulkier, the paper itself faded, its creases lending to the idea that this is an original copy; a photo of Bastion, nearly complete, in the background as a group of girls sit in the shade of a tree, with Chandrima and another woman sitting cross-legged in front of them; in a much smaller frame, a picture of two people holding a child between them, a rickety shack behind. They wear sandals and shawls, the sand below them emanating waves of heat, distorting their legs.

Annata motions for Curiesay to take a seat wherever she'd like, to which the Pilot declines, crossing her arms defiantly, hips half-cocked. "How much do you know about me?" Curiesay asks accusingly. In uncomfortable situations, she prefers to be the person in control, and making problems accomplishes that.

The young Steward grins and rattles off her answer at a clipped pace. "Curiesay Richardson, age seventeen, born the first of December, 2036. Height, one hundred and seventy centimeters, weight, sixty-five kilograms, as of last week. Diagnosed by her attending physician with bipolar personality disorder..." Curiesay's jaw tightens as the muscles feather themselves against her skin, "...convicted on two counts of attempted murder, sentenced to indefinite confinement at Wilted Rose Asylum for the Criminally—"

"Enough," Curiesay barks. "Don't think you know me just because you memorized my file." Brow furrowed, she menaces toward Annata, who's entirely unbothered. "So, you think I'm crazy?"

"Crazy is subjective. If I were to take the word of your prior attending physician, I wouldn't even be in the same room with you, especially not alone," Annata snaps back with a smile. "Luckily, I know better. Even if you are *crazy*, that makes you a perfect fit for me."

"Oh? You think you can rein me in? Have me do some fuckin' tricks for you?"

Annata cocks her head, looking straight up at her. "I won't take your attacks personally, for one." Curiesay grunts. "And two, a normal Pilot would be *boring*. You're much more fun."

Curiesay tries her best to rein in her temper, sensing nothing but goodwill from her Steward. An intoxicating amount. This feeling of reverence is foreign to Curiesay.

"Oh. Well... Thanks," Curiesay manages with some sincerity. She feels exposed, not receiving the negative reaction she had hoped for. Suddenly, she has the rising urge to flee to her room. She reaches for the door when Annata gently puts her hand over hers.

"It's okay, I forgive you. Why don't you stay for a while?" she insists with a gentle voice, like someone convincing a crawl-space cat that they won't hurt them. Glaring at Annata, Curiesay again attempts to elicit a reaction from her Steward, which fails as Annata grins back at her.

Curiesay steps past Annata, finding herself a seat on the sectional. At the table in the center, she can see that Annata's tablet is lit up, a notebook next to it. *She has nice handwriting for a child.* The notebook's current page is filled from edge to edge with rows of numbers.

Annata steps into her kitchenette and brings two bottles of apple juice to the living room. She passes one to Curiesay, who accepts it silently.

"I've kinda been working on a pet project," Annata starts as she takes a seat across from Curiesay, the table in between them. "I wanted to get your opinion on it." The Steward takes a sip from her bottle, then scoops up her notebook and flips the pages.

"Is this…my Arbiter?" Curiesay asks as she taps the tablet's screen with her finger. It shows her suit's parts breakdown. As a rule, her classes have included the basics of Stewardship, so she has a vague understanding of the software. "I don't recognize this screen."

"It's your suit's diagnostics. It's used to make fine adjustments to your systems," Annata says, still flipping through her book. Curiesay eyes the screen; it's different than the one she's seen in her classes, as it shows individual parts like her thrusters, cooling zones, fluid reservoirs, as well as weight distribution.

Seemingly finding the desired page, Annata slaps the book down on the table, oriented to face Curiesay. "Ah, okay. So given your current outputs, I ran the numbers, and I think I can get you moving even *faster* than you are now."

The page has a grid imprint in the background. A sharply drawn breakdown of Curiesay's Arbiter is in the center, as detailed as its digital brother on the tablet. Not being much of a math whiz, the numbers scribbled all around make no sense to Curiesay. She is smart enough, however, to recognize something beyond her own ability, and without *running the numbers* herself, she is inclined to believe everything her Steward is about to tell her.

"I'm sure you know that one of the limiting factors for a human's top speed is our stride length and maximum force output." *Uh, yeah, of course I know that.* "An Arbiter's force multiplication and external thrusters easily break those bonds but are still limited by..." Annata points to a long line of numbers written underneath the sketch's feet, "...friction. Every moment you spend touching the ground, you lose momentum to friction. But when you fought Parker, you were *skating*, your underfoots keeping you just above the ground. No friction, no lost momentum." Annata flashes a devious smile. "Where did you learn that?"

Curiesay rubs her neck, poorly concealing a nostalgic grin. "My uncle. He used to take me to a skating rink. I guess...I never forgot how to do it."

"He sounds like a good man." *He was.* Curiesay's somber expression halts Annata's bustling excitement. For a moment. "Anyway, given that method of locomotion, I think..."

Though logically she is following along, Curiesay has no educated guess as to where Annata is going with this and chooses to nod while her Steward rambles at a clipped pace. Annata points at the diagram, then scrolls on the tablet, showing some still images from Curiesay's fight with Parker. Curiesay neglects to look at Annata's work, opting to look at her face instead. Unaware, her Steward continues.

"...lose a bit of longevity, but in a tight spot, it could give you an edge. Of course we'd need to drop some of the less essential plating, and it's not exactly legitimate to change the configuration to that extent without approval, but—" Annata stops mid-sentence, looking up at Curiesay and seeing a pair of unfocused eyes. Much like their first meeting, Curiesay hasn't been listening particularly well.

"Are you all right?" Annata asks.

Curiesay gulps. "Uh, yeah. Yes. You…" She grabs the notebook and flips haphazardly through it; cover to cover, it's filled with notes, equations, drawings. Some hastily crossed out. Other pages were seemingly torn from the book—the jagged edges left behind indicate some frustration was involved. The occasional change in ink color marks several pen changes. "Did all this for me?"

"Of course," Annata says with a heartfelt laugh. "You're my Pilot." Curiesay nearly leaps over the table between them and wraps her arms around Annata, lifting her off her feet. "Wow," Annata squeaks out, her torso being crushed. "You really *are* bipolar."

"Shut up, you tiny idiot," Curiesay responds as she gently lowers her Steward back to the ground. Annata collects herself for a moment, adjusting her rumpled pajamas as Curiesay puts her hands on her hips. Curiesay points at Annata's bedroom. "Get changed. I wanna go see a movie," she says impolitely.

This doesn't seem to faze Annata, who skips into her bedroom. A few seconds later she returns, having thrown a zip-up hoodie on over her pajamas.

"Don't you want to wear real clothes?" Curiesay asks as Annata makes for the door, and in an unexpected show of manners, Curiesay opens it for her as they step out.

"Nope! It's my day off. I only grabbed this because the theater gets *really* cold," she responds excitedly as she runs circles around Curiesay. The two head to the rotunda and turn toward the Recreation Wing.

Curiesay smirks as her Steward bursts with youthful energy, zipping around her like an adolescent bird. A few Waifs pass by, dressed in their formals, and Annata exchanges a fervent wave. Her bubbly display draws some *curious* looks from other staff members, and while they aren't judgmental, Curiesay feels a sudden sharp urge to shelter this child.

"You sure are excited," she says, internally trying to temper her own spirits.

Annata grabs her hand and swings from it, drawing a flash of ire from Curiesay's eyes. "Of course I am! I thought you'd never come around!" she responds as they enter the theatre. "Oh, and I've been meaning to ask—what's your favorite color?"

* * *

The Pilot and Steward duo spend the rest of the day together in the Recreation Wing. Curiesay had been, up until today, hesitant to go there alone. The Third Floor is simply too big for her liking after having been cooped up for so many years in a dilapidating asylum. But she was willing to go with a...*friend? Is she my friend?* She supposes that she is. A friend of circumstance maybe, but a friend all the same.

They return late in the evening, having chided Frederic to simply give them an entire gallon of ice cream instead of bowls, to which he conceded with wide eyes. "It's very high calories, madams," he had said to their backs as they skipped away.

They return to Annata's room and share the couch, the two touching hips as they devour the gallon of Mint Chocco Chippy together. Annata put on some game show brain rot, in a language that neither understood, and they howl with laughter.

"Hey, I have a question," Curiesay says, turning down the volume a few clicks. "Since you seem to know everything."

Annata responds, the area around her mouth sticky with mismanaged confectionary. "It's true, I do."

"What are Scowls?"

Annata coughs bits of ice cream into the crick of her arm, speaking between spasms. "Why…ugh, why are you asking?"

"Just curious." *A little white lie.*

Annata regards Curiesay with wary eyes. "It's illegal to talk about it."

"Illegal? Why?"

Annata wipes her mouth on her pajama top. "Kinda defeats the purpose if I continue talking about it."

"I'm already in trouble anyway." *Okay, maybe two little white lies.* "I got caught watching a sermon from the Disciples of Willow."

The Steward turns her head to Curiesay, eyes wide. "You what? Why were you even watching that to begin with?"

"I searched for *Scowl* on my laptop, and it was the only result that seemed meaningful."

"Don't do that again. And *don't* believe a single word that they say. They're liars."

Curiesay has never heard the bubbly girl's voice so grave, but she opts to keep pressing. "I'll do what I want. I'm gonna figure it out either way, so you can tell me about *Scowls*—" Curiesay says loudly, prompting Annata to smack her knee. "Oh, should I not say that?" She draws in a deep breath, rolling her shoulders back.

"Okay!" Annata protests as Curiesay opens her mouth. "Okay, but you can't tell anyone that we talked about this. You have to promise me." Annata extends her hand and Curiesay shakes it with a satisfied smirk. "What do you want to know?"

"Everything."

"You don't know *anything* about them? Have you been living under a rock?" *Proverbially, yes.* Annata nods, quickly answering her own question. "For lack of a better word, they're superhumans. Incredibly resilient, exceptionally foul-tempered. Their bodies are denser than normal humans and it only increases with age. They can mimic any biological trait that they understand and become stronger the more that they learn. Each one presents differently, physically speaking, when threatened, and some even possess unique abilities, what we call their *Insigne Machina*, meaning 'notable machine' in Latin. Some think, and I count myself among this crowd, that they were the next step in human evolution."

"Were," Curiesay says slowly. "What do you mean 'were'?"

Annata exhales a defeated sigh. "They were thought to be myth for much of history, until one of them arrogantly made himself into a public spectacle, revealing his *Insigne Larva*, his Scowl form, in broad daylight." *Scowl form? Do they transform?* "Scowls were thrust into the limelight, in all their glory and grotesqueries. Mankind's leaders leveraged them for their own personal gain, using them as mercenaries. The results were..." she melts into the thick cushions behind her, "...catastrophic. Seeing the potential upheaval to the biological food chain, humanity hunted them to extinction. Men, women, children. It didn't matter. None were spared."

"The Culling," Curiesay whispers, recalling the word the Allsister used during her sermon.

Annata gives an exaggerated nod. "But they didn't turn out to be the boogeymen they were presumed to be. They were neighbors, lovers, friends. They were human. The few that managed to survive the Culling even fought against the Blight when it attacked, giving their lives for a species that hated them. So, in mankind's infinite shame, laws were passed to eliminate any mention of Scowls from every form of media. Like they never existed." Annata suddenly sits up and faces Curiesay. "I'll ask again: Why do you want to know this?"

"You were there that day. All of us were, but nobody has so much as mentioned it." Annata shakes her head in disapproval as Curiesay speaks. "I want to know how Arthur—"

Before she can react, Annata's hand is over her mouth. "Curiesay. Don't. You don't...understand."

Broaching this subject, and this subsequent moment, is the first time she's ever seen Annata's attitude fall into desperation. With great care, she puts her hands up in surrender, and Annata removes her hand. "I just don't get what the big deal is."

Annata lowers her voice to just above a whisper. "If word gets out that he's a Scowl, he'll be killed, or worse." *Worse? What does that mean?* "The Director trusts him, so I trust him."

Curiesay thinks that this girl is infinitely smarter than herself. She also thinks that Chandrima is a habitual liar and doesn't trust her as far as she can throw her. How Chandrima earned Annata's trust, let alone the trust of *anyone* she's encountered, she cannot understand.

But Curiesay trusts Annata. Moreover, she trusts Arthur. If he really is in danger, he must know. He put his life at risk, both by standing against her and by risking his exposure for someone he didn't even know. Curiesay isn't sure she would have done the same.

She doesn't respond to Annata's last statement. The pair sit in silence, the ice cream tub's dregs turning into sugar soup as it sits on the coffee table, and they watch TV until they fall asleep.

* * *

Late evening, October 3rd, 2053
Exclusion Zone

"You don't have to decide just yet!" Karima assures the girl. "I've memorized the book they brought me, so there's no rush." They've gone through hundreds of names, but the girl hasn't been able to decide on one. Karima

isn't sure she is even listening.

The emaciated girl, dressed in dirty and torn pajamas, nods, her jet-black hair falling in front of one of her eyes as she does. She runs the miniature brush through the doll's hair and cocks her head to the side. "Why are we doing this? Shouldn't we...brush our own hair?"

"Because it's fun!" Karima says with a giggle, tending to her own doll. "Didn't you have toys growing up?"

"No, not really. Just..." she motions to the dilapidated phantom apartment around her, "...what you see here."

Karima surveys the room. It's terribly unwelcoming. It could be anywhere, she thinks, where there is suffering. They're sitting at the table by the window, tucked in a half-nook. It reeks of stale cigarettes and body odor. And blood. "What, uh, is this place anyway? Why are we always here?"

"This is my home. Or was. And it is again, I suppose. There are no dreams for me. Only this, this...memory of hell." The girl drops the doll from her hands, letting it clatter to the dusty floor. "We're here...I'm here...because I'm being punished. This is..." The girl's eyes wander to the far side of the room, past the rotten mattress and the dated television, to a door. Karima had meant to ask her about it, about why it is adorned with so many locks, about why horror seemed to draft in from underneath. But the girl never looked at it, not even once, until now. "A bad place."

Karima speaks slowly and deliberately, her tone docile. "Why are you being punished?"

The girl stares at the door, lips trembling. "Because I won't bend to its will. That's why it left me in this city. That's why they don't come to visit me anymore. All...all I have is this. Every night. Forever. Because it needs me to see what it sees. It needs my approval. And I...can't give it what it wants."

"It?" Karima asks, watching the girl carefully.

"My Master. The Willow." A mighty upheaval strikes the room, sending

them tumbling off their chairs and onto the floor. The room quakes, an all-consuming rumble that leaves nothing for Karima to do but brace herself. The phantom boards squeal. The chairs topple onto their sides. It feels as if the entire realm they're in is being torn asunder and cast away into the abyss. Karima struggles to find her bearings as the girl scrambles to her feet, craning her head upward. "I won't say any more! I'm sorry! Please! Let her stay!" she shrieks.

As quickly as it had come, the quake is gone. Karima and the girl breathe heavily as they pick themselves up. "Don't ask me anything else like that," the girl growls through gritted teeth. Karima matches her gaze and can see a trace of the eyes she's seen so many nights in the physical world. For the first time, she's afraid of her.

"Okay, okay, I'm sorry," Karima pleads. "I didn't...mean... I just..." She struggles to find the words without broaching the subject again. She shakes her head incredulously. "I won't bring it up again. I just want to spend time with you." The girl solemnly nods as they right their chairs and sit. "All right," Karima says, clearing her throat. "We've done 'A' names thru 'C' names, now onto 'D.'"

"You're wasting your time. I can't decide. Why don't you just pick one for me?"

"Because it's your name! Most people don't get to pick their own, so consider yourself lucky!" Karima exclaims with a grin. "But the ones I've suggested so far are ones that I like. So, any of them that you pick, it'll be like I picked them too."

The girl looks at her, mustering a weak upturning of her lips. "Okay."

"I've actually been hoping we'd make it this far. I've been thinking a lot about you, and about..." Karima considers her words carefully, "...the path you've chosen. And what you told me proves it—you've never given up. Even with what you've been through. You still have light inside of you. You're choosing your own fate. This next name means 'to lead the way' or 'to guide.' It's for people who make their own way, and I think it

fits. You. Perfectly." Karima *finishes by enunciating her last three words, accompanying them with a matter-of-fact point of her finger.*

The girl's weak smile widens. It's the first time Karima has seen even the ghost of joy on her face. "I see. Well...what is the name?"

* * *

Clark can't help but revel in the contrast. Earlier that same day, the Yōulíng (Director Joshi's official designation for her) had gotten a whiff of another Blight in her territory. He should be used to it by now, but the sheer brutality of this frail woman was unbelievable. Slick with viscera, she had returned to her hovel, wet a shirt in a puddle from the recent rain, and wiped herself down like it never happened. He *had* to show the captain.

"Ugh, what is it? You lose track of her?" Pullhum groans as he rouses her from her slumber.

"Just come on," Clark whispers. He guides her to their spotting scope and motions for her to look. The captain lazily lays prone, taking a moment to let her eyes adjust.

"Oh my god," she whispers. "She's...smiling."

16

Move, Baby, Move

Chandrima has just arrived at the Observation Booth. Unlike most days where only the Stewards and Directors are present, today the booth is just as packed as it was during Parker and Curiesay's fight. Hundreds of lab coats, tiny Waif long coats, and camouflage uniform-wearing soldiers are in attendance.

Garrison Commander Cutter and Prefect Typher are present, the former wearing his fatigues, and the latter is dressed casually in jeans and a button-up shirt. They're standing behind the semi-circle desk at the front of the room, giving upturned nods to Chandrima as she approaches them.

"Gentlemen, good morning! Are you prepared to be impressed?" Chandrima bubbles, stepping up to the desk. She taps on the keyboard and logs into her terminal.

"Director Joshi, you had better hope that I am. I won't risk my soldiers' lives until you can show me that your *teenagers* can hold up their end of the bargain," Cutter says gruffly. Chandrima has always appreciated his bluntness. In their line of work, the stakes are always high, and she hates kiss-asses. Cutter provides the perfect forehead for Chandrima to press her own against.

Cutter waits for a response to his sharp-tongued statement, to which he receives none. "So…" he says, his tone a bit more cordial, "…how do you plan to show us?" Chandrima flashes a devious smile, like a child caught testing out the paint brushes they found on the spare television in the attic. Typher sees this and presses his thumb and forefinger into his eyes, rubbing them, as he steps up to the window. Zochitl is already there, watching the ruined cityscape in silence.

"You'll see soon enough," Chandrima says in sing-song.

* * *

"You guys don't think it's too gaudy, do you?" Curiesay asks as she, Arthur, and Parker walk down the long hall, dressed up to their necks in their Arbiters. Arthur's is still plain black, while Parker's is his usual navy-blue. Annata had taken it upon herself to have Curiesay's Arbiter painted during their day off, and hers is now a fantastic metallic purple with black undertones.

"No. I mean, maybe a little," Arthur comments.

Curiesay stops in her tracks. "I knew it! I need to go back." Arthur and Parker stop with her, having neared the end of the hallway, the latter rolling his eyes.

"Cut the shit, we have work to do," he says, motioning toward the Arena with his head. Curiesay vents a string of curses under her breath but does begin to walk, the three Pilots heading through the door to the Arena.

Curiesay has gotten used to visiting this space. It feels to her like discovering an abandoned shopping mall, stripped of its soul but still ripe for adventures, the musty smell inspiring fear and exploration. Denied this experience as a child, she has been thoroughly enjoying it as an adult. It's like a "rage room," except it's an entire city, and every day she gets to break something new.

Their titanium boots kick and crush rubble as they walk down the street. "So, what are we doing today?" Arthur asks.

"No idea, but…" Parker points to his left at the Observation Booth's window. Several people, including Prefect Typher, are standing up against it. "With an audience like that, I'm sure Chandrima has something fun planned."

Curiesay's face flushes red, the pores on her forehead seeping with anticipation. "Fun? Like the first time?" She makes a connection. "Oh! Think she's gonna tell us to beat up Arthur?" She taps the back of Arthur's armor—he smiles meekly.

"I doubt it. He can already use his Arbiter without Crossing," Parker responds as the trio continue down the street.

"Do you have any idea why? I mean, has this happened before?" Arthur asks.

"Our Arbiters are the Mark VI series. They were constructed using a novel technique which has lowered the threshold for syncing. I think that's why you're able to Pilot without a traditional Crossing. Hasn't happened before, *but* hopefully the next Pilots follow suit," Parker says. The three Pilots are still walking, approaching the center of the arena, a four-way intersection.

They notice something painted on the ground in the middle of the intersection. "Is that…an 'X'?" Curiesay asks as their speakers come to life.

"Good morning, my dears! I am so very excited for today; I have a team-building exercise in mind," Chandrima says through the microphone. Behind her in the Observation Booth are the three Stewards, sitting at their workstations. They exchange nervous glances upon hearing Chandrima speak.

The Pilots reach the intersection—below them, on the pavement, is a spray-painted giant red "X." "Shit," Parker curses.

"What's the matter?" Curiesay asks.

Parker grins with nervous skepticism. "Chandrima's idea of 'team building' is a bit unorthodox."

"Oh, Parker, you flatter me. Only Curiesay and Arthur are to complete this exercise, however. So, Pilot Parker, consider yourself an in-person observer," Chandrima follows up.

Arthur and Curiesay snap their heads to Parker, who lets out a terse chuckle. "Aww, what a letdown. Oh well, I'll be watching. Good luck!" Parker says light-heartedly as he waves. At the same time, four tendrils burst from his back. The ends of them manipulate themselves to appease his will, taking on a form like ice-climbing hooks. Looking up, Parker spots his desired vantage point atop the tallest building on this block, and with great force he leaps toward it. Nearly three stories up, he lands on the façade of the building and climbs at an astounding rate, reaching the twentieth story in no time.

Arthur and Curiesay watch as their comrade abandons them. Parker rarely asks questions, never seems surprised, and speaks to Director Joshi as an equal. They're used to his presence, giving the teenage Pilots a sense of security with his seniority. Now he looks down upon them from a great height, leaving them to the—what they perceive as *sinister*—machinations of Director Chandrima Joshi.

"The rules are simple; one of you will stand on the 'X.' When the countdown ends, you may move from this spot. Your adversaries will only pursue the Pilot who begins on the 'X.' You may disable or otherwise destroy your foes by any means necessary. Your goal is to survive for three minutes," Chandrima says through their speakers.

Arthur and Curiesay exchange worried glances. "So, when you say *survive*..." Curiesay says, leaving the end of the sentence open for Chandrima to fill in, which she doesn't. A dull humming noise approaches rapidly, and in a few moments, it is right on top of the two Pilots.

The drone stops ten meters from them, and ten meters in the air. Roughly one and a half meters across and one meter wide, the singular drone isn't all that imposing. It's held aloft by four propellers, and unlike when it is actively moving, it makes little noise while stationary.

"Is that…the only one?" Arthur asks skeptically.

It is not.

"Sixty seconds," the loudspeakers in the Arena boom.

* * *

"Don't you think that's a little overkill?" Cutter asks, eyes wide.

"Not at all. *Overkill* would be authorizing high-explosive rounds for live-fire training," Chandrima responds. Elva and Annata's ears perk up. They rapidly search through the Arena's cameras. One of them shows a great many blurs pouring out of a hatch high on the Arena's wall.

"Pilots! There's a *lot* more!" Annata yells.

"Aww! Don't ruin the surprise!" Chandrima responds un-seriously, feet stamping.

* * *

"Drones? Aren't those just, like, little plastic helicopters?" Curiesay asks as she eyes the seemingly non-threatening drone that floats before her.

"Not quite," Parker responds from atop his perch. The noise is overwhelming as the drones zip through the streets. The singular drone emits a mechanical buzzing sound, and a metal gun barrel extends from within its body, pointing forward.

"What the fuck? Are those real guns?" Curiesay asks aloud as more drones arrive and fill the airspace surrounding herself and Arthur.

"Of course not! They're *cannons*, and they're armed with high-explosive grenades that detonate on contact. So just don't let them hit you!" Chandrima responds.

"Forty-five seconds," the loudspeaker blares. The four streets around them are quickly filling with drones. Their propellers disrupt the air flow; they constantly bob back and forth as they adjust, with each new drone adding to the erratic air density.

"There's hundreds of them," Arthur remarks, eyes darting. In the booth, Annata and Elva can see their Pilots' heart rate and energy production begin to climb. The streets are abuzz with hundreds of drones, all fighting for a spot in the air. Arthur and Curiesay rapidly track and identify each one. The two still haven't decided who will be the target.

Arthur puts his fingers on his temples, wincing, then looks at Curiesay. "Okay, here's what we do. I'll cover you, and *you* stand on the X."

"How about you eat my ass with a spoon?! No way I'm gonna get blown up; you do it," Curiesay snaps back.

Arthur gives her a placating nod. "You're faster than me, I've seen it. Just focus on moving, and *I'll* keep them off your back." Unlike his usual timid tone, right now it is sharp and concise. Curiesay can feel this shift and blinks rapidly, ensuring it is still Arthur speaking to her. *He's been holding back.* She reckons he's just as fast as she is. *Why would he lie?*

"No, fuck that, *you* do it," she barks. She won't pass up this opportunity to watch him in action, let alone put *her* in a position where she could die. Her eyes, however, are not focused on Arthur.

She looks upward, viewing the incoming drones.

Before she can react, Arthur comes from behind and shoves her forward, directly onto the "X." She shoots him an incredulous scowl and is on the cusp of lashing out at him when she hears the drones simultaneously adjust their focus to her with a gust of air.

"You can kick my ass later," Arthur says flatly. "But I promise, I'll have your back."

It takes every ounce of learned willpower for Curiesay not to wring his neck at this very moment. She figures it's too late to do anything about it, and every second she wastes on him is a second she won't be preparing. But strangely, she has full confidence in his ability to keep her alive. If only she had that same confidence in herself. Stranger still is this sudden personality shift he's displayed. "Oh, you can count on that, fuckin' prick."

"You'd be best covering her from above," Elva says into Arthur's speakers. Much like Parker, Arthur's tendrils extend from his back, and he climbs the building nearest to the intersection. Curiesay watches him intently for a moment, and when she turns back around, she is astonished.

The streets surrounding her are filled with drones—she can see nothing but a swarm of metal. On the front of each is a spherical robotic eye, and the thousand or so of them are fighting for a view of her. All she can see in any direction is spinning blades, cannon barrels, and eyes. She looks skyward helplessly, the combined weight of the drones poised to crush her into the pavement.

"Thirty seconds," Curiesay's harbinger blares.

All at once, the drones chamber a round, their slides slamming home in a cacophony of metallic clicks, rattling Curiesay's teeth. Annata can see her Pilot's cortisol levels skyrocketing.

"You got this! Those changes we talked about yesterday, I'm implementing them…" Annata pauses, fingers dancing across her keyboard as she puts the finishing touches on her adjustment. "Now."

"Ejecting tertiary plating," a pleasant, yet unfamiliar, robotic voice chips into Curiesay's ear. She feels several dull thumps on the surface of her skin as the retaining bolts for some of her armor plates retract. Then, a flash of heat as they're ejected. Roughly one quarter of her plating, the smaller pieces on her joints and midsection, fall away. At the same moment, she nearly stumbles as her underfoot thrusters ramp up, almost lifting her off the ground.

"What...what just happened?" Curiesay asks as she examines herself, briefly taking her eyes off her adversaries. The same feeling of overbearing audacity as when she'd donned her armor that first day washes over her, filling her mind with a singular blindingly clear thought—*I can do this.*

"Less armor, less weight. Most thrust, more fast. Any other questions?" Annata says concisely. *Listen, you little shit.* Curiesay again curses her listening shortfalls but trusts her Steward's judgment. Kinda. Annata having that kind of control of her Arbiter concerns her. Her fear dissolving into abject determination—and the reason for the sudden change—makes her suspect that more than just armor plating has broken free from her suit.

However, she has more pressing matters to attend to.

She shivers as the veins in her neck and face thrust themselves against her skin, glowing brightly. Her irises flash to red and she exhales a lungful of steam as her body temperature shoots up. Whether she likes it or not, Curiesay stands in the center of the intersection, with a thousand unfeeling drones eyeing her with calculated anticipation, awaiting the line of code which will allow them to open fire.

"Fifteen seconds."

* * *

In the Observation Booth, the mood is electric. Like the final minutes of a football game, the crowd is bursting, eager to see how it will play out. Several groups have formed near the televisions or the main window itself. Zochitl grunts under her breath as a spectator accidentally bumps into her.

A group of soldiers stand not far from her, talking loudly as they lean up against the window. "So much for the *Pilot Regiment.* Guess we're not heading into the Exclusion Zone after all!" one says spitefully, his peers grinning with agreement.

"I'm kinda bummed. It's so boring here. I wanted to see some action," another says.

"And what a waste! Lot of money about to get burned in front of us. Could have used that money to buy us all new boots, and then some!" a third quips. He receives an elbow to his chest from another soldier who can see that Cutter isn't taking kindly to their remarks, his commanding stare silencing the group as he stands next to Chandrima.

She doesn't seem to be bothered by it, but when Annata makes the changes to Curiesay's Arbiter, the ear-to-ear grin she's sporting turns to tight-lipped shock. She snaps her head in Annata's direction, her cloudy brown eyes poised to burn a hole right through the young Steward. Annata shrugs innocently, as if she doesn't recognize the issue, and turns her attention back to her monitor.

The screens along the walls of the room show a variety of images, from the groups of drones to the empty streets a block over and, most prominently, Curiesay. Her fiery eyes and tooth-shattering scowl are front and center, the sweat on her face turning to steam as she smolders for all to see.

A collective gasp rolls over the room, Curiesay's wicked expression giving those in attendance a moment of pause. "Well, she's certainly intimidating," Cutter remarks aloud, shaking his head in impressed disbelief.

Annata shows her teeth with a vicious smile; though she herself may be small and unthreatening, the Pilot to whom she's linked is a fiery force of nature. She can't wait to see what she can do against impossible odds.

* * *

Piercing through the din of thousands of propellers idling, Curiesay's thrusters shriek to life. The intense heat tinges them bright blue as they gas off into the atmosphere. Crouching, she staggers to her feet, driving her toe-tips into the ground, coiling her legs beneath her and leaning forward on her fingertips.

"Five seconds."

She snarls like an animal having just recognized a predator that is too close for comfort—*flight* is the only option. She is poised to leap forward, directly underneath the mass of drones to her front. Wherever Arthur is, she hopes he's ready.

"Begin."

Curiesay explodes forward in a flash, the "X" being immediately engulfed in explosions. Dashing underneath the drones, a handful inadvertently fire upon their brethren, sending them crashing to the ground in twisted heaps.

Curiesay glides through the streets, her underfoot thrusters keeping her aloft just a centimeter off the ground. She feels impossibly light; losing twenty or so kilograms of titanium has her moving faster than ever, and the added benefit of "skating" across the ground preserves momentum. Unbeknownst to her, it also confuses the drones' targeting algorithm, as no living creature moves like Curiesay.

Like a great many birds of prey all seeking the same hornet as a snack, the drones pursue the deft Curiesay as she tears through the streets. Her backside is peppered with shrapnel as grenades consistently miss their target. In her periphery, she catches a glimpse of Arthur as he keeps pace, leaping from building to building. *Faster than you? My ass.*

She rapidly approaches an intersection and abruptly turns, driving her left tendrils into the corner building like stakes and swinging around. Although the drones *could* make the turn, there's simply too many trying to adjust their heading at the same time. Some rapidly slow to make the turn, and others crash into them, sending tens of them sailing down the far street that Curiesay just turned from.

The ebb and flow of their attacks tell her that Arthur is doing well— *He must be dropping ten of them every second.* She wonders if it'll be enough to keep her alive before one lands a lucky hit on her.

Breakneck speed. Approaching another corner, Curiesay turns hard, using her hand thrusters to redirect. She narrowly makes the turn. Glancing off the corner building, she bleeds her momentum fast. The drones zero in, their quarry having slowed. Her vision is consumed with fire, ears ringing. She dashes forward blindly to re-establish separation. As she emerges from the cloud, she crashes through a storefront at the bottom of a tall building.

The drones pour through the hole she created like a great many racecars screaming into the maw of a tunnel. Some are edged out and crash into the building's façade. Inside, Curiesay leaps and dives through the shambled clothing store, explosions sending burnt lingerie and wood splinters across her path. The low ceilings don't facilitate the movement of so many drones, and they begin to collide in their pursuit.

One crashes with such velocity that its ammunition case ruptures, causing a chain reaction of explosions—the line of drones light up like firecrackers. The plume of fire quickly overtakes Curiesay and her immediate pursuers. The building groans and lurches, the tired structure's back broken by a thousand straws made of high-explosives. It crashes down upon itself, taking hundreds of drones along with it as the rest frantically search the rubble dust plume for Curiesay.

* * *

The central display shows Curiesay's suit status, along with her current speed and a counter indicating the number of drones transmitting—the number drops rapidly when the building collapses. The soldiers up against the window are awestruck by the massive dust cloud. They look around, scanning for other surprised faces, for someone to make sense of what they're seeing. But anyone in a lab coat is simply watching intently, or taking rapid notes, as if this is just another day at the office.

"Nearly four hundred destroyed in sixty seconds?! What the hell are you feeding these guys?!" Cutter exclaims, his tone landing somewhere between scornful and lauding.

Chandrima chuckles. "Ask Frederic."

* * *

Arthur comes to a halt, strung up between two buildings by his tendrils. Two blocks are shrouded in dust and smoke. He wills his eyes to see, his Arbiter making them burn in their sockets. He can see the orange glow from the drones' exhaust as they zip around, frantically trying to reacquire their target. It's calm for a moment, and without knowing where Curiesay is, he is hesitant to throw another Gripe.

* * *

In the chaos of the collapse, Curiesay had climbed the side of a building and leapt into an open window. Third floor. Two beds, one bath. Persian rug in the living room. A trail of blood snakes down from her head, chest heaving. She is nearly at her limit, feeling as if she is suffocating. *It's been more than a minute. I'll just lay low until time is up.*

The incessant buzzing of the drones can be heard through the walls. Suddenly, the buzzing is *much* closer.

"Curiesay! They have thermal *and* X-Ray cameras!" Annata yells. *Yeah, I know,* Curiesay thinks as the drone bobs its way into the living room whose corner she has pressed herself into. The drone sharply turns, its mechanical eye sweeping over her. Her stillness has given the machine pause.

Curiesay, wide-eyed and nearly frozen, gives a wave worthy of a princess, slow and bland. "Um. He-hello," she stutters. Unbeknownst to her, Chandrima grins and waves back at the screen.

A passing drone is caught in the mass of debris ejected from the building as Curiesay is sent through the outer wall by a grenade detonating on her chest. *Aaaaand it's fuckin' broken.* Curiesay's poor damned sternum. It feels as if someone has struck her squarely over her heart with a sledgehammer. She's given no respite as the drones spot her and resume their pursuit.

Her tendrils slow her descent as she rolls onto the street and dashes forward. Hot on her heels, the drones fire away, peppering Curiesay's backside. The sound is overwhelming, the reverberations crashing through her soft tissues. *Just keep moving.*

She no longer feels confident enough to outmaneuver them, so she decides to try to outrun them instead. Curiesay skates forward at blistering speed, her rear thrusters shrieking out long trails of flames. Annata laughs nervously as she views Curiesay's current speed—two hundred and eleven kilometers per hour and climbing. Curiesay's rear thrusters emit so much force that any grenades that come close are tossed to the side or detonate prematurely.

"Curiesay, you won't be able to turn at that speed. The far wall is coming up quick," Annata warns. She's right. Curiesay, with drones in tow, is rocketing toward the end of the street and the Arena's wall.

"I don't want to turn. I want to go through *them*," Curiesay responds. Annata's nose crinkles, processing her Pilot's statement.

The drones have stretched their formation into a long line, the slower ones falling to the back. The entirety of their squadron is stretched longer than a city block. Narrowest at the front.

Light bulb.

Annata flips her notebook open and frantically jots out equations in sloppy, rushed handwriting. *Current velocity, acceleration, friction coefficient, combined weight, thrust, shock absorption, distance to wall.* "Okay, when I signal, start slowing down. I'm shutting down your cooling until then; the excess heat should overclock your thrusters," Annata says, viewing Curiesay's exact location on a separate screen.

Curiesay rockets down the street, the drones not able to keep up as their distance increases. Her thrusters scream with such fury that she worries she'll go deaf before long.

"Turn..." Annata prepares. Curiesay rockets toward the wall, every neuron screaming at her to slow down. "Now!"

The Pilot front-flips and twists her body in the air. Now facing her distant pursuers, Curiesay drives her heels and hands into the ground, ripping up the asphalt as she tears down the street. One hundred meters to the wall. As she slows, the drones close in, and without her erratic movements, their grenades land dangerously close to her.

"Arthur, move!" Curiesay shouts into her microphone, knowing he is likely directly behind the group of drones. Two meters from the wall, having bled all of her speed, Curiesay leaps, presses her feet onto the wall, and pushes off with all her might. The force she experiences is spiritually staggering—not only is she in disbelief that such a tremendous force can exist, but the fact that *she* is the wielder sets her heart aflame.

Her tendrils wrap around her like a corn husk.

Annata routes all her heat to her underfoot thrusters.

The two have created a living missile.

Curiesay crashes through the line of drones, her thrusters propelling her like a bottle rocket. Her teeth rattle as she impacts hundreds of them. The concussions are so violent it feels as if her bones will shake apart.

On Annata's screen, Curiesay's digital armor model lights up like a Christmas tree with damage. Bursting through the other end of the formation, Curiesay tumbles and dashes forward. She moves erratically, trying to confuse their targeting systems as she presses forward, but she has almost no strength left. Her body temperature is nearly ninety-five degrees Celsius. Arthur rains down upon the drones, with less than one hundred remaining.

Curiesay can tell that his attacks have slowed significantly. *There aren't enough left to shield me from him.* She takes a leap of faith, turns to face her pursuers, and skids to a halt.

She thrusts her tendrils in front of her, creating a solid shield the same size as her body. "Arthur, just finish it!" The pursuing drones stop and fire, hovering motionless. Arthur lets loose a furious barrage on the stationary drones. Curiesay disappears in a plume of smoke as the grenades detonate, and the last handful of drones crash to the ground in flaming heaps.

Curiesay hears the concussion of Arthur landing on the street and the footsteps that follow. She can sense that three of her tendrils have been blown off, and that her eyelids are heavier than even the strongest of sedative can boast. *It's so foggy,* she thinks for a moment, until she realizes that *she* is the cause as every joint on her suit pours steam, as do her heaving exhales.

She can hardly see Arthur through the fog, but he's there. Curiesay wants to be full of vengeful fury toward him, but she doesn't have the strength. And besides—*That was the most fun I've ever had.* As he materializes, a satisfied grin on his face, Curiesay can't help but smile back and give him a thumbs-up, even as her knees touch from exhaustion.

* * *

"With thirty seconds to spare! That's gotta be some kind of record, don't you think?" Chandrima says aloud as she turns to face Commander Cutter. Prefect Typher hears this and smirks, excuses himself, and leaves the room.

Cutter gives a half-hearted scoff, approaching the Director with his hand outstretched. "Don't know why I'm surprised. She's exceptional. They both are." They shake hands, with Cutter's calloused hand dwarfing Chandrima's. "All right, I'm in." His soldiers don't see this exchange, as they are too preoccupied with watching the crazed Third Floor staff jubilate around the room. Elva and Jordan accost Annata, lifting the Steward above their heads and tossing her into the air.

Unlike the rest of the staff, Zochitl stands motionless up against the window, having not moved a muscle since this all began.

* * *

"You're *incredible*, you know that?" Arthur says matter-of-factly as he approaches Curiesay.

She collapses to her knees, panting. "Well…you…also…" Arthur throws her arm over his shoulder and lifts her to her feet.

Parker drops down from his perch and walks to his comrades,

taking Curiesay's other arm over his shoulder. "Congratulations on surviving your *first* team-building exercise!" he says in a smarmy tone. The two carry the immobile Curiesay toward the Dock, stepping over burning drone carcasses. Curiesay has taken quite a bit of shrapnel to her face, and her Arbiter sacrifices what little biomass remains to heal her, the shards of metal dropping onto the ground as the wounds button themselves up.

"Arthur… Good…call…" Curiesay says, her breathing starting to come under control. They pass through the door into the Dock and bring Curiesay to her assembly area, propping her up as the technicians disassemble her Arbiter. Several of the plates have scorch marks. Others have been completely destroyed, showing artificial muscle fibers underneath.

After a few minutes, Curiesay is freed from her Arbiter, and she taps the two men to let her loose. "Boys, I need a shower. You're gonna have to wait outside," she says as she carefully walks toward the locker room at the far end. She's tired. She's hungry. She's ready to—*Goddamnit.*

Chandrima jogs up to Curiesay, throwing her arms up in celebration, with the Stewards right behind her. "Curiesay, that was amazing! You're unbelievable!" Chandrima puts her arms around her, her clothes getting soaked from Curiesay's sweat-dampened Interface suit.

"I appreciate that, but I stink. And I'm hungry. So let's save the celebrations for later. Also, please stop trying to kill me," Curiesay says, patting Chandrima on the back.

Chandrima tears up as she shakes her head, voice cracking. "No."

Curiesay pulls away from the eager Chandrima and trots to the locker room. As the door closes behind her, she isn't sure how she is supposed to feel. Her Interface suit grips her moist skin as she peels it from her body.

Did I...really do a good job? Everyone seems to think so. She doesn't feel that she's done anything special. In her mind, she's certain that Parker or Arthur could have done just as well, if not better. Her boisterousness seems to have been left inside of her Arbiter; or, at least, she thinks that to be the case. She adjusts the water in the shower to a lukewarm temperature—she's *much* too overheated for a hot shower.

Stepping in, she wonders if they're just playing up to her, padding her ego so that she falls in line, or holding their criticism so she doesn't verbally accost them. The water douses her hair, cooling her dry scalp as she leans her forehead against the tile. *Arthur...said that I'm incredible. He couldn't mean—*

The sound of footsteps cut short her train of thought. "The locker room isn't co-ed as long as I'm in here!" Curiesay yells as Arthur enters the shower stall opposite her, with Curiesay using the curtain partition to shield her naked body.

Arthur downturns his eyes. "Take it up with Chandrima, I don't make the rules. I'll just look the other way," he says cheerfully as he strips off his Interface suit and tosses it over the top of his shower stall.

Curiesay eyes him from behind her curtain. Normally, Arthur shrinks from conflict when Curiesay raises her voice or otherwise puts him off. Right now, he seems like he couldn't care less.

She can't help but notice the contrast between Arthur's normally meek personality and his body. He looks like he was carved out of marble, the striations of muscles seemingly bursting from beneath his skin. She has the brief notion that she is glad Chandrima didn't make them fight. Although she has never thought of him like that, Curiesay feels a pang in her nether regions as she watches him, ironically thankful that he decided not to respect her wishes. The water turns to steam as it hits his skin, rising to the ceiling.

He turns toward her, her eyes rising to meet his gaze before she retreats behind her curtain in furious embarrassment. "So, did you have fun?" *Maybe he didn't see me,* she wonders stupidly.

"If you call *almost dying* fun, then yeah," she responds nonchalantly. She showers in silence for a moment before Arthur speaks again.

"I left my curtain open, just in case," he teases, and receives a bottle of shampoo to the face for his troubles.

* * *

It wasn't five seconds after Curiesay left that Chandrima had kicked everyone out of the Dock, save for the Arbiters' technicians. Her cheery mood and signature smile were nowhere to be seen, and that was clue enough for her staff to quickly comply. Jordan had lingered by the door longer than the rest, but a stern glare from Chandrima shooed her away.

Annata watches the Director closely as the latter examines Curiesay's beaten Arbiter with the assistance of the Dock staff. "I know that it wasn't authorized, but just *look* at it," Annata says. Silence from Chandrima. She taps on the torso, and the workers quickly split it in half and lay it on the floor. "If I hadn't made those changes—" Annata implores before she chokes on her words.

From inside of the torso plating, on the back section, Chandrima carefully pulls something free. The technicians avert their eyes as she stalks up to Annata, eyes glaring. She holds it in front of her, so close that the girl nearly goes cross-eyed as she focuses on it—a single pale grey feather, tipped white at the end.

17

Comrades

October 8th, 2053

Bastion, Third Floor, Dwellings Wing

"Are you sure you'll be okay going alone?" Elva asks.

Arthur slips on his shoes and turns to face his encroaching sister. "I won't be alone. Parker and Curiesay are going with me."

Elva gives a curt grunt. "Yeah, I meant without *me*."

"I've lived on the Second Floor my whole life. I know my way around. We're just going to stretch our legs and show Curiesay the city, it'll be fine," he says as he moves to open the door.

Elva partially blocks him, eyes soft with concern. "I just want you to be careful with those two."

Arthur puts his hand on her shoulder. "I know they're a little… *rowdy*, but I'll be okay."

Managing a weak smile, she moves from the doorway. "Keep your phone on you, just in case." Arthur nods and the siblings embrace before Arthur leaves.

Just outside and leaning against the wall are Parker and Curiesay.

"Way to keep us waiting! You're a terrible tour guide," Curiesay teases. Since her arrival, she's had scant personal clothes to wear, opting for sweats on most days. It seems someone has donated some clothing to her, as she wears a yellow sweater tucked into her blue jeans, her poofy hair concealed by a dark beanie. Parker is dressed casually as well, wearing dark cargo pants, a plain green shirt, and a ballcap.

"Sorry, I had to convince her that you two weren't gonna jump me," Arthur says with a laugh.

Parker gives a lighthearted scoff. "Nah, that ain't me. At least, not when I'm not Piloting." The trio walk down the corridor, pass backward through the security checkpoint, and take an elevator to the Second Floor.

* * *

"Holy fuck, fuckin' hell," Curiesay squeaks out as the elevator descends and clears the Third Floor. The front of the elevator is clear, and as the concrete disappears from above them, they're revealed to be suspended hundreds of meters from the ground. The elevator runs along the angled wall of the dome, but is freely suspended in its carriage, keeping the bottom of the car level.

"Hell of a view, isn't it?" Parker remarks, his back pressed against the inside wall. The architecture below them isn't much different than the Arena but is larger by fiftyfold. With only so much room to lay their foundations, the layout of the Second Floor is highly efficient. No lot left unused. No building left unoccupied. The support columns here, which hold up the Third Floor, are completely covered by the buildings they support. Though roads cut through the city, there are almost no cars to be seen. City buses do most of the heavy lifting in the transportation department, and skyward trams run above the streets and through buildings.

Curiesay gulps, attempting to crush the handrail she grips. "Hard… to…believe…"

Arthur touches her hand gently with his, drawing her attention. "We're almost there." *He's…comforting me?* "Look there. Where those neon signs are? That's where we're headed." He points at the distant signs, their messages illegible from this distance. It's pre-dawn, and the lights from the city below provide the only illumination. Curiesay imagines astronauts must have the same view when observing cities from orbit. As they reach the same elevation as the nearby buildings, the view becomes less overwhelming.

The elevator car darkens as they reach the bottom, opening onto a wide sidewalk with hundreds of people ready to embark. The banks are fifteen-cars long, and it would be easy to get dragged along with the crowds if you're not careful.

Just beyond the sidewalk is a road, the few vehicles running on it being taxicabs. Curiesay spots them, face lighting up, and pushes through the crowd. "Oh! I know how to do this, I saw it in a movie!" she exclaims as she darts into the street while waving her hands, nearly being run over by a quick-witted driver with locked-up brakes.

"What movie is she talking about?" Arthur asks aloud and doesn't receive an answer. Parker is busy calming the curse-spewing driver with a few paper bills, nearly triple their intended fare. Curiesay is none the wiser, hopping into the back seat with excitement, followed by her male counterparts.

The taxi rolls forward, heading toward the center of the Second Floor. Curiesay peers out the window, her curious eyes absorbing all they can. This is her first time on the Second Floor, and *outside* of the Third—it is much larger than she anticipated.

* * *

The elevator has deposited the Pilots on the perimeter of this floor, where the civilian residences are located. They possess *some* flare—the occasional odd-set stairwell, a variance in the number and type of windows—but are largely "cookie cutter." The architects' top priority was to make room for everyone to live, while artistic liberties were put on the back burner.

The same can't be said for the innermost portion of the Second Floor.

The Arts Plaza consumes one fifth of the floor and contains everything from theaters to art galleries, museums to convention centers, concert halls, and even boasts a massive indoor park, complete with live foliage.

Less lively is the Government Sector, which counters the flare of the Arts Plaza with authoritarian architecture. Grey and imposing, Bastion's political and social organizers work here. Except for Prefect Typher, every representative is elected by Bastion's populace. Elections are held every year, and even popular candidates are voted out solely to keep the minds fresh. Politicians are relegated largely to ribbon cutting and press conferences, which most of them don't mind.

Aside from the aforementioned, the Second Floor houses all the amenities a person could want. Bastion was designed as if it were to be built on Mars. The best that mankind has to offer is on full display here, and Curiesay is soon to revel in the delight of Bastion's gooiest pastries.

As "day" breaks, Curiesay demands answers.

* * *

Curiesay rolls the window down and sticks her head out. "Whoa! What is that? It's so bright!" Light is cast down on the streets, a light that begins dull and yellow and then intensifies.

"That call it 'Hart,'" Parker says. "Humans don't do well without sunlight, so they designed it to mimic the sun's natural light."

Far above, half-mounted in the thick ceiling, is a massive orb, twenty meters across. It glows so brightly that Curiesay has to cover her eyes with her hand, and only accepts that this isn't the real sun when she again sees the ceiling above. "How come we don't have one?"

"Not enough vertical clearance on the Third Floor. 'Hart' and its sister reactor on the First Floor need quite a bit of room to breathe," Parker responds. Curiesay quickly draws her head inside the window, bumping it in her haste.

She rubs it with a wince. "Oh yeah, I guess it makes sense there's a First Floor too. Who—"

Parker cuts her off. "Soldiers. Farmers. Industry," he responds stoically.

"It must be nice to see the sun, huh, Curiesay?" Arthur comments, drawing her attention.

She's looking out the window as they talk. "It is. I've felt so cooped up since I got here." Though the Third Floor has plenty of amenities, it is isolated, dark, and unwelcoming. She felt as if its sole purpose was to keep Bastion's Pilots, and the rest of the staff, separated from the general populace. It doesn't even feel like the same city to her.

"I get it. Compared to this, the Third Floor is pretty lame. But now that we have three Pilots, we should be getting out a bit more," Parker says, looking straight ahead through the windshield, arms crossed.

Until now, Arthur has been peering out the window as the taxi trudges through the city. "Out? You mean, on missions and stuff?" he asks, turning his head toward Parker.

"That's the idea. We can conduct excursions into the Exclusion Zone now without risking too many military causalities."

"How do they feel about that? The soldiers, I mean. Elva said that the ones in the Arena Booth were watching us the other day and laughing. She said they seemed…spiteful," Arthur asks, and Curiesay turns her head to Parker as well.

Parker gives a long sigh. "They think we're freaks."

"That doesn't make any sense; they know we're on the same side, right?" Curiesay asks in a frustrated tone. *There's no way I'm gonna be painted as an outcast again. Not here.*

"It's not that they don't like us, they're just…*wary.* The discolored eyes, the tendrils, the…*aggression*… There's too many parallels to Class A Blights for them to ignore, I think." The cab slows down at a stoplight as they near the bustling city center. The streets are thick with people walking in every direction, with tall buildings rising from the concrete below on both sides of the street.

Arthur butts in. "Why are we so similar though? I mean, I've seen the pictures and the footage; we do kinda look like Blights."

***

Most of Curiesay's classwork has been, she thinks, bone-dry boring: land navigation; small-unit tactics; military history (*fucking yawn*); Morse code (*double fucking yawn*); basics of Arbiter operation. Five hours a day, seven days a week. She wonders if she can fit any more inside of her brain.

The only lessons she enjoys are the ones about Blights. They're shown grainy footage from the Calamity—*Fitting name for the Blight's war,* she'd thought—sixteen years prior, speculative research papers from top biologists, after-action reports from military commanders. Curiesay had never needed to know about Blights—and wasn't afforded much opportunity to learn before this—so much of this is new to her.

The Class C Blights are easily the most underwhelming. Almost entirely human-looking and adjacent, Chandrima says the Blight couldn't be bothered to alter their forms, opting to instead use them as numerous cudgels. They're heartier than the average human, but not by much. The majority of the Blight's victims are Class C rated.

Class B Blights, on the other hand, are an entirely different flavor of horror. Scientists speculate that the hosts must have had greater opportunities in their genome that the Blight took advantage of. It twists their bodies to suit its needs: shrieking, winged beasts that can strike down aircraft; canine-esque quadrupeds that attack in packs; pathogen-wheezing hosts that exhale infection into the air. Unlike the Class C's, Curiesay cannot imagine a world in which these Blights were *ever* human.

Then, there's their direct adversaries (as Chandrima had put it)—the Class A's. They can decimate a platoon of soldiers in minutes, and even if they're struck by gunfire, their bodies regenerate before they can be finished off.

Thick, raised veins on their skin. Tendrils. Capacity for violence. They're everything that Curiesay sees in herself as a Pilot. From the moment they'd appeared on the screen, she'd felt some sort of connection to them. What that connection is, she can't quite put her finger on. The exact question Arthur has just asked is something Curiesay has been thinking to herself every time she's in class.

* * *

Parker rocks his head. "I've told you before, the Arbiters were designed to mimic the abilities of the Blights. Humanity decided that the best way to combat the Blight is with hand-to-hand combat at *their* level, so they created the Arbiters."

"Cloned from Blight cells, right?" Curiesay asks. A skill she learned

253

underhandedly was how to "interrogate" people in a discreet manner. Inside of the white walls where she grew up, there were plenty of people with good hearts but bad habits. She knows most people aren't good liars, especially if asked a question flat out. A pang of regret is felt, but she pushes it down. She knows Parker lies to her, so she doesn't feel too bad about pressing the issue.

Parker's eye twitches. "Something like that."

"Chandrima has never said it flat out, but it is implied, right? I mean, we *do* look like them. Or they look like *us*," she says.

Parker doesn't budge. "The specifics of their construction are classified."

Curiesay motions toward Arthur. "Well, they can't be *that* classified, since it seems like you know more than we do." They both stare at Parker, who doesn't respond. Curiesay continues, her tone more curious than accusing. "I'm just saying. Kinda unfair that me and Arthur don't know if we're wearing Blight skin or not. Couldn't we get sick?"

"No. You won't get sick from wearing them," Parker answers flatly. Arthur seems uncomfortable with the conversation but doesn't interrupt.

Curiesay presses. "Are we immune in some way? Is that why we were selected to pilot?" Parker again doesn't respond. Curiesay knows he doesn't want to lie to them, because unlike Chandrima, she thinks he has a heart. Silence. *Am I...asking the wrong questions?* "Or are they not made from Blight cells at all?"

Parker snaps at her. "I don't want to talk about work all day! We're down here to relax, so just drop it." Curiesay and Arthur give reluctant nods and look back out the windows. *If he's that defensive, I must be on the right track.*

They ride in silence for a few minutes, feeling the gentle starts and stops of the cab, until they arrive at the shopping center.

They open the door to the cab and step onto the busy sidewalk. There are thousands of people: soldiers, businessmen, mechanics in mildly stained attire, all moving one way or another, in between each other and in between traffic. Curiesay has never experienced bustle like this—*I didn't know this many people even existed.*

This square of the inner city is entirely for restaurants: a traditional Italian kitchen which makes its daily menus a week in advance; a Korean barbeque with the aesthetic to match; a German brewhouse. Curiesay gawks at all the options she's never seen or had the opportunity to try. The scents combine and waft past her nose, curdling her stomach as they fail to complement each other.

"It's early, how about some coffee?" Parker suggests as he points toward a café with an outdoor patio, its tall façade being squashed by the gelato shop and the bakery that flank it. The sign above the door reads *Cup o' Dome.*

Arthur nods in agreement, nudging Curiesay as the three make for the door. "I've been coming here since I was ten. It's one of my favorites." It's rather busy inside, but it is clearing up, many of the patrons getting their orders to go—a caffeine pick-me-up before the workday begins. The vaulted windows and low lighting give it a cozy atmosphere, with dozens of seating options including tables, sofas, and lounge chairs.

Curiesay stands behind her counterparts, eyeing the long display of fresh pastries with a rapidly salivating mouth. Her uncle used to buy her baked goods when he would sneak her away, and she spots his favorite—strawberry shortcake, with fresh-cut strawberries glued to the top with whipped cream.

As the line moves forward, they're noticed by a young woman behind the counter. "Mister Adam Parker! In the flesh! And Pilots, what a treat," she says with an alluring smile. She eyes Parker in particular, straightening her slight shoulders as she grins.

Parker hesitantly waves. "Hi, Olivia. Are you going to let me pay this time?"

"Hmm…lemme think…" She touches her chin with mock contemplation. "No. What will it be?" Parker flashes a frustrated, yet thankful, smile as he ushers Arthur and Curiesay forward to order first, with himself going last. *Why is he so hesitant to be praised? It's like he's ashamed of being a Pilot.* When they're done, Parker pulls out a plastic card from his pocket, but the woman puts her hand up.

"It's a good thing you're handsome because you're awfully forgetful," she retorts with a wink. Parker blushes, turning away. The three Pilots find a secluded set of sofas near the back, a table in between. Parker sits in a recliner while Curiesay and Arthur take spots on the loveseat across from him.

"Hey, do we, uh…get paid?" Curiesay half-whispers.

"Yeah. We're not slaves. Have they not given you your card yet?" Parker asks.

Curiesay shakes her head. "If they had, I'd be down here more often." Parker nods in acknowledgement.

Arthur sits back, putting one ankle over his other as he scopes the café out. "You seem popular."

"I guess. She's one of the few who knows me. The Pilot Regiment isn't exactly *renowned*, but it seems…" Parker trails off, a newspaper on the table catching his eye. He grabs and opens it, his eyes glossing over the headlines. With pursed lips, he turns it to face his comrades, a bold headline printed on the front, along with a picture of Curiesay skating down the street of the Arena, the drones in hot pursuit.

NEW PILOTS SHOW OFF SLICK MOVES IN ARENA

"Well, I guess we are now," Parker says with a laugh. Curiesay takes the newspaper from him and examines it. Her dark skin conceals her subtly blushing cheeks—*I'm in the newspaper!*

"Why not? I mean, I've known about it since I was a kid," Arthur responds.

Parker shrugs. "There hasn't been much to know. It's been just me for a long time and we have had a few..." his eyes flutter, drawing Curiesay's attention, "...*mishaps.* I can't remember the last time the Regiment has been spoken about publicly." *Mishaps? Like when I tried to kill you?*

"So, what? They just pretend like you don't exist? What about the rest of the Third Floor?" Curiesay asks.

"The Third Floor does a lot more than just produce Pilots. It's basically the science arm of Bastion. But now that she has three Pilots, I think Chandrima wants to bolster our image, maybe try and get some more funding," Parker continues. A few tables over, the Pilots have a peeper. A young girl, eyes glistening with curiosity, watches them.

A waiter approaches the Pilots with their orders: coffee and a plain bagel for Parker, an espresso and a slice of coffee cake for young Arthur, and an iced coffee and a nostalgic slice of strawberry shortcake for Curiesay, as well as a separate tray of assorted pastries. Recognizing the café's good will, Parker attempts to hand the man a rolled bill, which he politely refuses as he excuses himself.

Their tiny spy has broken away from her mother's reach and runs up to the Pilots' table. "Hi," the girl says, having not thought any further than this moment.

"Hey! What's up?" Parker asks, exchanging his normally droll smile for a bright one.

The girl simply blushes and stares at him as her mother comes up from behind and scoops her up. "I'm sorry, she can't stop talking about you guys. They broadcast your training at her school yesterday."

Parker's eyes widen. "They *broadcast* it?"

"Um. Yes. It's been all over the news," she responds. The girl is fussing in her mother's arms, staring at Curiesay.

"Well, I'm Curiesay…" Curiesay motions to her fellow Pilots, "…and this is Arthur and Parker. So, what did you think? Pretty cool, huh?" she asks the girl.

"Yeah! You looked so mad. And then you were jumping around, and stuff was exploding, and there was a big whoosh and the building fell over!" the girl rambles off loudly, face alight.

"Well, I'm glad you liked it, it was a lot of fun!" Curiesay responds. The girl stretches her hand out to Curiesay, who looks to the mother for permission and receives it with a nod.

"Okay, well, it was nice talking to you all," the woman says as she takes her leave and returns to her table.

Curiesay notices Parker's smile dissolve into a stoic stare as he eyes the girl from afar. "You all right?"

"Yup," he responds flatly as he looks away, taking a sip of his coffee. The three make small talk for a while, with Curiesay asking non-stop questions about the Second Floor and Bastion. Arthur does his best to bring her up to speed while Parker opts to stay quiet, surveying the café as he drinks his coffee.

Eventually, two clean-shaven men wearing camouflage enter, glancing at the Pilots as they approach the counter. They order and are served shortly after, and approach the Pilots' table, with Parker noticing them first.

"Pilot. I hope we're not intruding," one man says as he motions that he would like to sit with them. Parker puts his hand out invitingly and the soldiers sit on a two-seat couch near the table. Curiesay perks up a bit—she hasn't met any of Bastion's soldiers yet.

"These are the new Pilots, right?" the other asks Parker.

"Yes, sure are," Parker responds shortly and motions for Curiesay to introduce herself.

"Hi, I'm Curiesay."

"And I'm Arthur."

The two men nod. "That's Stevens, I'm Martinez. I saw you two, yesterday during that…demonstration."

"Oh yeah? What did you think?" Curiesay asks.

The two men exchange glances and hesitate for a moment. "It was educational. I mean, we've had some missions with Parker, but I've never had front-row seats, so to speak," Stevens responds.

"Ah, well, you're not missing much. I'm the top Pilot, he basically works for me," Curiesay remarks as Parker rolls his eyes.

The two men nod skeptically, then look to Arthur. "You were pretty good too. Can I ask, how old are you?"

"I'm sixteen."

"What made you choose to be a Pilot? Most kids in Bastion sign up for the army once they are old enough."

Arthur opens his mouth to answer when Parker cuts him off. "Sorry, we can't really talk about selection stuff. You understand," he says flatly, and the men nod.

A silence falls over the group. Curiesay senses her need to instigate rearing its ugly head. "How do you two feel about Pilots? I heard the ones who came to watch us were pretty eager to see us fail," Curiesay says with what she thinks is an inquisitive tone but comes across as an accusatory stab. Parker, who had sipped his coffee a moment earlier, coughs, and coffee drips down his chin.

The two soldiers glance at each other before Martinez speaks. "I don't have a problem with Pilots, it's just…" Curiesay can't tell if he's searching for the words or for a nicer way to say that they hate her.

"We look pretty creepy in our suits, huh?"

The man hesitates for a moment before he speaks. "Something like that." She senses his tightlipped-ness, like a polite coworker denying that a peer's new outfit is in poor taste. White lies are a pet peeve of hers, as she feels they add pity to whatever insult has been neglected. Thinking herself shrewd, her speech picks up tempo, narrowly letting the man finish as she begins sentences anew. Her volume isn't of particular interest to the other patrons, but her tone is cutting, its antagonistic intent clearly identified by nature's most socially adept animals, drawing curious and cautious attention.

"Something like what?"

"What?"

"Should I speak up?"

"No, I just—"

"Just what? You can be honest, I'm not thin-skinned."

"You're just different is all."

"Aren't we all?" Parker's eyes are darting between Curiesay and the man, chasing the words from one's mouth to the other's ear.

"Not like that."

"Like what? You're being very vague."

"I mean, you're strong."

"That's good, right? You're a soldier, aren't you strong too?"

"Not like *you.*"

"Don't you want strong people on your side?" Curiesay's tongue dances behind her lips, readying itself for a swift retort. The man pauses, and Curiesay feels a pang in her heart. "You...do know we're on the same side, right?" she says, nearly breathless.

"Of course I do."

Unwittingly, her voice increases in volume. "Is it because we look like them?"

"I don't think you do."

"Well, don't say that. Of course we do!"

Again, the man pauses, his lips trembling as his mind races for a way to bypass the offense that has been dragged out of him. A second white lie. Shrewd isn't the word best suited for Curiesay's mannerisms—misguided is.

"It's not like we're *Blights* or anything!" she insists loudly. The ambience of the coffee shop drops precipitously, with ceramics shattering as people turn, neglecting their spatial awareness for an instant. Only the sounds of the percolating coffee machines now exists. All eyes and heads track down the source of the word, joints stiff and muscles tense. Parker nods to himself, massaging his eyebrows.

"It just seems unnatural is all," the soldier responds quietly. Curiesay's mouth is agape—nothing puts one's behavior into perspective quite like public humiliation. After a few moments, the ambience begins to well up, with patrons and staff continuing with their day.

"I'll let you three enjoy your time off," Stevens says. They stand and give a courteous wave to the Pilots, heading to a table on the opposite side of the café.

Parker runs his tongue along the inside of his cheeks. "We need to work on your social skills a bit." Curiesay's temper flares for an instant before embarrassment beats it down. *Way to make an ass of yourself on your first day in public, you idiot.* She drops her head, puts her coffee down, and leans back into the couch.

"I think she's doing just fine. She stood up for us," Arthur says abruptly. *That tone.* Curiesay's ears perk up. *It's him.*

"That's not what I'm saying—" Parker begins before Arthur cuts him off.

Arthur speaks matter-of-factly, cadence firm and steady. "We're not unnatural. We're gifted. We're going to put our lives on the line, right? There's no good reason to dislike us."

"I agree," Parker says, eyeing Arthur carefully.

Arthur turns to face Curiesay, putting a hand on her shoulder. "I'm glad you said something. You weren't rude, just upfront. No reason to be embarrassed." She looks up and meets his gaze. *They're different.* She stares into his green eyes, searching for something. Something that sways and burns behind his irises, but she can't make it out—it's like looking through a pinhole at the light from a distant star, so terribly bright, but nearly imperceptible.

Curiesay forces a weak smile. "Thanks. But Parker is probably right. I haven't been in *public* for my entire adult life. Spent too long around narcissists and sick people. I'm having trouble adjusting."

"No, Arthur has a point. You're a little rough around the edges, but you'll fit in just fine here. Just do me a favor and try not to yell the 'B' word out in public like that," Parker says.

Arthur gives a regal-sounding laugh and takes his hand from Curiesay's shoulder. "I think that's a good call." He turns away and reclines onto the couch. Something shifts within Curiesay, and she turns to face him.

Too often her ego would bluster in defiance or shrink like a child scolded, the two extremes of her rail-thin social skillset, but currently she feels vindicated. Not by his words, but by his presence. An impossible feeling bears down, a thick blanket caringly tucked over and under her, the indescribable embrace of acceptance. She feels that even if she were to shrink, he would see her all the same.

Curiesay always feels as if Arthur is holding his tongue, making himself smaller to accommodate those around him. But their battle against the drones seems to have lifted his spirits. As if the space that he is so wary to occupy is now his to do with as he pleases, regardless of what others may think of him. *I could get used to this. To him.*

Curiesay has been staring blankly at Arthur for an uncomfortable amount of time when she snaps out of it, realizing that Parker is watching. Arthur stares lazily out the window, feet crossed on the table, paying no attention to his comrades or where their eyes may have been.

Upon noticing Parker's eyes on her, her cheeks flush red for an instant and she quickly grabs for the remainder of not only her pastry, but several of the remaining pastries on the table. In quick succession, she compresses them with her hands and stuffs them into her mouth, filling her cheeks like a chipmunk—if chipmunks ate bear claws and lemon strudels. Arthur furrows his brow and turns toward her to ascertain why she would attempt death by pastry. She blindly grabs her coffee cup and downs the remainder of her drink, washing down the murder weapons.

"I eat when I get nervous," Curiesay says meekly as she taps her chest.

"Uh…okay?" Parker responds, his eyes narrowed with concern. *Distraction successful.*

Curiesay shoots to her feet. "Let's get outta here. I still want to go shopping." Her comrades nod in agreement and stand as well, with Parker discreetly leaving a tip under his coffee cup. The three Pilots leave the café, heading toward a long line of storefronts.

The trio spend the rest of the morning shopping and browsing, then return to the Third Floor after lunch. Curiesay heads to her room, carrying several bags full of clothing, jewelry, and electronics. It had been a long time since she had been able to choose what she wanted to wear, and as she put her clothes in her dresser, she smiles, reveling in newfound choices.

18

Checks and Balances

October 9th, 2053

Bastion, Third Floor

It's been quite a few months since Doctor Zora Manzurova has been on the Third Floor, and she doesn't mind that. Director Chandrima Joshi scares the shit out of her. Now, she's on her way to her office for unspecified reasons. Zora had chosen to forgo her morning coffee, as her heart is already trying to escape her chest.

She'd expected to be called up sooner, *much* sooner, considering what happened with the Class A she was supposed to preserve. Even if Pilot Parker had made the decision personally. Joshi doesn't approve of waste, and killing that Blight was certainly—in Joshi's eyes— wasteful. This morning, when Zora was summoned to the Third Floor by word of her boss, Giovanni, all the anxieties she'd since quelled in the wake of that day bubbled back to the surface. She's even gone so far as to write a farewell letter to her parents and left it on the counter of her apartment, though she's not sure if anyone would bother to post it for her should she fail to return.

And so, with all the courage she can muster, Zora strolls cooly down the corridors of the Third Floor to Chandrima Joshi's office, knocking softly. A voice instructs her to enter.

"Assistant Director Bottazzi, good morning," Zora says shakily as Zochitl's long figure greets her. *Shit.* Director Chandrima Joshi certainly scares Zora, but Assistant Director Zochitl Bottazzi provides a different kind of fear. To work with, and directly under, Chandrima Joshi requires a level of wherewithal and confidence that Zora cannot comprehend. Both of them being here doesn't bode well for her, she thinks. "Director Joshi, you'd asked to see me?"

"Thanks for coming on such short notice," Chandrima says cheerily. "Please, make yourself comfortable." She gestures to the couch on the far side of the office, and Zora reluctantly takes a seat. Zochitl plops down next to her, arm stretched behind Zora's back, legs crossed. Her proximity alarms Zora—her forehead perspires until her eyebrows are heavy with sweat. *I should have mailed that letter.*

Chandrima cocks her head and gives an innocent scoff. "Doctor Manzurova, if I were going to punish you, it would have happened already. You are here as our colleague. Isn't that right, Zochi?"

"Yes," Zochitl answers blandly.

Colleague? What could they possibly need from me that they cannot provide themselves?

Zora works in the basement levels of Bastion. Such levels are not technically secret, but they aren't spoken about commonly. Most people know better than to gossip about Bastion's most clandestine work. Researching a cure for the Blight requires "sacrifice"—as Chandrima Joshi had said when the studies began—and sacrifice they have. Thousands of captured Blights were preserved after the Blight's retreat, and in their desperation, mankind didn't allow itself any qualms about morality.

Zora had begun as a low-level employee, simply relegated to keeping the "patients" alive though their experiments, but she had shown, on more than one occasion, her disgust with the program as a whole. She received numerous write-ups for insubordination and sabotage—she purposefully pushed a tray containing vials of drugs onto the floor, shattering them to the dismay of the head researcher—and has often considered recusing herself from the position. She would, if she weren't certain that resignation would mean death.

"Why do you think that I've allowed you to remain an employee here despite your repeated attempts to hinder our research?" Chandrima asks. The question stuns Zora into silence. She's often asked herself that same question. "It is rhetorical, of course, because I know your true feelings about me. Even your home internet is monitored, by the way."

Fuck. Although Zora keeps her outbursts to a minimum at work, and doesn't directly speak about Director Joshi, she's made it clear to her family that she considers her a ruthless epistemophiliac—a person who obsessively pursues knowledge. She can feel Zochitl's arm resting on the back of her neck and wonders if she can feel her body shaking.

Chandrima smiles, but not in the way in which Zora is used to seeing. That is, perfunctory and fake. Instead, it looks…*somber.* "I don't disagree with your estimation. In fact, I think you're spot on. Back when I practiced religion, I knew I was walking the path of adharma. Do you know what that means? In Hinduism, it means I am acting in affront to the moral order of the universe. Someone like you is needed to provide balance. Otherwise, we are no better than our enemy. This fact is why you are here."

Zora feels herself relax ever so slightly. Zochitl's arm on her neck feels less oppressive and more inclusive, and when she turns to look at her, Zochitl returns a kind nod in the affirmative. "Um, well, thank you," Zora squeaks out. Feeling her confidence increase, she continues. "What exactly do you need from me?"

Chandrima brings Zora a tablet with a gallery of photos. The screen shows images of a Class A Blight, taken recently per the date stamps. She's skinny, starved, but sinewy muscles cover her body. A lamppost serves as a perch as she surveys the streets of a city. Crimson irises peer into the darkness—the whites of her eyes are not white, but obsidian black. "Meet the Yōulíng. She is our next Pilot. I need your advice in devising a plan to bring her back to us. To *humanity*."

Zora hadn't anticipated this. Not in the slightest. "Her eyes…" She thinks back to the Blight in the shed, how—unlike every other Blight they've seen—its irises were not only visible, but glowed bright red. "The one I met was the same way." *And she had exercised her own free will.* A bolt of regret strikes her. "You think we can save this 'Yōulíng,' which means we could possibly have saved—"

"Yes, but my Pilot made a decision that he deemed the most merciful, which is within his authority," Chandrima responds firmly, leaning against her desk, facing Zora and Zochitl. *I don't believe that for a second. There's a reason why you let him get away with something like that.* Zora recalls when she'd treated Adam Parker after his First Crossing, and wonders if Chandrima Joshi will ever forgive herself. "What would you have done if we could have brought her back?"

That question is something Zora has been obsessing over since it happened. Since the outbreak, doctors have been treating the Blight's sickness as a physical disease. It does indeed alter the host's DNA by adding a third strand of its *own* DNA to the mix. This fact alone—that is, the fundamental transformation of what makes us human—is why it's theoretically impossible to cure the infected. Humanity simply doesn't have the technology to alter the DNA of the trillions of cells that make up a human being.

But on the fringes of the scientific community, another theory has been gesticulating. A theory that the Blight is a sickness of the *soul* as well as the body, and that is something that Zora is personally subscribed to. "Using Pandora's blood transfusions *always* causes severe internal burns, with death following shortly after. But during the autopsies, the affected cells were indeed cured of the infection. I think that *after* death, the body isn't so resistant to change. That means the host is actively fighting against the cure. If we can also cure the soul at the same time, we may be able to cleanse them all at once. We need to access her Dominium Animae."

"We already have," Zochitl says abruptly. "Our Waif reports spending time with the Yōulíng in her Dominium. She seems to think she is seeking connection, though she hasn't had any sort of breakthrough."

"She's *speaking* to her?!" Zora shouts. Chandrima's admonishing eyes quickly adjust Zora's tone. "I mean, that's unprecedented. But then again, the one I treated spoke to Pilot Parker." She again wonders if killing that Blight was really the right thing to do. "Even so, it'll take more than conversations with a Waif to free the Yōulíng."

Chandrima nods in agreement. "So, what will?"

Part of Zora's duties involve interviewing and treating people left behind by the Blight. When the Blight fled, millions of hosts were left in its wake, their bodies shutting down in the absence of the Blight's signal. A few hundred thousand of those survived, albeit with severe physical, mental, and spiritual wounds. Their bodies provided no clues as to how other humans could be cured, but their recalled experiences did give some insight.

A German man by the name of Alden Einrich was one of these *Discarded.* Zora can still hear the sickening sound of his nails scraping his skin—a nervous tic he displayed when discussing his experience as a Blight. *I'm not supposed to talk about this,* he would say during their sessions, as if his prior master would hear him. As a young man, he saw abhorrent things during his time in the army. Regret weighed heavy on him.

He couldn't recall how he was infected or what he had done up until the point of release, but his spiritual experience was described in vivid detail. A voice implored him to concede. To dissolve. To meld. Horrors from his past played on repeat in his mind, as vibrant and real as they were when he experienced them. The moment when his squadmate Stefen, legs obliterated by mortar fire, bled out in his arms. When Alden had killed his first enemy who he swore looked just like the young boy at the bakery in his hometown. He drove a knife into his neck and apologized in tears.

But unlike those very real experiences, the Blight showed him something else.

A medic applied tourniquets to Stefen's legs in time, and they were able to bring him to the field surgeon, saving his life.

The boy from the bakery surrendered before Alden's knife struck, and he was taken as a prisoner of war.

The voice's bargain was clear—*Give unto me your soul, and I shall absolve you of your suffering.* Alden, like the billions of others, conceded. Of this confession he was most embarrassed, and begged Zora to burn her notebook after the session. She told him that she couldn't. He was found hanging dead by the neck in his apartment one day, his fingernails stuffed full of bloody skin.

Zora wonders if the Yōulíng is experiencing the same thing.

"Their 'master,' for lack of a better word, coerces the infected to do its bidding. The ones who don't comply experience..." Zora searches for a word to describe the horrors of relieving your most sickening moments for eternity, but comes up short. "Hell. They are terrified of the pain and will do anything to avoid it. Their loss, their sorrows, their suffering. It's a sickness of denial and shame, and the only way to free them is to make them face their fears."

There's a long pause as Zora finishes, her words left hanging in the stale air of Director Joshi's office. A smile forms on Chandrima's lips, a sly one, but not without a tinge of satisfaction. She keys the intercom in her desk. "I need coffee for three, and some lunch," she says cheerily. Zochitl stands, stretching her arms high to the ceiling as she pats Zora on the back. "Get comfortable," Chandrima chirps. "The three of us are going to be here for a while."

* * *

Dwellings Wing

Standing at Arthur's door, Curiesay waits. She has just knocked, and bangs her fist again, more obnoxiously than the first time. Nothing. She lifts her hand a third time, preparing a barrage, when the next door over opens.

Elva peeks her head out. "I think he went for a late dinner."

It's almost eight. "We had dinner a few hours ago," she retorts impatiently.

Elva laughs, leaning out of her doorway. "He gets hungry before bed. Do you need something? From him?" *Yes. I need his time.*

Again, too much free time eats away at Curiesay's sanity. They had classes earlier today, and some sparring, but were cut loose early. Besides having dinner with her fellow Pilots and Stewards, Curiesay has been alone in her room nearly all day.

"No, I..." *Don't open up too much.* "I'm just bored."

"What about Annata? Isn't she right next door?"

Curiesay rolls her eyes. Annata has barely interacted with Curiesay since her battle with the drones. *I think I'm coming down with something,* Annata had said before bailing on their prior made plans to see a new action movie. She's embarrassed to admit—to herself or Elva—that she is feeling quite lonely. "I see her all the time."

"You see Arthur all the time too," Elva says, some teasing in her

270

voice. Curiesay flushes red and turns to walk down to her room. *Fuckin' bitch.*

"But! You don't see me very much," Elva begins, stopping Curiesay in her tracks. "We haven't had much time to get to know each other. So why don't you come in and hang out?" Elva says, gesturing for Curiesay to enter.

Curiesay brushes past Elva as she enters her room. "I mean, I *guess.* Since I'm already here."

Elva is right—they haven't had much time to talk together. The most interaction they've had was when Elva pulled Arthur out of Curiesay's room, and she hasn't forgotten. Curiesay can see that there's *something* more to Arthur than he lets on, and she suspects his sister is helping him cover it up. *If she wants to play nice now, I'll be sure to get something out of it.*

Curiesay looks around critically as Elva eyes her. "Are you all right? You don't have to stay if you don't want to." Elva sits on the couch and pulls the small table in the center toward her. On the table are a handful of pencils, a pink eraser, and an open sketchbook.

"I haven't really been around people that I wasn't forced to be around for a long time. Still getting used to the freedom I guess," Curiesay responds as the sketchbook catches her eye. She takes a seat across from Elva and studies the present page. "Whoa, that's... Is that Arthur?"

"And you too! Way down there, see?" Elva says as she places her finger on the sketchbook. On it is sketched a bird's eye view of Arthur and Curiesay's battle against the drones. The subject is Arthur, slightly to the left, the view of his back, his tendrils extended and in various stages of throwing. Under Elva's finger is a smaller figure, Curiesay, who's skating across the streets, the drones in hot pursuit.

"That's cool. Did you go to art school or something?"

"No, just self-taught. I drew a lot as a girl, and I guess it just stuck.

Do you draw?"

Curiesay shakes her head lightly. "Uh, well, not really. My uncle tried to teach me, but I was never any good. The institution only allowed crayons, which sucked. Eventually I just stopped altogether, years ago."

"How long were you there?"

"Since I was eight. I was there for ten years, apparently. Annata told me I'm seventeen, so I guess that makes sense."

"You didn't know how old you were?"

"I never thought to keep track. I figured if I needed to know how old I was, they'd tell me."

"That's...sad. Birthdays are the best days of the year. It's a time to celebrate yourself."

"There's nothing to celebrate about me," Curiesay says dejectedly. *Don't let her in, you idiot.*

"Well sure there is, everyone has things about them that are worth celebrating."

Curiesay presses. "Like what? What do I have?"

"I mean, I don't know you that well, but you're really strong, I've seen that much."

"Yeah, well, I want there to be more to me than just breaking things and people," Curiesay responds with a scoff, and a short silence falls over the two. "I'm sorry...for being shitty. I'm still getting used to people being nice to me."

"It's okay, no offense taken," Elva says.

Curiesay's interest in getting to know Arthur has made her *very* aware of how Elva carries herself. She's polite, but hollow in a way. Like she seeks to avoid conflict because she thinks it's beneath her. During their classes, Elva spends most of her time preoccupied with what Arthur is saying or doing. Curiesay wonders how much she really knows about him.

"So, what else have you sketched?" Curiesay asks. "Do you have, like, a binder or something?"

Elva's face lights up. "I do! Lemme get it." She springs up and moves hurriedly to her room, returning a moment later with a brown leather bag with pouches on the sides and a long strap. She excitedly places it on the floor by the table, pulls a handful of papers out, and lays them out on the table.

The first one is in color, and shows a blue bird perched on a young Arthur's shoulder, the green grass in the background brightening up the sketch. The second is black and white and shows Arthur running across a baseball field and sliding into second base, narrowly avoiding the tag. In the background, Curiesay can see what looks like Chandrima, face pressed up against the fence as she cheers.

"Wow, you're really good. Are…these all of Arthur?"

Elva stutters, cheeks red. "Um, no, not… I mean, a lot of them are, but not *all* of them." Curiesay looks at her with amused skepticism. "Mom wasn't around much when we were kids, so we spent a lot of time together."

"I see. What's this one?" Curiesay asks as she points. It shows Arthur deep in a lush forest, crouched down and watching a deer drink from the creek.

"He really likes animals. He always wanted to go into the forest and try to catch glimpses of them. We had walked to the creek and saw this deer about to take a drink when we hid behind a tree. We watched it for a few minutes, and then it walked off. Arthur talked about it for *weeks*."

"I take it that you had a lot of animals at home then?"

"No, Mom didn't…" she pauses, clearing her throat, "…let us keep any animals in the house. I remember…" Elva starts with a chuckle, "…Arthur snuck a bird in once when he was young. He kept it in a little box and put a bottle cap in there as a water dish. He made me promise not to tell our mom, but, of course, the bird was loud, and so he only managed to keep it for a few days. I still remember him standing in front of the closet after mom heard cooing and confronted him about it. He told her that he was 'just practicing making bird noises.'"

Curiesay gives a huff laugh. "Here, let me help you put these back," she says as she grabs the pages and carefully aligns them with each other. Elva slides them into her leather bag and stands up to bring it back into her room when the side pouch opens and tens of drawings pour onto the floor.

"Oh shit," Elva says, dropping to her knees and frantically collecting the papers. Curiesay crouches down, ready to help.

"No! I mean, I've got it," Elva says quickly as she scrambles to put all the sketches away. *Why so panicked?*

Curiesay steps back, looking downward. A corner of a crumpled piece of paper is sticking out from beneath the couch. As Elva is preoccupied, Curiesay discreetly grabs the paper and examines it.

It's folded, brittle. Curiesay carefully unfolds it. The drawing is crude, done in crayon. In the center is a black figure with what look like twelve snakes coming out from its back. Surrounded by...black streets. *Bloodied* streets. Surrounded by *bodies.* Its head is unnaturally drawn. It almost looks like a goat's head, or something else with horns.

Elva snatches the paper from Curiesay's hands with a yelp. "Not that one!" Elva takes a step back, eyeing Curiesay down. *Was that Arthur too?*

Curiesay's eyes twitch as the two women lock stares. "Okay, well, thanks for showing me those. See you around," Curiesay says flatly as she leaves. Elva stands motionless, holding the drawing in front of her face, her eyes welling with tears, before finishing her cleanup and stowing her bag in her room.

* * *

Excerpt From 'The Waif's Handbook'

You won't mistake, if you see a Scowl,
Long dancing snakes, an expression most foul.
Bright red eyes, which glow in the dark,
Wicked, sharp, they don't miss their mark.
You'll feel a pit, you'll feel a chill,
With masks of bone, all submit to their will.
They are not friends, they are not foe,
If you see one, this you should know;
You do not run, you do not fight,
Avert your eyes, lest they be your last sight!

* * *

Early morning, October 10th, 2053
Exclusion Zone

They have made Hotel Narach their temporary home and have become exceedingly comfortable here. The two soldiers have done a significant amount of fortifying. Blockades. Booby traps. Motion sensors that Bastion sent, notifying them about movement in the sensor's range.

Having taken every opportunity to watch the Yōulíng, Karima has become skilled at operating the equipment, and her note-taking is already comparable to a college-level writer. As such, she watches her often.

Sometimes she sleeps. Sometimes she hunts. Most times, she sobs. Karima wants nothing more than to reach out to her in person, but she knows that what they share in her dreams is *not* how it would go in real life. Best-case scenario, she would flee the city.

Their courier, Ursula, had arrived the prior evening, and Corporal Clark is currently putting her harness on. Well, he's *trying* to, as Ursula seems more interested in cleaning the inside of his mouth. He spits repeatedly as he uses his shoulder to hide his face, hooking up the dog's harness blindly. Captain Pullhum glances over with amusement, sitting on the couch as she finishes up her written report.

"Geez, get a room," she says with a chuckle. Clark shoots her an annoyed look, then turns his attention back to the dog. He installs her reusable bladder, filled with fresh water and hooked to a tube that hangs near her mouth. It isn't much, only one liter, but enough to keep her going if she isn't able to find fresh water on the way back to Bastion.

Pullhum hops to her feet, rolling up the papers she had been dutifully scribing, and inserts them into a waterproof plastic cylinder. "Here, all done," she says as she walks over to Clark and the dog, who are near the door. He takes the tube and tucks it into the pocket on the harness of the same shape, zipping it shut.

Clark grabs a can of sausages and peels the top open. Ursula wiggles with excitement, but whether it's because of the sausages or the imminent night of running through the wilderness, the soldiers can't tell. "That's a good girl," Clark says as he firmly pats Ursula's side, watching as she inhales the pork links. They give her plenty of attention while Clark feeds her as their Waif lays prone by the window, keeping an eye on their quarry.

*

I think they're coming soon, friend. Just hang in there a little longer. It has been about three hours since the Yōulíng had fallen asleep, and Karima is feeling restless. Although she enjoys keeping an eye on her, she doesn't prefer it when she's sleeping.

Corporal Clark had told her that he'd take over once Ursula was on her way, and she can hear them praising her just a few meters behind, so it won't be long. Normally she wants to see Ursula off, but her friend has been tossing and turning, sweating and gasping. Karima knows she needs a friend and doesn't want to hold up their courier on her way out.

She isn't supposed to—as it is classified—but she had peeked at the last batch of orders from Bastion while the captain was sleeping. Talk of "making contact," "exact positional coordinates," and "landmarks" tells her that they're making a move soon.

She has hardly been able to sleep, like a young soul anticipating Santa Claus on Christmas Eve. Except it would be Pilots, and they would (likely) have to beat her into submission. *The city will rattle.* It won't be easy, but she is looking forward not only to returning to Bastion, but to seeing the Yōulíng safe and warm. She doesn't know if it's possible to cure her, but she assumes that's the plan. Hopefully, she thinks, she won't just be a prisoner to another master.

They're standing up. She hears the rustling behind her, the latch of the lock, as they prepare to open the door to their hallway and set Ursula on the path to Bastion.

The Yōulíng moves. Karima screws her eyes in tightly on her. She lies in a pile of dirty linens inside of a laundromat, and Karima can see her hand lifting. She often rustles in her sleep, but this is different. It looks like she's pointing—

* * *

Wooden floors. The smell of cigarettes. Body odor. Karima looks around frantically, finding herself in this strange, yet familiar, space. It's the same room, but something is different. Something is rotten.

The door that the girl won't look at rattles against its lock. "Please! You have to let me talk to her!" a voice sobs repeatedly from the gap underneath the door. The door shakes—something inside is desperate to get out.

Karima approaches slowly. Something is wrong. So wrong.

As she reaches the door, it falls silent. Such a silence that makes Karima's ears scream; a silence that empties her mind out from negative pressure. She lowers herself down, lying on her stomach, and peers under the door.

Dozens of black eyes peer back at her, fighting silently for dominance, for the right to look at Karima. "Where...where is she?" Karima whispers.

And they whisper back. Imperceptible at first, hardly more than a distant pin drop. But they rise. Before long, she can hear them talking over one another. She listens closely, trying to pick out the girl's voice from the cacophony.

The angel! He knows! Hush. Don't tell. We won't tell. You're like us. You could be one of us. He knows! No. Yes! Betrayer. Listen to me! Do you like it here? We do. It's nice here. Don't listen to them! All good piggies like it here. Are you a good piggy? Do you want to be? Don't listen to them! We could ask. Nicely. Listen to me! She lies. She belongs with us. All good girls do. Are you a good girl too? KARIMA, LISTEN TO ME!

Karima scrambles to her feet as the door flings open. The girl is there, a specter given form by a lungful of dust. For the first time, Karima sees her as she truly is: a ghoulish, wretched little girl. Skin and bones. Hollow eyes. Hollow soul. As tears well in her eyes, she grabs Karima, shrieking.

"He's coming!"

* * *

A tremendous crash snaps Karima from her trance as she flips over from her prone position and looks behind. The staccato report of gunfire pierces her ears for an instant before she's misted with blood. The tussle has knocked their electric lamp onto the floor, pointing its light toward Karima.

She can vaguely make out the figure of *something* past the light, obscured by darkness and dust. Holding her hand out, she covers the light and watches the figure as it walks from the doorway to what remains of their makeshift living area. The dividing wall between the kitchen and living room is just rubble now, and the being steps over it, reaches into a bloody hole in the wall it had created, and pulls a dripping corpse from it. Beyond the viscera, Karima can see the drinking tube from Ursula's harness hanging down from the mess.

This can't be happening. Karima remains perfectly still, too well illuminated to move without being spotted. She studies the room as the being does...*something* to Ursula. *Where are they?* Her eyes continue to search in vain for a moment too long. A moment she wishes she could take back. While there is no sign of Corporal Clark, Karima locks eyes with Pullhum, who is crawling on the floor.

No. Not crawling. Staring, blankly. Not at Karima, but at some spot on the wall behind her. Karima's eyes frantically search for the captain's body, but only the head exists, her eyes resigned to staring at that spot until time rots her eyes out from her skull. Karima purses her blood-misted lips. *Pennies. Oh God. Not like this.*

Giving it a few shakes, the being breaks the mangled corpse loose from the leather harness, with what remains of Ursula falling to the floor at its feet. Up until now, Karima has been frozen. As the being turns to face her, she can no longer pretend like she hasn't been noticed.

"Shame!" she shrieks as loudly as her lungs can manage. She scrambles backward onto her feet, picking up the spotting scope and throwing it toward the being, only able to see its outline as the lantern's light blinds her. The scope thumps against the being and clatters to the ground as it steps toward her. Her training takes over and she does the only thing she knows to do against the Blight.

"Shame! Shame on you!" she continues, throwing the tripod, her canteen, her knapsack. The being walks, footfalls nearly silent—Karima can feel the dull thuds of its weight. With a crunch, it steps on the lantern, crushing it and descending Karima into near-total darkness, her eyes still adjusted to the bright light. All that remains for her to despair are two piercing red eyes, glowing in the blackness, nearly as high as the ceiling.

Karima covers her eyes, her scolding unceasing. "Shame! Ashamed of yourself! You should be ashamed! Do you hear me?! You should—" The being grabs her face, its hand so large that its fingers touch behind her head as it lifts her off the ground.

"Oh, child," it says in a deep, somber voice. Karima's muffled scolds can still be heard as she kicks and scratches at the arm that suspends her. "I am."

19

An Intimate Experience

October 11th, 2053

Bastion, Third Floor, Medical Wing

"Today, you will be exploring Arthur's brain!" Chandrima declares with maniacal theatrics, throwing her arms open. Curiesay stares at her, perplexed. "What?"

Zochitl is off to the Director's side and speaks up. "More precisely, his *soul*."

"What?!" Curiesay repeats loudly. The Pilots and Stewards sit in two rows of chairs across from the Directors. Unlike most days, they are in a different room altogether. Nearly identical to the Observation Booth, instead of a large window, there is an enormous glass-walled room to the front.

"When you're properly synced with your Arbiter, you can enter a spiritual state where your mind and body occupy two different places. We call this a Pilot's *Dominium Animae*, Latin for 'Domain of the Soul,'" Zochitl says. Curiesay thinks back to her Crossing, to what she had seen, and *who* she had seen. She glances over at Parker who motions to the Directors with nod of his head. *Did you know*

281

about this?

"I remember… Parker was there. When I Crossed, I saw him, or, he saw me," Curiesay recollects. Her tone pivots sharply. "And I didn't like it."

"Well, it's a good thing that *you* won't have to share anything. How Parker entered *your* Dominium is exactly how you will enter Arthur's," Chandrima says.

Elva stands so violently that her chair topples over. "Why does it have to be Arthur?" Arthur stands as well, tapping her arm gently.

"We have a mission that requires the navigation of a Dominium," Chandrima says, stepping up to Elva. The young Steward doesn't falter as she meets Chandrima's eyes. "Arthur is the only one we haven't confirmed as having entered his Dominium, so he needs to prove his competency."

Much like her brother, Elva is normally quite reserved and proper. "Please," "Thank you," "May I." A young professional. Unlike the snide Curiesay, the unflinching Parker, or the hyper Annata, Elva's demeanor is a sort of demure self-assuredness. No bluster. No need for validation.

Right now, however, her tongue has sharp edges. "When was his competency ever in question?" Elva baits.

Chandrima doesn't bite. "Elva, your brother can't perform his duties safely unless he is experienced with all aspects of Piloting."

"He has been this whole time. This spiritual bullshit has nothing to do with killing Blights."

"You're right. It has to do with saving one," Chandrima says virtuously.

"Saving one?" Arthur butts in, brushing in front of his sister. "You—you want me to save someone?"

Elva scoffs at his undermining. Chandrima speaks to the impassioned Arthur, ignoring his Steward. "That's right. A woman. She's in the Exclusion Zone, infected with the Blight, and she needs your help," Chandrima says, ennobling him.

Elva reaches her arm across Arthur's chest and urges him back. "Arthur, she's playing you."

"How so?" Chandrima asks smarmily.

"You know he'll go along with whatever you want if you make it seem *righteous*."

"But she said someone needs my help," Arthur butts in.

"She says a lot of stuff," Elva spits back.

Chandrima locks down her tone the best she can. "And I'm telling the truth."

Elva scoffs. "That'd be a first."

"Elva, stop. I want to help," her brother implores.

"You don't under—"

The Director interrupts her loudly; it's two versus one. "I can't believe you have so little trust in me, dear Elva."

"And I can't believe *you* have no issue with messing with your nephew's head, *Aunt Rima*." A beat passes as the arguing trio absorb Elva's last statement.

This moment is all that Zochitl needs to step in. "Steward, if you continue to interfere, I will see that you are removed as Arthur's Steward and replaced with one more compliant with our orders," she imposes as she steps between Chandrima and Elva, towering over the young Steward. "This is not a place for family quarrels. Lives are at stake, and I cannot allow you to jeopardize our work with your petty reservations." Elva trembles in stunned silence as Zochitl's presence and words reduce her state to that of a disobedient child.

Squeezing between his sister and Zochitl, Arthur moves slowly and purposefully. He raises his hand, fingers extended, and silently presses them into Zochitl's chest, their eyes deadlocked. Curiesay can feel the hair on her neck flutter as Parker briskly walks over, gently separating the Directors on one side and the siblings on the other.

Blinking rapidly, Arthur puts his fingers to his temples. "So, um… when…when do we start? I mean, what next?" The group looks at him, heads cocked. Elva grumbles. Separating herself from the rest, she storms off to the far side of the room.

"Right now! You and Curiesay will need to get suited up, and then we can begin," Chandrima chirps, unfazed.

Parker moves back near Jordan, Arthur and Curiesay are ushered away by a few technicians, and the Directors are left standing alone behind the central desk.

Zochitl leans over to Chandrima, cupping her ear. "You need to get her in check. If humanity is to survive, you cannot hesitate."

* * *

Why didn't she say "we"? Chandrima watches as Zochitl walks to the makeshift Arbiter assembly area on the right side of the room. Six technicians scramble around Arthur and Curiesay, installing their Arbiters.

Averting her eyes, Chandrima walks carefully over to Elva. "I think we need to talk." Elva is half-facing the wall, arms crossed. Cautiously, Chandrima puts her hand on Elva's shoulder.

"I just don't want to lose him," Elva chokes out. "It's all happening so fast. He's just…growing up. I don't want to lose Arthur." She shakes her head, tears welling in her eyes.

"My dear, he's still your brother. He's doing good. He's doing the right thing, and you are too," Chandrima assures her, gently squeezing her shoulder. Elva sniffles, rubbing her nose, but refuses to face Chandrima.

"You know…" *Careful now.* "Your mother was adamant that he become a Pilot, once he came of age," Chandrima whispers. Elva's eyes widen. "She had told me that he was...*special.* Different. I mean, she never outright said it, but—"

Elva whips around, her wet eyes narrowed and tense. "I don't want to talk about this anymore; this conversation is making me uncomfortable."

Hands up in surrender, Chandrima tries to defuse the situation. "I won't tell anyone. I just want what's best for Arthur," she insists with a placating smile.

The Director is less threatening than her imposing counterpart, and Elva advances, her voice low. "Director Joshi, I can accept the conditions of Arthur working for you, but don't lie to my face." Elva steps close to Chandrima, their foreheads nearly touching. "If you wanted what's best for him, he wouldn't be a Pilot." Chandrima's normally cheerful expression devolves into defiance. Across the room, Arthur and Curiesay have finished donning their Arbiters, with Parker giving a whistle to alert Chandrima.

"Let's forget this conversation happened, shall we?" Chandrima says with a nasty frown, turning away from Elva and toward the group of Pilots and staff. *She's going to hate me for this.*

* * *

Curiesay had felt apprehensive about this whole process. She watched Arthur discreetly as they were fitted with their Arbiters. His expression was nearly neutral, but she recognized the subtle tells. Cheeks drooped, eyelids lazy, voice soft. *What are you so afraid that I'll see?*

Glancing to the far side of the room, she was barely able to make out the movements of Elva and Chandrima as they talked. Whatever Arthur is nervous about, his sister obviously feels the same.

Arthur and Curiesay have just entered the glass-walled chamber at the front of the room. It's off-putting: walls so thick the glass distorts the bright lights shining from the outside; technicians scrambling around them and hooking lines into their suits that hang from the ceiling; a gallery of people beyond the glass, watching with eager pens and eyes. It's like they're in a human-sized terrarium.

"Why do we need to be in here?" Curiesay asks aloud as Arthur stands a few meters to her right, sheepishly examining his surroundings.

"Just precautions. We don't expect any issues," Zochitl says. Herself and Chandrima are standing behind the main desk, with the rest of the observers, Parker and the Stewards included, off to the sides.

Pretty dire precautions, huh? She feels a bit like a circus performer. All eyes on her. Expecting her and Arthur to do some tricks. The technicians finish their work, hurriedly grab their tools, and make their way to the vault door off to the side. They file out, heaving it closed behind them.

She knows she should feel afraid. Afraid of Chandrima. Afraid of this *cell.* Afraid of why she's locked in here to begin with.

She looks off to her side, to Arthur, who has been watching her intently. "It's going to be okay." He forces a grim smile, like he's trying to convince himself and not Curiesay.

"Fuck yeah it is," she responds candidly as she turns her head toward the glass. "So, what now? And how long is this going to take?"

"Just a moment. We're running down the list," Chandrima says as the two women type away on their keyboards.

"Feeding is active at two hundred calories per minute, auxiliary heat sinks on standby, tertiary heat sinks on standby, electromagnetic reflectors waiting to calibrate. That should be it," Zochitl says, looking to Chandrima, who nods in the affirmative.

"Okay, you two, listen carefully. Dominiums only become habitable once you Cross. Arthur, since you haven't had to Cross yet, your Dominium may be more stable than Curiesay's. So Curiesay will Cross, and you need to let her in," Chandrima says into the microphone fixed to the desk.

"Wh-what, uh, what does that mean?" Arthur stutters. The observers can see his heart rate climb, but he stands motionless.

"I can't tell you because I don't know. This has never been done before. Just do what feels right," Chandrima responds, then turns her eyes and words toward Curiesay. "Curiesay, you need to bring your sync rate up."

And how do I do that? But she already knows somehow. Rising from far beneath her skin, she feels the heat welling up inside of her. Making its way to her suit, it bleeds off. Behind the glass chamber, a long row of cooling fans springs to life, pumping fresh cool air inside. The hot and cold air clash, swirling around the two Pilots as Curiesay turns up the heat. Watching intently, Annata eyes the Directors as they manage her Pilot's suit in her stead.

"Good, this is good. Curiesay, stop here," Chandrima says into the microphone, and Curiesay's temperature and heart rate quit rising. The tubes hanging from the ceiling in the chamber sway as the air whips around them. The waves of heat rolling off Curiesay further distort the light. Her irises have changed from hazel to red, piercing through the glass.

Curiesay cocks her head, smiling deviously. Inside her Arbiter, she feels indominable. Although normal people may imagine their peers in their underwear to stifle their anxiety, Curiesay's imagination has a darker twist. She flashes a regal wave to Chandrima, who returns it meekly as Curiesay stares.

One of the screens on the desk has the abbreviation *EMF* at the top. The screen is bisected, with two figures, representing Arthur and Curiesay, on either side. Waves emanate from Curiesay's effigy and crash into Arthur's at random.

"Okay, you two, close your eyes," Chandrima says as she presses a button on her desk. The screen shows additional digital waves coming from both the top and the bottom, reshaping Curiesay's until they no longer crash against Arthur, but wrap around him. The borders of the screen flash green, and all eyes are on the two Pilots.

Chandrima nods earnestly. "Now, he just has to let her in." The Stewards, Parker, the Directors, and the other staff stare into the glass chamber as the two Pilots stand motionless. The contrast between Curiesay's roaring heat and Arthur's stoic stance leaves some observers wondering if this will even work. Unbeknownst to them, the two Pilots are indeed communicating.

* * *

Dark. Distant.

She looks around, spinning slowly. Darkness. Nothing. NOTHING. More nothing than she can stand. More than she ever thought possible. Surely not even the entirety of creation is this vast, this desolate. Not knowing how long she's been here, she desperately wishes she weren't alone. Right then, she knows she isn't.

The feeling a deep-sea diver has when a submarine passes through their space but cannot see it. The whine of its propeller, the hollow pangs of its hull, creaking under the leagues of water seeking to crush its occupants. Moving above or below, both are nothing but a speck in an infinite and dark abyss. Something is here. She knows it.

"Arthur!" she cries out. Deadened, her voice doesn't carry far, nor does it return. She feels she'd be just as well served by screaming in space. Curiesay touches her chest lightly, calming herself. Looking down, she's no longer in her Arbiter. She doesn't even recognize these clothes. Demin jeans, a yellow short-sleeve top. This is what I'd wear. Wait, I can see… There's light?

It's distant, but it's there. I'll never make it. Taking a step, she gains an uncomfortable amount of ground. A moment ago, the light seemed as far away as anything could ever be, but now she can see him.

"Arthur," she repeats in a relieved whisper. Walking toward him, she realizes that the darkness isn't empty. The light diffuses, illuminating them. A few. Then dozens. Scores. More than she can count, more than she can believe. Doors. Hundreds of thousands of freestanding wooden doors are shrouded in darkness.

Though she can barely make them out, she knows they're all unique. Little quirks in their construction, in the wood grain, the knots. Different years, different trees. Triumph, falls. Love, desolation. Approaching the light, she feels the urge to run off into the darkness and explore whatever Arthur is so desperate to hide from the world. She stifles this. Mind. Your. Manners.

She walks, both feeling as if she has just begun her journey and has lived a lifetime walking. What she had thought was ground is not solid, but liquid. Blood, with surface tension enough to allow it to bear weight. She wonders if this is how Jesus felt walking on water, if she believed in such a tale. She's close now.

As her eyes adjust to the light, she can see it doesn't have a source. Or, at least, not one that she can discern. A ring of light is cast down from above, illuminating Arthur as he leans against a marble pillar. As she grows near, she can see more of them. Far fewer than the doors, but still too many to identify. They go up, up, up into the ether. Figures carved into them. Notions. She examines a few until she suddenly averts her eyes. That one shows a nude woman, and she feels as if it isn't her place to look any longer.

Reaching the light, Curiesay can see him clearly now. "Hey. I guess...it worked. Or something," Curiesay says with a nervous laugh.

"I can see that," he responds impartially. Curiesay has just passed the edge of the light, advancing toward him. He's taller. Older. He has a slight beard, scratchy and dark, and his hair is medium-length and tousled. He's dressed casually as well, wearing only jeans and a plain white shirt.

She steps closer. "Fuckin' sweet place you've got here. Not a lot of furniture. Very minimalist, you know, besides all the doors and the infinite nothingness," she teases, putting her hands on the small of her back. Arthur's expression remains neutral.

He's definitely Arthur, she thinks. Piercing green eyes, deep and sunk in his skull. He smells the same. He...feels the same. But there's something more. Is this who he's been hiding?

Curiesay twirls playfully, looking off into the darkness. "Sure are a lot of memories for someone two years younger than me." Again, silence from Arthur. "What's your problem? Don't want me here? Just say the word and I'll... I don't know. Click my heels together or something," Curiesay says scornfully. Arthur crosses his arms in lazy defiance.

As Curiesay takes a half-step backward, Arthur speaks. "Wait. Don't..." He pauses for a long while as Curiesay watches him avert his eyes, his cheeks flushed. "Don't leave me." Oh? Is that the flicker of emotion?

She rocks her head side to side playfully. "Then talk to me."

"Okay."

"That's not talking," she says in sing-song.

"I don't know what I'm supposed to say."

"What? Say whatever you want."

"There isn't anything I want to say. Why don't you just ask me something?"

"So, you do want to talk, but you want me to decide what we talk about?"

"You're the one who wants me to talk, why don't you—"

Curiesay quickly steps into Arthur's personal space as he presses his back up against the pillar. "I want you to make your own goddamn decisions for once and stop letting others make them for you. You obey Chandrima and your sister like they're your masters. But you do have your own thoughts. I saw it in the Arena. First time I'd seen you think for yourself since I'd met you," she says scathingly, with Arthur putting his hands up. After a few moments, Curiesay backs off, standing defiantly in front of an increasingly flustered Arthur.

Curiesay is surprised by this outburst. Though, every word is true to her. She's been wanting to scold him for every moment he concedes himself to others. She hadn't the courage to tell him face to face, but in this domain, the shackles that bustle against her heart don't exist.

"You don't understand," he says breathlessly, head shaking.

"Try me."

"I'm not who you think I am. I mean, I am, but there's...more."

"Go on?"

"I..." Arthur stutters, then begins to pace. "No. No, you don't belong here."

"Tough shit, 'cause here I am."

"Well, I don't...think that—"

"Why don't you just fuckin' tell me? You obviously don't want me to leave, but you don't want to talk about this? What are you so afraid that I'll see? Why do you treat yourself like you're less than everyone else around—"

"Because I am!" he booms. Curiesay jolts backward. Arthur's lips quiver as he eyes Curiesay bitterly.

"Why?" she asks quietly. "What makes you less deserving of compassion than anyone else?"

"I deserve nothing but fire and ruin," he growls as he takes a step toward her.

Unwittingly, she takes a step back. "You think you're the only person with problems? Lots of people don't like themselves. What makes you special?"

"Special isn't the word I'd use."

"Then what? What are you?"

Arthur's head swims. His eyes well. He opens his mouth, his truth on the tip of his tongue. He draws it back behind his teeth, then speaks. "It's time for you to leave."

"Nope! I like it here. Figure I'll stay awhile..." she says with playful

innocence. *"Maybe take a look around, find out what you're trying to—"*

Before she can react, Arthur has her by the throat. *"You're way out of your depth, Curiesay,"* he grumbles as he turns and presses her against the pillar. He's terribly strong—she feels as if her throat is in a vise, one screw turn away from collapse. *"But you're welcome to stay if you insist on being so flippant with your life."* Curiesay taps his arm desperately, but he does not relent, hoisting her up by her neck.

Slithering up over his shoulders, Curiesay sees his tendrils. His irises boil from green to red, thick veins bulging from his neck. *How... Is he Crossing? There is something more. Something new.*

What looks like a tendril, forked in two at its end, crawls up from below. *A tail?* From the flanks of his forehead, she can see the skin bubbling. Two mighty horns form themselves from the liquid he excretes. They twist around themselves like a goat's horns and go straight up, their bases expanding until they form a solid red and black bone plate around his head, with two holes through which his wicked eyes peer at her. Two pointy ears accompany them, covered with thick black fur.

Is this the being from Elva's drawing? Pressing his forehead against hers, she imagines this is what a fawn must feel like before it's torn to shreds by a lumbering bear.

"Well?! Is that what you wanted?! Can you see me now?!" he roars. *"Tell me, Curiesay, what do you see?!"* He relaxes his grip just enough for her to speak.

She draws in what breath she can—she'll need all of it to tell him. *"You're...beautiful."*

In a heap, Curiesay falls to the floor. She cradles her throat as Arthur stumbles back. His tendrils and tail vanish into ash, his bone plate helmet separates from his skull and clatters to the floor, his eyes fade to green.

"Why did you say that? Don't say that!" he pleads as he covers his face, pushing himself up against one of the many pillars. *"I wish you wouldn't... Don't...say that to me."*

Curiesay watches him carefully as she scrambles to her feet. She worries that she has wounded him, his figure withdrawn and unsure. The cracks have formed. Something's relented. Arthur, relented. She cannot understand it, but she knows that she has control now.

I see you, Arthur.

The balance of power has shifted, and a sense of giddy curiosity rises inside of her. She wonders what kind of agency she has in this place. With a snap of her fingers, a satin-sheeted bed appears beneath Arthur. He jolts, taking in this sudden change as Curiesay eyes him with a playful grin.

She approaches the seated Arthur, gently climbing onto his lap as he turns his head away. His lips move, but he doesn't speak. Only half-sounds. Shushing him, she takes his face in her hands, brushing his cheek with her thumb. He relaxes his muscles, allowing her to turn his head, and she presses her lips against his.

They kiss curiously for a moment. Arthur shakes his head, trying again to turn it away from Curiesay as his eyes well up. "It's okay. I'm not afraid of you," she says softly. Whether he believes that or is infuriated by it, she cannot tell. His pathetic eyes darken as Arthur side-eyes her. In a flash, he turns and pins her wrists down with vise-like hands.

He looses a hot, reverberating growl as he bears down on her. As kindly as ever, she smiles back at him. She does not fear him, and she wants him to know that. He grips and tears her shirt off in one swift motion. He presses his face between her breasts for a moment with a relieved sigh, one hand reaching up to her mouth. Curiesay takes it and kisses it sweetly as he breathes hot air onto her in short, panicked breaths.

He moves briskly down to her privates, undoing her button, loosing her zipper. She runs her fingers through his hair as he spreads her legs, pleasuring her as her eyes roll back and—

* * *

"Hey! There we go!" Chandrima exclaims as the two Pilots are engulfed in their own separate raging infernos of scorching air like invisible fire tornados. The waves of heat distort the Pilots' images as the staff view them from beyond the glass partition. Energy is produced with nowhere to go, and their Arbiters bristle with impatient kinetic fury.

The room vibrates beneath their feet, the thick concrete coping with the Pilots' show of force. Their heart rate, temperature, and energy production are in the upper limits, but no warnings flash for the Directors as they monitor them.

Zochitl eyes the screen showing the electromagnetic waves being shared between the two. To anyone else, the raw data is useless, but she screws her sharp eyes onto the screen and grins. "Oh really?" she whispers.

Jordan watches Elva carefully. She's fidgeting, feet shuffling, eyes erratic as they snap from screen to screen. Although Arthur's vitals had been mirroring Curiesay's, they rise, and the borders of his screens turn yellow.

Chandrima shakes her head, eyes narrowing. "What...what's happening?" she asks aloud and receives no answer. Arthur's energy production eclipses Curiesay's and continues to rise. Fast. The secondary cooling fans kick on, then the tertiary, and more cold air is pumped into the Pilots' chamber. On the central screen, the temperature of the chamber is displayed, and the value turns red as multiple screens begin to flash at once.

Elva bustles up to the desk, nearly knocking Chandrima over as she grabs the microphone. "Arthur! Arthur, are you okay?!"

The onlookers feel a chill as Arthur responds, low and despondently.

"No..."

* * *

Time is of no consequence here. Be it a fling, honeymoon, or a lifelong romance, it matters not to Curiesay. The two Pilots lust after each other for ages, their loving scent somehow filling this impossibly large space. In reality, Curiesay knows nothing of love, but she isn't herself. She is unbound, she is beyond.

Snap. How…am I here? *Looking on from behind a pillar in the distance, Curiesay can see herself leaning on Arthur's chest as she grinds her hips, the two speaking vulgar nothings to each other. Looking down to confirm, she has her clothes back.*

She's there.

And she's here.

Perfect.

She desperately hopes she can keep his attention as this other Curiesay surrenders to her feminine curiosity. Slinking back into the darkness, she tiptoes to the nearest door. Its frame is emblazoned with red roses, vines twisting around each other. The knob is smooth and slight. This one is as good as any.

Opening it, she's hit with a wall of steam. As the steam dissipates behind her, she steps inside. Wet, tiled floors. A communal bath, every showerhead pouring scalding water. She eyes the drains. Rivers of red drift with the tide of fresh water coming from the far side of the room. She can see them. A man and a woman, embraced in lust.

Arthur is as she had seen him. Tendrils and tail loosed, but there's too many. They're not all his. The two lovers' tendrils argue and clash as their bodies lust, the tiled wall behind them cracking from the force. Curiesay would suspect nefarious intentions if she had not just locked eyes with the woman. She has a mask too, borne from her own skull, adorned with red bone roses. The deviant smile she wears fades as she spots the intruder, her red eyes threatening. In a panic, Curiesay backpedals and closes the door behind her.

She bumps into another door. It's wretched, vile. Rotten wood threatens to disintegrate if she touches it too briskly. Curiesay firmly grips the cold iron knob and opens it.

She doesn't enter. She cannot. Or will not. Whatever this is, it grips her heart so tightly she worries if she furthers herself, it may rip it from her chest. It's dark. Cold. She lets the door open in on itself and her eyes drift up. And up. The figures before her are, for bipeds, enormous. One stands behind the other as the lower one gurgles and resists. Dread descends upon her as a flash of lightning illuminates Arthur. His eyes furious, his body nude and featureless, save for the blood, tendrils, forked tail, and horned bone crown. He howls into the night, choking the life out of his kneeling foe.

Slam! Who is this? Who is Arthur? He's...just a kid. Who—

She knows she should not look any further, but this mystery laid before her is too grand, too invigorating. Arthur, atop the other Curiesay, looks into the darkness. He knows something has happened. Turning his head back to her with her hands, Curiesay pulls him in, kissing him passionately as her other self continues her clandestine investigation.

"Don't look at me," he whispers.

* * *

"Tell her to stop!" Elva rages as Parker restrains her, dragging her from the desk. Both Zochitl and Chandrima are typing furiously, jumping from screen to screen. Not only is Arthur's energy production and temperature skyrocketing, but Curiesay's is as well.

"Curiesay! That's enough!" Chandrima implores into the microphone, but Curiesay either cannot hear her or chooses to ignore the order.

"They just passed one thousand calories per minute, Director,"

Zochitl says.

"Cut them off," Chandrima sharply retorts. Zochitl complies, commanding the Pilots' feeding tubes to eject. They do so with force, clanging against the sides of the chamber violently as they retract into the ceiling. The observers feel the heat beaming onto them through the glass. The Arbiters glow red at the joints as the suits begin to deteriorate.

"They'll starve!" Annata calls out from behind the group. The swirling heat and steam triggers arcs of electricity across the chamber between the two Pilots, carving red-hot lines into their armor as it licks at them. Curiesay hasn't moved an inch, eyes closed and body stoic as the storm she's ignited rails around her.

Arthur wails aloud above the din. "Don't look at me!" He stumbles like a man shot in the gut, doubling over. The group watches on in ever-growing horror as the spectacle continues unabated.

* * *

She cannot help herself. These memories are too real, too dire. Thousands of them does she invade, knowing full well that she is no longer welcome.

A deep blue hue strikes her eyes. She's seeing from his point of view. He's floating, submerged. He's an infant this time. Banging his clenched fists against the glass in front of him, he calls out. Muffled bubbles filled with sorrow. A hand appears, pressing itself against the glass as he presses his own opposite it. A face, sullen with regret, looks in.

Where now? Some...ditch. Some desert. It reeks of a corpse. The incessant buzzing of flies fills her ears as she looks on from a short distance. There he is again, grown. He kneels, sobbing wretchedly, like a dying steer as it's torn apart by a pack of coyotes. He cradles a corpse, wrapped in a blood-stained sheet. In his hand is a small wooden figure, but Curiesay cannot make out what it is.

And now, it's her again. The woman from the shower. Arthur lies in the field, impaled onto the ground. He's moving, barely, and looks up at his lover with incredulous eyes. Not his lover, not this time. She pummels him relentlessly with fists and tendrils. Blood spatters and mists. He does not protest. A wall of swirling grey, as loud as a freight train, descends and consumes them, and Curiesay leaves yet another memory behind.

One, final, door. This one is special. Reserved. The wood is immaculate, untouched. She has the feeling that no one has been here for a very long time.

The instant her hand touches the gold knob, she hears Arthur cry out from the distant bed. "Not that one!" Fearing that he'll thwart her, she quickly opens it and steps inside.

It's beautiful. A serene setting. An expansive green field, a gentle breeze licking at her skin. The sun is bright and high, showering the land with warmth. She's at the base of a hill with an ever-so-slight incline, and in the distance, she can see a robust red barn, front doors open.

"Arthur," she says as she sees a figure just beyond the doors. She runs, hoping to reach him before the other Arthur can stop her. Her footsteps are thick, moisture splashing her legs. She glances down in horror—the grass is saturated with blood.

Reaching him, he doesn't react to her presence. He doesn't move nor breathe. Kneeling, he stares into the barn's rafters in silence, frozen in time. Unblinking eyes pour tears. Curiesay's gaze wanders upward. It's much darker than outside, and her eyes struggle to adjust.

Pupils expanding, she searches for whatever Arthur is so singularly focused on. She sees them hanging, feet dangling and dripping with blood. Of all the grim sights she'd seen, this one she is most aghast to witness. Arthur's sorrow permeates into her mind, and Curiesay can do nothing except scream.

* * *

The Pilots burst with violent energy—a muffled shockwave ripples through the glass. The remaining tubes are torn from their Arbiters, along with some armor plating, rocketing them across the chamber.

"Ice!" Chandrima warns thrice as she slams her fist down onto a large red button. Liquid nitrogen sprays into the chamber, dousing the Pilots. Their scorching bodies and the nitrogen clash, sending violent wisps of gas lashing out. The contrasting temperatures crack the chamber's glass as the Pilots collapse onto the floor.

Their internal temperatures plummet—their suits' diagnostic screens struggle to fit all the warnings onto them. Medical personnel wait impatiently for the exhaust fans to purge the room of nitrogen gas before they enter. Carefully and with haste, they heave the Pilots and their Arbiters onto gurneys and wheel them away.

* * *

A short while later, Chandrima is standing outside of the clinic, with two security guards flanking her. She's speaking with a handful of other lab coat-clad personnel. A few Waifs watch from down the hallway, having heard the commotion. The heavy footsteps of Elva scatter them as she bustles up to Chandrima.

"Move," she says harshly as Chandrima blocks her path.

"Elva, listen. There's nothing you can do here," Chandrima responds in a docile tone.

Elva's lip twitches. "Oh, there's something I can do all right. I'm going to strangle that bitch." The other staff disperse around the two women as Elva encroaches on the Director.

"I understand, truly, but—"

"No, you truly don't. You…" Elva's spiteful words are tinted with sorrow, "…knew this could happen."

"We didn't *know* anything. I told you, we have never tried something like this before, and—"

"You're the only family we have, and you treat him like a plaything!" Elva's eyes darken with wrath. "Move."

Chandrima stands firm. "I cannot. You need to leave."

"The only way you're going to get me to leave is if you fucking drag me out of here!" Elva blusters, spittle misting Chandrima's face.

Stone-faced, Chandrima waves the guards forward. "As you wish."

Elva flails her legs as the guards restrain her, narrowly missing the stoic Chandrima's head. Her expletives echo down the hallway as the guards drag her away and out of sight.

The group who witnessed this outburst avert their eyes as Chandrima enters the clinic—she's seemingly done, or uninterested, with whatever they were talking about.

"How are they?" Chandrima asks the doctor who is waiting inside. They walk down the sterile hospital hallway, with personnel rushing every which way, doing something or other.

"We were able to remove their Arbiters without too much trouble. I'm afraid I can't tell you if they're salvageable or not. Arthur hasn't regained consciousness yet. Curiesay just woke up but she's still quite disoriented."

"Show me," Chandrima responds as they reach Curiesay's room and enter. The Pilot struggles pathetically with her attendants, disoriented. One injects a sedative into her IV, and she relaxes, lying back.

"Burns over most of her body, but thankfully none are too deep. The superficial nitrogen burns should heal quickly, but she's lost about four kilos—" Chandrima interrupts with a sharp whistle, and the staff scramble out in scant few moments.

"Ch-Chandrima? What…happened?" Curiesay manages as her eyes swim, her face splotched with cherry-red patches of skin.

"Everything is all right now, you're going to be okay," she responds as she leans over the bed rail.

"No…no it's not. I…" Curiesay shakes her head in disbelief. "Oh my God. I looked. He didn't want me to look."

"What did you see, Curiesay?" Chandrima asks insistently.

"Oh God. Oh fuck. Why did I do that? I shouldn't have done that. He didn't… I saw—"

The door bursts open, the overpressure popping Curiesay's eardrums. Chandrima, without turning to inspect the intruder and seemingly in a trance, silently slinks to the corner of the room, nose first.

The weight of Arthur's presence is crushing. The deep-rooted genetic preference to deter a predator if you remain completely still paralyzes Curiesay. His footsteps threaten her as he approaches.

Red, raw skin. Bloodshot emerald eyes. Curiesay feels that whatever he is here to do, surely she deserves worse. Although in this reality he is much smaller than he was in his Dominium, he looms. For Curiesay, she's never felt a greater threat. He leans on the railing, crushing the hard plastic as he grips it and bends toward Curiesay.

Before he can speak, Curiesay trembles. "Oh, Arthur, I'm so sorry." Over a few moments, Arthur's demeanor and posture relax. He presses a single finger to his lips as he eyes Curiesay, glances at Chandrima, and leaves the room.

20

Bittersweet

July 3rd, 2046
Bastion, Second Floor

"Mom said she's not coming home till late," Elva says as she sets the phone on the receiver. Arthur is sitting on the couch in their small Bastion apartment, staring at the TV. Elva moseys over to him, lovingly putting her hand on his back. "So let's go out for your birthday!"

Arthur whips his head around, his expression worried. "What if she finds out? You know she doesn't like us going without her."

Elva flashes a devious grin. "Oh, ye of little faith, I've been lying to Mom since before you were born. Besides, it's your birthday. You deserve to go and celebrate!"

Arthur looks at her skeptically, head drooped. "Mom wasn't home for my birthday last year either."

"She's busy. You know, saving the world."

"She doesn't miss any of yours."

Elva sighs and pulls a few folded bills from her pocket. "Aunt Rima gave me some money. She's no good at giving gifts, so you'll have to pick out your own. And if you're careful, we'll have enough left over to get dinner too."

This seems to catch Arthur's attention. "Okay," he says, side-eyeing his sister. "But I get to pick where we eat."

"Deal! Go get dressed," Elva responds as she jumps up. With that, the two siblings go to their rooms, change, and meet outside of their apartment door.

Bastion's climate control has been on the fritz, and this spring has been unusually cold in Eastern Europe. Both siblings are dressed in warm coats and hats. They make their way down the staircase in front of their apartment and down to the street. Dusk is approaching; the artificial sun mounted far above is gradually powering down, the light fading as they walk toward the shopping center in the town square.

This street runs the entire length of the Second Floor, wall to wall. It runs both wide and thin, depending on the density of the surrounding buildings. They walk hand in hand, following the sidewalk, as the streetlights flicker to life.

Inside Bastion's dome, each floor is relative to the available geometry, making the First Floor the largest, followed by the Second, and then the Third. Just under half of Bastion's residents live here, with thousands of apartment complexes wrapped around the edges of the floor.

Bastion's footprint is so large that here on the Second Floor, tens of square kilometers of space is available. On foggy days, you can't even see the walls.

As they near the market, the streets and sidewalks become busier, with residents shopping after their workdays finish. Seasonal produce, fresh cuts of meat, hot bread. Bastion is one of the few places in the world where humanity doesn't want for much. Rows of buildings line the streets, with vendors clogging up the sidewalks.

Restaurants, coffee shops, jewelers, butchers, produce stands. Abuzz with conversations and bargaining, the market bustles.

"So, where do you wanna go first?" Elva asks.

"I wanna pick out my gift before we eat!" Arthur responds excitedly.

Elva grins. "Okay, so what will it be? Jewelers, toy store, or maybe we can get you some new shoes?"

Arthur stops abruptly on the sidewalk, and Elva turns, bending to his level. "Are you all right?" His eyes don't register her as he stares at the butcher's stand they have stopped in front of. The merchant's wares hang from the awning above. Most cuts are unrecognizable as to what animal they came from, except for the pigs. They hang by their ankles, disemboweled, bisected in the middle, their ribcages exposed. What blood remains in them drips periodically onto the sidewalk.

Arthur steps past her without saying a word and walk up to the booth. "Young man! Have you come to pick up dinner for your family?" the butcher says with a wide smile, apron stained with blood. Arthur doesn't respond as the man steps from behind the booth and walks cooly to him. "First time here? Well, no worries, I know there's a lot to choose from, so let me pick the cut. *You* just tell me which animal."

Elva taps Arthur insistently, whispering. "Arthur…Arthur…" His eyes are glued to the corpse.

"Son, you okay? It's a bit graphic, but that's life. If you eat meat, this is where it comes from." The butcher's tone grows in disapproval as he puts his hand on Arthur's shoulder. Arthur doesn't break his gaze, his eyes locked to the drops of blood, counting the seconds in between them—a grizzly metronome. The butcher stands and gives Elva a stern glare. "Hey, kid, your brother is freaking me out. Probably best if y'all move along."

"Do you like it? Killing, I mean," Arthur asks emotionlessly.

The butcher's eyes widen, and he steps back behind his booth, waving the pair off. "I don't kill 'em, kid, I just chop 'em up. Now, get him out of here before he gets himself in trouble," he responds gruffly before turning to speak with an eager customer who has approached his booth.

Arthur finally turns to face his sister, smiling. "Let's go to the jewelers! I wanna see if they have anything cool-lookin.'"

Elva tries to hide her exasperation as she sighs. "Okay, yeah, let's go." The jeweler store is a few shops over. They walk up the short staircase and remove their hats as they enter—the shop is quite warm. The pair browse, cutting through the aisles as their eyes wander.

"You know, Arthur, we could get your ears pierced! They do that here," Elva suggests.

"Nah, that's all right. *I'm* looking for a necklace," he says matter-of-factly.

"Oh really? What kind of necklace?"

Arthur steps up to a display nearly overflowing with hanging necklaces. "The one I see in my dreams, the one Aashvi gave me."

Elva stops in her tracks. "Oh? What did it look like? I mean, what kind of necklace was it?" she asks hesitantly, eyeing Arthur from the corner of her eye.

"Well, the necklace itself was just string, but the pendant, she told me it was a Chital, you know, a deer. They live in India. That's where I met her." Elva nods her head as he continues. "They didn't have much in the village where she grew up, so she found some driftwood and carved it herself! Ah, I miss her."

Elva wets her lips. "And what…happened to her?"

"She died," Arthur says cheerfully. A beat later he yelps, collapsing to the floor. Elva rushes to his side. He poorly contains his groans—the shopkeeper takes notice and heads toward the pair.

"Let's go home and get you your pills," Elva says, patting him on the back.

Arthur's knuckles turn white as he squeezes. "No! That's not fair, these stupid headaches ruin everything. It's *my* life now."

"Are you two all right? Did he get hurt?" the shopkeeper says, kneeling next to Arthur.

Elva clears her throat. "He's all right, he just gets migraines. Bad timing. Come on, Arthur, let's go." Arthur doesn't budge. "Arthur…" Elva whispers, her lips approaching his ear.

"Please don't. I hate when you tell me what to do," Arthur pleads quietly.

Elva stops, then turns to the shopkeeper. "Could you maybe get him some water? I've got his pills with me, but he's no good taking them without a drink." The shopkeeper nods and briskly heads to a room behind the counter.

As soon as she's out of sight, Elva leans down again. "Please…it's his birthday." Arthur slowly stands, and with his sister's hand in his, the two exit the shop and head home empty-handed.

Later, they enter their apartment. Arthur trudges to the couch like a wounded animal. He falls onto it, curls up into a ball, and closes his eyes.

"Arthur, are you okay?" Elva says as she moves to the kitchen and grabs Arthur's pill bottle. She brings the glass and the bottle to the couch, setting them on the table. Arthur doesn't answer. "I've got your pills here, why don't you take a few, it should—"

"They're placebos. When I chew them up, they taste sweet. They don't make pills for what's wrong with me," he says defeatedly.

"There's nothing wrong with you! You're a perfectly normal little boy," she says as she sits near him and gently rubs his back.

"You and I both know that's not true. Days like this are…when I remember the most." Elva sits in silence for a few moments, unable to find the correct words to comfort him. Eventually, Arthur turns to face her and sits up, motioning toward the pill bottle. "I'm sorry. It's okay to pretend. Actually, I prefer it." Elva nods, opens the bottle, and pours two pills into his hand. Arthur downs them with a sip of water.

"Hey, I've got something for you. Lemme go get it," Elva says as she stands and walks to her room, returning a few moments later with a small bag. "I've been saving these for a special occasion. Since you don't have a birthday cake, this will have to do." She reaches in and pulls out two foil-covered treats.

Arthur cocks his head to the side curiously. "Is that...chocolate? Where did you get that?"

"I have my ways, dear brother," Elva says with a grin as she motions insistently to Arthur, who receives his treat with admiration. Of all the things mankind has lost since the Calamity, chocolate is one of the few remaining delicacies.

"Happy birthday, Arthur," Elva says gently as she "toasts" her candy against his.

Arthur smiles, and the two unwrap their treats, eating them in a flash. "Thank you for taking care of me. I love you," Arthur says as he hugs her.

Elva sighs. "I love you too."

* * *

Later that night, when Amiree gets home, the lights are off, and Arthur is already in bed. She enters the living area, tosses her jacket onto the rack, and turns on the light, revealing Elva, who sits sour-faced on the couch. She's the spitting image of her mother: slight freckles on fair skin, fiery orange hair, and serious grey eyes.

Not to mention her wicked temperament.

"You know, he does notice these things. Why did you have to miss his birthday *again?*" Elva spits, glaring.

Amiree suppresses a startle, hand over her heart, then speaks dismissively. "I had work to do; he understands."

"He *understands* that you treat him differently."

"Elva, I'm doing my best, all things considered."

"*Yeah?* No cake, no presents, and you weren't even here. Your *best* is shit."

Amiree stomps toward Elva, pointing a scornful finger. "That's enough with the mouth, young lady. I'm your mother, so watch your tongue."

Elva doesn't budge and instead stands to face her mother. "Arthur didn't ask for this. He hasn't done anything wrong, and he gets these terrible headaches and nightmares and—"

Amiree interjects. "It was the only way! And you're the one who keeps encouraging him like I *specifically* told you not to!"

"Because I care! We're all he has! He doesn't have anyone else to talk to about it!" Elva says, her eyes tearing up with anger. Both have been steadily raising their voices as their tempers flare.

Amiree rolls her eyes. "Oh! My! God! Elva, why do we argue about this all the time? Why do you pretend you don't know? He isn't—"

"Don't you dare!" Elva shrieks. "Don't. You. Dare," she repeats through bared teeth.

Amiree meets her glare, then scoffs. "I'm going to bed." She storms into her room and slides the door shut. Elva sits on the couch, staring at the wall, motionless. Unbeknownst to the two ladies, Arthur had woken up.

He's quietly crying, turned on his side. "I hate you…"

21

Death Knell

October 13th, 2053
Bastion, Outskirts

She enjoys these morning walks. Though Bastion was intended to be fully self-sufficient, able to be sealed up indefinitely from the outside world, there are many walking trails and sidewalks at her base. For a newcomer, it can be dizzying to walk alongside a nearly vertical wall, knowing that it trends ever-so-slightly at an angle, closing itself up at Bastion's apex.

Lately, Chandrima has been trying to be more active. She has put on some weight—a consequence of eating her mounting stress—and is determined not to let it snowball. Unfortunately for her, she is well known in Bastion as the "boss lady" of the Third Floor. If she has to wave at one more citizen on this walking trail, she is going to *scream*.

She's a few hundred meters from Bastion's walls, enjoying the mid-summer breeze as it rolls over the field of green. Taking a lesser-traveled path (because the sidewalk is uneven), she manages to isolate herself from the deluge of people out for some fresh air. To the north, she can hear the cadence of a military man, marching his troops in front of the Pale Wall. She wonders if they intend to beat their chests until the Blight no longer seeks to escape its home.

Her feet ache—new shoes. She walks quickly, sweat forming on her forehead and being absorbed by her bright violet sweat band, with an outfit to match. Unfortunately for Chandrima, her lack of social skills sometimes bleeds over into other areas of her life, like fashion sense. Dressed like a blueberry with a too-small sports bra and yoga pants, she hustles down the trail. She does feel a sense of freedom in dressing like a doofus—she doesn't enjoy the prestige that comes with being in charge.

These quiet mornings, however, also give her some moral misgivings. Since the Blight nearly wiped out humanity, there are many places on the Earth as tranquil as this. Human activity, especially in Europe and Asia, is a fraction of what it was. Nature was quick to reclaim its birthright, crawling up the sides of skyscrapers and bursting through city streets. Personal friends of hers in the scientific field had even cooked up clones of once-extinct species, their habitats now safe from human intervention.

Having been born at the turn of the century, when humanity seemed determined to rend the Earth from beneath its feet, she does feel some twisted sense of thanks to the Blight for staying their hand.

Albeit, with blood.

Her thoughts wander to Arthur. The boy has done everything that she's asked, even saved her life, as well as Parker's. She knows what she risks by making him a Pilot. Once he's healed, she intends to send him to the most dangerous place on Earth to face the deadliest Blight they've found in years. Scowl or no, he's just a kid.

But she's used kids before. Hell, she's using Karima right now. Protecting him over her for the sake of family is morally unjust. Between him and Curiesay, she's sure they will succeed. Should anything go wrong, Chandrima has confidence—

A green bench just off the trail serves as a perch for a large raven as it swoops down. "Oh!" she exclaims as she comes to a sudden halt. It startles her, giving her a moment of pause. *I need a break anyway.*

She reaches her hand out slowly, voice low. "Hey there, dear." She has always envied her nephew's proclivities for animal interaction and wishes to be a whisperer of his caliber. Though in all her years of talking to random animals, none had seemed all that interested in her words, let alone spoken back.

Except for this one.

The avian cocks its head. "Shame!" it squawks, giving Chandrima a jolt. She shakes her head in confusion, trying to place the voice. It dials in its impression. "Ashamed of yourself!" *Is that...a girl?* "You should be ashamed!" *That accent.* "Do you hear me?!" Chandrima's confusion devolves into abject horror as her neurons make the connection. *That's Karima's voice. That's—*

"You should—" Its words are cut off as it continues to vocalize, the muffled screams of Karima given dreadful new life by its tongue. Chandrima listens with bated breath to the death knells of one of her Waifs.

"Oh, child..." the raven says, its voice dropping precipitously. "I am." Chandrima stands motionless, eyes wide with shock, shaking in their sockets. The raven shakes its jet-black wings and scoots down the backrest, nearer to Chandrima, talons clacking against the metal.

It raises its left claw and drops a piece of fabric onto the bench. Chandrima moves to touch it but stops short. It's blood-soaked, but she can see the insignia; a heart, pierced by a nail, atop a wooden shield. *Her patch.*

The raven hops. Spins. Spreads its wings and gives a half-flap, sorting its feathers. Before it takes flight, it turns its head toward the frozen Chandrima. This time, a woman's voice is heard, and its beak does not move.

"You are running out of time, Doctor Chandrima Joshi."

***

"Any idea what this is about?" Commander Cutter grumbles as he and Zochitl meet unexpectedly in the hallway. Both are on their way to Chandrima's office.

"Nope," she says, the two walking briskly. "She hadn't mentioned anything to me."

"We aren't set to deploy until next week either; perhaps she's had a change of heart," he responds sarcastically as they reach Chandrima's office door, knock, and enter when they receive an answer from Parker. He is already inside and greets them with firm handshakes. Chandrima is behind her desk and doesn't acknowledge their arrival.

"Well, Director, you feel like telling me why you dragged me up here?" Cutter asks. Still, Chandrima doesn't speak. Her glazed eyes are locked squarely onto a nondescript point on the wall. Cutter's speech shifts, taking a grave quality. "Joshi, what happened?" This question stifles Zochitl and Parker—the guests wait silent and stone-faced.

Chandrima swallows hard, casting her gaze to the group. "The recon team is dead." Her puffy eyes flit between Parker and Zochitl before she drops her head. "Karima included."

Silence falls over the room—the group stares, dumfounded. Eventually, Cutter puts his back against the wall and rubs his face.

"Karima *can't* be dead," Zochitl says harshly, breaking the silence. "You're mistaken. The Blight doesn't kill girls."

Chandrima's upper lip stiffens, her eyes fixed on her desk. "You're right. It doesn't." She loudly whips open her desk drawer, grabs the clear bag within, and tosses it onto the desk. It's Karima's patch, still soaked in blood. "It was a Scowl."

"How do you know?" Parker demands. *A little birdy told me.*

"I'm sorry, but I…can't say—"

"Bullshit!" he bellows. Chandrima's shot nerves don't afford her a flinch. Hell, were he to drag her from her seat, hair first, she may not even protest. Zochitl backs up while Parker advances, making no effort to stop him. "How are you gonna say that they're dead and not tell us how you know?! And you're saying that there's a Scowl out there working for the Blight?! Why should we believe you?!"

Chandrima knew that, out of the four of them, Parker would take it the hardest. He's always been a problem solver, and problem solvers cannot accept situations they cannot change. Diving straight into denial, she knows that he thinks if he rages enough, she'll tell him this is all just a mistake. She raises her gaze to him, eyes dripping with sorrow, confessing the truth in the only way he'll accept.

Parker stumbles back, chest heaving. "Fuck!" he roars, flinging the door open before he storms out.

A moment later, Cutter makes for the door as well. "Commander," Chandrima says. "I am so sorry."

He pauses at the threshold, running his hand along the doorframe. "Me too."

Zochitl closes the door behind him. A squeak squeezes out from Chandrima's tight throat. Then another. They're chopped up as she begins to cry, ugly and wretched. She'd hoped that Zochitl would leave too so she could cry alone, but she doesn't have the strength to evict her, nor hold it back any longer.

In all the years she's known Zochitl, she's never considered her to be an affectionate friend. She's never even seen her hug another person, not even her Waifs. Except for Karima, who'd gone out of her way the year prior to organize a surprise party for Zochitl's birthday. She had been quite perturbed after the confetti bombs went off, marring her normally fashionable—and expensive—attire, but afterward, Chandrima saw her smile like never before. These girls are as much her children as they are Chandrima's.

"Zochi… I'm sorry," Chandrima mumbles out through her sobs. Zochitl moves to her side, and they embrace. Although Chandrima cannot see her face, she can feel tears on her shoulder.

They stay this way until Chandrima calms herself enough to speak. "I'm moving up the timeline. We're going after the Yōulíng," Chandrima manages, separating from Zochitl. She wipes her face with her lab coat as she continues. "If it went through the trouble of leveraging a Scowl against us, she must be incredibly valuable."

"I agree, but it was dangerous enough sending them into the Exclusion Zone to contact her. With a Scowl on the field, I don't see how this isn't a suicide mission," Zochitl responds, locking down her tears.

Chandrima's sorrowful expression cracks as her lips upturn ever so slightly. "He won't be an issue." She grins at Zochitl, silently saying, *I know something you don't know.*

* * *

She's keeping something from me. Chandrima hadn't mentioned the courier dog returning, and even if it had, the team couldn't write about their own demise, let alone return the patch to Bastion. How is she sure that they're dead? And to cast aside the dire threat of a Scowl so flippantly? Chandrima isn't a fool.

It's risky—she's already dove into her mind once. And this time, she's not concussed. But, more than anything else, Zochitl *must* know how Karima died. She takes a long breath, centering her own mind, before she thrusts it into Chandrima's. She watches her eyes flutter for an instant, for that is as long as she'll spend in there.

* * *

That raven. It spoke. She's seen it before. An unwelcome visit so many years ago. A promise of anonymity, and an unsure alliance. If I could only—

Wait, why am I remembering this now? I already know... I've already decided. So why—

I remember you! I...know you. Why do you decline to speak? Chocolate. Terribly hard to come by. What a foolish exchange, but I won't complain. Why am I telling—

* * *

"Gah, my head," Chandrima groans, slumping into her chair. *There it is again.*

"I trust your judgment, Director," Zochitl says.

"What? What...did I say?"

"You said we're going after the Yōulíng, and that the Scowl won't be a problem. I said that I trust you," she recounts. "I'm going to France. The Congress should be told in person, and I'm sure they'll be hesitant to move forward, but I'll smooth it over. And I'll..." she clears her throat with considerable effort, "...tell the Waifs...about Karima, before I go."

Chandrima puts a halting hand up. "No. It was my decision to send her out there. *I* will tell them myself." Zochitl studies her sorrowful eyes and nods in recognition.

"As you wish, Director," she responds, excusing herself from the room.

* * *

She *had* thought her episode on the night after Curiesay's outburst was from her concussion. But she doesn't have a concussion anymore. This was different. Violating. Someone had been in her mind. Her soul.

Zochitl didn't seem surprised that a Scowl had appeared. She didn't ask how Chandrima knew. She didn't ask how she planned to deal with it. She didn't do anything except agree with her. Wildly uncharacteristic.

Chandrima's sorrow blanks as the wheels of her mind spool up, running with frictionless efficiency. This is no longer a safe space. Her melancholy is replaced by waves of revelations, each one only adding speed to Chandrima's well-oiled gears.

Zochitl had fallen when she met Arthur in the Arena. *Did they see each other? How could she have known to look? Could she smell him?* Zochitl had been absent from the demonstration, but Chandrima remembers collapsing in her office. Hell, Zochitl had caught her. *She looked...at me. In me.*

Chandrima sits up sharply and slaps her keyboard, bringing her computer to life. She accesses the security system, reviewing the checkpoint logs. The scales had been meant to detect weight discrepancies for her staff; unnatural body densities. She can see every time Zochitl was screened at the checkpoint, and since the scales had been installed, the average amount of times she'd passed through decreased by sixty percent. *She's avoiding them.*

She reviews one of the videos, watching Zochitl carefully as they first scanned her with their handheld device. If there was a problem, the guards made no issue of it. They directed her onto the scale while she flashed her baby-blue eyes which, alongside her honeyed tongue, kept their attention on her face and not her feet. They were teetering on the edge of the pressure plate, her heel on solid ground. *She's fooling the scale.*

It doesn't make any sense to her. In fact, it's preposterous. She *couldn't* be a Scowl. Chandrima had vetted her personally, as did several other agencies. She wracks her mind, thinking back to their first meeting so many years ago.

* * *

July 10th, 2047
Bastion, Second Floor

"Doctor Joshi, it's a pleasure," Zochitl says as the women shake hands. The waiter slides her chair underneath her as she takes her seat across from Chandrima.

"The pleasure is all mine, Doctor Bottazzi," Chandrima responds, eyeing her interviewee. "Your necklace is beautiful."

She's right. It's tight, keeping Zochitl's slight chin raised. A choker, adorned crisply with hundreds of one-carat gemstones. Even as an internationally renowned scientist, this type of finery is well beyond her income. *Those must be cubic zirconia.* They're not.

"Oh, this old thing?" Zochitl says dismissively fiddling with her silverware. "Just wanted to make a good first impression." *She seems nervous.*

The restaurant is lowly lit and mysterious, with this section cordoned off for Chandrima's "business meeting." She is a bit ashamed, but she figures if she can write off this off as a business expense, she shouldn't skimp on the venue.

"First impression? Your reputation precedes you. Magna Cum Laude from Universidade de Sao Paulo, five separate letters of recommendation from the international scientific community, one from Doctor Nerezza Bellona, one from your *president*," Chandrima says as she shakes her head with satisfaction. "It's difficult to consider other candidates when I've several calls per day asking if I am considering Doctor Bottazzi for the role."

Zochitl touches her chest in flattery. "Please, I'm the one who should be reciting *your* prestige. Many of our colleagues say that without you, the Blight wouldn't have anything to fear. I wonder; do you suppose that you keep them up at night?"

Honeyed tongue. "I sure as hell hope so," Chandrima responds, cheeks reddening. The two share a regal laugh as the waiter arrives and takes their orders. He bows and recedes without a word. The Director's eyes crawl over Zochitl for a moment. Sun-kissed tan skin, flowing black hair, critical brown eyes. She's tall, lean. Built like so many South American athletes she's seen on television. Funny; she's surprised she hadn't noticed her athleticism when she reviewed her file.

"You know, we could have put this on hold," Chandrima says as her tone becomes tinged with sorrow. "I'm sorry about your husband."

Zochitl nods, putting a finger to her eye and catching a tear from the end of her lash. "Thank you. *I'm* sorry about Doctor Emerson. But you and I both know that our enemy won't participate in our mourning. Besides, without him, I've nothing left in Brazil. As I've always done, I'll lose myself in my work, as it fills my heart."

Chandrima nods in agreement. "I think you'll be a good fit here."

"I truly hope so," Zochitl says as their drinks arrive. Champagne. "So, what questions do you have for me?"

"None. I've already decided. The job is yours, should you want it," Chandrima says, and Zochitl immediately outstretches her hand. The two share a firm handshake.

"I accept. What will you have me do?"

"Foremost, the Waifs. They need a dedicated instructor. I'm not much of a teacher, and they're the key to humanity's defense."

"Ah, yes, the Waifs. Do you think it moral to use children as shields?"

Zochitl asks accusingly.

"Whether they stand in front of or behind us, we'll die all the same if the Blight wins," Chandrima responds, unbothered.

A satisfied grin stretches across Zochitl's face. "I see. Well, I suppose skipping the potty training is a nice perk."

"They're good kids. Orphans, all of them. I like to think…" Chandrima closes her eyes, thinking fondly, "…of them as my children. Well, them, as well as my Pilots."

"The Pilots. I've read some of the reports. They're not anywhere close to your initial projections, are they?"

Chandrima groans. "No. Not at all."

"They haven't been able to Cross yet," Zochitl says flatly.

Chandrima had been in the middle of a champagne sip, and it spews from her nose as she coughs. "How do you know that?" she manages as she frantically cleans her face with a napkin.

Zochitl doesn't miss a beat. "I'm thorough. Perhaps you have not pushed them far enough."

Chandrima ponders. *I suppose she works for me now, may as well…*

"The issue is the Blight cells are quite resistant to being governed. The Mark III features our highest sync rate, at a pitiful thirty percent. They're hardly stronger than the exoskeletons that the armed forces employ, and they cost twenty times as much," Chandrima responds dejectedly.

"Why Blight cells? I was under the impression that they mirrored the Americans' Prometheans?"

"Ha! No, unfortunately they did away with their source after the Culling. Quite shortsighted on—"

Zochitl grins as she interrupts her new employer. "They haven't. She lives."

Chandrima's narrowed eyes sharpen with skepticism. "I find that hard to believe. Why haven't they continued with their research then?"

"Once she found out about her role in the Culling, she rescinded her...*cooperation*." Chandrima stares with slack-jawed shock. "Her conditions are quite despicable. I'd wager, should you offer her better accommodations, she'd consider helping you. I've already spoken to Doctor Bellona about it, and she concurs. Perhaps you...*we*, should pay her a visit."

A long silence falls over the table as Chandrima downs the rest of her champagne in one fell swoop. "Doctor Bottazzi, I think you and I will be good friends."

"I do so hope that is the case, Doctor Joshi. If mankind is to have a champion, I cannot think of a more suitable set of shoulders for it to rest its hopes upon." Their waiter brings their meal, as well as a top up of fizzy champagne, and the two enjoy a long evening of small talk as they become acquainted.

* * *

October 13th, 2053
Bastion, Third Floor, Medical Wing

Why wouldn't she have told me? Surely she couldn't think I would sell her out. It's not adding up for Chandrima, and she doesn't like that. But her recollection of her surprise at Zochitl's physique just furthers her confidence in her theory—*Zochitl is a Scowl.*

Why dive into my mind now? What is she looking for? Zochitl has, in no small part, been instrumental in their success at Bastion. Now, she works against her? Something has changed.

Awake...

Awake!

She is toying with her mind. And that began *after* they received the letter. She hadn't considered that Zochitl is not only a Scowl, but that she's also sided with the Blight. And recent events have made it clear that the Blight can and will leverage Scowls against them.

Has she been a plant this entire time?! It can't be. All other doubts aside, Chandrima *knows* Zochitl cares for the Waifs. She'd never sell one out. The grief they'd shared, the look on her face. She wasn't surprised, she was *angry*. She must have known that this could happen. *Is she having second thoughts? What does she want? Information?*

Chandrima's train of thought stops dead in its tracks. It's been known that *some* Scowls possess the ability to influence a person's mind, but what Zochitl did was beyond that. *She can read my mind. Is that her Machina?* If she does it again, she'll find out that Chandrima knows. *What will she do then?* Her hands are tied. She can do *nothing* out of the ordinary, she can keep *nothing* from Zochitl, lest she grow suspicious.

Too much. Too much grief. Too much betrayal. Too much to do. The sorrow she had felt fully dissipates into an overabundance of calm. She must stay focused.

And she must make a trip to the candy store.

* * *

Night, October 13th, 2053
France

The door shudders as her guest pounds against it. "What an unpleasant surprise," Verlean chides as she opens it. Sadie stands on her stoop, face gaunt. Without a word, the blonde brushes past Verlean and into her apartment.

"Forget your manners?" Verlean asks snidely. Sadie doesn't respond as she tosses her briefcase onto the floor and plops down in the recliner. Verlean takes a seat across from her guest, crossing her legs. Sadie has apparently caught her just before bed; Verlean is scantily clad in a silk nightgown, her dark skin clearly visible through the fibers, a cup of tea steeping on the coffee table.

"She knows," Sadie blurts out bleakly, eyes closed, head resting on her hand.

"About you?"

"No. About the recon team," Sadie begins, then opens her eyes, a flash of red arching across her irises. "About how Samael killed them."

Verlean nods, pursing her lips in contemplation. "Well, it was only a matter of time."

"You knew."

"Yes, but not from you. Which pisses me off. What's the use of having a spy if you won't tell me when Bastion has a team in the Exclusion Zone?"

"Really? Really?! Samael murders one of my girls and you ask me why I wouldn't tell you?"

"*Your* girls? You're delusional."

Sadie springs to her feet. "Fuck you. I didn't ask for any of this, you—"

"Didn't ask?" Verlean interrupts cooly. "You took the job when I offered it. Did you think that was without cost?"

Sadie and Verlean went their separate ways after the Culling, and once the war with the Blight was over, Sadie was convinced that Verlean was dead. It wasn't until years later that Verlean contacted her, asking to meet in Brazil. What she had hoped would be a heartfelt reunion turned bloody as Verlean tracked down and killed Doctor Zochitl Bottazzi and her husband.

"What was I supposed to do? You'd already killed the woman and her husband, was I supposed to let that go to waste? You—" Sadie stops mid-thought, collecting herself. She had assumed the killing was part of Verlean's vendetta against those involved with organizing the Culling, but it is clear to her now. "You didn't kill her for revenge. You killed her because you knew I'd take the job." Verlean doesn't respond, raising her brows lazily in confirmation. "You're sick."

"I told you that you'd owe me. You took her place on your own accord. And you know the risks your *Waifs* take, what they're meant for. In truth, it's *your* fault she's dead."

Sadie scowls at her and leaps to her feet, irises boiling red. If Verlean is bothered by Sadie's stalking footsteps, she doesn't show it. "Don't you dare..." a stutter-step, "...tell...me..."

Verlean narrowly arrests her fall as Sadie faints, her serious expression softening, and gives a disapproving sigh as she heaves her back onto the recliner. She brings a glass of juice and a bag of salted nuts from the kitchen, setting them on the table.

Sadie comes to a moment later. Spotting the sustenance, she quickly gets after it, eating and drinking frantically.

Verlean plops back down on the couch, eyeing Sadie with heartfelt amusement as she eats. "You're too thin," she remarks seriously. "You need to be more careful."

Sadie quickly downs the juice and tears through the bag of nuts, belching unflatteringly when she's finished. "I'm done." Verlean stares at her unblinkingly. "Not with the food. With this spy shit."

"You'd really side with humanity over us? Over me?"

"There is no *us* anymore."

Verlean shakes her head with disgust. "No, there isn't. Only a handful of us remain after what they did. I still have nightmares about that day, about how you wept as I held you. I'd never heard a more agonizing cry. And yet you turn around and crawl into bed with our enemy."

"Our *enemy* is the Blight. What was left of our kin laid down their lives against it. And it consumed them all the same. It doesn't care about us, about you. You're only a means to an end. Why can't—"

"He's promised a world for us. A safe world, one where we can exist without fear of death."

"We all die, Verlean. That doesn't give us the right to annihilate every other—"

Verlean cuts her off with an upheld palm. "Enough. You'll continue your mission, unless you want them to find out what you really are, and what you've been doing."

Sadie's eyes widen in disbelief. "You wouldn't."

"Are you willing to take that chance, *Regalia?*"

Sadie stares at her for a long while. A sleek Persian cat leaps onto the backrest of the couch Verlean sits on, sauntering to its master on the backrest. She lazily scratches its chin as it rubs its head against her.

"Tell me what he's looking for," Sadie demands.

"*You* tell me what you know, and I'll decide if it's what he needs."

"Not gonna happen. I won't doom them. If I must die, then so be it."

"You think I'm bluffing?"

"I know you're not."

Verlean grunts, shooing the cat away. "A boy."

"A boy?"

"Yes. A Scowl. No name, in his teens by now. Green eyes, black hair. Very likely living in Bastion. Close with a redheaded woman and her daughter." Verlean pauses, conceding her frustration. "Seen anybody like that?"

"If I have, and I tell you who it is, do you swear to let me be on my way?"

"Do I really mean so little to you?"

"No. You mean a lot to me. Always have. But my girls mean more."

"They're not *your* girls."

"They're all I have. Swear to me. I want to hear you say it."

The two share a long pause. "Fine. I swear if you find me who he's looking for, I won't say a word to anyone about who and what you are," Verlean concedes resentfully, her hand over her heart. "So, have you seen him or not?"

"No, nobody like that. But Bastion is a big place," Sadie says as she leans back into the recliner. "If you'd told me this from the start, I could have been looking this entire time. Any idea what he wants him for?"

"You know, I didn't think to ask," Verlean says snidely. "You seem awfully relaxed now."

"The sooner I can put all this behind me, the better." Sadie checks her watch, then stands and grabs her briefcase. "It's late. I've got stuff to do tomorrow."

"Do you now? I thought you came all this way to see me. Can't spare any time for your master?" Verlean teases cruelly. Sadie knows that beyond Verlean's ruthless and unfeeling exterior, she'll have a glum night if she leaves now. But she cannot remain. The threats, the apathy. *The lies.* If she stays any longer, she'll let slip that she knows more than she lets on.

"I have to go," Sadie begins as she makes for the door, opening it to the cool night air. She looks over her shoulder, smiling somberly. "Because right now, I can't stand to fucking look at you."

***

Early morning, October 14th, 2053
Bastion, Third Floor, Administrative Wing

With Zochitl in France, Chandrima was free to root around her room. Of course, she'd waited until night, when the Third Floor entertained little more than crickets and a handful of overnight employees. Zochitl's room is adjacent to her office in the Administrative Wing, and all is quiet.

Chandrima had showered with near scalding water and scrubbed until her skin was raw. She couldn't chance Zochitl smelling her. If she suspects that Chandrima knows her true nature, Chandrima's life will be forfeit.

What a diva. It had been a while since Chandrima had dropped by Zochitl's dwelling. Original oil paintings, bronze busts of historical figures, boisterous antique rugs. Her room emanates high society and class. Though her own salary is considerable, Chandrima can't imagine how Zochitl affords these ornate furnishings.

Yet, she hadn't found anything suspicious. Her Scowl nature aside, she's known Zochitl to be incredibly particular about her personal appearance and belongings. She can't imagine that she'd simply leave evidence of her clandestine double-life.

She rooted through her study—a veritable Great Library of manuscripts—her kitchen, and her bedroom—the familiar regalia she'd seen Zochitl wear as well as some *questionable* personal aids. Last on her list was the bathroom.

Chandrima can't figure out how Zochitl could have fooled her so completely. Nothing about her past is suspicious in the least. Nothing shows any indication of having been fabricated. Her DNA scans are normal. Her *disposition* is normal. She helped develop the Arbiters, she leveraged the Americans to give up Pandora, she trained their Waifs. She *is* Bastion as much as Chandrima is.

Huh. That's strange. She's just finished going through Zochitl's bathroom, and it's surprisingly bare. Shampoo and body soap. That's it. No expensive lotions or sticky eyeliner or blush or brushes or makeup removal pads or lotion. Not even a tube of lipstick or a vial of nail polish. *Impossible.* Perhaps she'd taken some along with her, but surely not the entire menagerie of comprehensive beauty products that most women cling to.

I know I've seen her nails painted. I know I've seen her wear lipstick. It doesn't make any sense. How could a woman who values her physical appearance so grandly neglect to own a single beauty product? She knows that Scowls age gracefully, but this is beyond that. It's as if she doesn't *need* these products to—

Change her appearance. No. It couldn't be. That's why there's nothing in her past that suggests that she's a Scowl. Because *Zochitl* isn't. *She's an imposter.*

The revelation hits Chandrima like a ton of bricks. Her eyes wander to the sink. A hairbrush, one of the only implements in the bathroom, rests atop the basin. She examines it, her face contorting with confusion. *It's white.* The hair is white. Not greyed, not dyed hair that had washed away its aging coverup, but pure, dazzling white. Chandrima pulls a single hair from the brush and holds it close to her critical eyes. Since she's known Zochitl, she hasn't glimpsed a single grey hair on her head.

22

Intrusion

October 16th, 2053
Bastion, Third Floor, Recreation Wing

Nightmares, memories not of her own, have plagued Curiesay's dreams since that day. Her foray into Arthur's mind has only raised more questions, and she has less confidence in her understanding of Scowls. Not that she knew much to begin with.

She'd been released from the ICU after three days. Twice a day she had to receive her prescribed infusions of...*something*. Some compound, intravenously delivered, that darkened her already grave dreams. Its taste was familiar, her tongue tickling as it dripped into her veins. The same taste she has when she Pilots. *Peppermint.*

Arthur has been avoiding her. They'd exchanged glances in the cafeteria, but nothing more. She wonders how long he'll stay mad. *If it were me, I'd never forgive myself.* She hadn't intended to go so deep, to peer so intimately. Something about that place, his Dominium, dissolved her inhibitions. In that place, she felt free. Perhaps that wasn't a good thing.

She hesitates at the threshold. The Third Floor is bigger than she had thought. When she posed the question to Parker about Arthur's whereabouts, he'd responded, "In the Vivarium."

"What the fuck is that?" she had tactfully asked.

Located in the Recreation Wing, the door is at the far end of the hall. Apparently the Third Floor has more to offer than she's cared to see. She considers leaving him be, but selfishly, she cannot.

A deluge of warm, aromatic air strikes her as she swings the door open. The sounds of insects and cooing birds fill her ears as she steps inside. A concrete walkway snakes throughout the vaulted space, flanked by foliage from various biomes. Her skin tingles—*Is this what Eden was like?*

It's a large space, its ceilings vaulted. Nets are strung up between trees and the walls, and cables are used to help direct some of the livelier foliage to grow in more ideal patterns. *An indoor park?*

She traverses the path slowly. Not just birds, but insects as well, scurry throughout. Red-breasted robins dart to and fro, wide-eyed snowy owls perch on high, scanning for rodents. The sounds of their livelihood dissipate as she approaches, as if she emits an invisible force field dissuading them. Meandering through the Vivarium, she feels no ill will toward the creatures who avoid her—she'd do the same if she were them.

She almost misses him. Almost. Though his grey sweats clash with the vibrant foliage—and the butterflies that are perched upon him— he blends in like the natives. As if he himself has roots deep in the terra. He sits cross-legged and silent in a small clearing. She wonders if the butterflies think he's a statue, another artificial decoration.

She wonders if he belongs here.

His stoic expression melts into a smile as he brings his hand to his face to admire the blue morpho on his pointer finger. "What do you want?" he asks in a low voice. The wings of his guests stiffen as he speaks.

"I wanted to—" she begins, and stops short as half of the butterflies flee. "I'm worried about you," she continues in a whisper.

Arthur gives a disaffected grunt. "A little late for that. You should've…" He stands slowly, blowing gently on the blue morpho as he pauses between words, assisting its flight as it, too, finds a quieter place to jive. "Thought about that before you set yourself loose in my mind."

He steps out of the clearing, over the rocks that line the edge, and heads down the path away from Curiesay. She quickly falls in step behind him. "I didn't mean to. It just kinda…happened. I didn't…I've never done anything like that before. I don't know what came over me."

Arthur doesn't respond. He saunters down the path as Curiesay follows. She'd sensed his ire in the days since, even from a distance, even with a glance. And she senses it here too. But it's quieter. As if the tragedy has long since passed.

They walk in silence for some time. Occasionally Arthur clicks his tongue, mimicking the cry of the birds he beckons. More often than not, they heed his call. The orange-eyed eagle-owl lands atop his head, balancing itself as he walks. It leans over, examining his face. Its wings spread, and Arthur caresses it lithely, as if he is a gob-smacked first-time parent touching their newborn. It turns its head nearly all the way round and peers at Curiesay. She feels that it regards her with disdain. As if it, too, were wronged by her.

"They, uh, seem to like you," she manages weakly. If it were anyone except Arthur, she would be surprised with how willingly they flock to him. But right now, he floods the space with harmonious empathy, like he only remains corporeal because he chooses to.

Muscle-bound birds of prey, porous-boned love birds, steely eyed hawks, satin-smooth doves. Some linger longer than others, some sit across from their most fierce predators, some sit across from their tastiest prey. As if he's some sort of mediator, Curiesay doesn't sense their instincts when they're atop Arthur's head or shoulders.

"I like them too," he responds finally. He stops and turns to face Curiesay. He regards her with…nothing, looking straight through her. Her heart runs itself into knots—she wishes he would view her with contempt instead. He cocks his head, then a slight upturn of his lips. He vocalizes a series of high-pitched chirps and rolls, impossibly sharply delineated. *I know that call.*

A yellow-beaked bird swoops down and lands harshly on his outstretched arm. Curiesay can see its talons piercing his sweatshirt as it balances itself, but if it's hurting Arthur, he doesn't show it. "This one is a—"

"Peregrine falcon," Curiesay interrupts. She's enamored, not only by Arthur, but by his guest. A milky white, like when cream and coffee clash, colors its neck and breast. The same white is rolled over with lines of black down its legs, and on its wings and back the colors are inversed, with the grey-black majority being accented by the white. Tail feathers, sharp and long, extend from its backside. "I didn't know they lived in Europe too."

"They live everywhere except where its coldest. Too little food," Arthur adds. "How did you know what it is?"

Curiesay gives a modest shrug. "I used to have one. Not like, as a pet. Well, kind of like a pet." Arthur views her suspiciously, and she feels the falcon's eyes mirroring this sentiment. "I nursed one back to health when I younger. Hid meat from the orderlies to feed her, dug a hole near one of the far walls for her to nest." Her heart warms as she recalls her Orpheria—the name she'd given to the bird—as she was one of the only friends she'd made during the years she had spent interred.

"What happened to her?"

As quickly as it had warmed, her heart scalds over with ice. She thinks back to the feeling of sweat-covered hands on her biceps, an arm around her throat. A plea for mercy. "She died," she says flatly.

Arthur gives a short nod in recognition. "Would you like to see her? I could put in a good word for you."

"You…can talk to them?"

His chuckle nearly scares the falcon off, her feathers tensing. "I was being facetious; I know their calls, that's it," he responds with a teasing grin. "You can say no."

"No! I mean, yes, I want to see her," Curiesay says desperately. Such sharp lines. A living missile; the fastest animal on the planet. "I don't have anything to offer." Her friendship with Orpheria had depended almost entirely on food, though she hopes that it had taken her into her heart before the end.

Arthur reaches into his pocket and pulls out a piece of dried meat. "She won't prefer it, but it'll do," he says, tossing it to Curiesay. He performs another series of discreet avian noises into the falcon's ear, and though he'd said otherwise, Curiesay is convinced that he *can* speak to them. "Well…" he says with a hint of impatience, "…put your arm out."

Curiesay complies, raising her right arm. With gentle effort, Arthur urges the falcon forward and it swoops onto Curiesay's arm. Every conscious fiber of her being urges her muscles not to quake. The admiration, the memories, the deftness of its existence. She's entirely infatuated with this creature.

Making its way down her arm, it taps, not so kindly, on her head, and tugs on her hair. "Don't keep her waiting; she *saw* me throw it," Arthur says with a laugh. *Oh, right, the meat.* She presents it to the falcon, who, after a moment of examination, deems that it is worth consuming. It swallows it whole, then checks Curiesay's hand to see if anything remains. Disappointed, it pushes off with force and takes off into the "sky," returning to its duties or nest or whatever else it may choose to do.

Arthur turns away, lazily beckoning Curiesay to his side as he walks. They continue, traipsing through the trails. Birds and insects continue to follow, occasionally crossing paths, focusing solely on Arthur.

"I didn't know about this place," Curiesay says as a short, fat bird swoops by, nearly colliding with Arthur's head. "It's nice here."

"Yes, it is," he responds in a tone that Curiesay can't nail down. As they pass through an intersection, they spot a Waif, holding hands with a lab coat-wearing woman, admiring a chittering chipmunk on a branch. "I come here to think. Though we think ourselves better, we are still animals. Our self-imposed sequestration from our, for lack of a better word, *lesser* kin, only serves to dampen our souls."

Who is this? His manner of speaking is regal—some kind of overbearing confidence laced with a solemn modesty. Arthur is often soft-spoken, quiet, and unsure. What Curiesay would consider weak. It makes her sick most days, reflecting a part of her that she drowns out with aggression. But this is something else. Something in between the Arthur she knows and the Arthur she'd seen in his Dominium.

"What do you think about when you come here?" Curiesay asks, hoping that he'll elaborate on what the hell she'd seen in his mind. The woman whom he so lusted for, the Scowl he'd choked the life from, the corpse he'd wept over.

"Forgiveness," he whispers as he comes to a halt. Curiesay turns to him, his eyes lazily staring farther down the trail. "As much as we've tried, we have never been able to overcome our nature. Our proclivities for violence, for hatred, for selfishness, and our..." he turns slowly to face her, "...morbid curiosities." *Is that what he thought it was?* At that moment, one of the butterflies that had been mulling around Arthur is snagged by a sleek brown bird and its mate. They tussle over its corpse with greedy playfulness, tearing its wings from its body, before disappearing into the brush. "For them, you shouldn't attribute to a choice of cruelty what is very much their nature. Without the capacity for higher thought, their *crimes* are as much a choice as our hearts' choice to beat. But *we* are not without higher thought…" His eyes darken as he regards her. "Are we, Curiesay?"

The entire space falls completely silent. The same silence a forest concedes when a bear trudges through, waiting for any foolish meat to tremble in fear, giving away its position. Curiesay's skin tightens. Her eyes water.

"I do not fault you for curiosity," he says softly. "But it was not your place to look. You ignored my pleas. In my weakness, I could do nothing. You violated me."

Curiesay's mouth trembles. "Arthur, I'm so sorry. I fucked up." Their eyes lock for what seems like an eternity, his emerald eyes dancing with her hazel browns, a gaze of capitulation.

As if he can sense her next words, words that seek to clarify what she had seen, he steps closer. "Have you told anyone?"

"No, no, I didn't tell anyone. Chandrima asked, but I said it's still fuzzy."

"Here's what's going to happen," he growls, his breath hot on her face. "You don't tell anyone what you saw. You don't tell anyone *who* you saw. If anyone asks, tell them you saw memories about me finding my mother's body." *Your mother? What happened to—* "Focus!" he shouts. Curiesay's body stiffens, suddenly praying that the Waif and her companion are still nearby. "Can you do that? Can you keep this to yourself?"

Curiesay ponders as Arthur's gaze seems poised to burn a hole straight through her. "Who was that?" she asks, ignoring his question.

If she has had a moment of regret greater than this, she cannot recall. After what she's done, she's in no position to be demanding answers.

"Nobody," he responds quietly. "There is no one except Arthur. Promise me."

Her guilt outweighs her curiosity, and after her intrusion, the latter needs to take a back seat. "Okay. Arthur, I promise I won't tell anyone."

He takes a gliding step back, the sounds of life rising again as the thick air dissipates. His eyes soften as he shakes his head with a grimace. "I'm a bit nervous."

He's gone. The insects and avians return, swooping around him as he turns back the way they came. "About what?" she asks.

He raises a brow. "Our mission. That woman, the Blight. I… We'll have to go into her head. Like you went into mine. It's going to hurt her."

Curiesay has the notion that Arthur's uncertainty in himself isn't born of doubt, but reluctance. A fear of himself. He has no concern for his own safety, only the safety of someone he's never even met. *Selfless.* She feels terribly small next to him. She doesn't know what will happen when Chandrima inevitably sends them after the Blight, but she's glad Arthur will be going with them.

"She's already hurting. I don't know what they expect us to do exactly, but we'll do the best that we can. Together."

Curiesay glances at him. He doesn't turn his head, but she can see the blush rising on his cheeks. "Together."

The two take their time winding back through the maze of transplanted forest, not saying a word, smiling to themselves.

* * *

Bastion, Outskirts

Three months' salary, good grief. Confectionary ration cards aren't cheap. In fact, they're technically non-transferable. But everyone has their price. After a few hours of badgering her staff, she'd acquired enough for her needs.

She exits through the south gate, opting to take the long way around Bastion's circumference. Doing her best impression of someone who isn't in a hurry, she walks nonchalantly down the sidewalk that branches off into the surrounding fields.

Reaching the bench, she sits. And she waits. The nearest trail runners are barely perceptible. A rectangular box sits next to her. Red stripes, red bow. Although she can't smell them, she can imagine how they taste.

Wondrously crunchy chocolate-coated wafers, jaw-straining sticky caramel truffles, stomach-burning dark cocoa. *Three. Months'. Salary.* She beats down the urge to dig into the gift box.

It's a serene summer day; not too hot, nor too cold. Bastion sits like a grey monolith, its existence the only thing interrupting the rolling fields of green. Chandrima stares at her city for a while. *Her* city. Not in the possessive, but in fealty.

Maybe it's Bastion's isolated post, with her sister city being the only civilization in the region. Or maybe it's the power it permits her, a power she doesn't take for granted as the blood it derives from is not hers alone. Either way, she supposes this city will be her grave, as she fully intends to go down with the ship, so to speak, should it come to that.

She yelps as a grey owl lands forcefully on the backrest. She allows a quick glance before she drives her gaze forward. "I, uh…need another favor," she trembles. If the owl has heard her, or even cares, it doesn't react. "My Pilots are going into the Exclusion Zone soon, and—"

A whooshing sound is all she hears as the owl deftly grabs the box with its talons, taking flight on a northeasterly heading.

I suppose that's a yes.

* * *

Pale Wall, 1st Rampart

God this is so fucking boring.

The same thing, day after day. Rounds, reports, musters, and hours of staring at a forest. He doesn't figure there's many jobs worse than this, despite the relatively low effort. The corporal stares lazily into his binoculars.

Once the Blight had retreated into what is now called the Exclusion Zone, mankind was quick to surround it. Much like during the first World War, what began as a hastily dug series of trenches has evolved into a modern Great Wall of China. The Pale Wall encompasses the Exclusion Zone—at least until it reaches the sea—and the posts are cities in their own right. Three million soldiers man it year-round, and accompanying them are a plethora of permanent structures on the "safe" side of the wall.

It turns out that the Pale Wall was quite the overcompensation. The Blight seemed perfectly content with locking itself away and never expressed any intention of leaving its repose. The largest construction undertaking in human history—Bastion being the second largest—has been relegated to simply sitting in silence and pointing its critical eyes inward at a foe which has proved to be as aloof as it had once been deadly.

To add to their frustration, the Dreadwood began to grow. The Blight sought to keep humans out of *its* space. The forest grew rapidly and unabated by human intervention—artillery, napalm, tree growth regulators. Within a year, the Dreadwood stood stoically against the Pale Wall, a proverbial middle finger to all of humanity.

Angiosperms and gymnosperms alike dominated the forest. However, they were not the trees mankind had known. Twisted effigies of their once colorful and lush forms, while differing in some respects, all shared commonalities. Dull, grey bark. Black leaves, seeds, and needles. Terribly, encroachingly tall. Sequoia sempervirens, the tallest, stretched one hundred and twenty meters above, dwarfing its brethren. Humanity's scientists collectively scratched their heads, gob-smacked at the North American natives dominating this distant forest.

And so, day by day, year by year, soldiers peered inward into the grey expanse of privacy. Occasional eyes were spotted in the brush, sparkling in the sunlight. Almost always they were of some animal variety. On rare occasions, an errant Blight would make itself known, stepping into the fields between the Pale Wall and the Dreadwood. While they'd once ordered them struck down on sight, many commanders opted to let them be. What difference would it make, after all, against a foe which could reanimate and repurpose the dead?

"What do you think they're doing?" a man asks. The corporal looks off into the distance, to where the curving forest nearly conceals his view of the similarly curving wall. Trucks, tanks, white medical tents, thousands of men. They'd started arriving a day before and hadn't stopped.

"Something stupid, I reckon," he responds. Beyond the occasional "dead zone" check—ensuring that the minefield and traps between the Wall and the Wood were still in good order—humanity hadn't mounted an offensive against the Blight in years. Hell, there's a growing movement of people who think the Blight has died out, starving in its repose. *If it hasn't, they're gonna need a lot more soldiers than that.*

***

Morning, October 17th, 2053
Bastion, Third Floor, Medical Wing

An uncomfortable silence presides over the Pilots and Stewards as they sit. Behind them are a handful of uniformed soldiers, collars adorned with shiny insignia. In front stands Commander Cutter. Cross-armed. Silent.

Curiesay hasn't had the opportunity to meet him formally. She's seen him around on occasion, trudging through the Third Floor on his way to and from meetings with Chandrima. But today, he's in full view. And to her surprise, he sports an eerily familiar scar across his temples and the bridge of his nose. The same scar she'd noticed on Parker when they first met.

Cutter's gaze snaps to Curiesay so quickly that she hesitates to look away for a moment. There's something in his eyes, a recognition that she can't pin down.

The Directors enter the briefing room, dressed in their usual white coats. "All right, are you two ready for your first mission?" Chandrima chirps, drawing Curiesay's attention.

"Wait! You said two. Who's not going?" Curiesay asks, already suspecting the answer.

"Pilot Parker is staying here in Bastion," Chandrima responds. Some quiet murmurs are silenced as she speaks again. "It isn't up for debate, and I won't be explaining myself."

Chandrima and Zochitl approach the center podium where the Commander stands. "Figure you should tell them the *what* before I tell them the *how*," he says to Chandrima as he steps back.

"I concur. All right," Chandrima begins, then pauses for a moment as she collects her thoughts. "Your target is a Blight located approximately ninety kilometers northwest of the Pale Wall. Your mission is to make contact, subdue her, and bring her back to Bastion."

Curiesay is the first to interrupt, raising her hand a moment after she begins speaking. "'Make contact'? Like, talk to her?"

"I doubt she'll be in the mood to talk. No, you'll make contact via your Dominium. The Blight is telepathic, and with the help of your Arbiters, you are as well. The Blight invades their victims' Dominium and corrupts it, wrenching control from its victims. *Your* job is to enter hers and take control back, at least long enough to get her back here."

"Uh…okay. While we're doing…*that*, what will she be doing?" Curiesay asks hesitantly.

"Probably kicking your asses," Parker interjects. "Pilots are rated as Class A combat effective, while the Blight in question is estimated to have double A, if not higher, combat rating. It will take both of you to stand a chance." Curiesay looks at Arthur just in time to catch him rolling his eyes.

She returns her eyes to Chandrima. "If that's true, why isn't Parker coming with us? He's the most experienced and—"

"You two are plenty capable. Parker doesn't need to babysit you," Zochitl interjects. As much as Curiesay is frustrated by the manipulative and perpetually upbeat Chandrima, she much prefers her over her counterpart. Zochitl brings an air of superiority when she enters a room, and Curiesay wants nothing less than to question or respond to this cheap jab.

Curiesay continues her line of questioning, addressing Chandrima. "How are we supposed to convince her to come back with us?"

"Curiesay, while I appreciate your questions, I don't have an answer for you. No one has ever entered a Blight's Dominium, no one knows what awaits you inside, and no one who has fully turned has ever been cured before. Right now, you know more than I do." Although the thought of being without answers concerns her, Curiesay does enjoy the idea of knowing more than the omniscient Chandrima Joshi. "Speaking of, breaking her out of her Dominium probably won't heal her. We'll need to administer the cure as soon as possible once you have returned."

"Can't we just give it to her when we make contact?" Curiesay asks.

"Impossible. It must be administered here in Bastion. You worry about getting her back safely. Let *me* worry about the rest." For the first time, Curiesay feels as if she's part of a team and not just a big stick to be waved around.

Chandrima passes a folder to both Arthur and Curiesay. "We don't have high-resolution photos; too much interference." Curiesay flips her folder open and eyes the assorted stack of photos. A common theme exists: piercing red eyes. Just like hers and her comrade Pilots'. The biggest difference being the whites of the eyes are black instead. "It shouldn't be too hard to find her. She's likely the only Blight in the entire city," Chandrima continues.

Curiesay speaks without looking up. "Why is that? Rent too high?" she teases and allows herself a self-gratifying chuckle. Fear begins to work its way into her chest as she gets further into the folder. Although she doesn't suspect it is intentional, these photos play a lot like a "found footage" art project. Blurry, unfocused subjects. Red hues. Photos which seemingly show nothing, only to spot something malicious lurking in the background.

"Well," Chandrima says, then clears her throat. "She's not a big fan of other Blights." Curiesay flips to another photograph. The subject is their target, the red-eyed specter, out of focus. Around her are what *could* be corpses, but there's no way to be sure. Limbs and viscera wet the street as she stands threateningly in the center.

"She kills them?" Curiesay exclaims as she finally looks up.

Chandrima grins. "She kills anything that isn't cute and cuddly.

Except when she's *really* hungry."

Looking back down, Curiesay flips again. This one is different than the rest. The subject is curled up on a bench below a dim streetlight. She's rail-thin. Filthy. Laying on her side, a cat sleeps peacefully on the dip between her hips and ribcage.

"Okay. When do we leave?" Curiesay asks loudly as she closes the folder. Whoever this woman is, Curiesay is suddenly desperate to help her. To help *someone*.

Chandrima mimes her hands forward. "Let's not get ahead of ourselves. The Commander still needs to give you the *how*."

Motioning to Cutter, Chandrima moves away as the Commander steps forward. Two officers wheel a whiteboard behind the Commander and flank him. He speaks with impatience, leaving no beats for interruption.

"All right, Pilots Emerson and Richardson. You will be deployed via the Kinetic Deployment Apparatus into the Exclusion Zone, to an area south of the city where your target resides. It shouldn't take more than a day of walking to reach it, and you'll be staying at least two nights in the Zone." The Commander points to a topographical map on the whiteboard. At the bottom is Bastion, just above it being a red line that represents the Pale Wall. Farther beyond is a large red circle, their insertion point.

"Once you subdue her, you'll use these…" one of the officers brings a metal briefcase forward and pops it open for the Pilots to view, "…to signal for extraction. By then, your Arbiters will likely be exhausted, so my soldiers will come pick you up." The case is lined with thick foam, and in the cutouts are two pistol-shaped flare guns, with a line of thick shells flanking their sides.

"The red and blue ones are for you two to use at your discretion. Electromagnetic interference is guaranteed, so wireless communication is a no-go beyond a kilometer or so. These green ones are *only* to be used to signal back home to us. They're micronuclear charges, so be careful with them. They don't 'explode,' but they do emit radiation. Once fired, we'll be able to pick up the electromagnetic pulse and pinpoint your location. It shouldn't take more than six hours to reach you."

Curiesay nods along as he speaks, occasionally glancing at Arthur. He doesn't so much as twitch a muscle in his face as he listens.

"As for resistance, we will do our best to keep it to a minimum for you. We'll be launching diversion expeditions all around the perimeter which will hopefully draw Blights out to the edges. That, and this area has a low presence of Blights, thanks to your friend."

Friend. Curiesay supposes that she *will* be her friend soon. She dreads thinking what this woman's life must be like, how isolated she must feel. She recalls her many years at Wilted Rose. The desolation. The gallant knight rescue daydreams. Curiesay feels a sudden sense of camaraderie with Chandrima of all people. Just like Chandrima had rescued Curiesay, Curiesay would rescue—

"What's her name?" Curiesay asks as the Commander finishes his brief.

"You'll have to ask her. For now, she's designated as the 'Yōulíng,'" Zochitl responds.

Curiesay struggles a bit as she repeats the name. "You— Yōulíng? What language—"

"It means 'wraith,'" Arthur says flatly. Chairs creak as everyone turns to look at him with curiosity. "They're afraid of her." Curiesay catches Elva glaring at him with imperious eyes. *Let it slip, did he?*

"Yes, well, moving on," Chandrima announces loudly, drawing the attention back to her. Arthur winces, pressing his thumb and forefinger into his eyes. "You two will need to pack an overnight bag and any essentials. You're leaving at thirteen hundred hours this afternoon, so be quick. Dismissed."

In the afternoon, Arthur and Curiesay make their way to the hangar bay, clad in their Arbiters. They ride the elevator to the very peak of Bastion, the same hangar Curiesay arrived in so many weeks ago. As the elevator arrives, the Pilots, Stewards close behind, step out onto the hanger deck. Curiesay's eyes wander as they walk, glossing over the maintenance personnel, flight crews, and soldiers that mill about. Unlike the last time she was here, she no longer feels like an intruder—she feels like she has just as much right to be here as they do.

"Oh, my dears, I can't tell you how excited I am!" Chandrima bubbles as she sees the group approaching, clapping her hands obnoxiously.

"Lady, we're about to go fuckin' die, don't be too excited," Curiesay says, and Arthur stifles a laugh with a firm jaw. Elva glares disapprovingly at the back of her head.

"Curiesay, you must have faith! You two are ready, this will be fun! Your first real mission… Oh, I'm shivering with anticipation!" Chandrima shouts.

"Ew. Well, just stay over there then," Curiesay retorts.

Chandrima's eye twitches as she forces a grin. "You are *so* crude. But I think that's what makes you a good Pilot."

"Yeah, thanks, Mom," Curiesay responds sarcastically.

"So, as we discussed, your auxiliary feeding packs will give you considerably more time in your Arbiters. That is, if you keep your power usage down. We're also delivering feeding packs to your landing zone. You both attended the crash course the technicians gave you on how to disassemble the suit in the field?"

"Yes, Director," the Pilots respond in unison. On the backs of their Arbiters are said "feeding" packs. Large and rectangular, they're mounted high on their backs and add quite a bit of size to their suits. Curiesay learned about them in her classes—some pre-charged "battery" that feeds their Arbiters in lieu of their feeding tubes. She had wondered what exactly was in them, but didn't dare ask.

"Good. I recommend that you only Pilot them when you know you will be in imminent danger. Even with the feeding packs, your time in your Arbiters will be limited," Chandrima says. A handful of soldiers have been walking alongside them and motion to the Pilots to pass them the bags they carry, which they do with some reluctance.

"Hey, be careful with that," Curiesay growls.

"Oh, dear, you don't know *how* you'll be getting there, do you?" Chandrima says with a mischievous smile.

Curiesay shrugs. "Uh, a kinetic something or other?"

"And you don't know what that is, do you?" Chandrima responds. Curiesay shakes her head and glances at Annata, who is poorly concealing a giggle.

"Ta-da!" Chandrima exclaims as she points. Mounted mostly *in* the floor, a long black tube spans a quarter of the length of the hangar bay. It is slightly angled up, the breech of the cannon being recessed into the floor.

"A cannon? You're gonna fire us out of a cannon like fuckin' circus clowns?!" Curiesay rages with disbelief.

"Well *equipped* circus clowns! And this is the *Kinetic Deployment Apparatus.* That is also how your provisions and bags will arrive, so I hope you didn't pack anything too breakable," Chandrima says.

Elva, who along with Annata has been standing behind their Pilots and listening, steps forward. "Have you used this before? On Parker?"

"Of course. It is perfectly safe," Chandrima says. Elva waits for her to continue, which she does not.

As Elva begins to retort, Arthur puts his hand on her shoulder. "It's all right, this suit is tough. She could fire us through a building, and we would survive. Probably."

She glares at him skeptically before nodding. "Arthur," she says in a sharply serious tone. "Come back alive." Elva then turns her attention to Curiesay, pointing as threateningly as she can manage. "And you… No…uh, funny business!"

"Promise. I got his back." She puts up her fist to Elva, who reluctantly bumps it. The technicians usher the Stewards back from the cannon as the Pilots and Chandrima crowd around the breech.

"So, you two are on speaking terms again?" Annata whispers to Elva.

"Arthur told me to drop it, so I did. He said he trusts her."

"Good to hear," Annata says mockingly.

Curiesay holds her fist out toward Arthur. "Rock, paper, scissors?" Arthur rolls his eyes but cannot contain his smile as he puts his hands up. They play—Arthur reveals scissors and Curiesay reveals rock.

"Oh no, looks like you get to die first. When you get to hell, tell the devil to make some room," she remarks in an obnoxiously masculine voice. The technicians instruct Arthur on how to enter the cannon. They flip open the hatch on top, large enough for him to climb into the breech. He crawls inside, facing upward toward the hatch on the topside of the barrel.

"Okay, my dear, once we close the hatch, it won't be long until you are launched. Just try not to panic," Chandrima says. Arthur gives her a thumbs-up and the technicians close the hatch.

Curiesay leans over, using her hands to amplify her voice. "Hey, Arthur! I know you're about to be a cannonball, but *don't* panic!" The Stewards giggle at the absurdity of the situation as they cover their ears.

The barrel rises out of the floor, with hydraulic arms underneath bringing its bore in line with the targeting data. After a moment of adjustments, the barrel is still, pointing out of the open door at the end of the hangar bay. Beyond it, there is blue sky, and beyond that is darkness and fog and lightning. In the distance, the Exclusion Zone waits to receive its guests.

"Shot!" the fire control officer yells. Arthur is fired out at tremendous speed, so fast that Curiesay can hardly see him as he exits. The sound produced is a hollow *thump* which vibrates her teeth.

The cannon retracts into the floor as Chandrima ushers Curiesay toward the breech. "Quickly now, don't keep Arthur waiting!"

As Curiesay crawls inside, her breathing accelerates. There's barely any room to move at all, arms tight to her body. "Hey, lady, I don't know…I don't… I don't wanna do this." Uncomfortable memories of isolation bubble up. Tight spaces. Darkness.

Chandrima kneels at the breech. "My dear, you have come so far in such a short time. When I first met you, you were hiding behind a sheet. Now look at you; about to be fired headfirst into hell. If you weren't capable, I wouldn't send you."

Curiesay can't help that she is beginning to trust the Director, as much as it pains her to admit. This pep talk halves the butterflies in her stomach. "Okay…okay. Just…do it quick."

The hatch closes, and the darkness is nearly complete, save for the light from the end of the barrel. Her inner ear detects movement as the cannon adjusts, and she feels the hair on her skin stand on end. The smell of ozone.

A muffled yell is eclipsed by blistering acceleration as Curiesay is fired headfirst into hell. It's so violent that Curiesay fears her skin will be left behind in the barrel. She forces her eyes open; she's hundreds of meters in their air and rising. Looking backward, she sees Bastion's girth disappearing into the distance.

Looking ahead, her eyes burn. Wicked wind. Then, they burn even hotter. A translucent layer of skin rapidly forms over her eyes, shielding them. *Man, these suits are dope.* Below her, the Pale Wall approaching, and beyond it a thick wall of foliage. The trees' canopies are a sickly grey and give off a somber mist, the air above dark and tall.

Blazing over the trees, wind buffeting her ears, Curiesay's heart flutters. She'd always hoped that after she dies, she'd return as a creature with wings, and imagines what wings she would choose, if she could. Wings to fly away from her foster mother, to carry her over the barbed fences at the institution, to raise her to the heavens so that she may wrap them around her uncle Thomas. Wings like her wounded friend's who—

She wishes she had more time to enjoy this. She's reached the apex of her flight and begins to descend. Passing over the end of the sickly, dark forest, she can see the world open up. Green grass. Blue skies. Virgin lands.

It is strange to her to feel so at ease as she plummets toward the earth. Instinctively, she uses her thrusters to orient herself feet forward.

Two hundred meters until contact. Her underfoot thrusters scream to life, slowing her forward momentum. At the same time, she uses the ones on her back to arrest her vertical descent.

One hundred meters. She points her feet down, using her hand thrusters to orient herself into an upright position. Fifty meters. Thirty. *Too fast.* Ten. She kicks her right leg forward and sweeps it back violently, skipping off the ground. Then the same with her left as she comes back down—her knee nearly buckles. She points her left hand forward, landing sideways, and wills max power to the thruster as she digs her feet into the ground.

With the grace of a refrigerator launched from a trebuchet, Curiesay's feet dig a deep divot into the ground as she skids to a stop. Eyes wide. Accomplished. *I'm alive. But I probably need to work on my landing.*

"You need to work on your landing," Arthur says through Curiesay's speakers. *Yeah, I know.* She spots him standing on a small incline to her right, with no sign of a hard landing across the ground.

"I'm alive, aren't I?" she retorts in a playful tone, tinged with annoyance.

He shrugs and half-smiles as he makes her way to her. "I'm sorry. You did good for your first time." Curiesay can't help but notice his gait—he's light. Carefree. As if he's not in the most desolate place on the planet. Curiesay shares this sense of ease. No one around to tell her what to do, *and* she's with Arthur. The experiment they'd shared has intensified her growing attraction to him.

"Wish I could say the same about you," she teases. Looking around, she takes in the landscape. Off to the side is a road accosted by overgrown weeds, asphalt crumbling from inattention. There's a dilapidated town a ways down, the tops of the buildings drooping under the moss canopy their roofs are accommodating. In the distance, she can see small homes here and there, in a similar state of disrepair.

Above, she hears the gentle flapping of fabric. "Look! Presents!" A long green cylinder with a parachute attached is falling toward them. Several, in fact. As it lands, she uses her augmented strength to tear the canopy from the cylinder, leaving only the ropes behind.

"I think that's my stuff. I've got yours over here," Arthur says as he examines the cylinder that fell in front of him.

Curiesay blushes, dragging her cylinder to Arthur and leaving a trail of crushed grass in her wake. "How do you know it's mine? Did you go through it?"

"What? No, *your name* is written on the outside," he responds, pointing to the black marking on the side of it that indeed spells *Curiesay.* For the next ten minutes, the two Pilots search for and locate the rest of their supplies as more cylinders arrive, six in total.

They divide them up, three and three, and drag them as they

walk north. They don't talk much, focused solely on dragging their supplies. Even with her Arbiter, it's miserable work, and within four hours, Curiesay is gassed. Far in the distance she can see the cityscape over the horizon and figures it's their destination.

As late afternoon comes, Curiesay stops to catch her breath, sweat dripping from her brow and burning her eyes. Even with the weeks of physical fitness training, this is hard work. "Arthur, let's call…it a day." Seemingly no worse for the wear, he drops his ropes and scans the landscape.

Many of the houses look uninhabitable, even from a distance. Curiesay read a lot while she was in the institution and adored dystopian novels. Something about the desperation and brutality of those fictional worlds drew her in—she felt her soul would be more at home in struggle than in solace. *That blue one? No, the far wall is buckled.* As far as dystopias go, this world could be worse. *That one is big. Looks like the windows are all broken though.*

Things are alive here, just not humans. Although the homes aren't suitable for people, she is sure that *something* lives in them. *That one is half ash; I wonder how the fire started.* Perhaps a family of squirrels. *Oh! Besides the vines, that one looks all right.*

"Hey, Arthur, there's a nice two-story over—" Curiesay stops short as she turns to Arthur. He holds one hand out in front of him, flicking his thumb from right to left over and over.

"I can't do it alone," he whispers. Curiesay steps closer, quietly moving behind him, trying to gauge his sightline. "Together?" he says bleakly as he stares off into the distance. Curiesay sees it: a red barn, its doors open, sits half-demolished in the distance.

"Arthur," she says gently, placing a hand on his shoulder. "Let's head this way." This seems to snap him from his daze as he turns to her. He blinks a few times, and as if his eyelids have wiped away whatever recollection he'd been trapped in, he nods. The two pick up the cords from their canisters and drag them to the house.

Curiesay rattles the front doorknob—locked. They head around to the side and enter the unlocked door there. The house is quaint. Sparsely furnished. The bottom floor consists of a kitchen with some broken appliances, a table, a sofa in the living room, and a staircase. The pair drag the supply canisters in through the side door and close it behind them.

"Huh… I guess we should have been checking for Blights. I mean, we're in the Exclusion Zone, aren't we?" Curiesay says as she cautiously walks around the ground floor, the boards groaning under her weight.

"Probably. But they said the excursions should draw most of them from the interior," Arthur responds.

"They must have noticed us though."

"Maybe. But what can they do? Chandrima says they're smart enough to know when they're outclassed. Unless we run into some Class A's, I'm not all that worried." Arthur pauses, then shakes his head. "I…don't know why I said that. I haven't even seen one yet. I need to keep on my toes." Spotting a staircase, he leaves the canisters on the floor. After testing his weight on the first step, he carefully begins his ascent.

"Between the two of us, we'll be fine," Curiesay says, stalking her prey. "Let's check upstairs for a bed and see who's sleeping on the couch!" She bolts past him on the stairs, bumping him. He leans against the railing, which fails miserably under his weight and falls, crashing through the bottom floor and into the basement, leaving a comically Arthur-shaped hole in the wooden floor.

Curiesay freezes, cheeks drawn back and teeth clenched, as she watches the cloud of dust rise from the hole. "I think I know who's sleeping on the couch," Arthur says with a dull echo.

23

Rescue

Evening, October 17th, 2053
Exclusion Zone

"Hold still, it's jammed," Arthur says as he kneels. They've moved to the living room for the disassembly, and Curiesay stands in front of him, the arms and chest plates of her Arbiter having been removed. Arthur studies the directions intently, the drill and prybar on the floor next to him.

Curiesay gives a light-hearted scoff. "I think you just like being close to me." Arthur blushes as he glances up at her. She grins at the idea of *this* Arthur sporting the same helmet she'd seen in his Dominium. *Embarrassed, goat boy?* For once, Curiesay is the one providing the intrigue, and the butterflies accost her heart.

He finally looses the bolts for her thigh armor and removes them, sliding them through the back of her armor. They clatter to the floor as Arthur works on the pelvic plating. With Curiesay supporting the front and Arthur the back, he separates the plating, and they carefully lower them.

Curiesay pulls her fingers out from underneath as she almost

352

follows the armor plating to the floor. "Damn, these things are heavy. How much you figure they weigh?"

"Each Arbiter is different, but the manual says they're typically three times the weight of their Pilot," Arthur responds as he removes her calf plating, placing it aside.

"Amazing that we can even move in these things. I feel light as a feather when I'm wearing it though; that's still so strange to me." She puts her hands on his shoulders for balance as she allows Arthur to remove her boots.

Reaching upward, she lets loose a chirpy yawn as she stretches, finally free of her Arbiter. She's wearing only her Interface suit, which is black at her request.

They move the pieces of her Arbiter into the kitchen, neatly and in order. Her Arbiter, nearly sparkling with its metallic purple sheen, sits quietly without a Pilot and without a head, its limbs held together by nothing.

Arthur takes his place in front of Curiesay and stands with his arms straight out to his sides. "Okay, my turn." He waits. From behind, he can hear Curiesay giggle. "What?"

"Why are you standing like a scarecrow? I'm not a technician and I'm in no hurry. We're staying here for the night," she says, leaving Arthur standing awkwardly in front of her.

"The more time we spend distracted by this, the less time we are watching our backs. We're just regular people once these are off, and I'd like to not be snuck up on."

"Relax. We've got the gun," she says as she points to the black rifle leaning against the wall. It isn't much of a backup, considering Curiesay has only had a few days of marksmanship instruction during her training, but she's confident she can hold her own. Strangely, she had thought, Arthur had vehemently *refused* to participate, and stranger still, Chandrima didn't press the issue.

She continues, neglecting to remove Arthur's Arbiter as he stands stoically. "Plus, they sent those motion sensors along." They'd set up the small black sensors around the house before they'd started their disassembly. "If they try sneaking up on us, we'll know. It is kinda weird though. I figured we would have seen *something* by now."

Arthur turns around to face her. "Curiesay... Where are we?"

She half-laughs, shaking her head. "What? What do you mean? Like, this house? Or do you mean the Exclusion Zone?"

Arthur winces. "I... Never mind. Sorry, I zoned out for a sec. Let's get this thing off me." *Stay with me, Arthur.* She doesn't know why he seems to have constant headaches, but personal feelings aside, she needs him to be alert on this mission. Given that he'd stopped her from killing Parker without an Arbiter, she thinks he's the one who has the best chance of protecting them if something happens while they're unarmored. Curiesay grabs the drill and goes to work. Sometime later, his Arbiter is completely removed, leaving him standing in his white Interface suit.

Arthur stretches deeply and yawns, holding his hand over his mouth. "Just wearing those things takes a lot out of you. How many feeding packs did we end up with?"

Curiesay helps him move the pieces of his Arbiter into the kitchen, then counts the feeding packs that are laid out on the floor. "Two extras each, plus the two we wore here. So, six total." She presses a button on the side of the feeding pack attached to her armor and an LED bar lights up; only two of the five bars flash. "The ones we used today aren't completely dry yet, but by tomorrow morning our Arbiters will probably finish them off."

As they were shown, they enter the kitchen, portable tablet in hand, and "activate" their Arbiters. They'd laid the pieces out as if someone were inside, and as they press the button, the limbs snap together. Otherwise, without being attached to the torso plating, the limbs would "starve," the terminology giving Curiesay further misgivings about her Arbiter's secretive construction.

The pair grab their duffel bags out of the cylinders and go to separate rooms to change. They return to the kitchen, both wearing their prescribed sweat uniforms. Arthur's is all black while Curiesay's is purple.

She gives him a sour look. "Oh yeah, you still haven't decided on a color yet, have you?"

"What do you mean? It's black."

"Yeah, that's the standard. Is that what you want?"

"I don't see a reason to change it. What difference does it make?"

"I mean, you should want to make it yours. What's your favorite color?"

"Red, I guess."

"That would look dope. I'll tell Elva to have Chandrima change it, since I know you won't."

"I thought you wanted me to make my own decisions?" he says snidely, recalling their conversation inside of his Dominium. Curiesay's face turns beet-red. Up until now, he hasn't mentioned anything about what they talked about or what they *did*, and she suddenly wishes he would forget.

He tussles her hair with his palm. "I'm just messing with you. Red is fine I suppose." He steps past Curiesay and grabs a fistful of freeze-dried snack bags from one of the cylinders. Heading back into the living room, he tosses one blindly at Curiesay. Striking her in the chest, she manages to catch it before it falls. *Pretzels.*

The two take seats at the opposite ends of the green and decaying sofa. It's held up well, all things considered. Sixteen years of daily moisture changes took its toll; the cushions having dulled in color, a faint musty smell permeating the air around it.

Arthur and Curiesay open their respective snacks and eat. This is the first time they've been alone together, away from everyone and everything, since Arthur had knocked on Curiesay's door all those weeks ago.

"So…" Curiesay begins. He gives her an apprehensive glance, and she figures he knows where this is going. "You really don't want to talk about it?"

Arthur looks down, slowly chewing some almonds. "It's not…that I don't *want* to. I mean, I don't, but that's not why. I just…can't."

"Can't? Why can't you?" Curiesay asks as she turns more toward him, crossing her legs and pressing herself into the corner.

"It's complicated."

"Then let's work it out together."

"Why?"

"What do you mean 'why'?"

"Why do you care?"

"I just do, all right? I'm allowed to care about you."

"You…care about me?"

Fuck. Not only is Curiesay poorly skilled at speaking to people in general, but she's also woefully underequipped to talk to someone she likes. Whereas most people learn what *not* to say to their crushes during middle and high school, Curiesay never had that luxury.

"No," she insists. *FUCK.* "I mean yes. Kind of. It's not really like that… You know when… I mean, we see each other every day…so like it's not *that* weird if I like you. No!" she corrects. "*Care* about you. I don't like you. I mean, I do, but…" *I'm going to throw myself off the roof.*

Curiesay continues to say a whole lot of nothing, her cheeks flushed, speech rapid and nonsensical. She refuses to look at Arthur, who is enjoying the show that comes with his snack.

When she finally runs out of incomplete sentences, he lets her sit in the silence for much longer than she'd like. "Thank you. For caring.

Or not caring. Or something." Curiesay allows herself to chortle as she finally meets his gaze, his emerald-green eyes looking softly at her. *Stupid eyes.*

He crumples up his empty almond bag and grabs another pouch, not bothering to check the writing on the front. "I don't want to talk about anything that you saw. But we can talk about other stuff if you want."

She *can't* do that. At least, she doesn't think she can. Ten years in an asylum isn't an experience anyone else can relate to, and there's nothing outside of that place that *she* can relate to. She knows a lot about psychiatry. A lot about fiction. And a *lot* about Wilted Rose.

She knows that on Thursdays they bring in the baked goods for the week, and that anything left over by Monday is probably moldy or stale. She knows that Doctor Mattingly will *personally* see to it that Curiesay receives her shock treatments, even on her days off. She knows which of the staff smoke, which doors they use to sneak a couple of drags, and which ones will get handsy if they catch her alone at night.

Curiesay knows a whole lot about a world she'll never return to, and not much else. Things are easier in Bastion. Well, maybe not easier, but at least she's afforded a measure of freedom. And again, she finds herself with time. Her *own* time to do whatever she pleases. Say whatever she wants to say. And she can't think of a single thing she wants to tell Arthur. Why would he *ever* care about—

"Do you miss it?" he asks.

Curiesay had been staring at him blank-faced, as she often does. "Miss it?"

"You said you grew up in a mental institution. Do you miss it?"

"What? Why would I—" Curiesay stops mid-sentence, arresting her imminently raising voice. *Tell him the truth.* "Sometimes." Things were simpler there. She never had to think, never had to hope. Sure, it crushed her soul, but she'd grown used to it. The uncomplicated nature of being a living piece of furniture has become a part of her, and sometimes she feels like a coffee table that's gained free will. *What do I do now,* it thinks to itself, *and why would I do it?*

"What did you do there? I mean, what were your days like?"

Curiesay pulls her feet farther under her as she sits cross-legged in the couch corner. *What* did *I do there?* She starts off slowly, her tempo picking up as she becomes lost in recollection. "I read a lot. A book a day probably. They didn't really have a big selection, so I ended up reading a lot of the same books twice. I remember when the local library shut down and donated a ton of books for us. I read all day for weeks on end until they downsized our collection. Out of spite, I assume. But it was nice to, like, have a choice, you know? I read so many new books and I would stay up almost all-night reading. They didn't allow any lights past ten o'clock, so I had to turn my bed toward the window and use the lights from the parking lot to see. I managed to keep a couple of my favorites before they cleaned house, but I left them behind. Couldn't exactly peel up the floor tiles where I had them stashed while I was being rushed out the door. I do think about them a lot. The books, I mean. I did a lot of my growing up with those books. I miss them. There's one that—" Curiesay stops abruptly as she realizes how long she's been talking.

"I'm sorry, you don't want to hear me ramble all day," Curiesay says, averting her eyes. *How did he do that? How did he get me to—*

"It's not rambling if I asked you about it," Arthur responds warmly. "There's one that what?"

She stares at him in disbelief. "Well, there's one..." she begins, collecting her thoughts, "...called *The Road.* I've probably read it a hundred times. It's really sad. I mean, I guess it's not *all* sad. I mean...I mean, it is. It's super depressing. But, I don't know. Part of me felt happy when I read it. It's about this guy and his son trying to live in this, like, post-apocalyptic world. They never really say what happened, but it's hinted that it's a sort of nuclear winter. So, everything is super cold, right? No food, no civilization. Sucks ass. And this guy and his son have to find food and shelter. And that's…kinda the whole book. Just them trying not to starve. And then the dad dies, and the kid is sad about it, and then it's over. But that part is my favorite part in the whole book. Isn't that weird? Like, yeah, it's sad, but it's only sad because they cared about each other."

Curiesay pauses, examining Arthur closely. He hasn't moved an inch, or yawned, or made fun of her, or told her she talks too much. All the fears she harbors regarding vulnerability haven't made an appearance. Arthur doesn't speak. He just watches her as she decides whether to keep sharing. *How strange he is. He has so little regard for himself, but he'll sit there and listen to me blabber on.*

"You know, I read it so much that I used to have dreams that *I* was the little boy. I remember feeling very cold. And hungry. There's one part…" she taps her fingers over her heart, "…where they find this, like, cannibal house. And I dreamt that too. I was so afraid that I would be eaten. But he saved me. The dad. And even though I was more scared than I'd ever been before, I felt safe…loved. And I remember waking up alone in my bed and wishing I hadn't…" Her eyes begin to tear up as her voice cracks. "Because I'd rather be cold and hungry with someone I love, than be alone."

You asshole. Why'd you make me go and do this? Curiesay hates crying. She hates the way it stuffs up her sinuses. She hates how itchy her eyes get. She hates the greasy lines it leaves on her skin. And right now, she hates that she's doing it in front of Arthur.

But she'd never told anyone this before. She never really had anyone to tell. *Why him? Why does he care? Why does…* But she knows why.

His memory. Not only had she been able to see what he'd seen, she had felt what he felt.

The one where he floats. The one where he is drowning. The banging of his tiny fist on the glass. Not out of pain, she remembers. But out of fear. He was afraid of his last moments being desolate of connection. Of approaching that dark abyss alone. Of crossing the River Styx enraged, defiant. *Why is it that my last moments should be filled with rage? Am I not allowed to fade into the ether as the stoic?* When the other hand pressed up against the glass, he was comforted. He was content with death. It was that moment, his first, when he hadn't felt alone.

As Curiesay covers her face with her hands, Arthur discreetly scoots closer, and without a word he puts his arms around her. Relaxing a bit, she draws her legs up to her chest, holding them tightly with her arms. She allows him to embrace her as she stifles her tears. The first real embrace she's had since she was a little girl.

"Are you cold right now?" he asks.

"Cold? Uh...no?"

"Are you hungry?" he continues.

"No..."

"Do you feel alone?"

"I... No," she quavers, finally catching on. "No, I don't." Arthur holds her for a while as she regains her composure. As the sun creeps beyond the horizon, the two sit and eat and talk and laugh, careful to keep their voices down.

They pull up the coffee table and put the motion tracker tablet on it, its screen perpetually on. The rifle leans next to it. Curiesay wonders if it's wise to let her guard down like this, but she trusts Arthur. If he's not afraid, then she isn't either. She knows she should be, logically, but fear is the furthest thing from her mind.

As night comes, the two retrieve the thin blankets from their cannisters and sit on the couch, separated by the center cushion. "It's a shame that bed's no good," Arthur says as he backs into the corner.

Curiesay averts her eyes toward the floor. "Yeah." They had ventured upstairs earlier. A couple, decayed and embraced, were nearly melted into the mattress in the bedroom. Curiesay supposes they'd chosen to die together rather than be taken by the Blight.

"That was my first time seeing a body," Arthur says bleakly. *That can't be true.* She had seen so much in his mind. So much death. But she doesn't think he's lying. Maybe *he* has never seen a body. *But then, whose memories were those?*

"Me too," she responds as she curls up. Apparently, it's difficult to predict the weather in a place where no one ever visits. The olive drab blankets are subpar, and as the night carries on, the two can see their breath as they talk.

"You know, in that book, when it got really cold..." Curiesay struggles with the words as she turns away from Arthur. "They would... Well, so it's like, they slept close to each other. *Really* close. To, like, share body heat or whatever."

"Oh? Interesting proposal." Curiesay can't see his face, but she's sure he has some stupid grin on.

"It's not a proposal! I'm just saying that *this* reminds me of *that*. I'm not *proposing* anything," she insists. She's committed to freezing to death if she must. That sounds easier than...whatever *this* is.

She hears rustling. "Well, come on. I'm cold too," he says as he pats the couch cushion between them. He's extended his legs across the couch, laying long ways and holding his blanket open for her. He locks eyes with her for an uncomfortable amount of time. Usually, Curiesay's icy stare dissuades others from making prolonged eye contact, but Arthur doesn't seem to mind in the least. Curiesay feels like if she shows any more vulnerability today, she may combust, but she is quite cold.

She reluctantly crawls to his side and lays down in front of him.

Closing the blanket over her, he respectfully puts his left arm down across her leg instead of around her waist. *Liar.* He isn't cold. He's scorching hot.

They lay in silence as Curiesay tries to sleep, but she can't. She's too excited. Too embraced. She's never been this close to someone before. At least, not willingly. Like a child staying up to wait for Santa, she's afraid she'll miss this moment if she drifts off to sleep.

"Curiesay," Arthur whispers. "Why… In my Dominium…why did you come on to me?" *Quick! Pretend to be asleep!* She's changed her mind.

Moment go! Moment pass! Much to her dismay, Curiesay doesn't possess the ability to control time.

"I don't know," she responds curtly.

"Were you just trying to distract me?"

"No! No, I wouldn't… That wasn't why."

"I mean, I get it if that's why," he says bashfully. As if that isn't the answer he's hoping for. "I just want to know—"

"I just said that isn't why. There's more than one reason why people…do that."

"Like what?"

"Are you asking me why people have sex?"

"I'm asking why you wanted to *see* me."

She pauses for a long while. *I guess I've never really thought about it.* "You seemed lonely. Sad. And I…I don't think you deserve to feel that way. I guess…I was just trying to make it better. Fix it."

"Oh."

"Yeah." A silence falls over the two. From beyond the walls of this house, Curiesay can hear the night.

The haunting hoots of tawny owls echo across the landscape, striking fear into the hearts of the field mice below the grass. A chorus of crickets is so dense that she can only hear it when one of its members falters. A hefty breeze puts this old house's moorings to the test, buffeting the time-tested stone walls. Through their irregular bonds, more cold air seeps through, and eventually Curiesay completely covers up, head under the blanket.

She can feel Arthur's chest rising and falling against her back, its regularity comforting. The slight sound of air through his nostrils is melodious, and with its metronome, she drifts off to sleep.

* * *

The sounds of quick footsteps and rustling wake Curiesay from her slumber. Yellow light seeps through the tarnished glass windows. *Morning.*

She sits up, turning her head to the sounds' source. "Hey, why didn't you wake me? I can help." Arthur has already changed into his Interface suit and is rapidly packing away their supplies into their cylinders.

His mannerisms are aggressive, giving little thought to how the items are packed, forcing some into place with a closed fist. "I don't need your help. Get changed."

Curiesay cocks her head, watching him carefully. She considers that she may be overthinking and opts to grab her Interface suit and go into the bathroom to change. When she returns to the living room, Arthur has already dragged the pieces of her suit into the center of the room and stands impatiently with the tools nearby.

"Let's go. We got a lot of ground to cover," he says, directing her over to him with a tilt of his head. *I'm definitely not imagining this.*

"You'd better cut that shit out," she says harshly.

"I won't tell you again."

"What's your problem?" she says, not moving from the bottom of the stairs where she's standing.

"My problem is you. I would have been fine if you'd taken advantage of me because you were curious…"

"Take advantage of you?" Curiesay interrupts, but Arthur talks over her.

"…but you only did…*that* because you pity me. I don't need your pity. I don't need you at all," he finishes.

"I took advantage of you?!" she yells.

"Yes! What else would you call it?"

"Uh, how about consensual?"

"You *knew* I didn't want you to look, and you still did! Do you have any idea how close you were to—" Arthur's mouth snaps shut mid-sentence.

"To what?" Curiesay presses. "How close I was to what, Arthur?"

"Forget it. Just…*please* come over here so we can get suited up. We need to leave," he says in a conciliatory tone. Curiesay hesitates for a moment before she dejectedly walks over. Arthur begins to fit her Arbiter as she stands in silence.

She expected this days ago. His rage was thick in the air when he barged into her hospital room, and she was sure he'd hold this grudge for a long time. She had such relief when he seemingly got over it and had enjoyed his company yesterday. Now, she doesn't know how to feel. It's like he waited until she had opened up to him just to have the door slammed in her face.

It's hard for her to pin down who he is. He's meek, then he's confident. He's unsure, he's daring. He's warm, he's cruel. He holds her, he crushes her. It's as if there's Arthur, the man she'd seen in his mind, and a third hybrid of the two that takes turns making appearances. She begins to worry that he may belong in an asylum as much as she did. At this moment, she doesn't much care. Receding is a specialty of hers, and she has no issue walling him off. "I don't need you at all." *Yeah, that makes two of us, Arthur.*

A high-pitched beep interrupts her train of thought and they turn toward the tablet on the table. Another beep. Then a third, at a decreasing interval. Half-dressed in her Arbiter, Curiesay is worse off than being nude, as her leg armor severely restricts her movement.

"Arthur…get the gun." Without a word, he stands and walks to the front door. "Where are you going?" she whispers loudly, as he opens it and steps outside.

Curiesay clomps to the front window and peers outside. Beyond the grime, she can see a figure. She can't make it out, but it's certainly heading toward the house. Without a shred of grace, she rushes back into the living room, grabs the rifle by its barrel, and heads to the front door.

Arthur has stepped off the porch and onto the lawn. He doesn't seem concerned, or even awake for that matter. Curiesay feels as if she's watching another of his memories. He feels so far away. Sterile.

"Arthur, wait! Don't!" she yells. She can see it. A shambling mess of rot limps toward them. Dark grey sickly skin, an unsteady gait. Rotten teeth. Patchy hair. She can't tell its sex or age. Obsidian-black eyes glister in the rising sun, and although she can't make out a pupil, she knows it's looking at Arthur.

As it approaches, she can hear its breaths, gasping, raspy. She levels the rifle and pulls the trigger. Or at least, she tries to. *Safety, fuck.* She fumbles for a second, flicks the safety off, and brings the rifle up. *Bang.* The recoil pushes her back at the waist. Wide right, impact point unknown. Even with the built-in silencer, it's quite loud.

It looks to her like this person, this *creature,* hasn't exerted itself for many years. It moves like a wounded fawn, limbs foreign and weak.

"Stop!" Curiesay pleads. Arthur isn't doing much of anything, other than standing and watching the Blight. Curiesay lines up another shot. She barely knows anything about sight picture and doesn't know what range the rifle is zeroed at. This shot hits the ground in front of the Blight, evicting a colony of ants from the earth below.

Curiesay runs carefully down the stairs, flagging Arthur with the rifle in the process, and runs to him. The Blight is within ten meters now, its pace quickening. It pulls something from its pocket, holding it out front. Arthur raises his hand, palm toward the eager Blight.

Laying the barrel over Arthur's shoulder for stability, Curiesay fires a round through the Blight's head, dropping it in a heap in front of them. Arthur doesn't flinch or react at all, other than lowering his hand after a moment. Curiesay cautiously surveys the Blight, and other than some postmortem twitches, it lay motionless.

"Well done, Curiesay." He's quite blasé, nearly sarcastic as he congratulates her. A trail of blood snakes out of his right ear canal and down his neck. "You've killed your first one. How do you feel?"

Curiesay looks at him with astonishment. "Fuck. You." She bumps him hard as she turns and walks back to the house.

Thirty minutes of assembly later, the two Pilots have fully donned their Arbiters. They haven't spoken a word to each other. Haven't so much as made eye contact. The line of supply cannisters are neatly laid out in front of them.

"Let's go," Curiesay barks without looking at Arthur. They grab the ropes and drag, heading north, as the sun rises.

* * *

October 18th, 2053

Bastion, Third Floor, Medical Wing

"You know, it's quite difficult to defend you when keep secrets from me," Zochitl says. She sits across from Chandrima's desk, one long leg crossed over the other. "I thought you'd said Congress had authorized this mission."

"I did say that, didn't I?" Chandrima responds with a sly grin. "How much did they whine about it?"

Zochitl shrugs. "Quite a bit. You know, the normal talk about replacing you, sticking you in a prison cell. Stuff like that. They also…" Zochitl casts her eyes to the side at Prefect Typher, who is sitting next to her on the couch, "…asked if you knew about it. Said you weren't answering your phone."

"I've been busy," he remarks lazily. "Keeping tabs on Director Joshi is like herding cats. It's better if you just let them wander. Though I will say, Rima, that a little warning would have been nice. You should have known they'd be resistant about launching the first offensive in years on the Blight. And for what? Some sick woman who you aren't sure is curable?"

"You see, Typher, this is why I didn't ask permission," Chandrima says exasperatedly. "What they, and apparently *you*, don't seem to understand is that this is a war of principle. The Blight who brought us the journal defied the Blight's control. The Yōulíng has been doing the same. The reason the Blight is so feared is because it denies its victims' control. Strips their wills from their souls. The Blight with the journal was a black eye to our enemy, and I intend to give it another by taking the Yōulíng. If it's so adamant that we do not take her, then all the more reason for us to do so."

It's a difficult argument to counter, even with the risks involved. Sending thousands of soldiers to antagonize the Blight and risk their lives so they can cure one singular Blighted woman is a fool's errand. But Zochitl and Typher know that she's right. A win like this, to cure the uncurable, would be unprecedented.

"Does Commander Cutter know that he has, unwittingly, defied Congress at your behest?" Typher follows up.

"No. He will soon, I suppose. Hell, you could go tell him right now," Chandrima says as she points to the door. "It's not like he can pull his army back, not with Arthur and Curiesay still in play."

"You *think* they're still in play," Typher adds gravely. "You believe there's a Scowl on the field, correct?" Chandrima gives a curt nod. "He's the one who killed our Waif and her team. The same one who was watching the Yōulíng. And you've gone and sent two of your Pilots in to retrieve her. What's to say they're not already dead?"

Chandrima taps her mechanical finger against her chin. "Humanity's approach to combating Scowls hasn't exactly evolved since the Culling. And, without my own personal army, I was left with only one option. A favor." She pauses for effect, leveling her eyes onto the Prefect.

During the Culling, humanity's forces employed armored exoskeletons similar to the Arbiters to eradicate the Scowls. Even with a numerical advantage and the element of surprise, tens of thousands of soldiers lost their lives. However, a handful of particularly powerful Scowls defied even the most fervent attempts on their lives, leaving mankind to again resort to what got them into that mess in the first place—leveraging Scowls to kill one another. If Chandrima isn't worried about a Scowl killing her Pilots, it's because she has one in her pocket.

"The punishment for associating with Scowls, or not reporting their existence, is severe. As such, were I to delve into the details of this *favor*, I may, unintentionally, incriminate myself. And you, as a law-abiding citizen, would be left with no choice but to report what I may or may not tell you to the authorities. Do you *really* want to know what I've done?" Typher stares at her in disbelief, grinding his teeth. "I told you about the Scowl solely because you all deserved to know who killed Karima. But that information is not to be spoken of to anyone else. Cutter and Parker have already agreed. If you wish to confess your suspicions and my sins to the Congress, I won't think of you any differently. I only ask that Zochitl take my place, should I be removed."

Typher looses a long, dramatic sigh, rubbing his eyes. "These theatrics are of your own making, Director Joshi. As long as you've known me, I've been amenable to even your most outrageous requests. But your lies give me pause; why should I trust you when you don't trust me?" With this, the Prefect stands, buttons his suit jacket, and excuses himself.

"Are *you* going to ask me?" Chandrima asks Zochitl after the door has closed.

"Nope. Can't take your job if I'm complicit. Not that I want it. Too much paperwork," Zochitl responds grimly. She, too, stands, casting a wry glance at Chandrima before she makes for the door.

"They're going to do it, Zochi. They're going to bring the Yōulíng back, and we're going to cure her."

"For your sake, I hope you're right," she responds without looking and leaves the Director's office.

* * *

Exclusion Zone

She'd not found her body. Only Karima's female companion, the one in the periphery of her nightmares, lay where she'd been cut down. Even their courier hadn't been spared. But Karima's remains were gone. The Yōulíng had knelt in the blood and wept until she retched.

What now? So long ago she had abandoned the hope of ever having a friend. And when Karima arrived, the Yōulíng had been hesitant to let her in. To be seen. But Karima *had* seen her, and she did not shy. She did not judge. She was not repulsed. She became her friend. And they took her away. Perhaps this is her fault for letting herself believe that a warm sun would rise on her fate.

369

She does not know, and she does not care. It is decided: *I will be a slave no longer. If that means I am to die, then so be it.*

And so, she hunts. Whatever Blights remain in her city now become the subject of her furious ire. Tendrils and claws and teeth rip and tear and choke. She intends to run her body into the ground until not even her master can coax a breath from her lungs. But before she dies, she'll kill as many of them as she can get her hands on.

This night, she'd torn through tens of buildings, executing even the most docile of her *brethren*. Any who bore the same sickness as her had their souls cleaved from their bodies, their charnel cast onto the walls. She moved as her namesake suggests, dipping through holes in space and time, a cloud of smoke and a battle cry the only warning her prey received.

24

Big. Bad. Wolf.

October 18th, 2053
Exclusion Zone

Fortunately for Curiesay, her heightened senses make their silent trudge to the city more entertaining.

She hadn't noticed it much in Bastion, as the Arena is quite bland and unappealing to experience. But here, on the vast plains of the Exclusion Zone, colors dance like flames, sounds ripple as if they were still water accosted by a stone, smells twirl around her nostrils. A honeybee buzzes by at a distance, but she can smell the sweet pollen falling from its legs.

This place is so serene, so still. Apart from the curious wildlife that trails them, only her and Arthur exist here. She wishes they were on better terms. She wishes he wasn't such an asshole. And she wishes she hadn't let herself be vulnerable with him.

There is one solace to be had. That raven. It has been following them since they left the house. She'd first attributed it to another pair of curious eyes. But then she'd seen it again, stooped on the handrail of a sagging townhome. Then again, watching them from the canopy of a distant oak tree. She can't say why, but she feels safer having it watch her back, since she doesn't trust Arthur to do that right now.

Still, she wonders *where* the Blights are. This place is supposed to be the homeland of such a terrible plague that humanity built a wall all the way around them and spent years plotting to eradicate it. And yet, save the one she'd killed at the house, they hadn't seen any sign of them. *I guess the distraction they planned is working.* Or so she hopes.

Just past nightfall, the pair are approaching the city outskirts from the south. Curiesay is no longer angry. She is no longer anything. This is the longest she's worn her Arbiter, and it's taken a toll. She can feel it clawing at the oxygen her own cells require to live. She wonders who is using who.

They had stopped just after noon and swapped out their feeding packs. Already, the one she's wearing has less than a quarter-biomass remaining. With only one spare left for each one of them, she realizes that even if she were to turn back right now, she'd never make it home.

Her brain struggles to contribute any thoughts other than *We should stop and rest* and *Eat your bodyweight in chocolate bars*. Her Arbiter is sucking the life out of her, using her own energy to feed its muscles. Although it's the only thing keeping her safe, she wants nothing more than to be free of it.

Arthur's head turns up as they approach the city, pointing to a twenty-story building. "That one will work." It's the first one on the main street, and seemingly intact.

Curiesay grumbles. *Why don't you pick a taller one next time, asshole?* "Fine." They drag their cannisters through the broken doors and into the lobby. It's an overcast night, so inside, it's nearly pitch-black. Curiesay's heart skips a beat as she enters. Darkness. Her eyes burn as they adjust, her Arbiter giving her a gift in return for all the grief it causes.

She surveys the lobby—everything is the same shade of sickly green. A broken suitcase, the summer dress of its owner laying covered in dust. A corner table surrounded by leather sofas has plates atop it, the food having long disintegrated. Whoever had been sitting on the far end was—apparently—quite hungry, as an entire chicken skeleton is on their plate.

The two drag their cannisters to the staircase. "Let me give you a—" Arthur begins as he reaches for Curiesay's ropes.

She swats him away. "I got it."

After what seems like an eternity, they make it to the top floor. They enter a north-facing room and drop their gear unceremoniously onto the carpet. Curiesay collapses, back against the wall as she catches her breath. Surveying the city, Arthur stands at the vaulted window of this presidential suite.

Like many of the cities nearest to ground zero, this one is relatively intact. The serious bombings didn't begin until humanity realized the extent of the Blight's threat, and by then this city was far from the front lines. It has all the trappings of the setting of a psychological thriller where everyone has up and vanished. Doors are ajar, cars wait patiently for traffic lights that will never change, gusts of wind gather personal effects in tornado corners.

"Get comfortable. I don't know how long this will take me," Arthur says as he pops open a cannister and grabs his last feeding pack. The one already attached to his armor falls without warning, clattering to the floor with a thud.

"What do you mean?" Curiesay says, eyes closed as she slows her breathing. She feels Arthur tap her foot with his and looks up.

He's holding his feeding pack in front of him with insistent eyes. "You stay here. I'll signal you when I have her."

"Bullshit. You're not going to leave me here."

"I can handle it."

"Fuck that!" Arthur signals for her to keep her voice down, a gesture which has the opposite effect. Despite her exhaustion, she springs to her feet. "You aren't in charge here. We're gonna do this together. Like *we* said we would."

"We?" Arthur says with a condescending laugh. "There is no we."

Curiesay steps up to him as the two argue nose to nose—their tempers flare around them, too incensed to feel the eyes that spy them from the darkness.

* * *

Clumsy, loud fools. They are lucky she'd cleared the dregs that remained in the city, lest they be accosted.

Hanging from the side of the building's façade, she raises her eyes above the floor and peers in through the broken window. *What are they? What is that armor?* They smell familiar. *They will fall all the same.*

She feels the *other* gnawing at the edges of her mind. *The boy, him first. Separate. Yes, one, then the other.* A moment of hesitation crashes through one side of her mind and out of the other. These must be Karima's friends. They *must* be here for her. It's *their* fault she's dead. This revelation only deepens her conviction as a tendril slithers out of her back.

* * *

"You're a real fuckin' fuck-ass fuck. A fuckin' loser, you know that? No wonder all that bad shit happened to you," Curiesay spits.

"I could say the same about you. If my dear aunt hadn't rescued you, you'd still be eating stale oats and rereading the same books day in and day out. Hard to believe there wasn't anyone better to pick," he replies. She'd never heard his tongue ever suggest a drop of such petty cruelty before. Not that she is any better, but she had thought, had *hoped,* that he was.

"Someone better? Like you? Some little slave boy? Who'd rather play with butterflies and whine than be a real man. Even the Waifs have more balls than you." Curiesay doesn't know which words are true to her and which are pointed only for their own sake. She doesn't care much either way.

The two don't notice the tendril slithering silently in from the window until it is too late. It lashes out with blinding speed. Curiesay can only watch as Arthur is dragged by his ankle and tossed haphazardly out the window in an instant.

"Arthur!" Curiesay shrieks as the Yōulíng leaps into the room through the window and charges. Curiesay looses her own tendrils in an instant to defend herself, eyes flashing to red. Training with Arthur and Parker, Curiesay had realized that despite their inhuman speed, her enhanced reflexes made everything move in slow motion. But this woman, this *Blight,* isn't inhuman.

She's godlike.

The Yōulíng plows into Curiesay knee-first. She hadn't been able to see the strike at all. Curiesay is thrown against the wall and wills her tendrils and arms forward, deterring any attack from the front. But the next attack comes from below. The Yōulíng appears below her, accompanied by a puff of smoke, and rabbit-kicks her into the ceiling, sending her straight through to the roof.

Before she's hit the ground, the Yōulíng's tendrils wrap around her legs and fling her onto the gravelly roof. There is nothing she can do. She can't even see her. The Yōulíng is more than fast. It's as if she leaves one place just to appear in another. Curiesay scrambles to her feet and endures a seemingly endless flurry of attacks, blocking some only through sheer luck.

All over again, it's like she's back in the Arena on her first day, *before* her Crossing, when Parker had been pummeling her into the wall. But she's not the same woman she was then. After all she's been through, she refuses to let this be her end. She knows, however, that she won't last much longer. Every fracture, every cut, every teeth-chattering strike, wears upon her.

And so, she bides her time. The Yōulíng chips away at her with devastating force. She recognizes the pattern: *strike, reposition, strike, reposition.* The advice Annata had given her against Parker, sans one crucial element: *evade.* She sees the Yōulíng, then smoke, then she's struck. *Yōulíng, smoke, attack. Yōulíng, smoke, attack.*

There. She catches a glimpse of her attacker, then she's gone, leaving smoke in her wake. Curiesay wills the entirety of her available biomass into her palms, one Gripe in each, as big as softballs. *Smoke.* Out of nothing, out of no*where*, the Yōulíng appears in her peripherals.

She can't counter it in time, but she doesn't want to. *If I can't hit you, I'll blow this whole goddamn roof to bits!* With all the force she can muster, she claps her hands together, colliding the Gripes into one another. The roof erupts with blinding light and a terse crack, and everything goes dark.

∗ ∗ ∗

The force of the blast nearly tears Arthur from the side of the building as he desperately climbs his way back up. It's only been fifteen seconds or so since he'd narrowly arrested his fall, using his tendrils like ice picks.

He clambers onto the roof. The smoke obscures his vision for a moment until his eyes burn. Only one orange figure remains.

Scrambling to her side, he's careful not to move her too violently lest he injure her further. "Curiesay! Curiesay!" A groan of confirmation indicates that she's still conscious. No sign of their target. The roof is in shambles—not a pebble of gravel remains, and the parapets are cracked or completely gone. *Quite the display. Perhaps she was killed in the blast.* He doubts it. More likely she was thrown from the roof. *Which means she's still out there.*

Blood pours from Curiesay's ears and nose. The armor on her chest is cracked clean in half, her gauntlets scalded. Her Arbiter looks like she's been hit by a city bus. All this in less than twenty seconds.

Risk of exacerbation aside, he'll have to move her. He hefts her over his shoulder and opts to take the nearby stairwell rather than drop through the hole in the roof. He takes her to a room adjacent to their original one and props her up in the corner.

As he spends the next few minutes transferring their supplies to their new room, Curiesay comes to, deliriously muttering to herself. "Arthur…what…are you…doing?"

The feeding pack she'd been wearing was knocked off during her clash with the Yōulíng, meaning that between them, they have the nearly empty one Arthur had been wearing plus two fresh ones. He sets all three in a row beside her and rigs them in a series, utilizing the transfer tubes built into each unit. Then he plugs the last one into Curiesay's armor.

A rush of fresh biomass perks her up. Barely. "No, you need one too, you can't—"

"You can't stop me, so hush. Stay quiet. Stay safe. I'll signal you when I'm done." His heart tenders. To think that his last words to her would have been filled with such venom. He's glad she survived, if only so he can later apologize. But there is no time for that now.

The Yōulíng is out there. If Curiesay is this banged up, he figures the Yōulíng is off licking her wounds somewhere. *And she must be hungry.*

"Be careful," she pleads. "She's strong." She knows what he must do. If they bail out now, she'll never forgive herself. *He* won't forgive himself either. They'll return with the Yōulíng, or not at all.

He takes her hand in his, running his thumb over her equally armored palm. The mirror nerves in their gauntlets make it feel as if they're not there. "We said we would do this together. You did your part, now I'll do mine." He runs his palm over her eyes, urging them shut. "Please. Just rest."

Whether she accepts this request or is simply too tired to argue, he doesn't know. Eyes closed, her chest heaves as her battered body repairs itself. He's sure to clear anything flammable from around her before he leaves, lest her armor set fires from the waste heat it is producing.

Arthur watches her for a moment, his eyes regarding her as if it is the last time, before descending the stairwell.

* * *

The solar-powered lights are well constructed—every second one works to a degree. Although, their flickering is messing with Arthur's night vision, and he's more than fed up with them. Worse yet, the voice that so often flits at the edge of his psyche is louder than ever.

Feels like you're not up for this.

I am.

It's like a nature preserve. The foliage has long since crept into the city. Buildings accommodate great walls of vines. Grass and saplings have burst through the pavement. Arthur thinks it curious that he should see more wildlife than Blights in a place like this. For a land supposed to be the Blight's domain, it feels abandoned.

You don't even know where she is.

And you do?

Although he would never admit it to Curiesay, he does feel a measure of fear. It's physical. Threats strung up like invisible clotheslines that he stumbles upon. Whatever uneasiness has kept the rest of the Blights at bay weighs heavy upon his shoulders. He can feel himself recede. Become thin. Translucent.

You're not thinking.

Quiet.

He's been wandering for hours. He debates on returning to Curiesay, but if something were to have happened to her, he doubts he would be of any help now. And for some reason, he feels as if the Yōulíng wouldn't prey on an injured Pilot.

Why don't you let me handle this?

There is no "you." Go away.

Elva told you to come back alive.

I will.

I don't believe you. You're too soft. Even now. Even here.

Shut up!

My oath supersedes your autonomy. We have not failed her yet, and we won't now.

There is no "we"! Stop!

Arthur doubles over, groaning, hands covering his face. Motionless. Alone. For a moment, everything stands still. Not even a mote of dust whispers out a silent nothing.

A gust of wind whips past, tussling his jet-black hair. He straightens up, cracking his neck from side to side. Deep breath. Eyes focused. He turns slowly, searching. A clack, barely perceptible. *Have you forgotten your instincts, stranger?*

He bends his knees and leaps forward, crashing into the unsuspecting deer that had crossed his path nearly fifty meters away. They tumble across the pavement as he takes its back, wraps his arm around its neck, and rotates violently, snapping its spinal cord.

Its head lops sideways at an awkward angle. "I am sorry, friend."

He closes its eyes with a swipe of his hand and drags it under a streetlight by its ankles. It flickers incessantly. With a wicked strike, his gauntleted hand tears open the deer's abdomen. Guts spill out like an overturned butcher's bucket. With morbid indifference, he spreads the entrails and blood on the pavement beneath the light.

Satisfied with his work, he searches for a suitable place to wait. A four-way intersection nearby is the home of a long past fender bender, the two sedans involved creating a "V" shape. *Perfect.* Arthur squeezes in between them and sits.

And waits. He listens intently, with even the sounds of insects apparent to him, their subtle light-footed doings at the peripherals of his hearing. But he cannot hear her. An hour passes. He cannot *feel* her. Until there's an itch deep inside his mind.His neurons urge him to flee. *She's here.*

He stands, facing the streetlight and deer corpse. The figure hunches over as it begins to eat. Panicked sounds of desperation. *Best not to antagonize the hungry wolf.* But he must.

She's pathetically thin. Choking as she bites off more than she can chew, forcing it down with reckless abandon. Completely nude. Filthy, skin barely visible under the grime and dried blood, hands slick. Her small stature only adds to his unease. Like a deity's child, abandoned and left to rot with the rest of humanity. She brays with hunger, her yips of pleasure echoing off the buildings.

He watches her eat. In truth, he's hesitant to move. For a moment, he even reconsiders approaching her, but this fear only spurs him on. Without finesse, he hops over the car and lands with a thud.

The woman freezes, then whips her head around. Her eyes are neutral; brown and white. Whether she is afraid or livid, he cannot tell. As she looks down at her meal, he allows her a moment to piece it together.

That's right. All this, for you.

She turns to face him in shy defiance. A terrible message dances on her tongue as she hesitates to pass it along. His fear grows; *Are you my penance?*

She speaks in a foreign tongue. "You should have left when you had the chance. I'm so sorry... She's coming."

She emits a burst of energy, the shockwave hardly moving the stoic Pilot. "Let. Her," he responds in the same language. Doubling over, she vomits onto the ground—thick black tar punishes her esophagus. She stumbles, unwilling to submit. *Don't fight it. Let go.*

An instant of relief crosses her face as she looks skyward, her voracious howl being cut off by an eruption of black smoke and fire. The blast sends cars tumbling and spidering cracks appear through the ground below. As she Crosses, Arthur is enveloped in smoke, and he thrusts himself into her Dominium.

* * *

The wood splinters as he crashes through the door. Mildewed. The girl sits. Watches. Colorful childlike nonsense dances across the screen. She's ill-fitted for her clothes. Ill-fitted for this place. Across from the mattress she sits on, near the window, sits a man. The rotten smoke odor curls Arthur's nose hairs, but the girl seems unbothered.

The man uses one to light another, tossing the spent butt out the window onto the crowded, bustling streets below. Whatever his laptop is conveying, he doesn't approve. A tight band and a spoon will fix this. He coalesces, melting into his chair. This problem of his, it is a tomorrow problem.

The girl glances over, regarding him little, and turns back to her program. This isn't it. This is her, but this isn't it. But it is something. And there is someone. The woman from the streets rises from behind the girl. In this place, Arthur and herself are of equal stature. She may even be a hair taller, or a head, or a meter. Or maybe she looms over him. Perhaps she shall crush him underfoot!

Featureless pale skin, lower orifices smooth and non-existent, black veins pumping foul blood into her slender muscles. Like Arthur, her irises are red, but the whites of her eyes are jet-black. Are you allowed will? Are you allowed self?

Arthur steps toward the girl, hands outstretched. In a flash, the incensed woman strikes him, sending him crashing back onto the street.

* * *

"What? How did she…" he says aloud, shaking his head. He sees her feet leave the ground as she leaps, his mind calculating the time until she strikes. But it's wrong. Two puffs of smoke, and she's right on top of him. She delivers an earth-shattering kick that Arthur narrowly blocks with his forearms, the sound of metal versus flesh equivalent to that of two head-on freight trains. The city rattles. His forearm plating bows—he can feel the impact in his bones. She uses her tendrils for leverage, delivering another kick, breaking his guard and sending him stumbling backward.

Dancing around him, she uses her tendrils to keep Arthur within reach. Striking, pulling, dragging, striking. Her attacks are brutal, teeth chattering. This woman weighs next to nothing and whips around him like a sheet of paper in a tornado. Every time he thinks he sees an opening, she vanishes into smoke, only to reappear an instant later somewhere else. *Your Machina is beautiful, stranger.*

But she's sloppy. Inexperienced. Arthur studies her pattern and correctly predicts where she'll appear next. She pops into existence only to receive a punch to her sternum, sending her backward with speed. She crashes into a city bus, kicking up dust. Arthur quickly follows up, but she's gone. Vanished. He can still feel her, which means he can still reach her. He closes his eyes, his soul permeating the air as he finds her and again enters her Dominium.

* * *

Rosewood? Or Chinese oak? The door is thick. Foreboding. This place is the same, but darker. The girl is here. She's grown, some. Different programs, same rot. Her eyes are bagged, sorrowful. Her tiny chest barely seems to move as she breathes. Perhaps she lacks the desire. Arthur wishes that she had.

The man is there, in his spot. Ashtray. Litterbug no more. But he is not alone. A group of them, carrying on at the table. Drinks, money, needles. He looks a man defeated. Ashamed. He should be.

A knock. A man. He has money. One at the table has been working the spoons, two. The girl doesn't react as they stick her. Arthur hopes that the nerve endings are deadened. He hopes that her soul is deadened. The guest looks at the father, but he looks away.

The wretched man grabs her arm, body limp and careless, and drags her to the back room. Arthur watches, teeth bared. There's nothing to be done. He follows, and the woman emerges. This time, she is twice herself. She ducks under the frame as she steps out. The room grows to accommodate, fading out, back, away. She strikes Arthur with her fist, again sending him back from whence he came.

* * *

"Goddamnit!" he shouts. *Stubborn fool.* He whips around, ears on alert. He knows she's coming. He knows—

Throwing his arms above him, he narrowly blocks her strike. The pavement beneath buckles from the force as it travels down through Arthur's legs. She redirects herself, striking him in the abdomen with both feet. His own tendrils burst from his back, but the best he can do is defend.

She's otherworldly.

He's not sure that she even exists.

His armor does little to lessen the knee to the groin as she zips by, disappearing as his counterattack slashes the space she had occupied. She's learning at an alarming pace, no longer leaving any openings. He'll have to make his own.

She *only* strikes where he's left himself undefended. He baits his trap, leaving his frontside open, his tendrils and limbs ill-positioned to defend. Acrid smoke fills his nostrils as she blips into reality directly to his front, poised to slash him with her claws. It has been such a long time since he's had to use his Machina, and he knows she doesn't deserve what's coming, but *there is no other way.*

The entirety of Arthur's eyes flash red, lighting up the street. The Yōulíng is but a hair's length from him when the wave strikes her like a tremendous gale, and she's blasted backward. A thunderous crack like one thousand wooden bats striking in unison follows, turning the remaining windows on the street into glass shards. The force of the attack tears the Yōulíng's tendrils from her body, blasts the fingers from her hands.

Her skin is scalded lobster-red on her front as she struggles to stand, dazed. Her eyes tell Arthur that she'll die for this. He's insistent that she doesn't. He knows she doesn't want him to look. *I'm sorry, but I must see you.*

* * *

May as well be steel. Wood crushed into diamond. Its construction betrays its importance, and he laments his grim task as he lowers his shoulder and rams.

* * *

The woman stumbles. She cannot fight him in two places at once. Her vision narrows, and she falls to her knees in agony, weeping in the street.

* * *

Stubborn threshold! Relent! She is as mighty here as in the physical world. He pushes hard, the frame threatening its own failure. Arthur suspects what is beyond, and even if he cannot change things, he will not allow her to remain here.

* * *

"Stay the fuck out of my head!" she wails. But he mustn't. The two remain nearly motionless in the street as they struggle for control.

* * *

At last, it yields. The door falls inward, disturbing the layer of dust that had gathered. Dust, and little else. Newspapers obscure the windows, taped for privacy. But he is not alone. He casts his gaze to the room. The bad room.

This door is not of her construction. It is of man. Of malice. The locks that adorn it aren't meant to keep someone out. Then, a peep. A pathetic whimper. A cough. He desires nothing less than to look. He grabs the first lock firmly and tears it from the door.

The woman isn't here. But her shrieks tell him otherwise. These locks are all she has—they are everything that she is.

The second lock brings a chunk of wood with it as he pulls it free.

Hundreds of voices whisper to him, incessant in his ear.

If you let the light in, I'll melt. A horse. Don't melt me. I don't want it. Have you seen the sun? I have, a long time ago. It'll burn. Don't melt. Don't melt me. I'm hungry. It's okay. We like it here. Honest. It can't escape. I'll wait and wait until I'm swallowed. So hungry. But I'll choke! No, be very careful. And don't! Melt!

The final lock is taken and cast aside. The door is opened.

Macabre child.

Hungry, hungry horse! You'll melt me! I'll disappear! Poof! I'll disappear! Melted pile of shit! Shit, shit, shit. You can't bring me back. There is no me. Only us. Don't melt us, sir. Please. Too bright. I'm so hungry, I'm so hungry, I'm so hungry, I'm so hungry, I'm so hungry. Sun too bright, too bright for your eyes. Are those your eyes? Have you seen them, your eyes? I could eat your eyes. I'm so hungry. Hey, mister, let us eat your eyes.

The child kneels in blood. There must be three or four corpses, but he can't tell. Short a few limbs.

Ope! You saw me! No more eyes! You shouldn't look at me. Don't. Look. I'm so hungry, eyes? Your? Eyes? It's too bright, close that door. The door, the door. Oh, you brought more. I just ate. Too full! I'm spoiled, I know. This is where piggies go. Spoiled little piggy, playing in the piggy shit. Piggy shit, piggy shit. Ha ha! You stepped in the shit! You must be hungry too. Are you hungry, mister? I'M SO HUNGRY I COULD EAT A HORSE!

She hadn't been an only child. But she was the oldest and lasted the longest. It was four, then three, then two, and now one. They left them to wither and die, but one refused. Waste not, want not. She looks over her shoulder. Blood scowl, wet hands. Gorging on her siblings.

* * *

A tremendous shriek erupts from the woman as her suffering bursts forth. The pavement below her scalds red and her tendrils regenerate. They whip themselves across the ground, a tantrum of absolution and shame. The maelstrom heaves wicked gusts of scalding air into a cyclone around her, a force of nature fueled solely by pain. Her biomass is rapidly consumed—her grief given form.

Somber envy fills Arthur as he watches in braced silence. The heat burns his skin, discolors his armor. *This magnitude of suffering should be shared with the world—it is too great for one person to bear.*

* * *

The woman returns, wounded. Frail. Her eyes are less furious, more pathetic. He had looked. She told him not to.

"I want to help you," he whispers.

"You can't." She steps from beyond the girl, ushering Arthur back through the portal, and gently closes the door in his face.

* * *

The storm dissipates. Her knees touch as she holds herself upright, the pavement below pulsing red with heat. She will see this through, one way or another. Rushing toward him, she rears her fist back and—

Blood spatters below. Her tendrils lurch forward, but they're wet paper. Arthur severs them swiftly with the sharp part of his hand and backhands the woman, knocking out a tooth. She's slow, useless, and vulnerable. He follows up with an uppercut, paralyzing her diaphragm.

A hand may have beckoned surrender, but it is ignored as he grabs her arm and snaps it in two. Another jab, jaw. Knee shattered with a front kick, metal versus flesh. The champion boxer keeps his opponent standing only by the force of his blows. She gurgles out nonsense and a wicked cross silences her, sending her to the pavement.

The Yōulíng's rampage is over. The city block is in shambles, with chunks of molten pavement rapidly hardening all about. A clash between gods and the refuse of such leaves nothing but grim silence and utter destruction.

Arthur eyes his opponent for a moment, his own eyes red and furious, before he drops to a knee.

His Arbiter is wasted, having consumed all its biomass, the under-layer so thin that the plates clank against each other as he breathes. He can feel it chewing at his flesh, stealing his life to prolong its own. The young Pilot bares his teeth as he runs his fingers beneath the plating and pulls.

"Greedy fucking *leech*."

* * *

The sounds of their battle wake Curiesay. She groans to herself, head aching. *Arthur... Where is—*

That asshole! He fuckin' left me here. The feeding packs drag behind her as she stands and marches to the broken window that runs the length of the room.

Bursts of air carry on down the deserted streets; wicked howls echo off the buildings. The building's moorings groan as the floor shakes beneath her feet. *He found her.*

She remembers now—he'd given up his pack to heal her and went off alone. The feeling of abandonment roils into shame, then into desperation as the city finally falls silent.

He said he would signal. And so, she waits cross-legged at the window, peering over the dark city. This does give her some measure of comfort. Despite her ambivalence, she'd survived her first *real* fight. She wishes it could have been a win. She wishes she could have at *least* seen her opponent. But she's alive.

She examines her burned armor, the cracked plates. Raising a hand in front of her face, she twists it around lazily. *Armor. Like a knight.* For the first time since she'd arrived at Bastion, Curiesay feels like a warrior. And somewhere in this city, her brethren Pilot depends on her. She won't let—

She gasps as she springs to her feet—the blue flare lazily drifts toward the ground in the distance, obscuring itself behind the buildings. With a sense of direction that she feels isn't entirely hers, she knows exactly where he is.

Without hesitation, she throws herself out of the window and plummets toward the ground. She uses her tendrils to slow her descent, swinging from the building's façade as she redirects her momentum, gliding smoothly onto the street like a roller skater.

She moves deftly, leaving her fear behind. Her fellow Pilot needs her. *Arthur* needs her. As she blisters down the streets, there is not a force imaginable that she feels can stop her.

Rounding the next corner, she sees a figure at the end of the street. In the first moment, she considers accelerating and running right over her foe. In the next, she feels its aura wash over her as she approaches, demanding apology for her foolhardiness. It reaches far above, its presence extending to the dark skies above.

She nearly stumbles. This presence, this *creature,* will surely be her end. *Arthur needs you!* The young Pilot grits her teeth, her thrusters screaming as she accelerates, intending on going straight through the figure in the street. *Nothing will stop me from getting to—*

She begins to slow. "Arthur?" A few hard steps arrest her momentum as she skips to a halt on the asphalt. Arthur stands, wearing just his Interface suit, with a woman's limp body over his shoulder.

"Oh, thank God. Arthur."

25

Yōulíng

Early morning, October 19th, 2053
Exclusion Zone

It took thirty minutes to walk back to their campsite on the twentieth floor, and they didn't speak.

Where's your suit? Whose blood is that? Why did the city rattle so violently I thought the buildings would be brought down? She figures he'll tell her when he's ready. She can feel his presence, but it's different. He's shied, become thin. Most of all, she wants to know if he's okay.

"Here, it's soft," Curiesay says as Arthur and herself gently place the woman on a makeshift bed. Three sofas lost their lives to Curiesay to make it. Arthur wets a rag and wipes the woman's body down. Somewhere below the grime and blood is someone who hasn't felt a kind touch in a very long time.

"Could you bring her some clothes? They'll be a bit loose, but I think that's all right," he says, and Curiesay does as he asks. He's surprisingly neutral, she thinks. As if nothing has happened between them.

While she rummages, Arthur grabs a red zippered bag, retrieving the IV catheter, two vials of nutrients, and a saline bag. Curiesay watches from over his shoulder as he expertly places the IV in her right arm, injects the two vials, and hangs the bag. *Quite the skillset you have.*

Like caring for a newborn calf, Arthur's touch is delicate as he helps Curiesay dress the woman. They pull the blanket over her, place a pillow beneath her head, and step back. The Yōulíng's jaw sits at an unnatural angle, the middle parts not aligned. Her left eye socket is heavily bruised and bagged, and across the arm that hangs out from the blanket are deep lacerations, down to the white tissue below.

Arthur gulps. "Curiesay…what…happened to her?"

"I was gonna ask you the same thing."

"What? Why would you…" Arthur grimaces, taking a step back, "…ask me? Did I…did I do this?"

With eyes wide, Curiesay regards Arthur with uncertainty. "You fired the flare, and when I got there, she was already like this. Don't you remember?"

Arthur's lips tremble with worried hesitancy. "I remember… Oh. No, no, no." A hand of disbelief covers his mouth as his voice cracks. "It wasn't supposed to happen like this. She didn't deserve this."

Before she can react, he throws himself at her. Taken aback, she holds him, laying a careful hand on his back. "Arthur, it's okay. You did good. You brought her back alive."

"No, I've *brutalized* her. Look, look at what I've done. It's my fault."

"She's going to be all right. You did the right thing," Curiesay implores.

They embrace in silence before Arthur calms himself. "I'm sorry for being a fuckin' fuck-ass fuck," he says, coaxing a laugh from Curiesay. "I shouldn't have said those things to you. I haven't been myself lately. Something about this place…" He trails off as he pulls away from her.

Curiesay heads to the stairwell. "We'll be gone by this afternoon.

Get some food and chill out. I'm gonna head to the roof and fire the flare." She knows he's right about not being himself. She's curious about who he will be when she gets back. *Do I even want to know?*

* * *

Arthur puts on his clothes over his Interface suit—he can't be bothered to change. Its high collar peeks over his sweater, tight on his neck. He grabs several cans of food and some water and sits across from the Yōulíng as she sleeps. His eyes hyperfocus on her, as if she'll perish should they stray.

When Curiesay returns, the squeak from the door wakes the sleeping woman. She rouses slowly, speaking nonsense to herself. Upon noticing Arthur, she startles. She kicks her feet, pressing herself against the wall behind her. Foreign words slur through her broken jaw.

Holding her chin up, the joints steam and crackle as the bone repairs itself enough for her to speak clearly. "Who are you?! Who is that?!" she demands, this time in English. Arthur waves Curiesay off as she begins to approach, and she quietly slips back through the door. Unbeknownst to Arthur, she listens intently with her enhanced hearing.

"My name is Arthur. We're here to help you," he says gently.

The woman's eyes darken. "You can't help me, what part of that didn't you get? I'm a Blight."

"Oh? You don't look like one to me," he responds with a careful grin. Curiesay's sweats are baggy on the woman's emaciated frame, like a child wearing their mother's robes.

She bares her teeth. "What about earlier?" She can hardly hold herself upright, but she's still wildly defiant. Brown eyes determined, brow furrowed.

"What about it?" he says with coy dismissiveness. He turns, her eyes watching him critically, and grabs two bottles of water and a can of food.

She eyes them desperately. He cracks the bottle top and offers it, but she waves him off. "Just let me die."

"I can't do that."

"You don't get to choose for me!" Her eyes flutter but she keeps them open. Blunted daggers.

"I am sorry, that I had to look. I know you didn't want me to, and I shouldn't have," he concedes, bowing his head in apology. It clicks, and she remembers. The realization strangles a gasp from her, and she lies down with a thud facing away from him.

He scoots a bit closer to her. "I have things I don't want anyone to see either. But sometimes…" He looks across the room toward the door Curiesay is pressed up against. "You can't be helped until you're seen." He turns back to the woman and puts a hand on her shoulder. "I don't expect you to forgive me, but I'd like to make amends."

* * *

The doors of his mind swing open. An offering. She stands quietly, curiously. His eyes grant permission as he sits cross-legged, and she steps through the first door. Then the next. She drinks it in, a lifetime of love and suffering. Arthur sits stoically, silent tears streaming, as he apologizes the only way he knows how.

* * *

The woman jolts, whipping around to face Arthur as she sits up. "You… How…" she says breathlessly. Arthur offers no words, only an acknowledging gaze. "I'm sorry. About Aashvi."

"Me too. Do me a favor, don't tell anyone. Please."

She nods in agreement. "What do you want from me?" Arthur again offers her the bottle of water. She accepts but quickly drops it. Her fingers are gone down to the knuckles. Arthur motions for her to put her head back, which she does with some reluctance. He pours the water in her mouth, steam escaping from her nose as he does.

He tosses the bottle aside and takes a breath. "I work for a woman named Chandrima Joshi, she thinks she can cure you."

The Yōulíng's eyes brighten a bit. "Joshi? *Doctor* Joshi?"

Arthur cocks his head. "You know her?"

The woman shrugs. "I know *of* her." She sighs, a rueful smile edging at her lips. "That means that she was right."

"Who?"

"I…" The woman shakes her head, grimacing. "I can't say. I'm not supposed to talk about it." She eyes the other bottle of water. With his assistance, she drinks this one as well and spends a moment contemplating. She squeezes her eyes shut. "Let's say I go back with you. What happens if I turn again? I don't…I don't think I can stop her."

"We have medicine that will help."

"And if it doesn't?"

"What's your name?"

She pauses for a long while, then holds her chin up high. "Dai Lu."

"Dai Lu, if it comes to that, and you lose yourself again, then I will kill you."

She meets his gaze, staring for a few moments as she decides, and outstretches her hand. "Promise?"

"On one condition," he says with a soft smile as he clasps his hand with hers. "If I ever lose *myself*, you must promise to do the same to me."

She squints her eyes, then nods with determination. "Deal."

Arthur whistles and the door creaks as Curiesay enters. Dai Lu's eyes lock onto her in an instant with tight nerves.

"She's a friend," Arthur says as he observes this. "We both came all this way just for you. She's nice. Sometimes."

A heavy hand grips Arthur's shoulder a bit too tightly. "I'm glad to see you're awake. Can you eat?" Curiesay asks. Dai Lu nods and Curiesay grabs the can of raviolis and peels the top off with her gauntleted fingers.

"It probably doesn't taste as good as fresh deer, but it'll certainly be less messy," Arthur says, and Dai Lu manages a smile. Curiesay furrows her brow in confusion as she hands Arthur a fork. Dai Lu allows Arthur to feed her with less fuss, and within a few minutes, the can is empty.

The two Pilots exchange awestruck glances as Dai Lu's fingers begin to steam, little nubs appearing as they attempt to rebuild themselves. "Are you two okay?" she asks meekly. "I, uh… It's all coming back to me now."

"I'll live," Curiesay says with a smile. "But this one seems to have some brain damage. Not that I can tell the difference," she continues, lightly jamming the toe of her boot into Arthur's side.

"At least I got mine recently." This time the toe is not so light as it strikes him, and he gives a stifled moan as he waves Curiesay off.

Dai Lu leans back against the wall. "So, what now?"

Curiesay crouches to Dai Lu's level. "Our escort should be here in a few hours. Until then, you just get some sleep, and I'll keep an eye out for Blights. When I was firing the flare, I could see a couple of them lurking around."

Dai Lu's eyes grow wide with panic. "Please! Please don't let them take me back."

Curiesay nods firmly and gives a thumbs-up. "I got you, don't worry about it." Dai Lu sighs with relief, and a moment later her eyelids flutter. Arthur catches her as she falls, gently laying her back onto the bed.

Curiesay puts a hand on his shoulder. "She's nice. I'm glad we did this." Arthur stares at Dai Lu as she sleeps, his nose twitching. "Arthur, are you going to be okay?"

"Yeah, just…déjà vu."

* * *

As she patrols the roof, Curiesay wonders if he'll be back to normal when they return to Bastion. He's right—he's not himself. Or maybe he is. Since their experiment in his Dominium, he's been different. Wildly so, from one moment to the next.

But what he's done is nothing short of a miracle. Curiesay doesn't sell herself short for her role in making her way here, or squaring off against Dai Lu, but Arthur is…miraculous. He'd struck the Yōulíng down, the woman who'd nearly killed her in a matter of seconds, and then cared for her with the grace of a nun. How he could be brimming with such fiery brutality in one moment and such tenderness in the next is beyond her.

He's more than a Scowl. That only accounts for his strength, his resilience. She muses that perhaps he has a split personality but discards that idea. *I saw someone else in there.* And it *wasn't* Arthur. It looked like him, it *smelled* like him, but it didn't act like him. At least, not as he normally is. The times he'd snapped at her, *that* is when she made the parallels.

She considers her own Crossing for a moment. The feeling of a dark, vile part of herself making itself known. Her fire, her rage. A liberation from self-imposed restraints. Arthur feels different though, as if he's stuffed all his violent wants into a corner and covered it, and now it's grown legs and wants out.

397

Is that who he's so afraid of? Is that why he melts from confrontation? He didn't even remember fighting Dai Lu. Did the *other* Arthur take over? Is that why he wept? He'd even asked Dai Lu to *kill* him if he loses himself. To have such a deep fear of yourself must be exhausting.

She supposes that she cannot blame him. When she approached him earlier, she felt as if his aura would choke the life from her. Whoever that other Arthur is, she's afraid of him too.

His headaches seem to be getting worse. Often, he turns away as he grimaces, seemingly aware of her concern. *Is he fighting to keep it in?* Curiesay wonders how long it will be before Arthur becomes someone else completely.

Maybe it wouldn't be so bad. She's seen his happy medium; a place where his fear melts but his tenderness remains. At the café. In the garden. Caring for Dai Lu. *That is the real Arthur,* she muses. She nods to herself. *I'll be there, Arthur. I'll help you find your way.*

With that thought, she smiles as her cheeks redden, and she unwittingly hums to herself as she marches along the roof.

* * *

He can't believe that the humans' ruse worked. *Sadie must have known.* It'd taken him over a day to reach the forest, and now he must trudge all the way back. He grumbles as he walks. If he doesn't make it before they leave, he's fucked.

I let them linger too long. He'd known about the soldiers and Karima the moment the first Blight broke into their room. He curses his soft heart for allowing them to remain for so long. He didn't anticipate Bastion sending Pilots into the Exclusion Zone. At least, not yet. Again, Sadie either knew and didn't say anything, or she's a fool. He knows the latter isn't true, so it *must* be the former.

Impossibly, his footsteps are nearly silent as the giant approaches the city. He doesn't look behind, but he knows he's being followed. "You should have brought something bigger," he remarks aloud. A ways down the path he's taken is a thick brown bear, stalking him quietly. The man isn't attempting to conceal himself and walks tall, as if there is not a being in this land that can challenge him.

His dismissive grin fades as he passes a collapsed shed. Atop the rubble is a great grey owl, its eyes wide and squarely focused on him. He hesitates for a moment. The city rises before him as he nears, the dawn sun reddening the walls of the buildings. A bull elk joins the bear, lumbering and huffing loudly.

A falcon buzzes by the man at incredible speed, just out of his reach. Then a second makes its pass as his attention is drawn, its talons managing a razor-thin cut on his upper back. The land mammals stop in their tracks as he whips around to face them.

There's more than just two.

Prey and predator alike. There are tens, no, *hundreds* of them. He's surrounded. Eagles sit perched atop the shoulders of stags. House cats flank their larger brethren, their diamond eyes hungry. The man snarls as he spins, tracking his foes. Even a mighty grizzly has joined this alliance. It positions itself the closest to the man, and although it too would fall, it is no small threat.

"If you still want something bigger, I could bring a rhinoceros," a feminine voice says with a laugh. "That is, if you're willing to wait a few days." She sounds quite pleased with herself as the man turns to face her.

The *her* is indeed a "her," but not a human. An enormous white raven, three meters tall, stands before him. Wings tight to her body, she cocks her head as she examines him. She plucks a pest from beneath her wing with regal indifference, sending it down her gullet.

The man is infinitely more concerned with this new guest. "I thought you two had an agreement."

The raven preens itself, its beak not moving as she speaks. "Indeed, we do. I am simply out for a stroll, so to speak." Her speech is exceedingly condescending, especially when speaking to a man of his stature, with hands thick enough to squeeze water from stones. "Don't tell me that little brat has rescinded his open invitation—it would dash my heart."

"Don't fuck with me," he growls. The menagerie of animals around him tense in unison. The birds above either climb higher or land and hide behind their quadrupedal friends. "You know why I'm here. Step aside."

The raven shrugs, working diligently on her left talon. "How rude! I won't deign to *waddle* out of your path. You could simply go around, you know."

He ponders this for a moment and takes a singular step forward.

The raven's wings unfurl with wicked force. Like one thousand paper cuts, the gale buffets him.

Then. Calm.

His heart spills over with unbridled horror and reverence. It's been so long since he's met another who could match him. Though he fears the punishments his master has and would inflict, this creature terrifies him.

Wings so radiantly white they seem impossible to comprehend stretch before him. Their span is enormous, poised to blanket his entire reality under their well-groomed feathers. The red sun beams off them, blinding him with orange light. Stretching across his path, he cannot see the city beyond. Slowly, they crowd around him, and he does not dare make a move.

"My good will is exhausted," she croons, her beak unmoving, the voice coming from deep inside of his mind. "Turn back now, or I'll feed you to my Jötunn. And unlike me..." she whispers as she pulls him in close to her breast, "…he doesn't quite grasp the concept of 'mercy.'"

Her wings retract as Samael stands in stunned silence. If she can craft such an astoundingly beautiful form, he shudders to think of what she could do when beauty isn't on her mind. The force of animals she'd brought weren't to overwhelm him; *they're here to bear witness.*

His lip twitches as he fixes his gaze upon the raven. "What do you expect me to tell him?" he demands with exasperation. Seemingly, this is confirmation enough. The coalition of beasts dissolves, turning their backs to the man as they disappear into the distance. The birds take flight and commit to a single circular flyover before they, too, retire.

The raven and the man stare in silence as the dispersal finishes. An unnaturally cold breeze rolls across the land. It frosts the man's eyebrows. Burns his lips. Vanishes. The raven spreads its mighty wings and turns, poised to take flight.

"Tell him the truth."

26

Exposed

Zochitl can't quite put her finger on it. But something is off. The funeral is this morning. She steps lithely from the shower, trails of water snaking between the curves of her core muscles. It has been years since she'd last worn the dress she'd picked. It lies on her bed, awaiting its wearer. Deathly black, and modest, for once.

She rubs her hair vigorously with her towel, then runs it along her body and wraps her waist. The blow dryer whines as she dries her hair. She thinks of Karima, how she'd failed her. How the man she'd idolized had snuffed her from this world. How the woman she'd loved is complicit. How they'd sided with such a repugnant entity. She'd felt isolated since the Culling had wiped most of her kin from the Earth, but she's never felt as alone as she does now.

She smirks—*At least I have Bastion and my girls.* Truly, she's grown to love this place. Far from being a weapon herself, she's made the world better through wit and sweat. She doesn't know how she'll slip from her obligations to Verlean, but she takes solace in her role. And if Chandrima can accept that her nephew is a Scowl, perhaps, someday, she could accept her too.

No. She would never. Not if she knew *how* she'd gotten this job. Not if she knew she was a fraud. A liar of the worst degree. She sighs—*I can still do good here, even if I can't be myself.*

Hair dry, she exchanges the dryer for her hairbrush. *What...is that smell? The brush?* Over the years, she'd fallen into complacency, the chance of her being outed having dissolved as time dragged on. But her senses are as sharp as ever.

With great care, she brings the brush to her face. Inhales. *No. Please, no.* Inhales again. And again. As if the next whiff will wipe away the last. But it does not. The oils from Chandrima's skin had sunk into the wooden handle. Zochitl stares with wide eyes; *my hair.* Perfectly, overwhelmingly white.

The brush clatters to the floor. She backs herself up against her door, lungs heaving. She slides down, pulling her knees to her chest as she repeats her mantra over and over through tears.

"She knows, she knows, she knows, she knows…"

* * *

"You look good," Jordan whispers into his ear. "Far too good for a funeral, I reckon."

A weak upturn of his lips is all Parker can manage. "You're one to talk."

As he steps out of his bedroom, he can't help but admire her. Though today is shadowed by morbid rituals, he'll feel better with such a bright light by his side. She's terribly supportive, almost to a fault.

A Steward's formals are similar in style to the Waifs'. Her coat is not as long, extending to just below her waist. Slimly fitted, a shawl drapes over her shoulders, giving the outfit a sage-like appearance. As a standard, the shawl is a crimson-red, but today the one she wears is as black as night. She wears the same style berets as the Waifs, also in black.

Pilots, on the other hand, sport quite boisterous uniforms. The underlayer consists of high-waisted leather pants, and a black shirt tucked into them. A tailcoat, extending to his heels, starts loosely on his chest, flanked by lapels. A billowing hood hangs behind. The sleeves are intricately knitted with silver thread, effigies of flowers extending to his hands. Upon his shoulders, his cape is mounted, pinned by thick wrought-iron nails.

The Pilot and Steward pair silently examine one another, the latter letting a grin overtake her melancholy. "Karima would be proud. You know that, right?"

"I know. She was a good kid."

Jordan moves to him, pulling him in close by his waist, and urges his head onto her shoulder. "I'll do all the talking, okay? You just…*be.* It's gonna be all right."

* * *

She supposes she should have thought this through *before* sending one of her Waifs to her doom.

Commander Cutter, thankfully, had picked up the slack. He's quite the military historian and knows a plethora of rites and rituals for the dead. Although the ceremonies for deceased soldiers were set in stone, Chandrima had made no such arrangements for Waifs who fall, nor given them any thought. *Perhaps I hoped I'd never have to bury one of my children.*

Not that they have a body to bury. Karima, Corporal Clark, and

Captain Pullhum all remain in the maw of the Exclusion Zone. Chandrima curses herself for neglecting to ask her Pilots to retrieve their bodies. Though, she isn't sure they'd still be there at all. *I couldn't even be bothered to bring my baby home; what does that make of me?*

Director Joshi and Commander Cutter sit in the frontmost row. The Stewards and Parker join them, and on the other side of the congregation, two rows deep from the front, sit the Waifs. Roughly half were sent to accompany the distraction teams and—hopefully—keep their causalities to a minimum.

They'd opted to have the ceremony outside. A pyre is assembled in the field before them. When the ceremony began, all were invited to bring trinkets, photos, and letters to the dry wood in the hope that the cleansing fire would carry their love and kind words to the afterlife.

For Cutter and Joshi, the irony of holding a funeral for three people while thousands of soldiers and tens of Waifs are actively in harm's way isn't lost on them. They had met in private and exchanged some less than friendly words. But both had agreed that given time, they may not have the chance to honor their own again. They have the creeping feeling that the blood has only begun to run, and the privilege of honoring the dead may soon expire.

So, they sit and listen as the non-denominational chaplain talks of duty and honor and sacrifice and humanity. Waif Kashina, dressed in her formals, eyes heavy and wet, carries the torch down the path behind them. A soldier stands to her left and right, carrying unlit torches of their own. Reaching the pyre, they stoop, borrowing fire from the little Waif.

Three torches. Three lives. Together, they lay their torches upon the stacked wood laden with declarations of love. The flames spread fast, and a plume of smoke roils up from the wood. The soldiers take Kashina's hands and walk her back to her seat.

Chandrima can't hear all that well. Besides the grief that weighs so heavily that she cannot process external sensations, she's more concerned with Assistant Director Zochitl Bottazzi, who sits to her right.

The band plays a somber tune, its echo bouncing from Bastion's walls and disappearing into the open air. A traitor. A liar. A murderer. *A Scowl.* How could she, of all people, appreciate the sanctity of life? How could such an innately violent and blood-lusting creature possibly—

"We're gonna be okay, Rima," Zochitl whispers, laying her hand on Chandrima's knee. Chandrima stares aghast at the woman who she'd spent the last six years with. The woman with whom she'd co-parented the Waifs. The woman who'd propped up her fading ego when her doubts got the best of her.

From her perfectly lined and shadowed eyes, Zochitl stares sharply forward, tears running down her slight cheeks. Chandrima doesn't have to wonder if they are real tears—she can feel her hand trembling on her leg.

She lays her hand atop Zochitl's, interlocking her stout fingers with hers. "Yes. Yes, we are."

She cries silently. Not for the Waif whose memory she is supposed to be honoring, nor the soldiers who'd sworn to protect her as she protected them, nor her dear nephew who, when his nature is revealed to the world, will be in mortal danger.

She weeps because, by the end of this, she doesn't know if she or Zochitl will end up dead.

* * *

Exclusion Zone

Unless the Blight can drive trucks, that's gotta be them. A line of vehicles approaches from the south. Curiesay gives a deep sigh of relief—*We're actually gonna make it home.* The sun beams upon her armor as she stands, viewing the convoy from the rooftop. Allowing a moment of indulgence, she turns to the east and puts her arms out.

She knows herself too well. *This won't last.* The doubt will return. The pain will return. *Always does.* For now, the solace that she shares with the sun alone fills her with hope. Wrapped in flesh and armor, atop this silent building in this desolate land, the sun on her face warms her very soul, down to its coldest corners.

"It's beautiful up here," Arthur quips as he opens the squeaky stairwell door. She hears him place something down and correctly assumes that it is Dai Lu's still-sleeping body.

Curiesay doesn't afford him a glance. "They'll be here soon." The trucks are close enough that she can hear the faint rumbling of their engines.

"I know," he says as he quietly steps up to her side. She can sense him more than she can hear him. It doesn't feel intrusive, though he is indeed intruding on her solitude. Somehow, his aura seems to meld itself around hers, instead of fighting for its own space.

The two young Pilots lean on the parapet. Curiesay can't help but think how surreal this all is. Just six weeks ago she'd been a prisoner, forgotten at an underfunded asylum. Now she's a Pilot, tasked with fighting on the frontlines for humanity, and she's standing next to a young man who's terribly powerful yet is—normally—gentle as a mouse.

She isn't quick to forgive him, but she doesn't blame him for his mood swings or his cruel words, and not only because Curiesay is all too familiar with those same proclivities within herself. She's seen the terrible past he's been saddled with, and although she still doesn't understand who or what he is, she senses that foremost, he's a good person. If she must help him find that, that's what she'll do, if only so that she can find the same for herself. Together, they did the impossible, and they'll only do more—

"I don't want to be here anymore," Arthur whispers abruptly, his eyes turned east toward the risen sun.

Curiesay finally opens her eyes, turning to him. "Um, okay. Well, like I said, they'll be—" She stops mid-sentence upon noticing the tears rolling down his cheeks, joining at his chin and falling onto the weathered concrete parapet.

"I want to go home," he whimpers in a broken voice. Curiesay offers a hesitantly comforting hand, but recoils as he turns to face her. "This place…" Curiesay locks eyes with him as he peers back with crimson irises. Eyes filled not with fury, but with sorrow.

"…makes my head hurt."

Hey, you made it.

It feels pretty weird to be writing directly *to* my reader, but here we both are. Hopefully this won't be the last time we talk.

Are you wondering what my inspirations were for this story? Well, if you weren't, I've got bad news for you, because I'm about to tell you.

I must have been thirteen, waiting for the bus in the kitchen, listening to 101.5 WPDH, hard rock radio. "Renegade" by Styx came on, and I fell for rock and roll. Now, I'd always been a daydreamer, but something about music made it all the more vivid. This story, from inception to the end, is all inspired by my music tastes. A few of the chapters even bear the same names as the songs themselves.

In the interest in sharing amazing music, I'll list the songs at the bottom of this page.

I was quite the recluse as a young man, so I spent my time listening to music and daydreaming. But, over time, those dreams grew legs, and they wanted out. Things grew more complex as I got older. Fast forward nearly twenty years, and my head was filled with the lore of the world I'd dreamt. I'd tried several times to get it on paper but was met with nothing but failure and doubt. For a time, I resigned that I'd never get to share my story.

It took the loss of my closest friend, Jon, to finally spur me into action. I couldn't wait any longer, and so, I began to write. After more than two years of trial and error, I finally got it published.

The book you've read is the first of many, and the next one in the series is fast approaching, so keep an eye out. <u>If I can ask a few things from you, it is that you follow my socials, *please please please* **leave a review**, and tell your friends about my book.</u> It would mean a lot to me and would help me keep pushing my dream forward.

Thanks, friend, and take care.

If you're still here, the goods are down below.

<u>Chapter Seven</u>
"Good L_ck, Yo_'re F_cked" by Celldweller
<u>Chapter Sixteen</u>
"Move" by Pretty Vicious
<u>Chapter Nineteen</u>
"She Wants Me Dead" by CAZZETTE, AronChupa, The High
<u>Chapter Twenty-Four</u>
"Big Bad Wolf" by In This Moment

About the Author

Devin is a long time enjoyer of all fiction media from books to television and especially well crafted narrative-driven video games. From a young age, he'd always dreamed of turning his daydreams into consumable stories.

In his professional career he's worked many jobs, but takes the most pride in his years as a United States Marine where he worked on aircraft as an engine mechanic. As a civilian, he remains employed in the aerospace industry.

Born and raised in the lush landscape of northern New York state, he currently lives a far cry from home in Fort Worth, Texas. When he's not dabbling in books, television, video games or writing, you may see him on the road riding his Kawasaki motorcycle on the scalding Texas pavement.

You can connect with me on:

- https://www.facebook.com/profile.php?id=61570753493971
- https://www.instagram.com/author_d.a.masiero/?hl=en
- https://www.tiktok.com/@author_d.a.masiero

Subscribe to my newsletter:

https://preview.mailerlite.io/forms/2270429/184909277623747983/share